BUILD A GIRLFRIEND

BUILD A GIRLFRIEND

ELBA LUZ

SIMON & SCHUSTER BFYR

NEW YORK AMSTERDAM/ANTWERP LONDON
TORONTO SYDNEY NEW DELHI

SIMON & SCHUSTER BFYR
An imprint of Simon & Schuster Children's Publishing Division
1230 Avenue of the Americas, New York, New York 10020

Interior design by Hilary Zarycky
The text for this book was set in Sentinel.
Manufactured in the United States of America
First Edition
2 4 6 8 10 9 7 5 3 1
Library of Congress Cataloging-in-Publication Data
Names: Luz, Elba, author.
Title: Build a girlfriend / Elba Luz.
Description: First edition. | New York : Simon & Schuster Books for Young Readers, 2025. | Audience term: Teenagers | Audience: Ages 14 up. | Audience: Grades 10–12. | Summary: Eighteen-year-old Amelia revisits her past relationships to break her family's relationship curse, become the ideal girlfriend, and seek revenge on the ex who broke her heart, only to face unexpected complications along the way.
Identifiers: LCCN 2024030686 (print) | LCCN 2024030687 (ebook) |
ISBN 9781665942515 (hardcover) | ISBN 9781665942539 (ebook)
Subjects: CYAC: Blessing and cursing—Fiction. | Dating—Fiction. | Family life—Fiction. | Puerto Ricans—Fiction. | Romance stories. | LCGFT: Romance fiction. | Novels.
Classification: LCC PZ7.1.L895 Bu 2025 (print) | LCC PZ7.1.L895 (ebook) | DDC [Fic]—dc23
LC record available at https://lccn.loc.gov/2024030686
LC ebook record available at https://lccn.loc.gov/2024030687

For my sister, Jessie, my red pen. First for my messy college essays, and then for my even messier first drafts.

CHAPTER 1

To a stranger, the noise vibrating the foundation of the Hernandez household at five in the morning is chaos. For me, one of eight people in the five-bedroom and two-bath brick building, it's a typical day. All aside from my sister Sofia, we Hernandez women are hardwired to rise before the sun does.

Titi Sandra, the unofficial leader of the house, always says, "El camarón que se queda dormido siempre se lo lleva la corriente." Its exact translation is "The shrimp that falls asleep is swept away by the current," but in simpler terms, it just means, "You snooze, you lose."

I haven't done a lot of snoozing these days.

My girlfriend and I have been recreating our favorite moments from the rom-coms we watched last week. Yesterday we made cupcakes inspired by some random made-for-TV movie about a baker who falls in love with a divorce lawyer. Before that, we snuck into a park at midnight and painted our names along the slide. Today, we're going to watch the sunrise.

Depending on what music builds the earthquake under me and my sister Sofia's carpeted bedroom, I always know which aunt is in the kitchen. Daddy Yankee thumps under my sandals as I leave Sofia in the bottom bunk to snore, which means Titi Neva woke first to smack pots and pans around.

To get to our bedroom door, I hop over the 3D puzzle of colorful witches that's sitting at the center of our carpet. It's three hundred pieces, which would have taken me maybe an hour, but my little sister wanted us to do it together, and we're on day three now. Marisol's lucky that she's five years younger than me and her puppy dog eyes still work, otherwise, I would have never allowed my puzzle record to be ruined like this.

Like she hears my thoughts, Marisol jumps out at me when I open the door.

"Jesus." I slam my back onto the floral wallpaper, pressing my palm over my pounding heart. "What the hell, Mari, were you waiting at the door?"

"Amelia," she says, brown eyes wide, two space buns pinning her dark hair back, "do you want to read the next chapter of *Ghost versus Witch* with me? You promised we'd read chapter ten today." I'm pretty sure Mari's reading level is higher than Sofia's and mine combined. I caught Sofia making Mari proofread her essays multiple times this past year, and I'm not going to lie, I was pretty tempted to do the same after I piled up a few too many Cs.

"The day has barely begun." I rub her head, and disappointment clouds her eyes. "Later," I promise.

"You always say later."

"I always mean it." I ditch her to fly down the steps, Daddy Yankee's voice growing louder as I swiftly dodge Mom holding my one-year-old sister, Zoe, to her bare chest and enter the kitchen.

"Do not run in this house," she shouts after me, just as Zoe coughs up milk over Mom's knotted dark curls.

Titi Sandra had workers remove the doorway to the living room three years ago to make the kitchen even bigger, with a single L-shaped couch at the corner by the front door across a coffee table so we could pretend we have a sala.

You wouldn't know the long countertop is stainless steel with the amount of flour, bread, and pastries hogging the space like salchichas in a can. My family is opening a bakery beginning this fall in the very heart of West Springfield. Every day is nonstop practice perfecting the menu and paying the construction workers at the shop—and secretly testing their reactions to the dishes—with treats and flirting. The latter is led heavily by Titi Ivy.

Another thing the Hernandez women know how to do is flirt. That's easy. It's keeping a relationship that's impossible.

"My firstborn," Titi Ivy, in a shirt she wears like a dress, greets as she presses a kiss onto my forehead. "Settle the vote. I say scratch ticket, Neva says lottery."

The aunts love to play the weekly lotto and bicker over which gamble feels the luckiest that week. Usually Titi Ivy goes lotto—higher reward, less chance to win. She must be choosing to scratch now because she lost too many weeks in a row.

"Scratch," I choose, mainly because I like to be the one to scrape off the skin of the ticket with the "lucky" dime in the kitchen drawer.

"Perfect." She pulls me with her. "Come help me prepare the flan. You'll need to memorize the recipe for when you help out at the bakery."

Titi Ivy moved in four months ago when her third

husband died. The other two left. After eating a carrot cake, the third passed away, not knowing it was filled with his death sentence—macadamia nuts—because the bakery forgot to read Titi Ivy's special requests.

You can imagine the rise and fall of that party. *Happy Birthday, Michael; we love—oh no, oh no.* That's pretty much how Titi Ivy described it, her brown eyes brimming with unspilled tears. Which we didn't think was suspicious until the tears finally did fall—happy ones—when she told us how much money she got after suing the shop that will now allow my family to build their own.

Not that I'm accusing my aunt of being a murderer. Or uncaring. But I'm also not *not* doing that.

I rub off her signature red lipstick I know stains my head. "Sorry, Perri is almost here. She's taking me to the lake to watch the sunrise."

"Romantic," she croons while she leads me to the counter and shoves a powdered empanada straight into my mouth, "but breakfast is more important. Tell her to come and eat, and then you can go."

I only have the choice to chew or choke, so I chomp on the crispy edge of the pastry. Before the warmth of the sugar gets too dry, the filling of sticky, chunky pineapple meets my tongue. The edge of Titi Ivy's nail digs into my chin as she wipes crumbs from me, then finishes off the rest of the empanada herself.

Titi Sandra, an apron around her waist with the Puerto Rican flag running across it, rubs a hand over her face, leaving flour residue on her brown skin. A circle of it dots the tip of her square jaw.

"Knead the dough," she says to me, her chin gesturing to the ingredient on the table. Nobody in this family points with their fingers. It's always the chin, even if their hands are free. "I have to season the meat."

"Sorry, Titi Sandra, I have to go." I'm going to get hell for passing on an order from Titi Sandra of all people, but that's a problem for future me.

"What is this?" Titi Neva shuts the double fridge covered in sticky notes and awards from school. Mainly Marisol's, because I'm too busy talking my way out of detention, and Sofia is often pried away from whatever cheerleader she's making out with, so we're clearly not the academic stars here. "You think we're one of those white families in the movies slaving away in the kitchen for you to grab a piece of toast and run out the door? You sit, and I'll make you pancakes."

Titi Neva steps in front of me, placing her hands on her wide hips, the tight ponytail at the top of her head unable to tame her ashy-brown curls, a trait she shares with Titi Sandra—they're the only ones with the same father. They like to lie and say they're twins, though no one would ever think so. Titi Neva has a lighter complexion and dresses in vibrant maxi dresses with bangles along her arms, and Titi Sandra always wears dark pantsuits, as if the whole world is her courthouse. But another thing to know about the Hernandez women: All the sisters are mentirosas. Their true age is a mystery lost in time and shredded birth certificates. They all claim to be the youngest, and with their clear, smooth-skin genetics, I honest to God wouldn't be able to guess who actually is.

Titi Ivy waves a meticulously manicured freckled hand. We're the only ones with the random splatter of spots on our bodies, though I only have a dotting across my nose and cheeks, like someone sprayed them there and forgot the rest of me. On the other hand, Titi Ivy is covered in them, and no foundation can cover them up. "Neva hasn't gone on a date in years. She's just jealous of the joys of young love."

"That's not it!" Titi Neva presses a hand to her chest, the rainbow of bangles along her arms singing as she moves. I already know by the shift in her voice, when it gets all whimsical and narrator-like, she's going into one of her *moods*. The last time she was in one, she said we all had to bunker in the house because a storm was coming, and the sun ended up being out all day. "I don't have a good feeling about this *Perri*."

"Here we go," Titi Ivy says, ending the sentence with a yawn.

"You're both ruled by Mercury, mi amor," Titi Neva explains as she goes in to grip my hand—I make it to a fist before she tries to scan the lines of my palm for my future. "She is air; you are earth—she erodes you."

"If only being a Great Value fortune teller paid," Titi Ivy tucks her vivid red waves behind her heavily pierced ears, "then we wouldn't have to use my dead husband's money to start up our bakery." Her voice in that careless tone that again makes me not *not* think she had anything to do with it.

But if there's one thing living with a bunch of Puerto Rican women has taught me, it's to keep my nose out of adult business.

"The stars do not lie, *big* sister," Titi Neva says.

"I'm two years younger than you."

"You're older than both of us," Titi Sandra joins, and side by side, they could get away with claiming they're twins if you look past Titi Neva being a foot shorter and a little sharper, where Titi Sandra's face is rounded at the cheeks.

"Can I go?" My voice is a whisper among their shouting and Daddy Yankee.

"I've read the sky many times for you, mi amor." Titi Neva tries to pry my palm open. "The curse plagues you too. No love life. Girl or guy or pal. Just the scent of flour clinging to your fingers when you take over the bakery one day."

My left eye twitches as Titi Ivy swats Titi Neva. "Don't jinx my firstborn. She's not like us."

"Yes, she most certainly doesn't poison her lovers."

On that note, after scrubbing that sentence out of my skull (plausible deniability), I duck under their arms, and Spanish curses swinging along with them, to grab some napkins. The aunts continue to bicker as I find Mom rocking a fussing Zoe on one end of the couch.

After I sit beside her, I run the napkins through the drying milk in her black curls she hasn't so much as attempted to clean.

She glances up and smiles, her hazel eyes nearly disappearing over the bags beneath them. We're the only ones who have them, that swirl of brown and green, and it makes me feel closer to her, since the rest of me—the heavy spread of freckles, the thick brows, and the curved cheeks—all comes from my dad. Mom made sure I had *something* of her when I look in the mirror.

When was the last time Mom looked in the mirror? There's a box of unused dye in the bathroom that Titi Ivy got for the multiplying grays on Mom's head and a filled-to-the-brim pot of under-eye cream.

The more I study her, the more my stomach sinks. I doubt she's showered this week at all.

As if she reads my thoughts, and sometimes I think it's a supernatural-mom ability, she says, "I'm fine."

I'm not sure that's true.

The other day Titi Sandra called her a helicopter mom. After I Googled what that meant, the term has been stuck in my head. I wouldn't say she's obsessively protective—at least, not always. I know she's nervous because Zoe is so young, and she has had this weird cough in the middle of the night since she was born that gives me a heart attack every other day. Still, I'm pretty sure mothers are supposed to, I don't know, put their babies down every so often.

I rub my lips together, unsure of what to say that doesn't sound like I'm questioning her parenting skills. Which I'm totally not doing. I love my sisters an embarrassing amount, which means she did a pretty awesome job with us.

I'm saved and cursed when Titi Neva's bangles clatter as she lifts me from the couch and drags me to the hallway. We pass the countless framed photos of girls with crooked teeth, braces, and all the embarrassing moments the aunts decided not only needed to be on film but displayed to every guest who walks the yellow halls.

Instead of an entryway closet, meant for easily accessible jackets and shoes when you're running out the door, Titi Neva has transformed it into a shrine of salty crystals and oddly shaped trinkets she found at secondhand shops or the lawns of weird neighbors I'm not entirely sure were up for grabs.

Titi Neva's hand twists the blue crystal doorknob. The chimes hanging on top of the wood tinkle as the closet light flickers on, revealing an infinite number of crystals weighing down the shelves and the dozens of hangers holding the jewelry that Titi Neva runs a finger across, mumbling the name and purpose of each. She pulls a silver chain with a long black shape hanging off it, holding it above like she means for me to wear it.

"Black jasper will protect you from negativity," she undoes the clasp. "This should do just fine."

I shrug her away. "There's no negativity I need to block, Titi—" I collide with a soft chest.

Titi Sandra drags her hands over my head and curls. "Your hair is so frizzy. Did you forget to do your oil treatment?"

"No," I lie as she continues to roughly smooth out any frizz with whatever oil is clinging to her fingers. I sniffle and catch the scent of adobo lingering on her hands from her seasoning the meat.

Great. I'm going to smell like cooked chicken for Perri.

A quick clatter of heels comes from behind before Titi Ivy

grabs my shoulder and spins me toward her. I barely make out a word before she's swiping a gloss over my lips. "A little color wouldn't hurt," she says, piling on another layer. "Or a lot. I think I'll add some liner."

From the living room, Zoe starts to wail. Titi Sandra pulls me back and tries to tie my hair into a ponytail, muttering about how messy I look. If it wasn't strengthened from the daily yanking and spinning the aunts do to all my sisters before we leave the house, I'm sure my head would have zero chance of remaining on my neck.

"Fluorite!" Titi Neva chokes me with another necklace.

"When you get home, we're going to do a mask, my firstborn." Titi Ivy taps my cheeks twice. "Your pores are forming sinkholes. This is the future face of the Hernandez bakery."

Mom calls out, "Can someone grab Zoe's bottle?"

There's a tug at the bottom of my ripped shorts where Mari has appeared from thin air. "Can we read now?"

Three doorbell rings shudder through the halls. Perri's here, and I'm *literally* being pulled in different directions while the aunts fling their suggestions in the air to blend along with the pulsing reggaeton.

I've been in this position plenty of times, and experience has taught me to do the same thing firefighters coached me during elementary school: stop, drop, and roll. I nearly knock over Mari and ruin whatever progress Titi Sandra made with my hair, then do some horror show of a half-crawl and run to the front door.

I pull myself up, hand on the doorknob, then turn to my

beautiful family of women all facing my way, still rambling about my hair, clothes, skin, everything possible. Not with judgment; never that.

It's the love language of the Hernandez women: With every suggestion they're saying they love me—and that I could do with some more TLC, which is apparently not just a network Titi Ivy marathons in the middle of the night while eating hot Cheetos when she's stressed like I thought.

And I love them all. So much.

I don't hate the noise, the chaos, the hour-long waits to get in the shower, the company, the never-solicited opinions. It's just lately, there's this weird feeling that's trailing me. It's not exactly discomfort, but because I'm so used to *being* comfortable with our routine, it feels close to it. Like I'm a little off-balance.

There's this fluttering of nerves too, especially as Perri's and my relationship grows closer. I want us to work out so bad, but sometimes I can't help but worry it's impossible. Our family *is* cursed.

No woman in our family can keep a partner.

Whether it be a breakup, a move, or a suspicious allergy death, every single Hernandez woman, for a hundred years, has died alone. Which sounds so dramatic, I know, but even Titi Sandra didn't correct Titi Neva when she told—and continues to tell every so often—the story of our family's curse. Which means it *has* to be true. Titi Sandra is as serious as they come. She laughs once a year, during her favorite *Golden Girls* episode. There's no way she would lie about it.

Nobody really elaborates in detail about the Hernandez curse. Titi Neva told me it all started when my great-great-, and lots of greats after that, grandmother was left at the altar and swore that she'd never have another partner again. She'd practically tackle anyone who looked her way after the incident, and all her daughters (there are zero men in our family) and their daughters after that were taught the same. That's why the Hernandez house was built, so the women can all help one another.

I'm supposed to live here with my sisters until we have our own kids, then pass it down to them so they can do the same. I don't even want kids, and I find it strange that the aunts sometimes bring up Sofia and I having them when the curse exists. Like we're expected to be single parents. I don't want to be a parent. Or single. I want a life of my own.

I'm different—hopefully.

It's been six months with Perri, my second longest relationship. And my longest relationship was a year, even though I hate to think about it, since it sends my stomach into a full-fledged first-place gymnastics routine.

Still, that's longer than any of the aunts. Even Titi Ivy, who's been married three times now. I have a chance at a different life. One where I don't need steel muscles in my neck and live in a house that doesn't vibrate with music all hours of the day, to love and be loved. For the curse to be broken.

And she's waiting outside the door.

CHAPTER 2

Perri is the definition of sweet. Not only because of the thermos filled with hot chocolate she made me, warming the space between my thighs as she drives under the darkened sky, but everything about her. Even the taste of her lips. Each time we kiss, my mouth tingles with a cherry Jolly Rancher aftertaste. If I were to open her glove compartment, the sweets would avalanche onto my lap. Titi Neva is wrong—I don't need a crystal to protect me from Perri.

Perri, however, might need one for luck.

Her dad's Mercedes jerks like a sketchy carnival ride as she turns over *another* curb. Fourth time since we've left my house. A hundred-and-something times since I've been with her. Thanks to a particularly rough pothole, Perri and I learned how to change a tire last month after hers flattened on the highway.

Not that I'm any better. I'm not even allowed to drive any of the family cars after I crashed into the street sign at the end of my driveway. In my defense, it was a late night out with Sofia during an emergency midnight-chicken-nugget-craving run, and the streetlamp kept flickering so much that I jokingly told her it could be haunted. So I slowed down to examine it closely to try to freak her out, but then I started thinking it actually *was* haunted, which totally distracted me from the oncoming stop sign I VERY SLOWLY collided into.

Okay, I'm just a bad driver, but I have a hundred people in my house who can bring me to where I need to go, no biggie.

I hold up the empanada to her lips. No way am I going to risk her one-handing the drive; she can barely handle it now. "Want a bite?"

Perri nods, and I pull her strawberry blond waves behind her ear before she takes a chunk out of the crescent. She sighs, closing her eyes in the pure bliss my aunts' food creates to all who sample and—yup, that's another curb. Her eyes open, and she swerves, trying to straighten the car. My body sways with it, and the empanada flies out the passenger window.

"Well," I rub the place where my heart ricochets within my rib cage. "Rest in peace to that empanada."

"It lived a good life." Perri nods, her voice high enough that I know her blood pressure is spiking too. The car noticeably slows, and she flicks on the high beams.

"It will make a squirrel very happy."

"I'm sorry," she slows even more as she turns into a graveled lot. "You didn't get to have a bite."

"There's about twenty left at home," I say as she puts the car in park. "We can grab some after this." When Perri pulls the keys out of the ignition, the indoor lights flicker on, so I spot the red blooming in her pale cheeks. She opens her mouth, but I cut her off. "Seriously, it's totally fine. Don't worry about it. If there's not any left at home, I can make you some, and by 'I,' I mean my aunts, who *will* have a breakdown if they think I'm hungry. If I don't have breakfast, it sends them into a full-blown meltdown, like I'll wither away any moment."

She chews on her bottom lip. It distracts me from her big, blue eyes and perfectly round nose—so much so that I grab her heart-shaped face and pull her in for another kiss. There's a split-second hesitation, like I've surprised her, and then her lips work with mine. I get the taste of cherry, mixed in with sweet pineapple empanada filling, and it tastes so much better this way.

Perri pulls back with a giggle. "We'll miss the sunrise."

Part of me thinks it'll be worth it, but Perri is not a morning person, so it wouldn't be fair to waste her effort of getting up at what she considers to be an ungodly hour. Still, I give her a dramatic pout as I drag myself out the car, transforming her giggle into a laugh.

I move to grab Perri's hand before she leads us onto the path of thin trees and uneven terrain. Though she's a foot shorter than me, she has an easier time not tripping over her own feet as we balance on the rocks and roots. You'd think my four years of track would have taught me how to be steady, but instead it just thickened the muscles on my thighs.

"So"—I swat a gnat away—"have you decided if you want to come with my sister and I to check out the new ice-skating rink?"

"You and me in an ice-skating rink?" She grins as we reach the end of the path and the clearing opens up. "That seems like a disaster waiting to happen."

"For sure, but disasters with you turn into cherished memories."

Wow. Wrap me up in plastic and place me in the deli section because that was *cheesy*.

Perri glances at me, rubbing her lips together like she's

trying not to laugh, and I give her a *don't you dare say anything* glare, which only weakens her resolve, and she bursts out laughing.

I laugh too, though mine is a little forced. It was totally cheesy for sure, but I meant it. Perri isn't the best driver, but in general, she is a lot less clumsy than I am. Usually whenever I inevitably do something wrong, she only laughs it off. For the most part, I feel like she's laughing with me and not at me, which is more than I can say about past exes. Sure, I am a chaos magnet, but it never feels good to be the butt of a joke. But Perri would never do that to me.

I'm just lucky she sticks around with a mess like me.

We find a couple of flat rocks surrounding the dark lake to sit on and take off our shoes to dip our feet in the water.

"I came here with my mom the other day." Perri points at the rippling darkness. "It looks like the water is giving birth to the sun. It's cool."

"Sounds like it."

"Is your baby sister okay?" She traces a circle in the water. "I hope the essential oils helped."

After Perri saw some extra baggage holding up my eyes, I told her Zoe's cough has been especially bad this week. That night, Perri dropped off this mix of oils her mom used to run through a humidifier when Perri was sick.

I bump her with my shoulder. "Not a cough all night."

Perri rubs my arm. "Good." She wraps her finger around one of my curls and chuckles. "I thought you straightened your hair yesterday."

I wince at the memory. "The aunts are built-in smoke detectors. They found me halfway done and forced me into *two* deep-conditioning treatments."

The aunts were calmer when I was held back in sixth grade than when they caught me hiding in the corner of the bathroom, sizzling each strand of hair. I honest to God think they scratched off at least half my scalp trying to rub in the repairing cream and oils.

Perri laughs again. "That's a little excessive."

"It is." I nod, but it doesn't feel true. "Well, they don't want me to damage my hair. Titi Sandra's supervisor used to say her curls were unprofessional and forced her to flat-iron them all the time. It ruined her curls for years. And they have this thing about normalizing it, not letting us feel prettier with it straight. It's just—" I glance over at her, and she's smiling at me, but I can tell she's only nodding along to be polite. She doesn't really get it. And honestly, I'm probably being dramatic. "Never mind."

"Well, you look pretty however your hair is."

My cheeks warm. It's not that I don't think I'm pretty. It's impossible when I'm genetically related to the most beautiful women on the planet. But I know there are prettier people out there.

Exhibit A: polished, clear-skinned, rosy-cheeked Perri. Before we started dating, I thought we were on equal playing field. I mean, we're polar opposites in the looks department, but I had enough confidence to think I could stand beside her and people wouldn't think, *Wow, she's way out of her league.* It's like the closer we got, the more beautiful she was, and the more worried I became.

"You look better," I say, inhaling the cool morning breeze.

She doesn't respond, so we sit in silence as—like she promised—the lake births the sun into the sky. As it does, Perri links her fingers through mine. She keeps rubbing a thumb over my hand, and I turn to face her, but she's already looking at me.

At my raised brows, she takes a deep breath. "You know, we've been dating a little while now, and it's been so fun. At first, I couldn't get a read on you. It's like sometimes you'd talk so fast and heavy, but I feel like I wasn't getting to know you. Now I know you're funny and sweet."

"Thank you?" It sounds like a compliment, but the words feel unsure.

Her other hand is out of my view, but she glances over at it before going on. "And you're beautiful. Seriously, you definitely earned prom queen."

"What is this, a proposal?" I joke, then clear my throat.

Okay, so Perri and I have been together for half a year, but we've never had the *girlfriend* talk. We've never said the words. *Oh.*

It clicks in my head. It's finally happening.

My heart races, and my lips form a wide smile I just know is embarrassingly goofy. I mean, I always refer to Perri as my girlfriend all the time, but in my own head. If I'm honest, I wanted to have the talk months ago, but every time I tried to, my mouth got all dry and my voice got all deep and croaky like Titi Sandra after she sneaks a cigarette out back.

It's just, I'm always the one to ask for the talk, the exclusivity. So, I told myself this time, I wouldn't say anything. Yeah, it's been *killing* me remaining quiet. Silence isn't exactly my strong suit.

But it paid off. Take that, Titi Neva.

"You deserve one," her pitch skyrockets. She's as nervous as I am, and, God, it feels so good to have someone care as much as I do. I'm not cursed or unlovable. I'm the exception. "But not from me. I'm breaking up with you."

I blink, the smile freezing on my face. "What?"

"Oh my God." She pulls back and brings her phone to her face. "Sorry, I'm so sorry. I'm nervous and skipped ahead. I didn't want to say it like that."

I must look like a serial killer or something right now, because my smile is still on, but I feel the rest of my face go slack. I stare at Perri's lips as she goes on, but her words sound a lot like Daddy Yankee's rapping back at my house, but with elevator music as the instrumentals.

I think my brain is glitching, like when I let Titi Neva borrow my laptop and she went on too many sketchy *with just five small installments of 59.99 you can see your future* websites and my computer got overloaded with pop-up viruses.

I close my eyes the way I slammed my laptop shut and try to reboot.

"You're breaking up with me?"

She looks back at her phone, then at me, and—oh my God—she's been reading from it. She planned to break up with me and even wrote a speech to follow. "Yes."

I shoot up. There's this stinging pain poking throughout my skin, like a bunch of bees decided I'm hoarding honey under my flesh. "You brought me to watch the sunrise with you just to break up with me?"

She stands with me, hands out like she means to grab me, but I dodge her to pace. "I'm so sorry. I just wanted to do it in person, away from people. Your whole family is up, and I thought if you wanted some time for yourself, you could do it here, without them, and it's so peaceful here and—"

"I'd rather you have texted me this," I say, still trying to process what's happening. It shouldn't be allowed for happiness to wrap itself around me only for it to choke me seconds later. I mean, I thought Perri was going to make it official, not *officially* dump me.

She pulls out her phone and shows me my contact—no emojis by my name—and our text thread. "I mean, I wrote this whole essay about you, about all the ways I think you're great. Honestly, I think you're amazing and I want us to be friends—good friends. But I didn't send the text because that wouldn't be right. I wanted to do it in person. See?"

But I'm way beyond listening to her. All I hear is freaking Titi Neva. All I see is my aunts and Mom staring at me with knowing, sympathetic eyes. This can't be happening. This isn't real. This isn't a *thing*. I shove her phone away, but then my phone rings, so I yank it from my pocket. Any distraction to pull me from the humiliation.

This isn't working out . . .

Oh my God, I freaking sent Perri's breakup text by mistake.

"Are you *serious*?" As I whirl to spit fire at the universe, my sandal gets caught in the crevice of a rock.

Gravity—the dick—steals my body from me. There's wind. There's sky. A slap on the entire right side of my body. Then water.

Cold racks through me. I flail up, my head breaking the surface. I try to scream, but the lake water gathers in my mouth, and I swear to God something *slimy* hits my tongue. I go back under and spasm until something *swims* out of my mouth.

I'm yanked by my hair back to the surface. Perri helps pull me onto land.

"Amelia, are you okay?" she asks as I gag, my hair clinging to my face like some sea gremlin. "I caught your phone before you fell. So that's something."

"Something?" I repeat between coughs.

"I'm *sorry*." Her voice goes pitchy again. "Maybe this was the wrong way to do it. It's just, you're so into me, and I like you, that's not the problem. I didn't want to hurt you. I'm trying to do this right."

With as much dignity as a freshly dumped, soaking sewer rat with a leftover fish scale in her mouth can have, I snatch the phone from her and limp my way home, or hell, or wherever my bare feet will take me. I can tell Perri feels bad, and, well, maybe I would care more about it another time. If I weren't just dumped and my eyes weren't heavy with the risk of tears.

"Wait, I'll drive you home," Perri shouts at me.

"I'm fine," I mumble, my feet making a humiliating squelching noise as I move.

The curse *is* real. I am doomed to die alone.

CHAPTER 3

"You are *not* growing fish scales," Titi Ivy assures me as I'm freshly showered with my hair coated in deep conditioner under a warm towel, lying—wishing I were nonexistent—on one end of our L-shaped couch. I'm planning on staying here until I make a permanent Amelia-shaped imprint in the gray cushion. At least then I'll have made an impression somewhere. It's not like I'm making them on any of my partners.

"Spiritual scales, maybe. Every moment we live engraves itself within us. That fish might have been an ancestor, a savior, a—"

"Cállate, Neva," Titi Ivy snaps.

Mom rocks a sleeping Zoe on her chest, and the aunts all surround me.

Knowing eyes? Check.

Sympathetic stares? Check.

My will to live? Dwindling.

Mom, in a French braid Titi Sandra plaited for her, sits by my legs and rubs my thigh. "My poor baby, do you want fries and eggs?"

That is my all-time favorite meal, but I'm afraid even that cannot cure the vast, gaping pit where my heart once was. Cue the dramatic rain banging against the window. Hope is lost.

The Hernandez curse is real and has wrapped its messy web around my loveless future.

Perri and I spoke daily, nightly. I literally had to buy a portable charger to keep my percentage up from the hours we spent talking. Perri would use some ancient toy her mother gave her and make us beaded jewelry every week. I'd bring her boba tea while she worked at her father's guitar store. We'd make PowerPoints trying to prove which romantic comedy was the best of all time. All that *and* I let her see me with pre-diffused hair, which makes me look like the equivalent of a wet mop. That's how comfortable I was.

"Can I just listen to music and cry?"

"No," Titi Ivy says, "you need to find someone else ASAP. You know what they say. The best way to get over someone is to get un—"

Titi Sandra whacks the back of Titi Ivy's head. "She's eighteen."

"Eighteen was my prime."

"The pharmacy was all out of condoms that year," Titi Neva says.

"Enough," Titi Sandra snaps. "You two, go finish packing up the food for the workers. Elena, put Zoe down while she sleeps. It's a wonder she lets anybody else hold her without crying when you don't put her down for a second. Amelia, you have one hour to wallow. Then get dressed. You're coming with me to check on the construction site."

An order from Titi Sandra—whom I'm convinced is the oldest simply because she's the scariest and we all do whatever she says—is law. Which is why I'm surprised when the aunts don't follow it.

Titi Ivy leans over and runs her thumb under my eye. "Nena." She sucks her teeth. "You're going to need a few layers of concealer to mask these bags."

I wince as her print touches my raw skin. I managed to finish my crying on the walk here, but I did enough damage that I'm going to need to sleep with a pound of Vaseline to repair the raw skin under my eyes. "I don't exactly feel in the mood for makeup right now."

She pats my cheek twice, the same way she did whenever she spent hours trying to help me out with my English homework and I couldn't for the life of me figure out the difference between possessive versus plural. "When you look good, you feel good."

"Very true," Titi Neva chimes in. "It's a state of mind, a spiritual disposition. You are in charge of how you feel, and if you want to feel empowered, you need to look the part."

I rub my face and mumble, "Nothing about that sentence makes sense."

"Well, there will be plenty of days you don't feel great, but you'll need to put on a front anyway. Customer service is one of the most important skills for a blooming business," Titi Ivy adds.

Somebody claps their hands, and everyone scatters like a bunch of aunt-size mice.

Silence blesses the room—for all of fifteen seconds before the aunts reenter, whisper-arguing with one another. They are allergic to silence, long-term relationships, and the ability to read social cues.

Mom shuffles closer to me. I don't think she realizes that her arms are moving automatically, swaying Zoe side to side. Just like she probably doesn't realize her favorite rose-patterned shirt hangs loose where it once clung to her curves.

"Do *you* want *me* to make you fries and eggs?" I ask her.

She might be trying to glare, but her exhausted skin barely presses a dent between her brows. "I ate already."

"When, last week?" I eye Zoe living her best life in whatever dream she's sleeping through. "I can take her for a little."

Titi Ivy slaps my shoulder. "Always ready to take the baby, this one. You're going to be the best mother."

Titi Neva pinches my cheek. "I can't wait to have a dozen little Amelia-helpers running around here."

I stiffen and focus on Mom. She watches me for a moment, chewing on her lip. Her gaze flickers between me, Zoe, the doorway, and does another lap. Mom finally settles on me, and she gives me half a smile. "You're a good daughter, you know that, right?"

I flinch back at the compliment. I wasn't expecting it, and honestly, I don't really believe it. Because I wonder if she'd say that if she knew my secret plans for next year, about the money I've been saving up, about the real reason why I want to break the Hernandez curse so bad.

The Hernandez women love hard, and I love them, but I want a different kind of love in the future. The house and the curse are a pair. The reason the house filled with women exists is because none of them can keep a partner, so they only have one another. So, if I can break the loveless curse, I can break free of the Hernandez household too. I thought I was going to. With Perri.

Which doesn't make me a good daughter. Not that I say any of that. I'm a coward. That, and Mom holds out Zoe toward me.

"Let's make a deal," Mom offers. "I'll eat if you eat."

I pull my baby sister into my arms. "Deal."

She presses a kiss onto my forehead and walks off toward the kitchen while I smother the guilt down. Easy to do when Zoe's eyes slowly open, showing swirls of brown.

"Hey, beba." I boop her nose. "Do me a favor, never grow up."

Her babbling response is drowned out by the light echo of a guitar, growing louder as the aunts return to the living room. This time with ammunition. Titi Ivy drops the Bluetooth speaker by the doorway before the aunts swarm me.

Titi Sandra moves behind me and gives me half a second to secure Zoe before she yanks my hair back and starts *unnecessarily* aggressively combing it out. Below, Titi Neva tugs my foot and begins placing my toes into a foam spreader. Above, Titi Ivy lathers my skin with an "extremely hydrating primer," she makes sure to tell me.

In seconds, I become their personal doll as they polish me into a runway model. Zoe, who came out the womb hearing blasting reggaeton, falls asleep to the commotion. The aunts don't bicker with one another. Instead, Titi Neva compliments the pink eye shadow Titi Ivy chose. Titi Sandra tells Titi Neva she's got an eye for nail design. Titi Ivy requests the half-up, half-down twists Titi Sandra forms with my hair on herself. It's weird, but it's sweet that they're putting aside their usual differences and putting me first.

Instead of taking Zoe from me when Mom finishes her food, she sits beside me and hand-feeds me a forkful of fries, then takes a bite herself repeatedly until we clear the plate.

Finally, someone lowers the music, and there's a handheld mirror thrust in my face.

"What do you think, my firstborn?" Titi Ivy asks.

I think I look great. The foundation has blurred out any red spots, the blush brings some life to my skin, and my hair frames my round face perfectly. And, okay, I *do* feel better half a second after I see myself, but it's not like I got a choice in this. Maybe I want to be miserable and makeupless for a little while.

Another thing Hernandez women are allergic to: heartbreak.

I guess it works out. If nobody can keep a partner, then not being able to deal with the sadness is a perk.

"I love you guys," I say, which is the truth.

The truce between the aunts must be over because Titi Neva frowns at me. "Her eyeliner is uneven."

Titi Ivy gives her sister a dirty look. "As uneven as the French tips of her toes."

Mom leans in and whispers to me, "You better get out of here before they try to give you another makeover."

I give her a quick kiss on the cheek and use these track legs of mine to race up to my room. Sofia and Marisol are sitting on the floor playing cards until they see me and pop up.

Silently, I climb our white bunk bed and face-plant into my fur sheets. The footsteps on the bed stairs are light, so I keep a curse from my lips as I say into my pillow, "Go away, Mari."

"You promised we'd read."

"That was when I was alive." The fur sheets pop into my mouth and I know I'm going to have to wash off the makeup. I turn to say, "I am no longer a human being."

Sofia's manicured nails dig into the wooden frame by my face. Then her head appears as she hangs off. She's wrapped her black curls into a purposely messy bun, with two strands peeking out as bangs. "What are you, then?"

"A fish, I think."

"Your T-zone *has* been really oily lately."

"Bite me."

"I don't like salmon."

I groan. "Can everyone leave me alone to cry for at *least* five minutes?"

She rolls her black, heavily lashed eyes. She and Titi Ivy get them done together, something called a cat-eye. "Oh, come on, you're not actually falling for the family curse bull—" Her curls bounce as she freezes suddenly, and she looks to Marisol, then keeps the curse from her mouth. "It's crap. I mean, I love them, but look at them. They're all insane. It's no surprise they're single."

Marisol jumps forward, elbowing my gut as she does. "Shush," she tells Sofia as I cry out from the pain. "Titi Ivy will throw her chancla at you if she hears you."

"See?" Sofia points her thumb at our little sister. "Even Mari knows they're all crazy."

I try to shove Marisol off, but she pushes herself higher on my hips. "You don't get it," I tell Sofia, just one year younger than me, "you're definitely not cursed. You're beautiful and charming and fun and *interesting*."

"Oh, I like this."

"Shut up. It's not a compliment, only facts. You're graceful, and everyone and their sister wants a shred of your attention." With nearly everyone I've ever dated, I've been the one to initiate the relationship. They've all failed. Sofia, on the other hand, has never. She only opens her mouth to say yes or no. So many times, people have approached me to ask what she likes, do I think they have a chance, will I put in a good word for them. Even my freshman-year crush asked for a reference . . . *after* I dated them.

Maybe it's the poise to back up her confidence. Sofia isn't clumsy like me, and if she actually tried, she'd probably be valedictorian. Aside from math; she sucks at that. Which is probably the only thing she's not good at. Maybe that's how it works. You're either good at math or you're interesting.

I bet when people find out we're sisters, they're shocked that we're so different. Or maybe not. Maybe they think we're twins, and Sofia just sucked up the best parts. I mean, if anyone is free of the Hernandez curse, it's her.

She has drive and direction and a bright future. She's known what she's wanted to do since she was eight, arguing with the aunts about why she should be able to sleep over at a stranger's house. As for relationships? She leaves a trail of broken hearts like breadcrumbs in her path.

Whereas the rest of us repel, Sofia attracts. It doesn't hurt that she's a few inches taller than me and has the sharpest cheekbones only using a filter will allow me to have. *And* she never gets a spot of acne on her golden skin. Though that could be because of her ten-step nighttime routine I'm too lazy to replicate.

I'd hate her if I didn't love her so much.

"Not to shift the focus from me, because, God, I love it, but you are also beautiful and fun and charming and—"

"Ew, shut up. I'm *boring*. And I'm charming for all of five seconds before I get too cocky and stumble over my words, you know, if I'm not physically stumbling over something because I'm *clumsy*. And yeah, I'm not particularly scared of anything, but I'm not *good* at anything. So you're going to be this renowned, unbeatable lawyer, and what will I be? Spending hours counting change for an order at the bakery?"

"The register will do all the work."

I groan, unsuccessfully trying to push Marisol off.

Shifting tactics, Sofia's lips purse. This means a more thought-out response is coming, a trait she earned from too many astrological discussions with Titi Neva.

"You've already broken the curse. You dated Le— Mari, bad word."

Like a programmed robot, Mari stuffs her pointer fingers so deep into her ears that I worry she'll pop an eardrum. In this house of bantering women, curses are inevitable, and whenever we remember, we have Mari stuff her ears so she doesn't repeat them. "Bad word" is code for: *You're not allowed to hear the rest of this sentence.*

Sofia continues, "You dated Leon for over three hundred and sixty-five days. You were disgustingly in love. He was too. Had to be. Remember when he made a necklace out of the Naruto eraser you gave him in study hall? Peak romance."

Hearing *his* name sends my heart into a frenzy. As soon as my brain starts to piece together those oceanlike eyes, I scrape the memory away. There are only two people who know of *him*. Me and Sofia, who knows every single thing about me. Secrets between us are like a bad Bad Bunny song. They just don't exist.

Well, *almost* everything. Just one thing. One secret.

"I don't really feel like going through my dating history."

"We would never have enough time to."

"I hate you," I say, though it'd be impossible to.

After every breakup, Sofia always showed up. If I was too miserable to comb through my hair, she'd braid it for me. When I was too anxious to walk past an ex in the hallway, she'd hold my hand and power walk through the halls—oftentimes having a carefully crafted insult at the ready when we passed my ex.

Me? Aside from being good at math, there's nothing I excel at. My future? There's nothing that's ever called to me. I've never had a passion for anything like the aunts, who like to bake, Mom likes to be a mom, Mari reads, and Sofia debates. The only thing I love is seeing the world from other perspectives.

It's why I'm obsessed with romance, the way it pulls you in and whisks you away from reality. Anywhere, whether it's in books, games, movies, comics, TV, I've always been obsessed with it. Sometimes I act out the parts of a scene differently if I think it could be done better. Before bed, I make up these romantic scenes in my head and have full-blown plots and twists and endings that continue for days until I have a new story.

So I guess I love love, even though nobody will fall in love with me.

Whomp.

Marisol rubs my arm. "I don't think you're cursed, Melia. I love you."

Ah, well, I guess there's not exactly a gaping hole in my chest. There's just an inch of warmth. For the fam. For Marisol and those bright, caring eyes.

"Well, that means a lot to me. But in thirty years, when I'm old and wrinkly and living in a house with ten dogs, I'll want to have someone else to love me too. You know. Like a fiancé or something."

"Have you seen our aunts?" Sofia says. "You'll never get wrinkles, especially not thirty years from now."

"It's okay." Mari snuggles up next to me. "I'm going to read to you. That'll make you feel better."

"No—you know what, fine. Let's see what Lucely has gotten herself into."

We finish two chapters when I start to doze off. Mari jabs me in the stomach, effectively yanking the tired out of me. I remove a pillow from behind me and throw it at her, then I take the one I'm lying on and press it over my face.

"What's that?" Mari asks, and I pull the pillow down to peek at her. She's pointing at the headboard behind me—I shoot up, blocking her view, my heartbeat thundering.

"Nothing." I discreetly maneuver the pillow to block the shape carved on the wood behind me.

There are two hard knocks on the door. Titi Sandra enters the room and says, "Two minutes."

Marisol, thankfully distracted, perks up. "Can I come?"

"Put your shoes on." She turns her sharp gaze to me. "You too. Now."

I pout, catch the flash of a warning on her face, then remove said pout because I value my life and follow her commands.

There's no time to wallow in the Hernandez household. And from the looks of it, I'm probably never going to escape it, so I might as well suck it up and get used to it.

CHAPTER 4

arisol sprints down the steps, sucking all the enthusiasm from the room as I follow her, hunched back, to the SUV outside, where the aunts are shoving packed treats into the trunk. They're placing them into coolers to prevent melting from the sun.

I can't believe even the weather has betrayed me. My world is a rumbling dark fog. I should at least get the respect of a drizzle, a cloudy sky. I mean, if I'm going to be miserable, I want the full effect so I can stare out the window and pretend I'm the main character in a music video.

I hop into the passenger side, connecting my phone to play sad indie music to mourn. Titi Sandra joins me, and Marisol sits behind her. It always smells of vanilla in here, so I breathe it in and lay my head back to wallow.

Titi Sandra switches the music immediately to a merengue station, so I guess my wallowing party isn't meant to be. Much like my dating life.

"When we get there, you'll bring the coolers out front. The men know to take a treat when they're hungry. Marisol, you stick by me, and we'll make sure the workers are on schedule."

Marisol salutes. "Yes, ma'am."

"How long is this going to take?"

I'm lucky Titi Sandra has a strict rule of two hands on the wheel, face forward when driving. I don't think I'd be unscathed if I were on the receiving end of that scowl. The last time I got it was when I forgot to take the chicken out of the fridge, so when Titi Sandra got home from work, she didn't have any meat to cook for dinner. "However long it does."

"I have things to do."

"You crying into a pillow is not more important than the family business. You need to start paying more attention if you want to take over it in the future."

Out of all the aunts, Titi Sandra has always been the harshest. Not that she means to be. She's a lawyer and mainly deals with divorce, which probably has some deep-rooted connection with the Hernandez curse, but Titi Sandra doesn't talk about that much. We just know when she's dealing with a particularly annoying client when she comes home smelling of cigarettes and criticizing the contestants' answers on trivia shows.

I groan. "Would it kill everyone to give me more than sixty seconds to be upset?"

"You can be upset and still live. Pointless to waste a day on tears, especially for a young girl like yourself. You have your whole life ahead of you."

"Yeah," I pick at the skin around my nails, "how exciting to know no matter what I do, I'm going to end up alone anyway."

"Never alone." Titi Sandra turns a corner to the long strip plaza where the bakery will be born. "Family is always there."

"Well, I can't make out with family."

"Amelia," she snaps, in a way I imagine she interrupts a newly filed couple.

Marisol's here, right. "Fine, but I'm going silent in three, two—"

"Good."

I know Titi Sandra is trying to make me feel better. Everyone has their way. Mom feeds me. Titi Ivy makes me dance. Titi Neva rubs crystals. And Titi Sandra gives me tough love. But right now, I'd like something else. Like medium love, mild love. Something other than *tighten up, Hernandez*.

The aunts always say what they feel as they feel it, and once they say the thing out loud, they're free of it. For them, nothing builds up, which means no explosions, no anger, no regrets. And they expect us to be the same. But I'm not like that. It doesn't matter if I talk about my feelings out loud. I always store some of it somewhere inside me.

Every heartbreak, fear of never breaking the curse, guilt for wanting to break the curse, every emotion I go through leaves a scar. I'm not sure what it looks like. I only know when I feel it forming, the heat behind my chest that swirls until I manage to merge it with the rest of the emotions I store away until it's faded enough that I forget about them. It's there now, trying to hide behind my rib cage. Hurt, embarrassment, and of course, the worry that something is truly wrong with me.

Usually, I can tuck it away smoothly and quickly so nobody notices. Until something rattles me. Then things get ugly.

I forget about guilt or my conscience and explode. My emotions scatter like a dandelion feathering away in heavy wind.

Sometimes I lose the point I'm trying to make. Instead, I want to take out all the anger inside of me and place it on someone else, even if they don't deserve it. Just if they're near. In the heat, I think, better them than me.

The last time it happened, Sofia didn't talk to me for a month straight.

Mari tosses me her hardcover book and asks me to read a chapter as we go, and I hurriedly push all those emotions to the side. A problem for future me.

We pass the line of trailers and enormous steel boxes and trucks all packed into the strip of road—usually reserved as extra parking for the football field a mile away—and I frown at the workers putting up colorful tents and flags for the Big E. Every summer the block transforms into the biggest state fair on the East Coast. People from all over come for the food, the rides, and social media-worthy photos from the weekly fireworks show.

At the very end of it all, the cherry on top, is a tiny plaza where Hernandez Café is being birthed, along with the already-grown-up jewelry store, ice cream parlor, and sports bar that have been there since I was born.

The plaza does good business, which is why the aunts had their eye on it, but opening midsummer during the Big E, when thousands of people are going to flock over, is going to make them bank. If the construction gets finished in time.

We park between two red pickup trucks. I take a deep breath before shuffling out.

Titi Sandra grabs a cooler and starts for the corner, and I

let Marisol grab the other end of mine, and we waddle together toward the café. We drop it down beside the first, and Titi Sandra holds open the glass door for us—men shouting, tools drilling, and sawdust wafting from within.

"Come," Titi Sandra says when I shuffle back. "Let's see how it's going."

I sigh and shove all thoughts of this morning to the side. Not that I do a good job. There's this phantom, slimy movement I keep jumping at in my mouth, and yeah, it's my tongue, but try having my hell of a morning and not cringing whenever you remember a fish swam in your mouth.

After being dumped, of course.

Ugh, shut up, brain.

I've only been to the café once before renovations. Back when it was a tiny karaoke spot with mismatched carpets and what Titi Ivy described as *gawdy* sculptures hanging on green wallpaper. It was such a mistake that the naked wooden walls and ashy planked floors now are much-needed improvements.

A bunch of men in hard hats and goggles all greet Titi Sandra, and one even presses a kiss onto her cheek before going toward the door to collect some snacks, I assume.

It's scientifically impossible to find a person who isn't obsessed with the aunts' food. Titi Neva's ex-girlfriend sometimes is *walking through the neighborhood* right around dinner and poor Titi Neva hands over a plate and doesn't realize the woman leaves right after she gets a container each time.

"Hey!" a man with a dark beard shouts. All the tools shut

down, and I jump at the sharp silence that leaves a ringing in my ears. "Take a thirty—no, an hour. You guys have earned it."

The dozen men start for the door. Some take off their helmets to bow and greet me as they do—which has Marisol hiding and giggling behind me.

"Connor," Titi Sandra greets the man in charge as he nears, sweat beading down his brown skin and pooling at the collar of his red shirt, his face mask protecting him from the air thick with dust and debris. "You've ripped the walls off already? You guys work fast. I was worried you wouldn't be able to manage working here while setting up the Big E, but I was wrong."

He winks at her. "Told you my guys were good. And you're doing us a favor. Lots of my men need extra money." He shrugs. "Anyway. Want to tear this place apart as much as I can so electrical can get in. That's what is going to take up a lot of your time."

"You've met Marisol." Titi Sandra grabs my arm and brings me closer. "This is my oldest, Amelia."

Not oldest *niece*. Just oldest. All the aunts refer to us daughters as their own, and nobody ever questions it. There's no need. They're as much a mom as Mom is. We're the daughters they'll likely never have. It's kind of awesome having the choice to pick who disciplines you when you do something wrong.

Whenever we did bad at school, Sofia and I knew to have the teachers call Titi Neva because she hates not only school, but authority in general. If we, and by "we," I mean *me*, knocked a curb hard enough the bumper of our car came off, Titi Ivy has a *situa-*

tionship with a mechanic who can fix it before the aunts see.

"Good to meet you." He offers his hand, and I shake it.

My brows pull together. There's something familiar about his blue, evening-sky eyes. And I swear his are filled with recognition too.

"Come," he tells Titi. "Let me show you what we've done to the kitchen. Marisol, why don't we find you a mask? All this sawdust isn't good for a young girl."

"Cool." I wave as they head to the back door leading to the kitchen, leaving me alone. "I'll just breathe in the poison. Who cares about *my* health?"

Certainly not Perri. Or Ruby and Taylor and Daryl—

Okay, I am *not* going to go down the list of my failed relationships.

Besides, what good will it do me? It's not like they have anything to do with one another. Or maybe they do. If everyone I've ever been with has dumped me, there has to be a reason why. But the only common denominator among all the failed relationships is me.

If that's the case, then there must be something I'm actively doing to be a relationship repellent. I just don't know which exact ingredient of me is the active one.

I drag myself along the carpetless floor and inspect the bare walls.

Seriously, even the ceiling has been ripped out, and there are thin strips of light pouring through the tarp, acting as a temporary roof. This has to be one giant safety hazard.

Metal clashes against metal in a loud *clap*. I jump, whirling to watch a bunch of tools on a chair fall onto the ground. One screwdriver rolls under a folded tarp.

To save a worker from looking for it, I go to grab it, walking past a giant yellow sign.

"Hey," a voice shouts, and my heart gallops yet again.

I spin on my heel—and nearly pass out. A ghost, he has to be. Or a figment of my imagination formed by my panicking brain trying to remind me of every failed relationship I've ever had.

But he speaks, and so, he has to be real. *Right?*

"Amelia?"

His blue-and-black—ah, now I see the familiarity—eyes widen as he looks me over. He's taller than the last time I saw him, which should be impossible since it was a pain sophomore year to look up at him, and he's doubled in size, muscle, specifically.

Guess football paid off.

"Leon." The sound feels foreign on my tongue. I haven't said the name in so long.

Thought it? Now, that's a different story. When that happens, though, I look for the nearest item, my phone, a remote, a book, a sister, and desperately distract myself before the name becomes a full-blown memory.

"Get over here."

Wow. He dumped me via text two years ago, ghosted me with no explanation, and he can't even form a greeting. "Whatever happened to hello? Hi? Howdy?"

"First, get over here." He holds out his hand like I'm supposed to run to him and grab it, as if seeing him doesn't make me taste the fries Mom hand-fed me. I open my mouth, but there's no snark to give. My words get tangled in my throat, so I resort to a glare.

His thick brows pull together. His wavy hair is caught on the sweat of his forehead. "Stop," he says as I take a stubborn step back. The opposite of whatever he wants me to do will work best here. If he told me to run, I'd walk. Jump, I'd lie down.

He takes a step forward. I take a step back.

Or try to.

The tarp that was folded there is not for future use. Instead, it was placed on the ground like a warning. Like a makeshift floor. I realize that too late.

My foot falls through, shoving the tarp in the hole, and I fall backward. I swing my arms forward, but the only thing I catch is the stool, which comes down with me. I land on my side above a weak plank, sending tiny little splinter-daggers into my ass.

"Are you kidding me?" I breathe out, the shock stealing the air from my lungs. I'm pretty sure the vibration in my chest is my rib cage shuddering.

Something light slaps on my skull. Clumsily, I grab it. It's the yellow sign I passed earlier.

Ah, it was a *warning* sign. Good to know after I passed it and am now in a hole, ass aching, head throbbing, and wishing the rest of the building would come down and bury me.

Especially when Leon's head appears from above.

"No, thank you," I say as he starts to reach to grab me. "I think this is a perfect place to die."

Unfortunately, he reaches farther until he grabs my wrist. I let him, because a concerning amount of sawdust floats from the ground, and my vision blurs. He lifts me with a grunt, and my face presses into his chest.

Musk and earth and fruit. The same scent that clung to his skin two years ago. I can't use the strategy of grabbing whatever is nearest to me to get Leon out of my brain, seeing as Leon *is* the closest thing near me. Which forces me to do this weird hug to myself like I'm trying to reach my back for a scratch.

"What hurts?" He pulls away, hands on my shoulders to inspect me.

"A lot." I swallow. "But most pressingly? My pride."

A quick tug of his full lips and—oh no, *don't you dare stutter, heart.*

"I remember you had a lot of it."

"Do you remember how fast I was?"

He frowns. "What—"

I run.

Literally and figuratively, you know, from my annoying, pounding heart. Leaving both the scene and the boy in sawdust and confusion.

It takes twelve miles, two and a half hours, and fifty-two fries for my heart to return to its normal pace.

CHAPTER 5

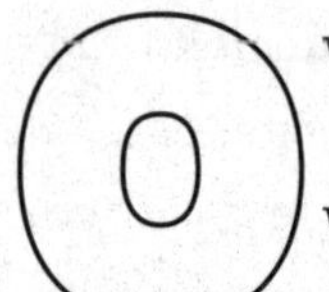

w!"

"Enough." Mom whacks the back of my head when I twist my body to get away. "I've only got one left."

After Leon pulled me out of the hole, I ran thirty minutes straight, then took turns jogging and walking the next couple hours when my chest felt like it was going to explode, until I made it home. It seemed the best idea at the time, but I'm sure it just pressed all the splinters deeper into my ass.

My ass, which is currently out, as I'm starfished on the couch in my underwear as Mom collects the splinters with tweezers and drops them on a cotton pad. This has to be rock bottom.

"Ow," I yelp. "You said there was only one left!"

"Yes, one, and one, and one more," Mom says, her accent thickening. All the aunts have hints of an accent, but the more frustrated they are, the heavier it saturates their words. "I swear, Titi Neva needs to do some sort of cleansing for you. Too much bad luck."

"Isn't that our thing? We're all cursed."

"Mi hija, you seem to be cursed all around."

"Love that for me."

"Mom." Sofia enters the sala, her lengthy hair pinned away

from her face. "Don't tell her that. She's already miserable." She holds up a yellow striped sundress toward me. "What do you think?"

"Mom," I ask, "can you grab one of those splinters and stab it through my eyes?"

"What? Why?"

I point my chin to Sofia. "That's the ugliest dress I've ever seen."

Mom turns, sees Sofia without our baby sister, then straightens stiffly. "Where is Zoe?"

Sofia rolls her eyes. "I left her on the side of the road. What do you think? She's sleeping in her crib."

Mom jumps up, dropping the tweezers on my thigh. "You can't leave her alone. What if she chokes? What if she—" I don't hear the rest of her worries since she torpedoes away to her shared room with Titi Ivy and Zoe.

I sit up, and Sofia plops beside me. "She's so dramatic. She barely sleeps. She's too busy making sure Zoe is taking exactly thirty breaths per minute."

"She did the same for you."

"And you." She drops the dress over my thighs. "Look, this would look great on you. Besides, I've been in your closet. Oversize sweaters are not, nor will they ever be, in. This is a date-worthy outfit."

I gesture to my bare legs. "I'm not really up for a date right now. Or you making fun of my style." Then I process her words. "Wait, what date?"

"I set you up with someone. It's my friend's friend's friend,

Dev. He goes to Capital Community College, so like, older guy, hot."

I rub my face roughly. "I was dumped literally five seconds ago."

"Exactly. Let's not let the pain marinate. My girl told me he's pretty funny, and you like to laugh."

"A match made in heaven," I mutter and blow out a breath as Leon's face appears in my head again. No matter how fast I ran, or how few breaths I had left, I couldn't escape him. The concern etched on his skin when he pulled me from the hole. The quiver of his lip like he was holding back a laugh. The way my heart decided to make a remix of its regular rhythm like it forgot all the ways it ached when Leon left me.

I thought I'd never see him again. Worst of all, I thought I'd never *want* to see him again. I'd be lying if I didn't admit there was this odd wash of relief. Just for a moment. A quick *oh, look, he's alive and healthy and didn't get abducted by aliens.* Quickly squashed by the reminder I thought he was the love of my life, and he thought my heart was a treadmill.

I sit up. "Don't you want to know *why* I ran after falling in the hall?" I shake my head. "Or even *why* I fell into it in the first place?"

"I've witnessed you fall *up* a flight of stairs. I don't need a wild imagination."

I suck my teeth and gesture for her to come closer. She gives me a weird look but sits beside me, and I whisper, "Leon was there."

"Shut the fu—"

I slap my hand over her mouth, panicking as my gaze darts

around the room. No aunts, no baby sisters. But the walls have eyes. And the aunts have supersonic hearing.

Like I'm being timed for it, I give her the world's quickest play-by-play. Every few seconds I have to press my palm down on her lips harder when I feel the buildup of another squeal.

She slaps my hands a few times, but I raise my brows twice. She sags her shoulders and narrows her gaze, and I can read the *I'll be quiet, I swear* sentence in her pot-of-honey-brown eyes.

"Okay," she says quietly, "I'm Titi Neva's niece, so I have to get this out of the way first. Don't you think it's some kind of cosmic sign? You and Leon reuniting?"

Ugh, if Titi Neva knew of Leon and this, she'd say the exact same thing. Sofia is younger than me, and she is already morphing into them. There really is no hope.

"If the universe is dropping any signs, the only one that makes sense is that it hates me."

"So, you're not at all happy to see him again?"

Stealing from Titi Sandra—oh no, *I'm* morphing into them too—I give her the meanest glare I can pinch together. Sofia knows all that happened between us and exactly how it ended. I should shave off her eyebrows for even suggesting that.

She rolls her eyes. "Oh, come on, it's everyone's dream to bump into their ex."

"Only when they're doing better, not freshly dumped," I shoot back.

"Or when they're hotter than ever. Your bangs grew out, and you fit into Titi Sandra's clothes, so your jeans aren't high-waters anymore."

"If we don't talk about something else in the next five seconds, I'll tell the aunts who really drank the rum and filled it with water last month," I threaten.

In one of Sofia's more ridiculous moments, she thought the aunts wouldn't notice the switch, as if Titi Sandra doesn't have a glass every Thursday during her meeting-heavy shifts and Titis Ivy and Neva never play beer pong with it because *our bloodline handles the strong stuff.*

"Anyway," Sofia quickly moves on, "I'll drop you off on your date." I do have my license, but nobody lets me drive one of the three family cars after I popped the tires driving over curbs. But that only happened once. Twice. Okay, it happened five times.

I flick her wiggling brows. "Are you listening to me?"

"Unfortunately."

I hold out my phone. "I'm going to Google the word *cursed,* because I'm not sure you're getting it."

She slaps her hands over my cheeks, squeezing my face so I probably resemble the fish that made my mouth a home yesterday. "Stop it. You're *not* cursed. Or unlucky. Okay, you've had bad luck, but that doesn't mean you're plagued with it forever. One of us has to prove these women wrong."

"You're doing a good job," I say, but the words are muffled since my lips are squashed together. Something flickers in her face. Sadness? Irritation? Hard to tell when she squeezes so hard my cheeks block part of my vision.

"As the oldest, you have to set the example." Sofia finally lets me go. I rub my throbbing cheeks. "If *you* can keep a date, then maybe all the aunts will realize they can too. Last week,

Titi Ivy dumped a guy on their third date because she thought he would first. And Titi Neva was muttering something to her crystals the other day. And, well, you *know* Mom needs to get out of the house."

If generations of Hernandez women haven't broken the curse, the odds aren't looking great for *me*. Honestly, I'm starting to think the curse clings to me harder than anyone else. Or maybe it's because unlike the aunts, I keep trying.

You'd think the aunts would give up on dating if they know it's not going anywhere, but ask any of them and they'll say it helps pass the time. Titi Ivy always claims she likes the free dinners, but she, like the rest of the aunts, has zero commitment expectations.

"Come on, Sofia. Why don't you do it? I mean, if you stopped leaving a trail of broken hearts, you'll be set. Do you know how many times your exes have stopped me in the halls trying to get back in your good graces? If anything, you're the chosen one." I gesture to her with my chin. "You'll be fine. It's skipped you. Maybe your dad's genetics are special."

Like the aunts, Sofia and I don't share the same father. Hers, Mom met on a quick trip to Puerto Rico. Every other summer, Sofia visits and stays with him, and he sends monthly checks for her, but Sofia says it's all obligation. She can tell he never really wanted her, but at least he acknowledges her.

My dad? Mom doesn't talk about him. Only says he was the equivalent to a son of anarchy, and I have no idea what that means, only that she has no clue where he is now.

Maybe I should care more, but it's not like I've ever known

him to miss him. That and the aunts would all act like I'd summoned a demon and mutter a prayer of protection, whenever I used to even mention him.

"You're probably right," Sofia says, her lips forming her signature *you didn't instantly do what I wanted* pout as she yanks the dress from my lap. "You're doomed like the rest of them. You've already dated more people than our own mother has. If there was a chance for you to be different, the metaphorical clock has already struck twelve. The buzzer has gone off. The ticking bomb has blown up. There's really no point of you dating ever again."

"All right." I glare at her. "Let's tone it down." A weird ringtone, a mix between a beep and a buzz, jingles through the air. I frown as Sofia hurriedly takes out her phone, then I snatch it from her. "You're on Beedle? Seriously? Have you already dated everyone you know?"

Her heavyweight foundation covers where blush would arise on her skin, but I recognize the twitch in her eyes and know if I wiped her cheeks clean, I'd see it there.

"You make me out to be some kind of serial dater. Maybe I want to meet people I *don't* know."

"I should do the same," I say bitterly. "At least when they dump me, it'll be less embarrassing if we don't have any mutual friends. Perri and I have half the same followers."

Sofia snatches the phone from my hand, her claw-shaped nails tapping rapidly on the screen. "So what? You broke up, it happens."

"It *always* happens," my voice rises embarrassingly. I do

this weird thing where the more embarrassed I am, the louder my voice gets. Titi Sandra is still scarred from me screaming that I was dying when I got my period for the first time. "What if it's not the curse? What if there's something deeply wrong with me?"

Sofia rolls her eyes. "What could you possibly be doing wrong?"

"I don't know, you tell me. You've known me our whole lives. If anyone can figure out what's wrong with me, it's you."

She winces. "This feels like a trap. I don't think—" Her eyes brighten as excitement shudders over her face. "I have an idea."

The last time Sofia had an idea, I ended up in the ER with three stitches in my forehead in what we refer to as the "Scarface incident," where we raced outside on skates and tried to do flips on the curbs when neither of us can even do a cartwheel.

"I have a deep, widening sense of doom."

"Dramatica," she notes while typing rapidly on her phone. I let her do it for a few minutes before I give in and ask what she's doing. She claps her hands together and pinches her features into a Titi Sandra–esque expression. "Maybe you *are* doing something wrong. Or maybe you're just crazy when you're in love."

"Are you plagiarizing Beyoncé or just trying to make me feel bad?"

She ignores me. "Maybe it's less about what you're doing *wrong* and more about what you *should* be doing *right*." She smirks. She knows I hate when she gives me the little half smile that means *I'm the little sister, but I'm so much better than you.* I mean, she's only *one* year younger, but she plays it like I'm already knocking on death's door. "Like any muscle, with some training, it'll be stronger. You just don't know which workouts to do. That's where I come in."

"Sorry." I rub circles into my temples. "There are too many metaphors going on in whatever it is you're trying to say. Is there a point you're trying to make?"

"Obviously," Sofia starts, but Titi Neva dances in, a hand on her low-cut blouse patterned with roses.

"Mi amor, I had a feeling something bad happened to you."

"Aka a text from Titi Sandra," Sofia mutters. She's probably sour Titi Neva has interrupted whatever spiel she put together in the three seconds it took her brain to come up with it. "And this feeling, I feel it still." She grabs my hand and brings it to her chest. "The wind tells me you should stay home."

Titi Ivy saunters in after her. Another T-shirt turned dress hanging above her knees. Honestly, she saves so much money when shopping since she doesn't believe in pants and also doesn't pay full-dress prices. "What it should be telling you is to take off those damn bangles. I can hear you walking from upstairs."

But Titi Neva keeps her orange-shadowed eyes on me. "Bad things happen in threes: this morning, afternoon, and tonight. So stay home, mi amor. I mean it."

Even though the curse is obviously real, I usually pay little attention to Titi Neva's ramblings—and that's on the advice from all her sisters, who have dealt with her way longer than

I have. She's way too gullible with all she reads and watches, throwing science out the window. The less science an idea has backing it, the more likely Titi Neva believes in it.

But, man, if she isn't freaking me out right now.

Titi Ivy points a finger toward me. "The carpenter's son? Why weren't any of us informed about this?"

"*What?* Who told you?" Sofia interjects.

Ah. I should have figured a lecture was coming. Running off before finishing helping wasn't my best idea.

My brain races up to speed and processes the end of the sentence. "Wait, what?"

Busted. Maybe I should have told them all about my year-long relationship with Leon, but the first couple months, I was worried that mentioning something becoming so precious to me, so different from anything I've felt before, would jinx it.

Then, each time I actually worked up the courage, something major happened. Zoe was born and her being sickly took up all our attention for months. Sofia earned several new academic awards. The aunts officially put a down payment on the bakery. It felt selfish to try to wedge myself between all the major things going on. It became less of a secret and more of me genuinely not having a proper chance to.

Then Leon and I broke up, or more realistically, *I* was dumped by a text that took me less time to read than it took me to actually unlock my phone and pull up the message. It seemed pretty pointless to tell them of *another* failed relationship.

"Leon said you seemed a little sick," Titi Ivy explains. "He's the one who told us you left. He wanted us to check on you." Her voice goes even quieter and tinged with curiosity like the ending sentence is part question.

Check on me. He didn't do so for years. What makes this moment so special?

"Yeah." I try to look away, but Titi Ivy places a gentle hand on my arm. "It was sophomore year till the beginning of junior."

During that summer, Leon's father sent him off to Arizona to live with his mom. It was for them to develop a better relationship, and his new high school was supposed to have this amazing football team sure to land Leon a scholarship. We were going to be thousands of miles away, on different time zones and schedules, but Leon *swore* we could make it work. That distance would only make us realize how much we loved each other.

Which is why reading his breakup text felt like my world flipped over.

"Why didn't you want to tell us about him before?" Titi Ivy asks softly.

There are no secrets in the Hernandez house. And not because anyone forces truths out of the other, but because everything here is a safe space. Instead of rules and secrecy, we talk through everything—and yeah, Sofia and I have been scolded many times, but never severely. Mom and the aunts always say they'd prefer to know what is going on with us, even if they disagree, so that they can help. *Better to be in the know than in the worry.*

I shrug. "Well, it didn't work out, so why bother?"

Mom joins us again, this time with a sleeping Zoe in her arms. "Heartbreak is never easy. We could have eased some of the ache." She frowns as she stands beside the aunts.

The front door creaks open, and half a second later, Mari bullets into the room, Titi Sandra's thin heels clattering close behind. "I've learned Connor is a good man since we started working together. And I've seen how much his son respects him," Titi Sandra says.

"What's his sign?" Titi Neva asks.

"Don't start," Titi Ivy warns her.

"Well"—Mom rocks Zoe—"I'm sure you had your reasons for breaking up, but that boy seems so nice. He helped put together Zoe's newest car seat last week. Remember, Sandra?"

Last week. That means Leon's been back seven days, and he didn't tell me. If he's been around my aunts, he had to have thought of me at least once. Yet nothing. I can't tell what's worse: him remembering me and deciding not to reach out or him not thinking about me at all.

For someone who had two years to heal from heartache, it still feels like someone's twisting a rusted knife into my chest. But I'm in a better place now, despite being freshly dumped. So I methodically remove the rusted knife and toss it in the metaphorical trash, where Leon should live.

"Amelia," Titi Ivy says, "invite him over for dinner."

"You're just saying that because you want *Connor* to come over," Titi Neva adds.

"Before we have anyone over, this house needs a deep clean. Elena, you need one most of all," Titi Sandra says.

Sofia elbows me again. "This feels like a perfect time for you to listen to my idea."

"Melia, can we *please* read—"

"Enough!" I snap, standing quick enough that vertigo slaps me so hard stars dance along my vision. The sensation reminds me I forgot to take my iron supplements. Everyone stares at me, the silence as loud as my order. Good. It's about time they *actually* listened to me. "I don't want to read, or talk, or clean the house so that I can invite my ex-freaking-boyfriend to dinner."

My voice grows louder, and heat climbs my neck. My hands turn to fists at my sides as I go on. "He *dumped* me. Everyone does, and everyone will because of a family curse that I have nothing to do with. So no invites and no questions. Because there's no point. I'm going to die alone with my sisters and a hundred dogs, so, please, *please*. Leave. Me. Alone."

Everyone is quiet as I storm out, climb the stairs, and slam—then lock—the door to my room. Good. Silence. For once in my entire life.

CHAPTER 6

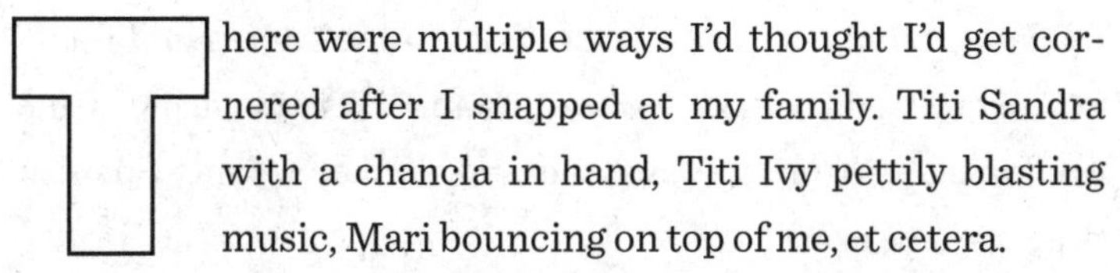

There were multiple ways I'd thought I'd get cornered after I snapped at my family. Titi Sandra with a chancla in hand, Titi Ivy pettily blasting music, Mari bouncing on top of me, et cetera.

I lay awake for hours, gaze glued to the door, waiting for whatever consequence of yelling at everyone, but nothing came. And aside from some whispers and footsteps, there wasn't much shaking the usually vibrating house. So I let myself push out a good cry over Perri, a harder cry for my loveless future, and a guilty wallowing over yelling at the only people who will remain by my side while everyone else leaves me. Then I took a nap.

Before I awoke to the smell of smoke.

A quick stab of panic pierces through my chest at the burning. Zoe, Mari, Sofia, and the aunts' faces all flash through my head rapidly. My eyes open and I shoot up and slap my forehead on someone's arm, nearly knocking an incense stick from their hands. The fear flickers into annoyance as the first whiff of salty ocean water invades my nostrils and open mouth.

"Titi Neva." I cough as the smoke attacks my lungs. "What are you doing?"

"Cleansing," she answers simply, blowing out the end of the stick. "Your mind and body are tense. I believe Sofia said *your vibes are off.*" The mix of quick movement—I really need to take my iron—and the rainbow stripes all over Titi Neva's dress make my head spin.

After I manage to clear out my throat from whatever essential oils Titi Neva soaked the sticks in, I straighten up. A series of clatters follows the movement, and I look down and find a pile of crystals and rocks over my blanket. Titi Neva picks one up and slaps it on my forehead and mumbles some Spanish prayer about peace.

"Am I being punished?" I ask, rubbing the space between my brows when Titi Neva takes the rock back.

"Punishment? I use my best oils and crystals on you, and you use such a nasty word in thanks. Maybe I need to do another."

"No, no. Thanks, Titi Neva," I try to put some excitement in my voice. "I feel, um, clean."

Titi Neva slaps a rock on my palm. "This one is for you to keep. It attracts love, joy. You need it for your lessons."

"My lessons?"

"Hurry up and go downstairs. Your sister is waiting for you."

There are multiple questions that pop into my skull once my throat clears and my head stops throbbing, but Titi Neva narrows her eyes at me, her nostrils flaring. That means something is off with my aura, according to her. Which will lead to another rock on my forehead, and honestly, I'm not sure how I don't have a permanent dent there from the amount of times Titi Neva has found the need to cleanse me. The last time she did it's because she overheard me calling Sofia some, well, *colorful* adjectives after she stole, then lost, my favorite sweater.

I crawl past her, still a little dizzy from the quick movement, and nearly tumble down the bunk stairs. Before my face meets the sharp edge of wood, Titi Neva grabs the collar of my striped hand-me-down pj's and saves my lips from splitting open. She doesn't let go until we're both upright and my hand is reaching for the door.

Before I can touch the knob, Titi Neva's bangles jangle together as she grabs my wrist. "Do you know why I always call you *mi amor*?"

My body tenses as I brace myself. Titi Neva's questions are never really straightforward. They're either rhetorical, philosophical, or meant to lead whoever is on the receiving end of one into some kind of ritual or lesson.

I try for the obvious. "Because you love me?"

She smiles, and it's not the *gotcha, time for a lesson in astrology* one, but one that crinkles the corners of her hot pink–eyeliner. "It's because you are so filled with love." Her hand moves to my cheek. "Your whole life, you've given that love out like you were born to. To your sisters, your family, your friends, strangers. It is not a bad thing to love, mi amor."

My throat constricts enough that it hurts. Now, even more than when she was slapping rocks on my forehead, my feet itch with the need to leave the room.

Titi Neva looks at me like she can see all my thoughts and spot my hidden box of emotions. It makes my stomach tremble like it's filled with static. If she looks any deeper, then she'll know secrets I try so hard to keep from them all. She'll know I don't want to stay in the house she helped raise me in. She'll figure out how ungrateful I am for the life they've given me. The most I can do is nod.

As I open the door, Titi Neva adds, "You would do well to share some of that love with yourself."

I hurry out, taking the stairs two at a time. A voice so quiet I can barely hear it, or maybe I don't really *want* to hear it, asks, *How can I love myself when I don't even know myself*?

Which is a ridiculous thought. Of course I know myself—I think. I mean, it'd be crazy not to. I deal with my own thoughts every second every day.

I know that I like how it feels when someone laughs at something I say. I know I hate when people forget small things about me, like being allergic to kiwi. I know I like the look in someone's eye, the way it shines enough that the colors seem to change after you get them a gift so perfectly suited to their personality. I know I hate losing anything, sports, games, arguments. I know I like waking up to the smell—not taste—of coffee.

I know a collection of tiny things about myself, but for big things, like my dreams and my goals . . . I'm not so sure.

As soon as I step into the living room, a horn blares in my face. I jump up so high my head hits the top of the doorway as a colorful array of streamers tangle themselves around me. Before I can catch my breath, music blasts from beside me. The loud pop instrumental threatens to burst my eardrums and I step back, but my bare feet slip on a streamer as it falls, and I drop on my ass—it's got to be bruised at this point—in the span of two seconds, a ribbon spilling over one of my eyes.

The music shuts off, and Sofia, dressed in a tux that's swallowing her, appears above me. "Ugh, no, this is not my vision." She thrusts her hand out, and when I don't take it, she grabs my wrist and pulls me up and into the living room. "Mari, you were supposed to wait until she was *in* the room, and, Titi Ivy, the volume was supposed to be at five. Some of us still have our hearing."

"Cuidado," Titi Ivy warns, sitting by a foldout table pushed in front of the kitchen.

"Amateurs," Sofia mumbles.

After I pull my blindfold free, and the shock of it all settles, I finally realize the sala has been transformed into, well, I'm not entirely sure what.

The L part of the couch has been pushed to the side to make room for a chair holding a projector casting Sofia's desktop wallpaper, a pic of her photoshopped next to BTS, on her makeshift screen—the back of the carpet from our room, duct-taped at the corners on top of the bookshelf only Mari uses.

Now that my eardrums have stopped pounding, I can hear the music of some game show I can't remember the name of lightly playing as Sofia makes her way over to the table and grabs some flash cards beside Titi Ivy.

"What's going on?" I ask, unsure if I really want to know what. I'm still bracing myself for some sort of consequence, but Titi Neva didn't do anything, and Titi Ivy winks at me when I sneak a glance her way.

Mari, in leggings and a blazer, jumps up and starts, "Welcome to—"

Sofia catches her midjump and spins her around. "Oh no you don't. That's *my* line." She drops Mari, and she gives Sofia the cutest, most nonthreatening scowl on the planet. "Anyway, take a seat." Sofia claps her hands twice and then huffs out a breath. "Mari, that was your cue."

"Oh, right." Mari gallops toward Titi Ivy and picks up the chair the same height as her, then drags it to me. She pushes me until I sit on it and face the hanging carpet.

Again, I ask, "What's happening?"

With jazz hands, Sofia stands into front of the DIY screen and sings, "Welcome to the Hernandez Romance Boot Camp."

"The what, now?" I look around, hoping to find confusion on a face that must mirror mine, but everyone is normal. Like this is a daily occurrence we meet for before breakfast.

Still in her announcer voice, Sofia goes on, "I'm your host, Sofia, but you can call me Your Highness—"

"Not doing that."

"—and I'm helped by my assistants, Ivy and Marisol!"

"That's us," Mari says, standing by the desk beside Titi Ivy with a buzzer from one of our board games in her tiny palms.

"Now, I know you people in the audience are wondering what exactly this boot camp is about. Well, let me explain," Sofia says, and I look around to see the invisible audience she speaks of, but it's just me. "Titi Ivy, *hello*."

"Oops," Titi Ivy says, then the screen behind Sofia transforms into a PowerPoint with the words *Romance Boot Camp* dancing on the screen. She even typed *by Sofia Hernandez and Co* underneath.

Maybe I'm still dreaming. Or Titi Neva's incense was too strong and now I'm seeing and hearing things. This is too weird, even for my family.

Mari comes over, shoving a tiny, pink bound journal into my hands. The cover of the book has the words *Hernandez Romance Boot Camp* in bubble letters Sofia must have drawn. "For your notes," she whispers before going back to Titi Ivy.

The screen changes, and a picture of our whole family lights up the frame. "First things first," Sofia explains. "The curse. You know the story, so we'll skip past that, but is the curse permanent? Well, my assistant Ivy can explain more."

Titi Ivy crosses her bare legs, her T-shirt dress hiking up farther as she speaks. "Technically speaking, nobody has ever tried to break the curse, so there's no reason to think that it's permanent."

"Or real," Sofia mutters so only I can hear. She doesn't believe in it, but she knows *I* do. Which is why she's put together whatever I can classify this as. A class on love? A lecture on what I'm doing wrong? I mean, I'm surprised Sofia doesn't believe in the curse, with all our track records. There's no evidence *against* it. "So, to the audience watching—"

"Sofia, please." My left ear begins to heat. "I'm half asleep and my throat is burning with essential oils right now. I can barely focus on anything but my never-ending humiliation, so can you get to the point?"

"Fine." She rolls her eyes. "None of you appreciate the flair of it all, anyway." She leans down so we're level. "Look, you want to break the loveless curse. We love you, so we want to help. Factually speaking, it's not looking like you're on the way to breaking it anytime soon—"

"Thanks."

"—so we've put together a PowerPoint to help." Sofia gestures at Titi Ivy, and there's a *click,* then a Venn diagram appears on the screen. "We've put together all our favorite ships, why they work, why they last. Both fictional and, of course, the power couples still together. We've got BuzzFeed quizzes, interviews, the works. So, Mari, hand Amelia a pen because we're about to make her the perfect girlfriend. So perfect, nobody will ever even *think* to break up with her."

It takes a moment for me to realize that, one, this is all not a dream or delusion, and, two, they're all serious about this.

My stomach bottoms out.

My family adores me so much. That's what their massive love is: ignoring your beliefs to help someone solidify their own. They're all feeding into Sofia's game show host make-believe, trying to help me find love—even though they believe in the curse.

If only they knew part of the reason I want a relationship is because it's another step in my dream of getting out of the house. They don't have the slightest clue about that, or about my biggest and only secret—from Sofia, at least.

That I've been accepted into a gap year program that starts next year. That I'm around five thousand dollars away from my program fee. That I'm planning to leave this house for an entire year, by myself. Guilt pokes at me, but before I can think about it, Mari comes over with a bundle of glitter-gel pens and colorful highlighters. She tells me, "I think you're perfect the way you are already."

"Me too," Sofia adds sourly, like she wanted to say it first. "And you are, but these people you're dating, they can't see that. Dating is an act, a dance, a courthouse. If you don't play it correctly, you lose the part, the case." Again with the mixed metaphors.

"So you want me to *act* like the perfect girlfriend?"

"No, you already have all the traits, you just don't know how to use them. I know you. You get too nervous and you mess up your words, say the wrong things. This isn't to change you, but to guide you."

There must be something wrong with me, more than all the stuff I already know about, because a flicker of hope blinks within me. I've always been a hopeless romantic. I love love. Netflix strictly recommends rom-coms to me because I've never watched another genre on the app.

I've always been obsessed with love. Probably because nobody in my family has ever been in it, so every time I read a book with it, or watched a movie, I was amazed. All the characters were always content, but not fully happy. They were on the brink of it.

Then they'd find their soul mate, and everything *clicked.* Everything in their life became more meaningful, fun. That's how I feel. I'm not unhappy, not even close to it. But I feel on the brink too. Like I'm right at the climax of a movie, but it's stuck on pause before it can finish.

The aunts, my sisters, they don't feel like that. They already heard their *click*. They found their happiness with one another, in their bakery, in their passions.

The aunts view love through a singular-lens telescope. That's where it lives. Love is Titi Neva hanging protective crystals over us while we sleep so we don't have nightmares. It's Titi Ivy learning the contours of our faces to make sure our makeup suits us perfectly. It's Titi Sandra rotating the weekly dinner menu to ensure everyone gets their favorite meal at least once. It's Mom learning how to sew so she can tighten the waistbands of pants that don't ever fit our hips perfectly. To them, love is counting seven pairs of shoes by the front door.

For me, love is meant to be viewed like a kaleidoscope—there are dozens of shades of it. Family is orange, strong and reliable, a force as powerful as the sun. Friends are green and peaceful, solid ground to lie on to relax or have fun with. Relationships are blue, sometimes a gentle wave, other times scary, like the North Sea, filled with a depth meant to be explored but never able to be comprehended fully.

I love them all so much, and yet I know there's more to be found outside this house, outside this one lens.

But . . . what am I doing? I'm just getting my hopes up to be shoved aside again. I'm cursed if not by familial culture than by my own unlovable personality. I mean, I'm hot, so it can't be my looks.

Oh my God, I am conceited. I'm too arrogant. That's another one to add to my list of traits. It's getting quite long,

Amelia's Dumpable Qualities. I could make a book of them. Okay, fine, more like a short story, but whatever.

"Hey." Sofia appears so fast, I have no chance to dodge her hands pinching my cheeks. "None of that."

"None of what?" I try to pull away, but she only twists harder.

"I know what's in your brain. That's your 'I'm going to be unnecessarily mean to myself' face."

My words come out muffled since she's squeezing my entire face into a raisin. "I don't have an 'I'm going to be unnecessarily mean to myself' face."

"Yeah, you do." She pulls away and holds a hand up to frame her face. Her eyes go a little glossy, far off, like she's trapped in a different memory, and her bottom lip disappears as she chews. Then she blinks and she's back in the present. "See? Mean face. We're going to work on that. No negative spiraling allowed."

"I wasn't spiraling. I was slightly declining."

"Be quiet. You're ruining my pace."

Okay, maybe I *was* doing that, but I didn't realize Sofia picked up the skill to know when I'm doing it by expression alone. She's so observant and smart. Most definitely, Sofia isn't cursed. She's got everything going for her. If I can learn to be more like her, then maybe I won't be either. It's worth a shot.

"Okay," I say, then my pitch grows louder. "Okay, I can do this. I can become the perfect girlfriend. I can break the curse."

"Yeah." Sofia raises her hand for a high five. "You can."

I stand up and slap her hand with mine, full force. "I can!"

"You can!" Mari jumps in.

A new thought hits me and deflates all the hope expanding in my chest. "Well, maybe not," I blow out a breath. "Even if I manage to become a perfect girlfriend, who am I supposed to test it on? I'm single, and I'm not going to lie, I've dated enough people that I don't have that many left."

Sofia snaps her fingers and smirks like she knew I'd think of this and already thought of ten different solutions. "I've made you a Beedle, and I have a bunch of people ready to set you up with."

I chew on my bottom lip. "But if I'm trying to impress them on the first date, wouldn't they do the same for me? I mean, I have no problem with first dates, or seconds. It's keeping it going that's the problem."

We've never had a puppy or a cat, but I assume if we did and anyone accidentally stepped on their tail, Sofia would wear the look currently pulling her face down. "Well. You see. I guess. Hm."

We all look around, and clearly none of us have an answer. This is all good in theory, but it's no use now. If only Sofia came up with this last week, while I still had Perri. Maybe then I wouldn't have been dumped, literally and metaphorically, into a lake. Maybe there was something I did that Perri didn't like. Or something I didn't do enough of.

It's not like I can just ask her.

A light bulb flickers in my head. Or maybe the noise is the new upbeat sound playing on the speaker. "What if I tried to date someone who knows me already?" I say aloud, talking more to myself as I work out the idea. "The people I've already dated have no reason to pretend to like me or try to impress me. If I can get them to like me, wouldn't that mean I'm on the right path?"

"That's brilliant," Sofia says, back in her stride. Then she tilts her head. "Then again, that's a lot of people to juggle." She paces, mumbling different ideas.

A tingle of determination straightens my spine. Instead of sitting around doing nothing, this is a chance to change my fate. If I do it right.

"Okay, let's have some clear guidelines here," Hope greases the wheels spinning in my head. "Realistically, I can't spend all my time hanging out with exes."

"More realistically," Sofia cuts in, "they all probably won't be so willing to hang out with you." At my glare, she holds up her hands. "Exes are exes for a reason. How often has an ex tried to go watch a movie with you?"

"At least once." It sounds so much like a lie, I add, "I'm pretty sure. Maybe."

"Sure," Sofia says dismissively enough that I have to fight the urge to pull her hair. "How about we reach out to as many exes as we can to see who is willing and set you up on dates with them?"

Sending off a chain message to exes asking for second chances feels a bit like begging, but I'm not really in the position to give in to embarrassment. "So some say yes, I go out with them and see if they want to go out for a second date. That'll be a way to tally a win."

Sofia gives me finger guns. "For every win, I'll take you out for ice cream. An additional incentive to do well."

"Amazing."

She rubs her thumb along her chin. "For the ones who *don't* want to go out with you, we should still see if we can learn anything from them. Figure out what went wrong enough that they're opposed to another meetup."

My gaze travels to the PowerPoint on the wall. The only time I've ever done presentations like this was during school.

I snap my fingers. "We can do, like, case studies for some. Debriefs to look back on. Like a study sheet."

Sofia's fingers dance on her hips. "Okay, okay, this is coming together. We should schedule dates close enough not to lose momentum and long enough for a breather between them. How about every four days? We can speed them up or slow them down depending on your mood."

"Lovely." Titi Ivy interrupts us, reminding me we're not the only ones in the room. "This is great and all, but, my girls, it doesn't sound like you have an endgame here." She watches one Avengers movie with us and has a new word to use against me.

Sofia frowns at her. "I thought you were here for support."

Titi Ivy shrugs, then pulls out tweezers and plucks some hairs around her brow without a mirror. Mari grabs my hand and squeezes. "We should set you up with the best date of all. Like the first-place prize."

I should be more concerned about having my younger sister so actively involved in my love life, but before I can voice it, Sofia shakes Mari. "You're a little Hernandez genius. Leave it to me. I'll find you the perfect person, Amelia. But let's not worry about that yet. We need to focus on what's up first. Who are you going to date, well, *re*date, first?"

"Who wouldn't I? I've got a long list of exes to choose from."

"Which means a whole lot of practice," Sofia adds.

We lock gazes and smile. We can do this. I can do this. I can break the curse and finally be in a lasting relationship. Then my life can begin.

My stomach flips as I try to continue to match Sofia's smile. She's doing all this to help me because she loves me and wants to be happy, but she doesn't realize that my happiness lies outside of the Hernandez house. She hasn't pieced that together yet, and I won't say it because I don't want her to call the whole thing off.

Sofia always talks about us living together and being crazier than the aunts, decorating the house the way we want, less cooking and more eating out, parties all the time. Just like everyone else, she sees her future here, with me, with the rest of the women.

If I was a good sister, a good daughter, a good niece, I'd tell her the truth. But I only keep my mouth shut and take notes in my new journal as the PowerPoint begins.

CHAPTER 7

HRBC Lesson #1: How to Be Chill
Sofia: Unless it's life-changing news, keep your voice at a certain (lower) level. It gives you an air of mystery.
Mom: For first dates, even if they annoy you, do not let it show. They can be nervous or say the wrong thing. Just let it slide.
Sofia: Unless they're assholes. Then text me to pick you up and drop-kick them.

When Sofia came up with the whole Hernandez Romance Boot Camp, I thought I'd have, I don't know, more than just three days before she thrust me back into the dating world. I texted a few of my exes who hadn't dumped me harshly, since they'd probably be nice enough to at least hang out with me in general. Henry, who made me realize tutoring people in math is, like, my *move,* since I met him and nearly every one of my exes that way, was the first one to respond.

When he asked me to meet him at Bee City's Adventure Course, I nearly backed out. I'm the exact opposite of an extreme-sports girlie. I get woozy on the highest level of a two-step ladder. But dates are the time to try new things, and nobody else has responded to me so far, so Henry is my only option. I guess my desire to be the perfect girlfriend outweighs my fear of heights.

Bee City is an adventure course and is technically part of the second level of an arcade since the middle is floorless while the hanging obstacles of rope-ladders, zip lines, and hurdles overlook the people playing games below. Totally not scary.

I swallow the lump in my throat and drag my feet along the carpet toward the starting point, where a small group of people surrounds the entry to the obstacle course. When I reach the group, Henry spots me and breaks free from the circle, meeting me before I join the rest of the climbers.

"Amelia." He grins, still missing one of his incisors after falling down a mountain while hiking with his family. He runs a hand over blond curls that now reach his shoulders since I last saw him. "I'm so glad you could make it."

I rub my now-sweating hands over my hand-me-down leggings. Though Titi Sandra insisted on doing a sun-kissed no-makeup-makeup look on me, I figured a loose white T-shirt and sneakers would do for an active date. But the brand-name check mark is bright on Henry's tight-fitting matching set, and his sneakers don't have a hint of dirt staining the white. He's straight out of a fitness commercial, and I'm straight out of a laundry basket.

"Thanks for letting me join."

"It's no problem." He leads me to a rack of harnesses. "Sorry to spring it on you. I'm just practicing for the courses at Catamount. There's a timed event this weekend, and this is the closest I can get to training, but after we can grab some dinner and really catch up."

Henry gathers my equipment and kneels, holding out two circles. I catch the cue and place my hand on his shoulders, positioning my legs in the gear. My neck begins to warm, but the closeness isn't too awkward. I mean, we definitely did more in the back seat of his car on several occasions after a tutoring session. Still, that was a year ago.

"I was a little nervous you wouldn't want to see me again," I admit as he straps me into a harness that cups me *incredibly* uncomfortably in some sensitive areas.

"Why?" He tightens a final strap by my thigh, then stands up so we're eye level. "We were pretty cool, weren't we? If I'm honest, I've thought about you a couple times since we broke up."

His "since we broke up" translates to "since I dumped you the day before prom, and you had to take your sister as a date." He did say he did it then, so I didn't have to crop him out of any photos, which may be what he considered *pretty cool*. Before that, though, we were.

Henry would drive out to his family's beach house, and we'd get to ride on their boat on the weekends. We'd eat pizza and watch the waves crash into each other. It felt like a constant vacation with him.

I guess that's what he thought too. I was a vacation, fun for a little while, but not forever.

My eyebrow twitches involuntarily, my telltale tick that my annoyance meter is rising—the exact opposite of today's mission.

"Rule number one: Be chill." Sofia used a chancla to tap the

picture of ice on the makeshift screen. "There's nothing less appealing than complaining on the first date."

Titi Ivy said, "I can think of several things less appealing than complaints. I once had a first date who finished every sentence with a barking noise and asked me to wear a collar at the restaurant."

Mari added, "What if they chew really loud? Titi Sandra says that's bad manners. Can she complain then?"

Sofia pinched the bridge of her nose. "Mari, that's unhelpful. Titi Ivy, that's . . . You know you don't have to share everything with us, right?"

"I, for one," I said, turning toward Titi painting her nails a bright green, "would like for you to finish that story."

"Everyone, focus," Sofia demanded. "Write that down, Amelia. Be chill*."*

If I asked every single human in the world who knows me to use one word to describe me, I would bet all my savings not a single soul would say *chill*. But if chill is what Sofia and every rom-com movie she made us watch during my romance boot camp says, then chill is what I'll be.

"We were," I say, all airy, like I easily agree and hardly care about the additional *I've thought about you*. That's a good thing. And way more than Leon, who couldn't pick up the phone to text me, well, anything, even though he was around *my* family. Not that I should expect that, seeing as he ignored every single one of my texts and calls pathetically asking for an explanation for his cold ending to our warm and sweet relationship.

Ew, what, there's no reason to be thinking about Leon

when I'm out with another guy. Or at all. Definitely at all.

Henry throws an arm around my shoulder like nothing has changed, then leads me back to the huddle of people. There's a young girl in braids with an orange staff shirt and a harness with the group. She does a head count and then declares, with a beaming smile, "Great, everyone is here. Now let's go over some safety procedures and general tips."

I straighten out my shoulders as a hot, *someone is watching you* feeling creeps along my skin.

When I turn, it's worse than the sense warned.

I whip back so I'm facing the employee, but her voice is distant as my pulse grows loud enough that my ears pound with its rhythm. Everything in me wants to turn again, but I try to remain calm, keep my face clear of any emotion, as if seeing him is no big deal.

With all my focus on masking myself, I barely pick up any of the instructions. The gist of it all is *stay clipped and don't die*, or something along those lines.

Henry removes his arm from me. "Hey, no need to be nervous. It's totally safe."

"Totally," I reply, my pitch skyrocketing—but not for the reason Henry thinks it is.

Everything is fine. It's all one strange, annoying coincidence. I don't have to acknowledge his existence. He certainly didn't acknowledge mine. I'll just pretend he's not there. No problem.

"Amelia," a deep voice says from behind me, too loud to ignore without Henry noticing me actively ignoring the owner of it.

Out of all the places to plant himself, Leon positions his body right in front of mine, blocking my view of the path everyone walks—toward the platform to start the hanging course. The only person I see is a redhead pausing beside Leon, her gaze trained on him.

The last time I saw him, he was covered in sawdust, and his hair was sweaty and sticky on his face. Today, there's not a wrinkle on his dark jeans and black shirt. And his hair is doing that Superman curl over his forehead, the one I used to twirl with my fingers whenever we cuddled together.

My stomach flips at the memory, and if I could kick myself, I would. But that wouldn't be very chill-girl of me.

"Leon!" My voice mimics a whistle-note, and it's enough that Henry frowns between us.

"Friend?" he says, like he senses it's not true.

"Acquaintance," I grab Henry's wrist before he recognizes Leon from school in an attempt to begin pulling him away, but he doesn't budge easily. I know they didn't have any classes together; except for math, Leon was in AP freaking everything, and he transferred before junior year. Hopefully that's enough time for Henry to forget his face. "He's working at my family's bakery is all."

Leon reaches out, his hand aiming for mine, the one that's wrapped around Henry like he means to remove it, so I yank Henry away, but not before I spot the redheaded freckled girl eyeing our interaction in the same way Henry just did. From the way I catch her eyes narrowing at me, I'm pretty sure they're on a date.

The wave of nausea crashing into me is because I reached the start of the course. Not because I care that Leon's seeing other people. *I'm* seeing other people. Kind of.

The course has a level, then above, more ropes and lights. The platforms that hold people are glass, with flashing lights blinking under them. There are so many lights, with the largest being a bright blue, that it looks like we're all fish in an aquarium.

Except instead of salt water, it only smells of sweat.

I focus on Henry as he lines up to follow a group of people climbing the metal ladder at the start. He's stopped from clipping his harness in by the employee, who points up to the course above.

"Only two people per platform. It's a weight thing," she explains.

"Good thing we work out." Henry elbows me lightly.

When I don't respond, he gives me a weird look. Then I realize it's a joke. I'm trying to think of the punch line. Is it people who don't work out?

I can hear Sofia's voice in my head telling me *be chill.* But it's not very chill for the thud of irritation pounding behind my ear to be hard enough that I can't think of a response that isn't *grow up* or *who cares?*

Whatever comes out my mouth is definitely not a laugh. Close. It's just, laughs aren't usually loud enough to make the person next to you jump in fear, but the employee quickly recovers and gives me half a smile.

It's our turn, and Henry doesn't hesitate to clip his harness onto the rope hanging off the side of the ladder.

"Lame joke," a deep voice says from behind.

Because I'm so bad at everything, I do a terrible job at pretending Leon doesn't exist. Despite trying to be a chill girl, my voice is fast and snappy. "Nobody asked you."

My gaze unwillingly searches for the girl he's with and catches her speed walking toward us from behind him, like Leon walked off without checking for her.

All my annoyance with Henry lands on Leon instead. There's a tiny part of me that is embarrassed Leon doesn't have a problem critiquing Henry when I couldn't form a word. He's not worried about being chill. He's worried about being honest—and, it seems, annoying me.

"I didn't *want* to hear it," he says, sounding put out as if I offended him personally. "And since when do you find those kinds of jokes funny?"

At that, I turn on my heel. He's so close, the metal parts of our gear collide and ring out against each other. My entire body feels supercharged, like I ran around a furry carpet and the next thing I touch will be electrocuted. It's such a stark difference from having to force myself to breathe evenly in the name of "being chill." My whole body is still in defense mode.

"Since when do you have a right to speak to me?" Somehow, the more I try to relax, the more Leon makes my body want to do the opposite.

"This doesn't count as 'speaking to you,'" his jaw twitches. "I've been trying to speak to you, but you won't let me."

I go on my tiptoes, but it's still annoyingly not enough to reach his eye level. "I'm pretty sure I gave you plenty of chances to."

"You *literally* ran from me last time I saw you."

From the platform above, Henry whistles down at me. "Come on, Amelia, what's the holdup? Scared?"

But I'm too busy dealing with my flurry of emotions to respond to anyone but Leon. "I was referring to when you left me high and dry."

"I'm going to start without you," Henry shouts as I latch gazes with Leon.

At my response, Leon's jaw unlocks, and he takes a step back. He chews on his bottom lip, eyeing me in a way that makes my shoulders tense up. It reminds me of how he acted before he told me he was considering transferring schools for a better chance at a scholarship. Cagey. Wrong. Only this time, there's this added layer to his gaze. I can't pinpoint whether or not he's judging me or annoyed with me. Two things he rarely ever made me wonder about before.

The girl he's with places a hand on his shoulders and gives me a *stay back* look while her voice sweetly asks Leon, "Someone you know?"

"Not anymore," Leon says so quick and sharp it stings my very core. Pain vibrates my rib cage fast enough I can't keep from flinching. I'm not a friend and not even enough to be a past acquaintance. Just somebody he doesn't know at all anymore.

I barely have enough time to process this before I feel tears prickling my eyes.

I can't believe my body is reacting this way. It's been so long since we've spoken to each other. Leon's right. We aren't friends, and I practically said the same to Henry. But he sounded so appalled by the idea that it brings up all the same hurt from when he left. The same confusion, the same frustration, the same sadness, because what right does he have to think of me that way? When I'm the one he left, I'm the one who doesn't even know what I did wrong?

He must catch whatever embarrassing look is on my face because all the harsh lines on Leon's face vanish, and a concerned expression replaces it.

He says my name so softly, if we weren't so close, I'd miss it. The way it sounds on his tongue almost feels fragile. Like he's scared to say it any louder, but I turn, hurriedly clipping myself to the rope and ignoring the strain of muscles as I ascend the ladder to make it on the first course.

When I reach the top, Henry is already clipped on one of the two lines to the first obstacle to reach the next, higher platform. "Awesome, Mels. Keep up that speed and we'll be finished in no time."

I let out a breath as if the climb was tiring, rubbing a hand over my face, trying to wipe away stray tears as discreetly as possible.

A giggle erupts from me, earning a tilted head from Henry. My brain sends conflicting signals to my body. I'm nervous but still trying to implement the Hernandez Boot Camp strategies, which would be so much easier if seeing Leon, talking with him, being so *close* to him, hasn't made me feel like I've just escaped from being in a high-spun washing machine. I have to shut my eyes for a few seconds before I feel the world stop spinning around me.

When everything is balanced, I open them again.

This high, the people down at the arcade are close to becoming ants. We're not even at the highest level. I probably won't be able to make out the shapes of their forms when we reach there.

Henry hops off the square glass and grabs the metal bars, leading up to the next platform. Without his weight, the glass vibrates. I jerk back onto the pole.

My nails dig into the metal wrapping it. I really shouldn't have eaten half of that flan Mom made me. It doesn't taste as good climbing back up my throat.

Just as Henry reaches the next platform, Leon climbs up to join me on the glass that's even smaller now that he's here. Somehow my irritation with him overwhelms the dread settling underneath my skin.

It's a benefit and an annoyance. At least I'm less likely to throw up. Barely.

"You couldn't have waited until I reached the next platform before coming up?"

Leon gives me a pointed look, then the next platform, then me. "I was beginning to think you were caught on something and couldn't go."

"Ha ha." I swallow, then move. It's more of a shuffle, but it still gets me to the edge of the glass.

"Why are you up here?" Leon asks as Henry calls for me to hurry over.

"To freaking meditate, Leon, what does it look like?"

"But you're afraid of heights."

Again, a shock of emotions jolts me, and my throat starts to close.

I hate the reminder that Leon knows so much about me, more than I've told anyone else I've dated, and I hate it even more how he throws it in my face now like it's nothing. Like we're two causal friends and he can bring up things I told him in confidence. Even when moments ago he said we weren't.

"You don't know me anymore."

I keep my gaze trained on my shaky hand as I clip myself the same way Henry did so I'm secured on the long line. That way, if I fall off the course, it'll catch me in half a second. Hopefully. I'm too young to die.

I'm sure if Leon's body weren't an inch from touching mine, I'd cling to the pole the way Titi Neva claims Titi Ivy used to. Instead, I lunge forward and grasp the bars, using momentum before swinging to the next one. I nearly slip off with my clammy hands but tighten right before I plunge to certain death.

Just keep it moving, Amelia.

In a surprisingly graceful way, I make it across the bars as fast as Henry did. Mainly because I have two motives for speed. One, finishing this as soon as possible before I throw up. And two, the bigger reason, to get away from Leon.

When I land, Henry is waiting for me. "Wow, that was faster than I did it. Why don't you take the lead?"

Chill girl that I am, I pick up my brick feet and join him on the edge.

There are three different lines leading to different paths on the obstacle course. One for hard, intermediate, and easy.

Hard would be the chill-girl move, but seeing as it will lead me to have a full-on meltdown that would guarantee Henry would block me, intermediate it is.

Before I can clip myself onto the line, Henry grabs my arm. "Come on, that course is way too easy. Let's challenge ourselves. It'll be boring if we don't."

Boring isn't exactly an adjective I want to be referred to as. *Chill*, absolutely. And chill Amelia goes with the flow, even if that flow feels like it's rapidly transitioning into a whirlpool as I watch Henry fasten himself onto the line leading to the hard path.

Before I give in to the panic drumming in my chest, I attempt to follow. It takes me three times to get my hands still enough to clip myself onto the wire and follow Henry.

The first course is a scatter of not-at-all stable-looking blocks, tiny and lined horizontally like a death ladder. It's slightly swaying with Henry's graceful walk across it. He doesn't even grip the safety line above him for balance. He practically skips his way along while I try to breathe through my nose and think about how unlikely it'd be for my safety equipment to be the only set that's somehow broken and will lead me to my death.

When I finally find the courage to place my foot on the first step, Henry is already halfway done. "Come on, Meli. What, are you scared?"

Unlike him, my slick fingers maintain a death grip on the wire above for balance. I don't let up while I place a shaky foot on top of the first block. By the time I manage to place my weight on it, I can feel the burn on the palms of my hands.

My heart races faster than ever. And that's just the first part of the course. I'm supposed to do this for how much longer? I'm too young for a heart attack.

Metal clashes with metal right behind me. Startled, I turn and find Leon about to jump onto our path. My stomach twists sharp and quick with panic. It's supposed to be two people per platform.

What happens if there are three? Do the wires drop us?

I try to clip myself onto the closest line, but my shaky grip misses the wire twice before it snaps into place. I hear a rustle of metal, Leon's intake of breath. I jump forward before he reaches me.

I land on a tiny circle of wood that nearly tips me over if I don't grip the thin pole hanging on an even thinner rope. It's like an oversize spinning top.

Every time I *think* about moving, the entire thing leans and I'm half a second from falling over. I can't help but look down, and we're in the center. If I fall, I'll drop right at the top of the high-striker—the tall structure of lights and numbers that measures how strong you can strike down a hammer at the circle sitting at its base. I just know my spine would break right in half. It's not like it's made of anything sturdy in the first place.

"I want to go back," I say, water building at the corners of my eyes. "I'm done now."

"You can't go back," Henry calls over, his voice way too distant. "There's too many people on the platform behind us. You have to finish it."

I look up and realize he's already on the other platform, standing by the pole, waiting for me to cross over. He didn't even slow down for me. Didn't offer an inch of support.

"I don't *want* to finish it," I practically scream. The chill girl is gone, and after another near-fall, panicked girl takes her place.

"Amelia," Leon grabs the rope above with one hand, leaning forward and reaches out toward me. "I got you."

While I momentarily freeze, trying to gather a coherent thought, I hear Henry shout to me, "Whatever, I'll do the hard course and meet you at the end."

"Wait," I say as he starts walking around the pole, where I can't see him anymore. "Don't go."

But he does.

Leon calls for me again, but this is all humiliating enough.

I'm crying, obviously this time, because I was just ditched by my date, in front of my ex, who also ditched me (in the past). I'd say this is rock bottom, but there's still the arcade waiting underneath me. I only have two options: I can reach out to Leon and panic, or I can try to finish the obstacle course and run back home to avoid any more embarrassment.

Before I chicken out, I lunge toward the next spinning top. And meet God.

At least, that's what it feels like when my body flips completely over right as the wire catches me. My scream catches in my throat as the world literally flips over.

My clip gets caught on something—I can't tell since I'm *upside down*. My mouth is an O, and the blood rushes to my skull at the sudden stop.

Now I'm grateful how tight the harness is because I'd slip out and fall on the people a story below playing a zombie-shooting game. I'm also grateful for my thick thighs that keep me in—aside from the slightest slip that has me screaming.

A girl on the platform I was *supposed* to be on starts shouting for help. Some people below me start pointing and yelling, and I scream louder when they pull out their phones and begin to record me.

I swear I'm slipping, and if I weren't upside down, tears would be spilling down my cheeks. From fear and from the pain blooming in my core as I try to use it to swing my body upright to grab the zip line and right myself again.

Strong hands wrap around my waist, and Leon helps yank me vertically until I'm upright again.

I wrap my arms around Leon, who's somehow managing to hold me and keep us balanced on the few inches of space we have. My feet are on top of his, and I'm pretty sure I'm going to have his skin under my nails, but all I feel is relief that I'm not going to plummet to my death anymore.

"This doesn't mean anything," I mumble into his shirt, my voice shaking with adrenaline and not because his hard body presses against my lips. "My terror just overrides my hate for you is all. Once we're off this thing, remember that."

It's the truth, but it feels like a lie when my hands finally have the ability to unclench themselves and my heart remembers it doesn't have to beat like it's trying to come first in a race.

His body stills. "You hate me?" He turns so his back is facing me. "Never mind. Let's finish the course. I'll go first, then you."

"Okay."

"By the way, your date's an asshole," he adds, and I can't tell if he sounds glad about it or is making fun of me because of it. Maybe both. Hard to tell without seeing his expression, but his voice is sharper than it has been this whole time. Interesting because *I* haven't spotted *his* date since we began the course.

"Whatever," I huff out, the momentary relief Leon offered quickly fading away.

For the next hour, I ignore every twist and turn my stomach takes each time Leon and I touch. Which is easy since Leon is silent until we make it to the end of the course. Even when I swallow my pride and turn to thank him for patiently waiting and helping me finish each path.

He just carefully removes all the gear from my body, puts it on the rack with the others, and leaves.

Safe to say I do the same and did not earn a second date with Henry.

CHAPTER 8

HRBC Lesson #2: Humor

Sofia: No matter how lame the joke is, if they say one, laugh.

Titi Ivy: Unless the joke is at your expense, then ask them, "Can you explain that to me?" and enjoy as they crumble.

Sofia: It's okay to make your own jokes, but try not to go off laughing at them. (Remember when you laughed for thirty minutes straight after you told Perri a pun? Let's not repeat.)

"Put your phone away," I snap at Sofia, who is positioned toward the window so I can't see her screen as we sit in the back seat of the SUV.

"I can't be on my phone?"

I try to snatch it away, but her palm smacks my forehead, so I switch to pinching her. "I *know* you're watching the video again."

"What video?" she asks innocently, blinking her pink-shadowed eyes like I don't recognize the sound of commotion coming from her speakers. I've watched the video of me hanging upside down screaming for help a thousand times since it was uploaded last night.

The original, and the remixes changing my scream into a beat drop, the duets. All of them. And yeah, *some* of them were funny, but it made me mad at myself for laughing.

I glare at her and she sighs. "Fine, but just so you know, I was *reporting* another upload. It's called damage control."

"It's called adding to the views." I snatch her phone, catch the twenty-seven thousand likes the video of me has, then turn it off. Leave it to my sister to be a thousand of the views.

"Hey, you need a better sense of humor," Sofia points out. "Have you already forgotten lesson number two?"

"Is it my turn?" Mom asked, popping her head in on day two of Hernandez Romance Boot Camp. "I heard the Golden Girls theme song. That's what you said is for me, right?"

Sofia, in one of Titi Sandra's pant suits, waved her in the living room and said, "Actually, it's for all of you. Four old ladies for four old ladies."

From thin air, a chancla zipped through the room and slapped Sofia in the chest. Thin air, because Mom walked in with Zoe in her arms, so it couldn't have been her.

"Well." Mom ignored the PowerPoint behind her with the four old ladies smiling in a living room. "I think people try to make others laugh to impress them. So maybe you can laugh extra loud when they tell jokes."

"That's surprisingly pretty good," Sofia said, earning a glare from Mom. "My bad. Anyway, she's right. I guarantee they'll try to joke around. Lots of times they'll try to make some light jokes about you, so laugh at those too."

"You want me to laugh at a joke about *me?"*

"Joking and poking fun at a date is flirting, not malicious.

If your voice gets pitchy, they may say something like Wow, you seem nervous. *It's playful. It's banter. You don't get offended, you laugh it off and say,* Maybe.*" Sofia sucked her teeth. "Do we have to watch* The Princess Diaries 2 *again?"*

"No, I get you."

"Good," Sofia went on. "Humor goes both ways. You have to flatter the people around you, but you also need to be able to laugh at yourself too. No self-deprecation jokes though."

"But those are my favorite ones."

I'm sure I would find the video funnier if I didn't know Leon was right there to witness it in person. Good thing it cuts off right before Leon saved me. I can't handle Sofia asking me about him again. I'm still stewing over the fact that he helped me.

Titi Sandra brakes way too hard into a parking spot, and I drop Sofia's phone as the two of our faces smack into the back of the seats. "I have a headache, and you two are making it worse," she unlocks her seat belt. "Grab the cleaning supplies and *behave.*"

My sister and I are quiet until Titi Sandra hops out and shuts the door.

Sofia flicks my arm with her heavily ringed fingers. Seriously, she always has at least three minimum on one finger. I think she's growing tiny muscles around them. "There's no need to be embarrassed. I've seen seagulls poop on your head at the beach. Twice."

I slap her hand, trying not to compare how my nails are missing skin around them and hers are a perfectly summer color and claw-shaped. I *really* need a manicure. "You're not the one who was trending."

"I wish I was. You've gained a thousand followers since."

"If you watch it one more time, I will rip off every single extension on your eyelashes."

Sofia rolls her eyes, shrugging so her orange spaghetti strap slips off her shoulder. "As long as you promise to put them on yourself. Are you out of mascara?"

Titi Sandra slams on the window and we jump hurriedly out the car before she loses the little patience she has. From the number of threats she was mumbling into her Bluetooth headset, I'm pretty sure whatever case she has is *not* going well. The last time she had this attitude, it was because she was working with a divorced couple and neither of them wanted full custody of their kid.

That's the ultimate sin for a Hernandez woman, not taking care of a child. If the impossible happened and the aunts all split up, they'd all fight to keep us with them. When the case was over she sat Sofia and I down and told us when we grow up and have kids, we damn well better treat them with the love and respect we've been given since birth.

Not a problem for me for plenty of reasons, mainly because the mere thought of having a child makes me want to literally die. Not that my aunts would know that.

After we grab the boxes filled with supplies from the trunk, we follow Titi Sandra inside the bakery. There are fewer workers inside today, and the hole I fell into now has an actual wooden plank to walk across. Wallpaper lined with delicate lattice tree branches with birds, butterflies, and insects of all colors decorates the walls now surrounding the construction workers.

This time when I walk in, I scan the room, searching for Leon. I'm not going to get snuck up on again. I'll spot him first, and then I'll . . . I'll find another hole to fall through.

Now that I've had some time to stew over it all, the way he helped me through the course, abandoning his date while mine left me, I realize how embarrassing it all was. I know it wasn't from the goodness of his heart.

I bet he had the best time watching me so miserable. That's why he came on the same course, to get a front-row seat to the action. He probably had to put so much effort into keeping himself from laughing at me.

Or maybe it was his way of trying to make amends for what he's done to me, but we're still not even, we'll never be, and I'll never forgive him.

Mom says keeping a grudge only anchors the holder down, but I'm pretty sure I'm strong enough to stay afloat. I'm a great swimmer. I've got island genes. I'd be banned from Puerto Rico if I didn't know at least a butterfly stroke.

I hold my breath to prevent breathing in the sawdust floating in the air and follow Titi Sandra into the kitchen.

Titi Sandra and Leon's dad are standing by the long steel countertop covered in boxes, surrounded by oversize stoves and fridges. The sight of them is kind of funny, Titi surrounded by dust particles and unfinished walls in an all-black pant suit and Connor covered in debris, sweat pooling around his loose top hanging over his paint-splattered jeans. Titi Sandra's shoulders are still tense from whoever she's been arguing with over the phone, but she smiles when Connor speaks.

"That's the last of the equipment, and everything should be up and running in this room."

Titi Sandra blows out a breath. "You do such good work. I thought electrical would take weeks in here."

"I'm good friends with Danilo, so I made sure he kept a good pace. Besides, they only focused on this room here. Might be another week to finish the front, but we're more than half-way done."

Sofia and I place our boxes on the floor. We're on cleaning duty today, which normally would have me fake a headache to get out of it. Sofia hates when I do that because nobody can ever tell if I'm lying or if I actually have a bout of vertigo. The only good thing about being anemic is that you have a go-to excuse for getting out of plans.

Maybe that's why I have bad karma. Using a condition to get out of plans sounds shady, *but* Titi Sandra was the one who taught me anyone who doesn't use all the tools in their disposal is sure to lose. Sure, she was talking about her court cases, but a lesson is a lesson.

"Maybe we'll start making food in here early," Titi Sandra gestures toward me and Sofia with her chin. "Whenever these two get finished with deep cleaning, we'll be able to use the stove."

"Deep cleaning sounds intense," Sofia says.

"Yeah, how about a *mild* clean?" I add.

We earn the Stare, so we shut up, put our gloves on, and make our way toward the corner of the bathtub-size sink.

Titi Sandra and Connor continue conversing about numbers, time frames, and general snooze-inducing topics while Sofia and I start scrubbing bleach on every surface.

For us Hernandez women, if something isn't squeaky clean, it may as well be hazardous waste. Doesn't matter if the thing has never been used before. With all the people who've touched it—from the store, during travel, to delivery—it's officially "dirty." If there's even a fingerprint here when we're done, Titi Sandra will make us start again.

Halfway through our first round of bleach, the door swings open, and Leon walks in, momentarily bringing in the noise of hammering and chatter before the door shuts and it muffles again. He approaches Titi and his dad with a box. "I brought some of the bathroom tile choices you wanted."

I duck behind the counter before he sees me. I'm not sure *why I do it,* only that I can't let him see me.

Sofia gives me an *are you serious?* look, and I give her a *shut up* one in return.

Some people say sisters can hear each other's thoughts, but Sofia and I can communicate with a look alone. This particular skill is used most often at the dinner table when we're trying to bet on which aunt is in a mood.

"Look at you," Titi Sandra says softly, like she's giving him a once-over. I wonder if she's looking at him with a new perspective now that she knows about us. "Planning on taking over the family business?"

Leon clears his throat. "Yes, one day."

For the record, I am trying very hard to pretend Leon doesn't exist, but that part makes my ears perk up.

Last time I checked, Leon had dreams that didn't involve constructing anything but the perfect no-look throw. He was going to get a scholarship, then drafted, bench for a few years to prove himself, and end up being the greatest NFL quarterback of all time.

"Steady career, good work ethic," Titi Sandra notes, like she's going through a list of benchmark character traits and he's checking all the boxes. Ugh. A part of me wants to scream, *You don't even know how he hurt me.*

I kick Sofia and she yelps, then waves at everyone who's probably staring her way now. "Leg cramp," she lies. Then she spares me a look and whispers, "What?"

"Get him out of here," I say through my teeth.

The best thing about sisters is the unmatched, unbreakable loyalty we have to each other. We don't have to get why the other person wants something, but when a sister needs help, the other is ready. ASAP.

Sofia says, cavity-sweet, the same voice that got us in to *multiple* eighteen-and-up bars before Titi Neva found out and promised not to tell the others if we never went again, "Weren't we supposed to have ceiling fixtures by now? They're a few days late."

I hear Connor's voice say, "We got an email the fixtures you ordered arrived at the store. Just need to pick them up. My guys are all getting ready to clock out in a few minutes. I've got some work to do at the Big E after this, or else I'd grab them for you myself."

"It's no problem," Titi Sandra says, back in her lawyer voice. "Sofia, take off those gloves. You'll come help me pick them up."

Sofia gives me a wide-eyed look I'm sure matches my own. "But I'm cleaning."

"I can help with that," I hear Leon say, and I shoot up, forget I'm under the counter, and bash my head into metal. Both my skull and the counter rattle. Sofia grips my hands and stops me midsway, helping me up. "I'm good on my own!" I say automatically, then Sofia grips my shoulders and spins me to face Titi Sandra and the others, so I repeat, "I'm good."

"Me estás desafiando?"

It's the second time today Titi Sandra has given me the Stare, and I do not want to get to a third. I stand at attention. "No, ma'am."

"Good," she says, but what she really means is *good, you get to live another day*. "Sofia, vamos."

Sofia mouths *sorry* before, and I can't blame her, running to follow Titi Sandra out the door. Connor pats Leon shoulder and says something by his ear I can't hear, mainly because my skull is still rattling within my head.

I'm going to start wrapping myself in Titi Neva's crystals if this is the kind of joke the universe wants to keep playing on me.

It's like I'm being real-life haunted by him. Even the two years without him, I'd have these moments where I'd wonder what he was up to, compared whoever I was dating at the time to who he *used* to be, passed by his road and pretended not to feel the quickening beat of my heart.

And now he keeps showing up to torture me.

I'm so in my own thoughts, it takes me way too long to realize I'm staring at Leon. And he's staring at me. There's no longer a sound of construction work hammering beyond the walls. Just us two.

"You can go." Thankfully I keep my tone at a normal human pitch. "I can clean by myself."

He approaches me. "I said I'd help." He has the audacity to *smirk*. "Hiding from someone?"

"Dusting under the counters. It's a very neglected spot. People always forget to clean down there."

He looks me up and down. "No duster? Rag?" I open my mouth and immediately shut it. Can't lie when I don't have a good one to form. Nothing is in my gloved hands. His smirk turns into a full-on grin that shows his single, stupid dimple. "Something wrong?"

"Plenty," I manage to get out, wishing for a better comeback and for something toxic I can throw in his face.

Instead of elaborating on that, he stares at me so intensely I replay the past ten seconds and hope I didn't say anything embarrassing aloud, but then he passes me to put on the gloves Sofia removed.

"That's it?" I watch as he has trouble fitting the latex on his big hands. I don't realize my eyes are trained so hard on him until I unclench my jaw. "You have nothing else to say?"

"I'm not sure if I can say anything to you." He gets one glove on, and a thousand different curses spring to my lips but I shove them all down. "Last time I tried, you shut me down."

I mirror the irritating smirk on his face. "All right. Silence, then. Perfect."

I still want to snap at him, but it's hard to argue with someone who I'm claiming I don't want to speak to at all. So I mimic him and keep my mouth shut as I grab a rag and start scrubbing the counters.

If *he* wants to act like there's nothing that happened between us, nothing to talk about, then I can do the same. I can do it *better*. If my brain can manage to finish a thousand-piece puzzle in under an hour, then it can most definitely force me to be *quiet*.

Whenever our bodies are near each other, I—dramatically, of course—dodge him. He glances at me each time but doesn't say anything, not even when I start humming his least favorite song—some country one his father would play to annoy him when he didn't wake up on time. Instead of speaking, he starts to whistle the melody of the theme song of my least favorite show. I want to throttle him.

After ten minutes of trying to discreetly annoy each other, we both get lost in our tasks, cleaning side by side. Once upon a time we made a great team. It's weird and sad to see that hasn't changed.

Halfway through brushing the bottom of the oven with my soggy rag, I have to close it and rest my forehead on the cool metal. I can't tell if it's the cleaning solution or my confusing feelings that are making me dizzy.

"Amelia?" Leon's shadow hovers over me.

"Go away," I say bitterly. "Don't you have a date to go on or something?"

That sounds like I care he was on a date. Which I don't.

"I don't have a date," he says casually, all carefree like it's something I want to hear. "I was with my cousin yesterday, to make myself clear. I'm not dating anyone else. Why would I?"

I move too quick and smack my head on the stove.

"Are you okay?" he adds, concerned.

"Ugh, I'm fine." I pull myself up, discreetly checking the labels of the bleach I used to make sure I didn't mix up the chemicals and create a bomb. That would be concerning. The room isn't exactly spinning, but it's not as steady as I'd like it to be. If it's not the chemicals, it's probably because, yet again, I forgot to—

"Did you take your iron?"

I whirl on him. He's got some nerve acting like he still knows me—even if he's right. "Don't talk to me."

"Why don't you go outside and get some fresh air?"

"Why don't you stop telling me what to do?" I slam my finger so hard on the self-clean button, my bone cracks. "I *will* go outside, but *not* because you told me to." When he rubs his lips like he's hiding a smile, I jam my now-throbbing finger into his chest. "And you don't get to laugh at me, with me, whatever. We're not friends, or close, or anything. I wish you'd leave me alone."

"Easy for you to do when you barely give me a chance to talk."

"Okay, talk," I say, and as he opens his mouth, I add, "But

only if you speak about why you left, why you ghosted me, why you came back and didn't say a word, and why you're popping up now like nothing happened at all."

His lips slam shut. I hate that it sends a pang through my chest. Hate that my change in pitch makes it obvious that I still care.

"That's what I thought." I turn on my heel and storm out. The cool night wind does make me feel better, and the pettiness in me is mad that he was right to suggest it.

I kick a nearby pebble as Leon follows me out.

"It's been two years." He doesn't say it, but I hear what he means: *Get over it already.*

I open my mouth to say something snarky, but all that comes out is a harsh laugh. We rarely ever fought. Sure, little things here and there, like me never remembering to use a turn signal when he was helping me learn to drive, and me telling him to remember to eat instead of studying all day. We could barely stay mad at each other for more than a few minutes before either of us cracked with a laugh, a kiss, a hug.

Two years is a long time to be mad at someone.

And yet it's not long enough.

"Try again in twenty years. Maybe I'll be over it." I look up until my eyes adjust as stars pop up one by one and freckle the sky.

"I meant it's been two years and I'm different now." Then he adds so quietly I might have missed it if not for the breeze lifting his words to me, "You're not over me?"

I jerk back. "No. I mean yes. Yes, I'm over you. But I'm not over what you did." Which sounds as if I still have feelings for him. "You know what? Just be quiet." There's no point in arguing. Not only will it get us nowhere, it'll get me nowhere—aside from closer to a headache.

He blows out a harsh breath. "Don't you think you're being a little unfair?"

Never mind.

"Is this a joke?" My throat burns like I swallowed sandpaper. "Unfair? Did you think I'd welcome you happily? You're just a coward. A jerk. A fu—"

"Do you think you're the only one who was hurting?"

My jaw drops. I can practically feel the bubbles of my boiling blood, hot enough to leave burn marks from underneath my skin. He's truly standing here, acting as if *I'm* being unreasonable.

"May I remind you that you broke up with me? You ghosted me. And then you physically exited my life and left without so much as a goodbye. So, yeah, I'm pretty sure I'm the only one who was hurt."

I watch his full lips purse, his jaw clench. His gaze feels hot on me, and yet here he is again, not saying anything.

I laugh because this is going absolutely nowhere. He'll never truly understand what I felt, and I'll never be able to forgive him anyway.

It just sucks that he gets to get away with it, without any real consequence. So many people do too. Heartbreakers get to go along without facing their actions, without caring about the hearts they left to bleed.

People who hurt you should have to feel the same hurt you felt. It's the only way they'd understand the damage they did.

"Stay out of my business," I tell him, my anger stirring into something new.

"You are my business."

I have to physically grab my chin and push it up. I laugh because it's so ridiculous I'm not even mad. "You think you have some kind of claim on me? After everything?" I laugh again. "You know what, in some way, I think you're brave to have all this nerve. It's amazing."

He reaches into his pocket and pulls out his phone, frowning at his notifications. "I have to go," he turns away, ignoring every single thing that I said. Like he's been ignoring my feelings all this time.

After stirring up all these emotions, after *pissing me off*, he just walks away.

I don't know why I'm surprised. Leaving me behind is something he's good at.

CHAPTER 9

HRBC Lesson #3: How to Be Mysterious but Not Unattainable

Titi Neva: When you answer questions about yourself, lean toward smaller answers. This makes them more curious and they ask even more.

Sofia: Sigh and make a far-off look sometimes so it's like you're lost in memories. (They'll want to know what memories they are.)

Titi Sandra: Listen more than you speak.

Since I did the wrong proportion of solution to water, all the steel counters and appliances in the kitchen are lined with streaks. As punishment, Titi Sandra makes me and Sofia stay behind to clean up. Again.

It's evening by the time we finish, and Sofia is driving us back home. Our stomachs are growling, and our patience with each other is growing thin. Yeah, it's my fault we had to stay behind, but Sofia's singing as we cleaned made me want to drink bleach.

When we get home, all the aunts and Mari surround the kitchen table, laughing and eating the spread of empanadas lining the steel. I move toward the table, ready to stuff my face, and then I trip over my feet.

At the end of the table, sitting with my aunts, is Leon and his dad, both of them listening to whatever story Mari is enthusiastically telling with her hands.

He's traded his working shirt for a plain, wrinkleless white one that clings to every curve of his muscles. He spots me before anyone else does, and a smile fills his face.

It reminds me of our mornings at school or on the weekends. I called it Leon's *eternal prom look.* The moment he saw me, every time, the first moment, he always gazed at me warmly, fondly, like I was walking down the steps in a prom dress, like in all the movies we watched together.

I catch the aunts watching Leon, tilting their heads, furrowing their brows, then following where his gaze is currently stuck on. That's when everyone else notices me.

Without looking away from Leon's gaze, I ask, "What's going on?"

Titi Ivy, who is moving toward me at a speed that lets me know she had way too much to drink and needs the bathroom ASAP, answers, "Thank-you dinner. They've been putting a lot of hard work into our shop."

Okay, fine, valid reasons to invite my ex-boyfriend to our home, but I'm annoyed that the one place I shouldn't run into Leon has now been stolen from me. Since our breakup, it's been a Leon-free sanctuary, and now he's infiltrated it.

I know it's not entirely his fault, but he *could* have said no to the invite. So I have to ignore my first instinct to shove an entire empanada down his throat. Instead I simply walk toward the group and help myself to one without any powdered sugar coating it.

"Isn't this a *lovely* surprise?" I say as Leon moves around the table. Closer to me. I chomp on the end of the pastry, sweet pineapple filling my mouth. "Sorry I missed it."

"Oh, don't worry." Leon grabs the empanada from my hand before I can snatch it back and takes a bite where I just did. "The party's only started," he adds with his mouth full, somehow not looking or sounding ridiculous while doing it.

I try to pull my gaze away, but it snags at the appearance of his dimple, makes a pit stop at the tiny crumb by the bottom of his lip, and fully crashes at the sight of his tongue running along his mouth.

Before I can form a curse, the aunts shout.

"Sofia!" Titi Sandra calls out, drinking what I hope isn't one of Titi Neva's potions. Last time she made her *crystal-infused moonshine*, Sofia and I had to take turns holding the aunts' hair back as they did unforgivable things to the toilet. "Start gathering up the plates. You're on cleanup duty tonight."

"Ugh," she groans. "Why is it *always* me?" She leaves to begin, forgetting that it's always her because she keeps trying to get Mari to clean up for her and the aunts keep catching her. Mari can barely reach over the sink. She's broken three plates this week.

Like she senses my thoughts about her, Mari bullets toward me so quick some of the sparkles dusting her middle part float in the air behind her. Most of them sprinkle the shoulders of her white dress. "Amelia, can you believe Leon *loves* puzzles like you?"

Leon doesn't love puzzles at all. It's the one thing I couldn't get him to do with me, because he would get so frustrated not being able to finish it fast. He'd sit around and wait for me to finish. I send him a hard look. "Oh, does he ,now?"

"Yup," he says happily. "Mari and I were working on the frog one before you got here. It's really hard, though. I think we need a professional like you." He kneels down to my little sister's level. "Isn't that right, Mari?"

Mari's eyes widen with affection, and I have to keep my hands in fists before they give Leon, who gives me a quick wink before patting Mari's head, the middle finger.

"Yeah!" she turns to me. "Will you finish the puzzle for us, Meli?"

"Yeah, *Meli*, will you finish the puzzle for us?" Leon repeats, batting his eyes. *Batting his freaking eyes* like some flirty little puppy dog demon.

"I'm a little tired."

"*Please*," Mari begs, pulling on the belt loops of my jean shorts. "I want to see how it looks." I open my mouth to say the picture is on the box, but Mari must have some mind-reading skills because she goes on. "In *real life*."

I groan. "Fine."

I turn and walk toward the circular carpet by the couch where—did they even *try* to put this together? None of the pieces are separated by the shade of color, corners are mixed in with middles, some are upside down. A few are piled together like they tried to build a tent with them. A *crime*.

I sit down and start arranging them in organized piles. The top of the frog is the lightest green, so that gets its own;

the sides have slimly scales, so those are iridescent.

It's the first step to any puzzle, building the foundation. Without it, the process becomes frustrating, which is why I think a lot of people don't like puzzles. People don't like what they don't understand.

But since I was a young kid, I've always loved them.

It started when I didn't know about the curse and would ask where my father was. The aunts would throw puzzles at me to distract me, and it always worked. Each time it was used as a distraction, it also became a sort of remedy for my confusion.

I would pretend each piece was a possible outcome or reason why my life was the way it was. They were all different, but together, they made something whole. I liked to think that maybe parts of me and my life were scattered puzzle pieces, and eventually, once everything was placed correctly, it would create this beautiful picture.

That, even if something didn't feel right at the moment, one day, it would.

Now I'm not too sure. I have so many pieces of my life's puzzle, and I can't figure out where they fit. The corner pieces are there, as they always have been, and they're my family. They're the easiest and strongest to place, but the rest? I have no idea where they go.

Still, no matter how frustrating my life is, there's something soothing about taking your time, putting something together that takes hours, sometimes days.

Before I remove my phone from my pocket, a flash goes

off. I blink, and Leon has his phone out, the lens pointed at me. "Want me to send it to you?"

Something tugs in my stomach. Melancholy, maybe. "Why would I want that?"

I swear he has freaking ESP the way his lips pull into a knowing smile. "It'll drive you crazy when you finish and can't get the satisfaction of looking back at how you started. I'm helping you."

"Don't need help and won't go crazy." But my hands twitch with the urge to take out my phone. There's no way I can sneak one in without him seeing.

"Okay," he dramatically tapping the screen of his phone. "I'll delete this photo."

I clamp my teeth together and focus on arranging my piles. When I'm almost finished, Leon's fingers cover a chunk of the pieces and mix them up.

"What are you doing?" I snap, and Mari, attuned to my tone, slowly picks herself up and leaves. Smart enough to pick up on the tension, and even smarter not to be in the cross fire.

"Spreading them out," he explains, messing up more of them. "This will make it easier for us to grab them all."

"You're ruining them." I place my hand over his to keep him from messing up the corner sections. My palm barely covers his, and I don't put any weight on it, but he stops.

Oh—leaning over to stop him has brought us *way* too close. Our noses are practically kissing, and I can smell his lavender shampoo, still the same one he used two years ago, swirling with the peach dessert he must have had. It's sweet and soft and heavenly, and I close my eyes to breathe it in.

It brings me back to, well, every moment between us.

Like looking through a kaleidoscope of each time we were close enough I could smell him, taste him, touch him if I wanted. The way this warmth of safety would follow, like nothing wrong could happen because I was with Leon and anything was possible, anything good.

My eyes open, and Leon's watching me carefully, our noses a hair's breadth from kissing, his gaze flickering down to my mouth, to my eyes.

I jump back so quick the side of my hip lands wrong and sends pain signals up my back. Wincing and ignoring Leon watching me, I reorganize the pieces.

Leon's reaches out toward the puzzle again, so I snap, "If you mess up my piles one more time, I will shove these pieces in every crevice of your body."

He smartly pulls his hand away, though a quick glance up shows he's not at all intimidated by my threat, if his smirk is any indication. "Since when did you become so violent?"

"Since when do you love puzzles?"

"Touché," he says, then softer, "but I've always loved watching you do them."

I drop the piece I'm holding and cross my arms against my chest. "What is this?" I frown at him. "You disappear, you come back, you refuse to offer any kind of explanation, and now what? You're going to annoy me because you're bored? What's your endgame here?"

"It's a secret." He positions himself so one leg is up, and he uses it as a rest for his elbow. He places his chin on his arm like he's bored of the conversation, but there's a glint in his eyes. "But for now, I'm having fun."

"With *my* feelings." He blinks, like he hadn't thought of that. Leon, the guy I used to believe was the most thoughtful and kind human to ever walk this planet, didn't think that I'd be at all effected by this. I laugh because if I don't, I'd probably scream. "I can't believe this. You can't even attempt a simple *sorry* and think I'm supposed to play along with you because you're *bored*?"

He chews at the bottom of his lip. I wish I could read his mind as easily as he can read my feelings. His gaze lands on mine, free of any amusement. "If I did, would you forgive me?"

A great question. If he said sorry, it's not going to take back the months I spent wallowing with my fingers aching from the millions of times I unlocked my phone in case he called me.

Would he even mean it?

If he was so eager to leave me, he shouldn't bother to give me attention. He's staying here and figures he can hang around me when he's bored. Which is the worst thing I can think of. Being a default choice when he used to make me feel like anything but. I leave his question hanging in the air—we both have our answers.

Leon shakes his head and a determined look etches itself on his face. "Well, I'm back now," he says, "and I'm not leaving. Not again. So, things will be different. For now, I'm going to make up for the two years I've been gone. And I want to be your friend."

He left for two years, deemed me unlovable, and tosses the word *friend* at me like I'm leftovers in the fridge nobody wants but they have to finish anyway.

It makes my eyes burn, but I don't want him to see me cry. *I* don't want to cry. I can be strong, too, like the rest of the Hernandez women. "I'd rather lick a rusty water fountain in an all-men's gym."

Instead of taking it as the insult it is, his lips pull into a smile like it was a challenge. "We'll see."

"Get out." I sigh. "Lie down in the middle of the road or something."

Instead, he holds on to his knee and twists his body so his back cracks. My gaze lands on the word *staff* written on the back of his shirt. Right, he's working at the Big E too.

Noticing me watching him, he smirks before he returns the favor, looking me up and down, making my body warm.

I wish he could know how it feels to have your body betray you because of the boy who betrayed you. That'd be closure for me and my constantly crumbling heart. Maybe then I could finally, finally move on.

An idea comes to me in one quick flick in my head.

It's my turn to be the heartbreaker. I'm going to use everything I learned from the Hernandez Romance Boot Camp and become the perfect girlfriend.

What better practice than to see if I can make my ex fall back in love with me? And when he does, I'll do the same thing he did to me.

I'll throw it all in his face.

CHAPTER 10

Date Debrief #2
What Worked: Told him his hair looked sexy pushed back. (Sofia: Good job, flattery always works.)
What Didn't: Accidentally ran over the top of his fingers. Not sure how I haven't been arrested. (Sofia: IS HE OKAY?????)
What Could've Gone Better: Safety skates. (Sofia: Seriously, does he still have his fingers??)
Total Rating: 2/10. He left after, but he still said bye, so adding a point. He didn't, like, ignore me. (Sofia: DID HE GO TO A HOSPITAL?) (Titi Neva: My crystals tell me he's okay.)

ou did *what*?" Sofia shouts. I grab the pale sham on the couch and shove it over her face. I swear to God the only person who knows how to whisper in this family is Mari.

Luckily, Titi Sandra is too busy moving around pots and pans in the kitchen now that they've dried and putting them in the cabinets.

I let Sofia struggle for breath maybe a little too long before I release her, and she answers the attack with an elbow to my gut. Air whoops out of my mouth, but I keep it quiet—and keep a hand pressed on where she hit.

"Getting revenge on your ex was *not* in my presentation." She pauses, and her lips purse like she's thinking back on what she created. "No, definitely not."

"It makes sense. It's how I'll know everything I'm learning is working. An ex is, like, the toughest person to impress. That's what you said."

Her eyes are wide as she nods and shakes her head in this weird yes-no motion. "Right, remind me of the part where I said to break the heart of said ex."

"I read between the lines."

Marc Anthony begins to lightly play from the speakers as the sound of a knife slapping against a cutting board bangs in tune with the rhythm.

"Okay, Titi Neva," Sofia shoots back.

"Oh, like you've never done something mean in your life. I've seen you eat everyone else's fries and then save the untouched ones for yourself."

She taps my cheek. "Not the same thing."

"Come on, you know what he did to me."

"I do. Which is why I feel like we're losing the point of this whole exercise." She pinches the bridge of her nose. "Have I been failing as an extraordinary romance counselor? Have I not emphasized the importance and fragility of the human heart?"

I give her a look, then decide not to point out the dramatics. "How? I'm learning how to be a perfect girlfriend, aren't I?"

"The point was to help you grow and find a new love, not break someone's heart."

"Well, I'm tired of my heart being broken all the time. When is it my turn to do the heart-breaking?" Even though I say it a little petulantly, I see Sofia's mouth clamp shut. For once, she doesn't have a comeback. "So you won't help me?"

Now she looks at me like I'm out of my mind. "When did I say I wouldn't help you? Remind me to add *communication* to our next boot camp lesson."

"I—wait, you're going to help? This whole time I thought you didn't agree."

"Obviously I disagree. This has *mess* written all over it. But unlike a certain ex, I can't leave my sister high and dry."

"Then why didn't you start with that?" I shake my head. "You know what, never mind. I'm glad we got here."

"Ride-or-dies." Sofia holds out her hand and wiggles all her fingers. It's our little handshake, so I put mine out and wiggle along with hers. "I do want to point out this probably isn't healthy, and you're lucky that I love you!"

Mari runs over, hopping on the couch with us. "Titi Ivy is busy, and she said you guys have to take me to the movies now."

Sofia looks at the imaginary watch on her wrist. "Isn't it past your bedtime?"

"It's *Saturday*." Mari rolls her eyes. "I can stay up forever."

Sofia claps her hands together. "I'll go if you can weasel extra money from the aunts for the popcorn."

"Deal." Mari zooms off as my phone buzzes in my pocket.

Automatically, I check the notifications. It's from my email, the headline: *Urgent: Change in Dates.*

I tilt my head to the side and read the email.

Dear Amelia Hernandez,

We hope this email finds you well. We wanted to bring an important update to your attention regarding the payment for the upcoming Bridge Year Program. Due to unforeseen circumstances, we have had to make some adjustments to the deadline for payment.

The new deadline for payment is now August 31, which is earlier than originally communicated. We understand that this change may be unexpected, and we apologize for any inconvenience this may cause.

Please make sure to submit your payment by the new deadline to secure your spot in the program. If you have any questions or concerns, do not hesitate to reach out to our team.

We are excited to have you join us on this enriching journey, and we look forward to all the amazing experiences that lie ahead.

Thank you for your understanding and cooperation.

Best, The Bridge Year Team

That's *one* month from now.

My heart sinks like it's falling into quicksand. The music muffles like the speaker drowns underwater. Even the scent of browning onions wafts away.

Something yanks my arm once, twice.

Mari drags me toward the door, but my limbs are heavy. Even my blinks are slow. There's a ringing in my ears that seems to be getting louder and louder, until all I hear is that high-pitched noise.

And then, suddenly, reality comes crashing back when I hear Sofia call out, "Mari, bring some smushable snacks to sneak in."

"Okay," she calls back.

Focus, Amelia.

"I'll be right down," I call to Mari, who sprints to the kitchen.

As if all eyes are on me, when I know *no* eyes are on me, I try to walk at a normal-yet-fast pace while I make it back to my room. When I get there, I shut the door gently, so nobody hears it slam.

One month.

I climb up to my bed, my hands aching as if they've been kneading dough all day. I move my pillows to the side, revealing the small, thin, rectangular line on the headboard of my bed.

I grab the sewing pin I always leave pushed in the corner of the frame, high enough that my head wouldn't hit it, and sneak it through the crevices, wiggling it around until the wood tips out enough so I can remove the block completely. My secret compartment. A wad of cash spills out, and I catch the stack of hundreds gripped tightly in a pink rubber band.

The last time I counted was a couple of months go, after I got extra cash for dog walking one of Titi Sandra's clients. Logically, I know I couldn't have made a substantial amount of money doing that, but I can't help it. I unwind the rubber bands of cash and begin counting.

One month.

I lose count after five hundred and start again.

Two thousand dollars' worth of cash in this band. I grab

another stuck in the two-inch hole, and behind it, beside it, are four other ones I count. I start again when I hear a blaring of a horn from outside.

It's about ten thousand dollars in total.

Every single thing I've earned over the past three years. Babysitting jobs, three summers working at the summer camp Marisol went to because she was too nervous to go on her own, tutoring sessions with desperate jocks, birthday money, Christmas money. Everything I've earned, here. It had to be cash; since the aunts added Sofia and me to their account, I couldn't risk them seeing how much I saved and asking about it.

These funds were meant for me to move out. I was saving money even before I asked Leon to make this compartment for me when we were together. I had a few grand hidden in a pair of socks, but when Sofia almost tried to wear them, I knew I needed a new hiding spot.

When he made this compartment, it was with the belief that after high school we'd move in together. This stash would help us secure a nice apartment wherever we ended up. But when we broke up, that dream vanished, and I needed something to else to put this money in, to look forward to.

Then I found the Bridge Year Program.

After I got a D on another one of my assignments, my teacher Mr. Donaghy asked me what I was planning to do after graduation, if there were any schools I wanted to go to.

When I told him I had no clue, he smiled and told me about the program he did when he was my age. Granted, he became a teacher, something I would never do, but he said, "When I was given the freedom to do *anything*, I realized exactly *anything* could be a dream."

Freedom. Dreams. A year of traveling abroad, exploring, learning, and growing. Along with a bunch of people doing the same. I realized that even without Leon, staying here wasn't something I wanted to do.

I had to write the most humiliating, long-winded essay to get in. I spend so much time keeping my deepest fears to myself, but I had to be honest when writing. It felt I was in too desperate of a situation not to.

I'm not sure what the people who read my essay looked like, but even the blurry silhouettes my brain crafted still cringed at the thought of them not only reading my feelings but judging them, too. Listening to my big dreams to see the world and my small ability to make any of them happen was the first time I've ever admitted it to anyone. To strangers. But I *got in*.

What Mr. Donaghy failed to mention was the fifteen-thousand-dollar fee that went along with it.

But I was supposed to have until winter to save up the rest. I had it all planned out. I'd work some more dog-sitting jobs, find a part-time job at the mall, and while I was doing that, the aunts would think I was in class at the community college fifteen minutes away.

Studying business, to *take over the bakery*. And take care of my sisters. And live in the house we always lived in. And have children, more little girls to follow in the exact same steps as me and everyone else in the Hernandez family.

Going off on my own is pretty terrifying. But a future that's set in stone, one that I don't have any choice in at all, is the scariest thing. And now, after this email, I'm back to square one.

There's zero chance of me earning five thousand dollars in a single month. It's not like I can ask the aunts for any money, because then they'll know I've been secretly planning on leaving them while they prepped me to become the next Titi Sandra. Eldest-daughter fate.

My throat closes so tight, I gasp for air. My eyes are burning with the risk of tears.

This must be a sign. It's my destiny to live with this curse like it's my destiny to head the bakery, stay in this house, have a kid, and just be a Hernandez woman. I was crazy to think I could do something different.

"Hey." Sofia kicks the door open, storming in toward me. "You think gas is cheap? Get your ass up," she says in a thicker accent and deeper voice. Her Titi Sandra impression. "No, but seriously." She crosses her arms. "I'm hiding empanadas in Mari's backpack, and I need them to be at least semiwarm for me to enjoy them."

I can't think of anything to say, and Sofia jumps on the seconds of silence. "What's wrong?" Her gaze softens. "Are the dates getting overwhelming?"

"No, no," I say, doing so well in keeping my voice normal I nearly trick myself. "Seriously, I'm good." I shove my blankets on top of the money, the headboard. "I'm coming."

Sofia is up the steps and has me by the ear right after I pile my pillows enough so the opening is blocked. "The movie starts in twenty minutes."

"Wait." My tone skyrockets.

"I can *feel* the temperature of the empanadas decreasing." Sofia's sister telepathy may have picked up on my mood first, but she still can't really understand me fully. At least, not as much as I thought.

I finish hiding my stash and follow her out. Away from a dream that never got to be anything but.

Not even a hottie in a Spidey suit could steal my attention from my downward spiral, though I welcome the break from the house. It makes it easier to breathe without the weight of guilt I feel or the resentment brewing inside me.

I know it's wrong. To be angry at my family, especially when it's not their fault the payment date got pushed. But the pressure that lives in our house, the assumptions about who we are and who we're going to be. I love my family, but they make it so hard for me to be honest with them. I'm here having a meltdown and I can't even ask for comfort from the people I love the most.

I was hoping by the end of the movie, I would have stored up all the nasty emotions welling within me and hidden them away in a place where they can't affect me. But that didn't go as planned.

Marisol's tiny palm nestles in mine as we walk out of the stale bathroom for the second time since the movie started. She's got the bladder of an eighty-year-old woman, and Sofia refused to miss the end of the film, so I brought her.

She yanks me down and we pause on the carpeted hall. The

blue LED lining of the ceiling pours over the glitter between her space buns. “Can we get popcorn?”

“The movie is almost over.” I try to pull her under the neon *7* where the entrance to our movie is playing.

She pulls again. “But I’m hungry.”

Well, I’ve already seen the movie, and I’m pretty sure some romance is about to play out on the screen. Which will only remind me, on top of the fact that I’m never going to leave the family house, I’m also going to die alone. Probably. So, I lead Marisol toward the concession stand guarded by a single uniform-wearing guy handing some dude in a yellow sweatshirt a box of popcorn.

For Mari, the sight of concessions is like a new book in the library—or a new crush for me—and she ditches my grip and dashes forward. I call after her, but she’s locked on to the popcorn machine and bullets forward, which wouldn’t be a problem if she knew how to pump the brakes. But she hurtles into the guy holding the holy grail of snacks.

The popcorn rains down like confetti over her, the carpet, the counter. She instantly opens her mouth, trying to catch the pieces like snow during a flurry. She really has her priorities in order.

I snatch her away, pinning her in place when she attempts to pick some from the floor.

“I’m so sorry,” I blurt out as the last of the popcorn rain drizzles.

The guy shakes crumbs out of his ashy-blond hair before brushing it aside, and I’m startled by how blue and round his eyes are. "It's okay. I'm as into popcorn as this little one is."

He blinks at me, and the smile faulters. "Amelia?"

Now I blink. "You know me?"

"Ah, well, yeah." He swallows, moving the lump at the center of his throat. He rubs his lips together, and whatever embarrassment burns within me from Mari cools as confusion snuggles up in its place.

I mean, I would totally recognize this guy if we met. I may not be the most attentive person around, but when there is a tall, pretty boy with a million-dollar smile, well, I'm obviously going to focus.

He's quiet for so long, so I step forward like a robot and point to the popcorn machine as I face the cashier. "Two popcorns, please. And if you have a broom, I can clean up the mess."

The concession worker starts pouring the snack into the boxes. "Don't worry about it." She hands them to me. "It'll give me something to do."

Carefully, I hand Mari a box. "Spill one piece and I'll spoil the end of *Ghost versus Witch.*"

Unbridled terror widens her eyes. She holds the snack as delicately as she would Zoe—if not even more. I offer the other to the guy, who now seems to have two pink dots blossoming on his cheeks. "Um, for you."

He takes it and straightens, like he's come to a decision. "You were trending."

I laugh, because, what? But his face doesn't change, and I cough. "That's impossible."

"Not, like, globally or anything," he adds. "But I saw this

video of you. It was on this influencer's page. You're the girl who got stuck at the adventure course."

Lucky I wasn't holding the popcorn because I'd have caused another flurry. Of course, that video is still making its rounds. The universe is making a point to punish me in every way it can. My upside-down-puppet moment should be old news by now. Shouldn't there be a new, more interesting trend?

"If you'll excuse me, I'm going to walk into traffic. Sorry about the popcorn."

"Wait." He grabs me as I lead Mari away. "I'm sorry. I didn't mean to spring it on you like that. I just didn't want you to be weirded out that I knew who you were."

"It's fine." Ah, yes, the familiar heat of embarrassment rushes to the back of my ears. "And you know, it wasn't even my fault. Not fully. If I hadn't been on the worst date in history. Well, not the worst date. But what kind of guy leaves a girl hanging upside down thousands of feet in the air? Okay, hundreds of feet, tens." I shake my head, sinking deeper into humiliation. "You know what? Doesn't matter."

His fingers tap over his jeans like he doesn't know what to say.

"So, about this video. Can you send me it?" I can't help but wonder what influencer found the need to duet one of the countless videos of me hanging helplessly. Maybe I can report it.

"Sure." He pulls out his phone. "What's your number?"

I read it out to him, and a few moments later I get the buzz at the back of my jeans. "Thanks."

"The date wasn't mentioned in the video," he says, and I

wonder how much I'd have to contort my body to fit into the popcorn machine. It's probably soundproof. Then I wouldn't have to hear this conversation.

"Yeah, well, at least they let me have a tiny bit of dignity."

"I could take you on a better one."

I don't register the meaning of his words. Not until the rest of his face goes red, and he adds, "You know, a date. I could take you on a better one. Hopefully one that doesn't end up with you suspended in midair."

"You're asking me out?"

"Yes."

"Like, *me*, the girl from the video?"

"Yeah."

"Amelia." Mari nudges me and I jolt, forgetting she was there. "I have to pee again."

"No," I answer.

"But I have to *go*—"

"No, not to you, Mari." I face the—wow, I don't even know his name and he asked me out. My deep conditioner really must have done something to my curls. "I'm sorry, I can't go out with you."

"Oh—"

Before I can hear the rest of his sentence, I grab Mari and drag her down the carpet, almost missing the bathroom before circling back. Because wow. Desperate Amelia said no to a date. With a hottie. A hottie who knew what a mess I was and was willing to subject himself to it.

As we enter the stale air and red-and-white stalls, I take

the empty box and toss it as Mari hurries into the room. It'll be the last time I give her a large Coke.

For something to do, I run my hands under the faucet.

"Amelia, why'd you say no to the boy? You always say yes."

There's a snicker from the other end of the room and I slap my hand over my face. Of course I have an audience for this.

"I don't know," I answer, but the words that bounce along in my head are *You'll never be free anyway, so why bother?*

CHAPTER 11

HRBC Lesson #4: The Princess Peach Effect (per Sofia)
This is a case-by-case basis, but if your date claims to be good at something, even if you are good at it too, make sure you become an amateur.
Dates will love to teach you things. It makes them feel important.
Trip into them, be scared of the dark, anything that makes them feel like they have to protect you.
(The reverse is true too. Pick up on if your date is Peach and become their hero.)

What does *trending* mean?" Titi Sandra asks as she drives past the nearly finished festival, toward the bakery. After hearing Sofia and me arguing over whether going viral is good or bad—for the third time since morning—Titi Sandra demanded a debrief on "what the hell we are talking about."

"It's when something gets so popular that—" Sofia starts explaining, and I punch her arm for bringing it up *again*. Maybe I do it too hard, but she doesn't know the extra emotions I'm dealing with.

A night's sleep has not cured a single bit of misery from that dream-crushing email. I cried about it for a while last night, but as Titi Sandra would say, el camarón que se queda dormido siempre se lo lleva la corriente. So, I woke up, patted aloe into the raw skin under my eyes, and blamed the redness on dryness.

She yells, elbowing me. Sofia's already printed out the screenshot, twenty-five thousand likes later, and framed it in our room. As if it's something I want to *remember*.

"Trending," Sofia sings in my air.

I pinch her arm and twist until she yelps again.

"Oh, come on." My sister slaps my hands. "You can use this to your advantage. Thousands of people know you now. You can be, like, an influencer or something."

"Totally." I grin as my fingers pinch her skin. "I'll just go around tying my legs to a rope and jumping off things."

She screeches as I twist and we pinch and slap and wrestle like toddlers and not the young "adults" we are until Titi Sandra snaps, "*Enough.*" And we both straighten in our seats like we're her soldiers.

"So," Sofia says because she cannot remain quiet for the life of her. You can hold her at knifepoint and she'd probably laugh in your face. Something in her brain that's *supposed* to be connected to her sanity is probably cut. I mean, same. "Mari tells me you met a cute guy at the theater."

"I'm going to take all her favorite books and put them on the highest shelf."

She rolls her eyes. "Please, she wants you to have fun. I can't believe you said no. I didn't think you even learned the word."

"I got too nervous." *And too depressed.*

I glance up toward the mirror, but Titi Sandra isn't looking my way. I lower my voice anyway. "I think the Romance Boot Camp needs to be put on pause for a while." Or forever. At least until I'm less miserable about not being able to afford the gap-year program. I need an emotional break.

"Oh my God, people would give good money to be as famous as you are right now. There's nothing to be sad about. It's the perfect time to get out there and take your mind off things. Have fun. Don't be a bore." But Sofia doesn't know there's plenty to be sad about.

"Well, joke's on you," Sofia looks out the window. "Because I already planned some new dates. Only the gods can stop me." Then she wiggles her brows at me, and I hear her unspoken *actually, not even the gods can stop me; I'm too powerful.*

Before I can laugh, we pull into the lot and Titi parks right in front of the bakery, next to our other SUV. The other aunts got here earlier while Titi Sandra was stuck on a work call before she brought Sofia and me.

She heads straight inside while Sofia and I hop out. We go for the back of the vehicle, where coolers of food and boxes of decor wait. We take each end of the first cooler and Sofia drops her side, nearly chopping off her exposed toes.

She screeches, and my fingers ache as the weight of my side grows heavier. "It's not that bad."

"I can't get a good grip with my new nails," she whines, holding out the coffin-shaped claws she pressed on herself last night.

"Grab the bottom, then, genius." I gesture with my chin. "I'm holding my side with *one* hand."

"One *manicure*-less hand."

"Hey," a familiar and voice reaches from behind. Leon, his pale jeans and shirt dusted with sawdust, joins us. "Need help?"

"No." I panic as Sofia sings, "Yes!"

"I can do it," he offers, a single dimple making an appearance.

After being ditched two years ago, it should be illegal for my throat to catch at the sight of him, but I chalk it up to the relief that he's already falling for my trap. Already back to being the same guy who helped first, asked questions later.

While Sofia jokes that I don't have *no* in my vocabulary, Leon's life purpose is to say yes to everything. *Yes* to helping his Dad with a job. *Yes* to staying behind and putting away all the tennis balls after practice when he wasn't on the team. *Yes* to eating the whole meal at a restaurant even when they got his order wrong.

Yes when I asked him if he loved me.

But that last one turned out to be a lie.

The bitterness in me reappears like an old friend. It's better focusing on that familiar feeling rather than letting the sadness about the program cling to me. Misery does love company, and what better company than a pretty ex?

"I don't need help," I tell him.

Sofia grabs a small box of decor. "Well, I do. I'm not risking my manicure." She winks as she passes me, sauntering her long legs showing under her miniskirt into the bakery, leaving Leon to pick up her slack without a thought.

"Hi," I say, my tone laced with annoyance. My sister

betrayed me for her nails. I'm going to clip them off when she sleeps.

"Hello," his dimple deepens. "You look beautiful."

I nearly drop my side of the cooler. It would be a lie to say I didn't try a little harder with my makeup today. Mainly because I needed a pound of concealer to cover the redness from crying into my pillow last night. Then the rest of my face didn't look right, so I did *all* the makeup. And it's second-day hair—which is scientifically proven to always look better than day-one hair.

"Thanks." Not *thank you.* That's trying too hard. *Thanks* is sufficient, to the point. Not cocky, but not ungrateful. I think that was Titi Ivy's tip for How to Be a Cool Girl™. I'm not entirely sure I'm remembering it correctly. We didn't officially get to that lesson yet and Sofia ripped a couple strands of my hair when she caught me going through the slides of her PowerPoints while she was in the shower.

I know I just told Sofia that we should pump the brakes on the HRBC, but I do have to admit that focusing on my revenge helps me forget about my hopeless situation. My head is scrambled with too many emotions right now anyway.

"You cut your hair," he goes on. Which I haven't *recently,* but he adds, "The front."

I bring my hand to my bangs. They've grown out to my chin, but when my hair's curly, they stop right at the tips of my brows. This is different from the last time he saw me.

"Yeah, well, the last time you saw me was two years ago, so."

My throat clenches into something painful.

So what if Leon noticed something different about me? So

what if it reminds me of how he never missed one detail about me, even a change in nail polish color, a different parting of my hair, or a new pin on my backpack?

I didn't know being outdoors could feel so claustrophobic.

He doesn't respond to me, only reaches down to take Sofia's place and lift the cooler. I wave him off. "I can handle it."

He looks at me, the cooler, then me again. "This thing is probably more than half your weight."

"I'm stronger than I look."

"There's nothing wrong with admitting you need help, Amelia."

Something about his tone, how soft and sweet it sounds, makes my stomach flip. Then my blood starts to simmer at my body's reaction to the sound of his voice. I should be cool and unphased. "I don't need help. Just you watch."

A glint of mischief flickers in his eyes. He stands straight, crossing his hands against his chest. "Okay, Amelia. It's all yours."

It takes all of my willpower not to stick my tongue out at him.

With all the strength I have, I pull the cooler. It doesn't even do me the solid of pretending to budge.

Unable to stop myself, my gaze travels to Leon and his lips are already pulled into the widest smile.

Using my now-boiling anger, I go for another pull. The muscles on my arm stretch, and the skin feels tight and stings, but the cooler only moves an inch before my strength gives out.

Leon yawns and holds his arms straight in the air. The

veins in his arms protrude deeper under his skin, his muscles twitching, and he stretches.

I huff out a breath. "Are you seriously flexing right now?"

"Me?" he asks innocently, *slowly* returning his arms to his sides. "Not at all."

We're at a weird standstill. I need help. He knows I need help. He wants me to admit it. I would rather chew off my own arm.

With the spite of a thousand aunts, I pull. The abandoned half drags on the cement, leaving a dusting of ground plastic in its wake, and I know Titi Sandra is going to scold me for it later, but I need to keep it moving.

"Doing all right?" he asks.

"Phenomenally," I say, then start humming loudly to mask my heavy breathing until I get my half on the curb of the sidewalk. The song grows louder as I switch places, careful not to touch Leon, whose hands still remain out like he's going to grab the entire cooler himself. Instead of pulling, I'll try the opposite. Maybe it'll be easier.

When I push, nothing happens.

"Need help?" he says, a smug olive branch.

"No."

"I'm right here."

"Obviously." I use both my hands to gesture to his largeness. Overly nearness. Overly *hereness*. God, I'm not making any sense, even to myself.

I push at the cooler so hard I feel sweat beading at my temples—why isn't it budging? Not only am I under the blazing sun right now, but I'm even warmer under Leon's scrutiny.

After a minute or two of pushing without any luck, my breath catches in that way that tells me I know I'm about to cry. Please, please, please, stupid feelings, not now.

"Hey, is everything okay? You seem a little off." He approaches, blocking the sun so that I finally have a moment in the shade.

"What?" I cross my arms against my chest as if that'll soothe the increasing beating. "I'm only trying to show that I'm strong and capable. If I can't move a cooler on my own, what can I do, you know?" *Nothing, you'll never amount to anything.*

He looks at me carefully, and it's so strange. It feels like he can see every emotion running through me, hear my every thought, while not showing a single one on his own face. I remember in the early days of when we were dating and I was so concerned with looking and being perfect he'd get this look—like he's trying to figure me out. Like he's already figured me out.

"I'm sure there are other ways to prove you're strong and capable," he says.

Yeah, like picking up this cooler and dropping it on you.

God, I'm going to *kill* him. He's so good at falling into place. Picking up as if we never parted, as if he never dumped me and ghosted me, as if he *still* isn't leaving me in the dark without any kind of explanation.

The door swings open and Sofia saunters out, a scowl on her face. "Titi is already complaining how slow you're being. Come on, Leon, if you want to be useful, get this inside."

I hurriedly go for the trunk and grab the smallest box I can find as Leon brings the cooler in with so much ease it annoys me even more.

Sofia joins me. "I would ask if you're charming him, but the frown on your face says it all."

I raise my brows and feel the wrinkle smooth itself out. "Ugh, I'm so bad at keeping my face blank."

"Just pretend frowns are lava," she says, offering no real help. "You should ask him to hang out. You know, as 'friends.'" Sofia does the most obvious wink on the last word.

"He already asked me to hang out."

"But you didn't set up a time and place. You're a starter, Amelia Ivelisse Hernandez, but definitely not a closer."

I open my mouth. "The whole government-official name? Is that necessary?"

She slaps her hands around my face, squeezing my cheeks together. "He literally dumped you. Left you. He probably deleted your contact number from his phone. But you're too nervous to ask him out?" Her brows press together. "Are you sure you want to do this whole Operation Break Your Ex's Heart like He Did Yours?"

"Only if you think of a better name than that."

"Operation Dump Your Ex's Ass," she offers.

"Too crude."

"Operation Revenge?"

"Too simple."

"Operation Heartbreaker?"

We both cock our heads to the side. "Winner," we say at the same time.

Sofia lets me go. “Okay, go get ’em, then. Date him. Dump him. Break him.”

I give her a look. “Calm down. I knew you were always going to help me, but I thought you were against this whole plan.”

“He broke your heart, and based on your face after every interaction you have with him, he’s still doing it, so he’s got no love from me. My sister’s enemy is my enemy.”

She salutes me as I turn to enter the café. I pause when I see her heading the opposite direction. “Where are you going?”

“To lie on the hood and tan for as long as I can before I get yelled at.”

She’s braver than me. I salute her, then make my way into the building.

I had a lot of questions dancing around in my head since I found out Leon was back, no matter how hard I tried to ignore them completely. Why did he leave me? Why didn’t he say anything since? How long has he been back? How long is he here for?

And the most terrifying question of all: Why do I care?

Maybe I’ll be able to figure some of that out during all of this.

I enter the kitchen. Titi Neva is in a green-and-orange-patterned maxi dress with bangles strapped to her forearms. Titi Sandra in a light gray pant suit, unbuttoned at the top, and Titi Ivy in her signature red lip, with a matching red button-up barely covering her thighs.

They don’t notice when I enter and snake my way to the back. Neither does Leon, who looks like he’s getting a talking-to from his dad, but, unlike my aunts, Connor knows what a whisper is, so I can't pick up what they're saying.

The aunts are speaking in Spanglish, weaving in and out of their native tongue, but I can understand what they're saying perfectly. I've had my whole life to learn—how else would I be able to know if I'm being talked about?

"We should start putting up postings for part-timers now that everything is coming together," Titi Ivy tells Titi Sandra.

"No need for plural. The girls will work when we don't."

I close my eyes, picturing myself behind the register here. My face gets older, and wrinkled, and gravity yanks my smile more and more until it's upside down. That's what the future looks like. Me, withering away behind the counter.

"Sofia can come after school, but Amelia will have to study. You know she'll struggle a bit the first semester. College is a lot more than the work she's done so far, and you've seen her grades." Her heel taps on the floor, hands across her exposed chest, her button-up only held together by luck and a single pin by her belly. "Let's not put extra pressure on her."

The tips of my ears heat. God, I haven't even attempted college, working at the bakery, and they already expect me to be mediocre at it.

"She'll adjust," Titi Sandra says, no room for argument. "She'll have to."

I mean, I know I'm not great at things like Sofia, or smart like Mari is becoming. I'm basic, normal, nothing special.

But maybe, with the Bridge Year Program and some distance, I could have realized I could be more than that.

"Amelia!" Titi Sandra snaps me from my thoughts, catching me.

I open my mouth to speak, to lie and say I wasn't eavesdropping, but nothing comes out.

"Go outside. The adults are speaking," Titi Sandra says, clearly annoyed that my eighteen years of training weren't enough to keep me out of adult business.

Connor pats Leon's shoulder, shooting away from the dust clinging to his burgundy top. "That means you too."

"But I want to help," Leon says.

"Leon," Connor's two salt-and-pepper brows furrowing into one. "I told you, you need a break. You know what your doctor said."

Leon reddens, and I perk up like a cat. Doctor? What's wrong with Leon? I thought he was fine. He certainly looks the part. Is he sick?

"Leon." Titi Sandra smiles in a way that doesn't *feel* like a smile. "Your father was telling me the Big E is nearly set up. Do me a favor, show my oldest around. She's been moping about for a while. Maybe a bit of fun will cheer her up."

"I wouldn't use *moping*," I say as Leon says, "I'd love to."

"Now," Titi Sandra says as I beg her with my eyes to let me stay. But she uses her chin to gesture to the door, ignoring my plea.

Leon holds the door open. I march forward out the bakery, chin high so I don't *look* like I'm moping. Sofia is nowhere to be found, so I make my way toward the back of the plaza where there's an opening to enter the end of the Big E.

Leon keeps my pace, even when I quicken it, and when we

reach a tall fence with a couple of men setting up an *Employees Only* sign before the gate, he greets them both by name.

"Leon, my man, here to sneak a couple more fried doughnuts our way?" one of them asks.

Leon throws his head back to laugh—did he just wince? He coughs, straightening himself out before saying, "If Daisy still has the shop open, I'll bring you guys some."

I smile awkwardly at the men who wave at me as I follow Leon in. If I hadn't known when opening day was, I'd think the festival started already.

People—mostly teens—roam about with giant pink *E*'s etched on the side with the word *Staff* written on the back of their shirts. Some work at hanging up signs by whatever tent or pop-up shop they stand by. Others sit cross-legged on the concrete, laughing with their coworkers.

This place is more than a festival—*festival* is too small a word. This is a mini-town turned carnival on steroids. The buildings—normally used for town hall meetings or random school events—are now occupied by food and jewelry vendors. Last year at the very end of the strip was an off-brand version of the Roman colosseum, with metal balconies and a stage occupied by C-list celebrities paid for in publicity and fried food.

"So," I say, because the doctor comment is digging its nails in my brain, "are you okay?"

Leon jumps, like he's surprised I spoke to him. "Yeah, fine."

"Then why do you need a doctor?"

His face clears of all emotion.

"No reason."

I watch him, trying to do that mind trick that he always did with me. I can tell by the way he refuses to look my way that there's something going on, but clearly he doesn't want to talk about it—and why would he? I'm his ex.

"Whatever," I say, but there's no *whatever* feeling running through me.

He grabs my arm and pulls me to a stop. "There is something bothering you, though."

To the side of him, between a water gun setup and dart board hosted by some kid who looks way too young to be holding sharp objects, stands a corkboard with *HELP WANTED* in hand-cut letters, and a bunch of fliers for local available jobs.

My gaze lingers on the postings.

Five thousand dollars.

That's all that's keeping me from a dream of a dream. My ticket to the start of my future is at risk of being shredded all because of five thousand dollars. If I got a job, and worked overtime, I could come up with enough before the deadline. I wouldn't be starting from zero. I'm literally so freaking close.

My pulse speeds too quickly, and my vision tilts. Adrenaline and I'm sure another missed iron supplement on my part. But five thousand dollars doesn't seem too unattainable. Not now, with the bottom of the fliers flapping in the light breeze.

Hope blooms in my chest and nothing is more terrifying. Nothing feels as dangerous as hope because whatever it is you're hoping for isn't guaranteed, yet you can't help but long for it anyway.

I don't want to give up the program. I don't want Titi Sandra to expect more from me and Titi Ivy to expect less and Titi Neva to read my palms with a worried look on her face or watch mom glued to Zoe and hear Sofia talking about what we'll do when we're in charge of decorating the house.

First, I'll find a job. Next, I'll think of a way to tell my family I'm ditching them for a year. Last, I'll end the summer and be on my way to travel the world. I have to.

If not, I'll spend my gap year working at the bakery, in the Hernandez house, alone but never truly alone, and miserable. Guilty too, for being miserable.

With all my focus on the fliers, I pull the fringe ends of the pinned papers where the numbers and emails of the contact information of the poster's owners are.

I make a promise to myself. *If I can pull this off, then it was meant to be and I won't have to be so guilty for it all.*

"Amelia." Leon jolts me from my thoughts. He goes on, "You should work here. The Big E always needs staff, and you could move around and do something new every day, plus you get free food. I could get you a job. Dad is friends with the hiring manager—"

"You can get me a job?"

"Of course." He uses a warm tone that used to melt me into a disgusting puddle of love and heat. I keep myself from going boneless by sheer willpower alone. "I can figure out a way to get you anything you want."

He steps close to me, like anything I need he not only can get done, but will do with full enthusiasm. It flicks the switch of a batch of memories.

Most of the time we were together, Leon was always willing to do anything that would make me happy. This time, there's a little desperation to it. Like he *has* to do this for me.

Strange.

"A date with Mackenyu." My favorite actor from the live-action *One Piece*.

A throaty laugh escapes his lips. My hands turn to fists while, annoyingly, the rest of me warms at the sound I haven't heard in so long. I feel a small smile tugging at the corners of my lips. Traitor body.

I start to walk away but can *feel* Leon right at my heel.

"So, should I ask my dad about a job?"

I don't want it to be obvious *how* much I want this job. It's not that I have any shame in needing his help. The money is most important at the end of the day. It's just . . .

It'll feel weird owing someone who I'm trying to break.

We pass by a group of guys playing ring toss, but the two workers under the tent keep jumping around trying to block them from making it to the bottles. Right as we go by their speaker blasting music, the blond in the group grabs Leon's shoulder.

My feet lock in place.

"Leon, come on, Chad's betting his PS5 nobody can beat his high score."

"Not now, Arno," Leon says, and the popcorn guy from the freaking theater, *Arno*, faces me. His eyes widen with recognition, and then he smiles—charmingly awkwardly. I did reject him. Not because he isn't ten out of ten, but *he* doesn't know that.

"Amelia," he says, "what are you doing here?"

Leon frowns. "You two know each other?"

"Yeah." Arno's smile falters. "I asked her out on a date and she rejected me."

"A date?" Leon repeats softly, slightly confused, as if he's unfamiliar with the word.

"I didn't mean no," I can't help but say. I mean, *I* know what it's like to be rejected. It's like lying at the end of a bowling alley and the center of your stomach is considered a strike and everyone is lining up for a chance to get one. And to have to relive that rejection again when you least expect it? I feel bad for Arno. "I just got nervous."

Leon looks between us. His furrowed brows slowly separate as if now he remembers what the word *date* means. His mouth opens, then shuts. His hands go into his pockets, then through his hair, and his brows furrow together again. It's like he doesn't know what to do or how he feels.

Why would the idea of me being asked out on a date throw him off this way? Since he's been back, he's had this new, more confident air about himself.

For a moment, it seems like he's going to say something, but he shakes his head instead.

Oh. Huh.

With an inkling driving me, I focus on Arno, who has such a dumbfounded look on his round face, and move toward him. I can feel the heat of Leon's gaze following my every movement.

"Well." I laugh, and there's this weird thrill running through me. "What are the odds we meet here like this?"

Arno nods. "I don't know, but I'm glad for it." He smirks in a way that sends a zing through my body.

I laugh and all my nerves settle. Well, *most* of them. Behind me, I hear Leon scoffing way too loud not to be a distraction.

Arno doesn't even look toward Leon. "Will you be working here over the summer?"

"Yes," Leon answers for me. When I raise my brows at him, he adds, "What, you are, aren't you?"

One of Arno's buddies rushes over and wraps his arms around Arno's neck in a position that makes me flinch. "You're holding us all up." His friend drags him away, while Arno tries—and fails—to fight him off.

He's barely out of earshot before Leon and I face each other.

"What was that?" we ask at the same time.

The shock of it makes us both blink and then laugh. A real laugh from me. As soon as it's out, I wish I could swallow it down and the little flutter of wings at the pit of my stomach that attempt to fly off.

He scratches the back of his neck. "Well, I was surprised you knew that guy."

That guy. Like Arno suddenly doesn't have a name.

"We met briefly Saturday. It's no big deal."

He takes a few extra seconds before replying, "Kind of is, since he asked you out."

"I don't know how it's any of your business—as my 'friend' and all. Friends would be happy their friend is hot enough to be asked out by cute strangers."

He laughs, and it's so hearty and easygoing that I question

if I made up the tension from a minute before. "Of course, I'm happy my friend is getting asked out by cute strangers. I think they should be lining up to."

"Oh." I'm weirdly disappointed by the response. "For some reason, I thought you sounded a little jealous." Friends tease each other like this, right? This is totally not me flirting, even though this is one of the oldest tricks in the book, right?

"Nah," he says easily. "We're friends. I want you to be happy." The quickness of the response, and the sincerity in the words, makes me pause.

I'm on a roller coaster. Trying to get Leon to fall for me, avoiding falling for him, trying not to feel so hurt when his responses make it seem like he only wants to be my friend and the swift worry following that he won't see me romantically anymore. It's all giving me a headache. And a desperate need to cling on to hope.

"So." I shift gears. "About that job."

CHAPTER 12

Date Debrief #3

What Worked: Waited three seconds so she knew I was listening. (Sofia: Maybe dial it back some. One second is okay.)

What Didn't:

—Kept eye contact for too long, my eyes got too dry and my contact popped out. (Sofia: Pirate life.)

—Laughed way too loud at a joke. In hindsight, realized was not actually a joke. (Sofia: At least she knows you have a sense of humor.)

What Could've Gone Better: My skirt was way too tight. (Sofia: That's because it was from middle school.) So every time I moved, I waddled. I'm sure she thought I had to use the bathroom the whole time. (Sofia: Next time, I'm preparing your outfit.)

Total Rating: 7/10. Got asked hesitantly on a second date. (She probably just felt bad.)

When I asked Leon to get me a job at the Big E, I figured I'd hand out stuffed animals in the game section, take people's tickets before they fearlessly entered a ride that came from a *box*, maybe even scoop up some ice cream. Sitting cross-legged under a striped tent across from Eric, a part-time clown from a traveling circus sticking around for the summer, with a helium tank by my foot is not what I imagined, but beggars can't be choosers, and there's a hot dog stand nearby for hunger emergencies.

Literally two days after I told Leon to get me a job, he did. He knocked at the front door—because he's too good for texting—to gleefully let me know I start at four o'clock the next day, for training.

After he asked, "So, want to grab breakfast to thank me?" I slammed the door in his face. But maybe my karma for not being able to utter a thanks is being given the strangest possible job at the Big E. Mom always says whenever someone does anything for you, even the smallest of things, you have to thank them.

But a freaking balloon blower?

Technically, I'm an assistant, so balloon-blowing isn't my only responsibility. Yet, instead of sending me off to get him coffee or snacks or setting up the table with a variety of balls and flowers and squeaky toys, Eric has me doing the frustrating task.

First he had me blowing up balloons for him with a stopwatch and wanted me to be able to make thirty in under a minute—yeah, I'm in the balloon-blowing Olympics. Those were long ones for him to make balloon animals and half of them were okay and the other half kept blowing away before I could tie them. Same goes for the oversize balloons with confetti in them.

Now, since I've lost his trust, he just wants me to blow

regular balloons that some girl Sophie will use to make decorations somewhere.

"It's not that difficult," he says sternly, and I'm trying hard to take him seriously, but with the two red circles on his pale cheeks, and a sparkly bow tie, it's especially difficult. "You just grab the end before you take it off and it won't blow away."

"I'm doing that."

"If you were, they wouldn't be blowing away. Do it again." He leans closer, and his overwhelming Axe body spray invades my nostrils. "Just one. Just do *one* balloon."

He's already told me a child could blow balloons better than me, so I guess it's time for the positive reinforcement approach.

I grab from the giant pack of flat balloons and place it on the tip of the machine. The red expands, growing and growing.

Okay, it's big enough. I lean to grab the tip of the balloon. And it spits wind in my face, swirling in the air four times before landing on Eric's dark curls.

He leaves it there as he glares at me. "You know, I think the people at the pig pen need help."

"I'm not sure I want—" His glare heats, and I swear I feel it melting into my skin. "I think I'll check it out."

He gives me directions and starts picking up all my failed balloons with my final murder still on his head. No big deal. Just one failed job. The Big E has countless jobs for me to do. There's no way I can be bad at *all* of them.

As I'm walking past tents, people wave and greet me. Some rush to me and ask me my name, where I'm stationed. The staff shirt is a magnet. Maybe I'll start wearing it on dates. For good luck.

There's only a week till the grand opening, so the setup is nearly done. The rides are out and being tested by screaming staff members. The Ferris wheel I saw Leon's dad working on looms in the distance. A death trap for sure. It came from giant boxes. There's no way it's safe.

Past a corn dog stand are two long trailers with cardboard-cutout letters that spell HOG RACE hanging unevenly between them. There aren't any pigs in the curved dirt track circling the ground across the sign, but I follow the oinking and chatter behind the trailers. More staff stand around, but some are inside the pen of baby pigs and chasing them around the mud, laughing.

It's cute, sure, but some of the pigs keep bumping into the gate surrounding them or trying to jump up as if to climb out. I wonder where their mom is. For some reason it makes me think of Mom and how she'd react if someone separated her from Zoe.

Oh God, *Amelia, don't you dare get emotional at a pigpen.*

"Amelia." Leon appears beside me, a little out of breath and, more distractingly so, shirtless. "How is your first day going?"

"Fine," I try to swallow, my throat suddenly dry. "You do know shirts are meant to be worn and not wrinkled in your hand, right?"

His dimple makes an appearance and we lock gazes for a moment. A good thing, since my eyes need something to focus on besides his naked chest.

"Sorry." He pulls the colorful top over his head. The moment his face is covered my gaze can't help but try to spot all the new lines and dents on his body. I'm just a girl, not a god. I can't help my instincts. "Some kid ran into me, a full cup of slushie in hand. One of the shop owners let me have this."

When I get the full view, my lips pull up at the corners. It's the brightest green, impossible to mimic even with a highlighter, and an array of pink flowers covers the oversize button-up. "Now, this is a look. I can't believe anyone would give this out for free."

"I practically begged for it." Leon straightens up, smooths out the imaginary wrinkles on it. "Was on my hands and knees."

It makes me giggle in a comforting and easy way that's hard to explain. Like the laughter itself feels effortless and natural, and it makes my heart warm.

Ugh, I'm supposed to be doing this to Leon, not the other way around. It's hard to apply any of the HRBC methods to him when my traitor heart keeps falling for his old tricks.

Leon links his fingers through mine, pulling me back so fast I nearly trip over my feet, but he easily pulls my weight back up.

"Do you *want* me to twist my ankle?" I ask, knowing I should pull my hand away but unable to bring myself to.

"Sorry." He gazes forward. "One of the pigs came from behind the trailer and ran straight to you."

I follow his gaze and see the medium-size pig right by the fence. It drops on its side and instantly lays itself out.

I roll my eyes and walk forward, making a big show of caressing the barrier of the fence.

Leon scowls. "It's pretty big. What if it broke through?"

"Leon," I say, and he looks anywhere but at my face. It makes my throat tickle with another laugh. "Are you scared of these cute little guys?"

"Of course I'm not scared," he says, in a weird pitch that screams the opposite. "I'm not a fan. They seem a little too unpredictable." When I only look at him, he adds, "And they're dirty. I can't risk ruining my new shirt."

It reminds me of all the times Leon spotted a spider and would pretend not to freak out but slowly start moving as far as possible from it. I would always ask, "How can someone so big be afraid of such small things?" And he'd always respond, "I'm not scared, but if I was, it'd be nice if someone who wasn't helped me." And I'd have to collect the spider and bring it outside, not kill it, because Leon would also always say, "Live and let live."

"Hey." Leon nudges my arm, bringing my back to reality. "You okay?"

Yes and no. Both the answers will fit.

"Do you ever think about the past?" I ask him, still a little foggy with flashbacks replaying again in my head. "All our memories?"

"Always," he answers, like he doesn't have to think about it. "They're my favorite ones."

I blink. "Which ones?"

"Every single one with you."

My stomach somersaults, and I feel every scar and crevice on his palm in mine. My gaze lands on the sky. "You say that so easily."

"You make it easy." I realize our fingers are still linked together. "It's always been easy with you. Even when I moved. Thinking about you brought comfort, because *being* with you is comforting. Like this moment now, and later. We can make more memories too." Something in the words, or maybe something in my face, must set off alarm bells for him because he removes his hand from mine and rapidly adds, "As friends."

I rub the space above my heart. "You say I'm comforting; most people say I'm a headache."

"*Most* people who have a working brain think you're clever and funny and a charmingly clumsy puzzle-solver."

I can't keep letting him talk about me, so my first instinct is to talk about *him*. "Yeah, well, *most* people would say you're an observant, massively kind, good at everything, and a weirdly excellent juggler." Why am I complimenting him? *Focus, Amelia.* "Can you still juggle?"

In answer, he grabs my phone at the front of my pocket and his, along with a pencil hidden in his jeans and demonstrates. He goes faster, and faster, until his eyes go wide and he's moving around, wide-legged, trying not to drop anything.

I'm laughing, he's laughing, and I forget that I'm supposed to be mad at all.

CHAPTER 13

HRBC Lesson: #5 How to Listen Better
Mom: It's okay to be excited if you make a connection, but don't interrupt even if something connects back to you. Let them finish speaking.
Sofia: Ask at least two follow-up questions so you fully understand whatever your date is talking about.
Titi Ivy: Keep eye contact. Flutter those lashes.

I've lost my mind.

One thousand percent, there's very little logic in my skull. Just chaos. Me asking Leon to hang? Even though Leon doesn't know I'm treating this as a date, *I* do. Still, I'm standing on this plot of green, holding a rusty club, playing mini golf with the ex who broke my heart. This is pretty weird but strangely not awkward at all.

I swing, smacking the baby blue ball way too hard, and it goes flying over the tiny border surrounding the green, then flies over a slope toward two guys surrounding a hole. It whacks directly on one of their backs. They jump, whirling around to find me at the top of the hill, waving.

"Fore!"

Leon grabs my arm. "You're supposed to shout that *before* it hits someone."

I blink, trying not to get distracted, because this close, the way the sunlight hits, a fleck of gold glints in his eyes, or maybe it's the way the hue of blue on his shirt pulls out the colors. "My bad."

He calls down an apology to the couple, then pulls me away from the ledge. For *mini* golf, this layout sure is elaborate. There's even a bridge over water on the crisscross layout of this place. This is the third time Leon's pulled me away from a near tumble.

"I don't think I'm good at this," I tell him as he rubs his lips together to keep from laughing.

Even though his club is way too short for him, he has been getting a hole in one each time we move to a different spot. It's irritating being around someone so good at everything, and worse, being impressed by him.

"Let's grab a snack," he says, "before you give someone a concussion."

I drop the club like a toddler throwing a tantrum. He chuckles, picking it up and following after me. We drop it off at the tiny tent where some miserable teenager picks at a scab on the side of their face.

Shelton's Valley is home to a golf course, go-karts, ice cream parlor, and shack of all snacks. This place was my friend Alex's go-to spot for free weekends, but since she's spending the summer visiting her family in Texas, I haven't come since she left at the beginning of the month.

"What do we want to try?" I ask as I make it to the center plot of land, where the surrounding food shacks all wait at the end of every path. "Hot dogs made with question-mark meat? Nachos covered in three-day-old cheese? Ice cream?" In this heat, I'll probably end up having it melt and drip all over my new white crop top—and by "my," I mean Sofia's, which I stole this morning. "Scratch that, we can try some fried dough, or I think they just sell corn dogs. Actually, I could eat anything, or all of it. I skipped lunch."

I stop when I catch Leon watching me, half a smile on his lips. Right, I'm talking too much.

"I'm not sure I like this," Mom said, Zoe asleep in her arms as she sat on the edge of the couch. "I don't think you should change for a date. You're perfect the way you are."

Sofia, in another pant suit I'm sure I saw Titi Sandra in before, frowned at Mom. "The rule was you had to come with advice, or you weren't allowed to join." Behind her was a giant loading screen of Sofia's favorite rom-com series couple looking adoringly at each other. We watched the entire set of movies before Mom came to the living room to join us.

"My advice is to be yourself."

Titi Sandra walked in and dropped a stack of papers on the table with the rest of my notes I wrote down. Sofia stormed over and grabbed the set. "Magazines? What are we, in the Dark Ages?"

After Sofia took several steps backs from earning the Stare Titi Sandra managed to give her while tucking her blouse into her trousers, she said, "You said to come with advice. I brought Cosmo. *Pick a page, you'll find something." Then her heels clattered on the floorboards until the front door shut and she was gone.*

"It's like they think this is a game," Sofia complained to me, as the elevator music played in the background while she skimmed through the magazine. She found an advice column, then held up the page for me. "Seven positions to make him stay—"

Mom somehow managed to keep Zoe in one arm and ripped off the page Sofia was reading from.

Sofia rolled her eyes and flipped to another one. "Okay, this is a good one. Don't talk too much. People love to talk about themselves, and if you talk too much, it's—" Sofia frowned, then held the page to make sure she pronounced it correctly. "Unpalatable."

"This is definitely for an older crowd," I pointed out.

"Experienced," Sofia corrected. "Write this down. Listen more."

That's what *Cosmo* said was an issue, talking too much. Maybe it was for Leon too. I mean, what better way to shut me up than to ditch me and block all forms of contact.

Hm, suddenly I'm not all that hungry anymore.

I scratch my arm. "Sorry, you pick."

He frowns and waits like I'm going to say something else, but when I remain quiet, he gestures to a shack. "Hot dogs?"

I'm not sure if a response to a question is considered too much talking so I play it safe and just nod. He watches me for a moment, carefully, and I rub my lips together to hold back my laugh. All this time Leon's been gleefully getting under my skin and now, it's finally my turn to do the same.

When we get to the clump of wood passing for a hot dog

stand, Leon greets the older man. "Two hot dogs, one with chili, the other with onions, lots of onions, and mustard, no ketchup." He looks back to me, smirking. "Right?"

"Actually." I pick up on his whole *I know you better than anyone* vibes. "Plain for me."

"Boring," Leon says as the man puts together our order. "What's next, you'll want to drink *water*?"

I *was* going to grab a Coke, but I grab a bottle of water from the shelf and let Leon pay. Then he holds out my hot dog and we pick an empty bench overlooking the larger golfing area meant for experienced players who actually know what *fore* means and ride around in trolleys, shushing people for breathing too loud.

"I'm starving," Leon dramatically opens his mouth and takes a giant bite out of his hot dog. He moans in pleasure, chili bursting on the side of his lip.

I eye the toppings and then try to bite my plain dog with the same, annoying enthusiasm Leon did. I clearly don't sell it because he holds out his hot dog toward me, waving it by my mouth.

"Want a bite?" He's not laughing and holds back his smile well, but the words still sound like a laugh to my ears.

My hunger nearly has me taking a chunk out, but I sense Leon would be way too pleased with that, or he'd snatch it back just as I went to eat it. Instead, I wipe my hot dog on the excess chili on the side of his lip and then take another bite.

We finish at the same time, but before I can get up and toss out our trash, he turns so most his body faces me. He grabs my stuff and places it to the side so our legs touch, and I remain as still as possible. He's wearing long jeans, but my legs are exposed from my shorts and I know he couldn't possibly feel the heat in my thighs from touching, but, you know, just in case.

"So tell me what I missed while I was away."

It takes me a moment to understand his question, mainly because I'm too busy watching the way his dimple eases in and out as he speaks. "Prom?"

He cocks his head to the side. "I meant with you. What's happened these past years with *you*. I know what *I've* missed."

I place my hands under my lap to keep from slapping myself on the forehead. "Well, nothing much. Or at all."

He rolls his eyes. "Come on, that can't be true. You still adding to your secret savings? Found a puzzle you *can't* solve? Tell me something new."

"Not yet," I answer, "*but* . . ." I give him jazz hands until I have his devoted attention and he raises his brows. "You're looking at the newest holder of the fastest Rubik's Cube solver title in the Guinness World Records."

Leon's eyes grow wide. "No way."

"Yes way. Two Christmases ago. To be fair, I'm tied with the other holder, but still, I finally beat my record." I don't mention the only reason I got that good is because I would absentmindedly solve it after our breakup because I needed something to do with my hands. Though I do wonder how it would make him feel, if he would even care.

"Wow, I can't believe I'm hanging out with a celebrity." He looks toward an older couple walking by us. "No pictures, no autographs, please. She's on break right now."

"Shut up," I say but can't help my laugh as the couple speeds up their pace. He's grinning at me, and there's none of that charming smirk he's been planting on me since he's gotten back. He's genuinely beaming, having a good time.

Falling for me, possibly.

And listening to me, interested in me. I know not to let my real guard down, but it feels nice to speak to someone and have the freedom to say anything I want, and not with any guilt, either. "Want to know a secret?"

"Absolutely," he answers.

I have a split second of hesitation, but then he smiles, a small one that doesn't even make his dimple appear. But it's somehow encouraging, and then I tell him about the gap-year program. About all that I saved, about the secrecy from the aunts, about the impending due date to pay.

"Ah, that's why you wanted a job at the Big E." He looks down at his lap. "And you haven't told anyone else?"

I shake my head. "It's too hard to."

"Don't you think it will be harder once you have to leave?"

Once I have to leave. Not *if*. Like he believes that I'll be able to, just like that. "It probably will, but I'm too much of a coward to deal with it yet."

"I don't think someone willing to break the mold with their family and go off on an adventure in a different country on their own can be classified as a 'coward.'"

My gaze travels to the side of his face. It's a nice thing to say, and it feels even nicer that it sounds like he believes it because it makes me kind of believe it, too. I mean, it is pretty brave of me, parts of it, I guess. Maybe.

"Okay, not coward. I'll downgrade to scaredy-cat. I still need to work up the courage if I ever can."

"You will," he says, so sure.

The urge to poke the side of his cheek, since he still won't face me, is too strong. I press where I think the dimple lies hidden until it appears. He finally looks at me, but when I get a full view, it seems a little sad.

"I'm coming back, and you're leaving, weird isn't it?"

If he is sad about me potentially going away, it means my mission is off to a great start. Sort of. I'm being funny and we're having good banter. And we're also opening up to each other more. Maybe a little too much on my end.

Next up from the HRBC lessons on keeping a partner, make sure you give them space to talk too. "What about you? How's your life been? What kind of impact did Leon Alistair make in Arizona?"

The smile wipes clean off his face. "Who cares?"

I jerk back. "I was just asking."

His face softens a bit. "It was different. And it's different being back. I feel like an outsider in my own neighborhood."

"You? An outsider? The guy who made friends with the old man who took out a baseball bat to swing at you for hitting his car?"

Humor lights his gaze again, lifting his lips. "Last time I checked, *you* hit his car while trying to parallel park—"

"Not how I remember it," I lie, but Leon was trying to teach me how to park in his beat-up Camry and I drove right into the Honda next to us. Leon lifted me out of the driver's side so fast that when the old man yanked the driver's door open, it was Leon in the hot seat.

"Besides, he was nice. He was just having a bad day. Once he calmed down, he was easy to talk to. Remember he gave me some fresh apples he picked?"

My lips pull into a smile. "See? You find the good in everybody, get along with everyone. I can't imagine you being an outsider anywhere."

He looks at me, and suddenly, we're back to the way we used to be. He's gazing at me like I was made in a lab specifically to love him. Or maybe that's what I felt about him? Everything is getting lost in my head and me in his eyes, and it's making me a little dizzy. Or it's possible I forgot to take my iron. Again.

I feel like I'm forgetting something very important.

"What happened over there? Wasn't that the big plan, play football, get scouted, free college? Bond with your mother? What happened?"

The light in his eyes vanishes. His body tenses up, the veins in his arms tightening as his fists do. All the ease between us is replaced by taut, heavy air.

"Stop." The single word is low and clipped.

"I don't understand you." I pull away. "One minute you're spending all your energy being nice to me, and then the next you shut down. What do you want?"

"Right now?" he says softly. "Quiet."

Oh, *that's* what I was forgetting. The point of this all. I'm here to break Leon's heart. I'm glad he's become such a jerk to remind me it's what he deserves. "You're a dick."

Before I get more than a step away, Leon blocks my path. He moves so quick, my body collides with his. "I meant in my head," he says quickly. "Not from you."

That makes me pause.

Sure, it turned out I didn't know Leon as well as I thought, but I know deep down the person I knew wasn't entirely a stranger. The parts I saw of Leon, some of them, had to be real. We were together for an entire year, you can't fake it all the time.

It's not that Leon wasn't thoughtful back then. He's always been observant, always takes a second to listen before responding. But now, it's like he's got a chip on his shoulder. Like there are way more worries bouncing around in his head, enough that he gets a little lost in them.

"What are you thinking about?" I ask.

He chews on his bottom lip before forming an answer. "I'm thinking about how I want to move forward, not back. That talking about the past doesn't change the present, but it feels wrong to do that when I know I have to make up for my part in it. That I hate that I hurt you, and sometimes it feels like I still am, and sometimes I see it on your face. That I want to be a better friend to you, now more than ever. That I *will* be better. That you look so pretty today."

My brain loses touch with all of its processing systems.

Maybe I've been so hurt that it's been hard to even imagine Leon being genuinely sorry—if he's telling the truth. It still might be an act. I have to remind myself that at one point, I trusted him and loved him, and he still left, completely ghosted me without an explanation. So, it would be too gullible, too naive of me to believe him.

Wouldn't it?

Besides, would being sorry be enough to make up for the hurt?

No, it won't be. Not as much as getting back at him. *An eye for an eye.* That's what Titi Neva says whenever someone crosses her. That's how things will be even. A heartbreak for a heartbreak.

But why does it feel like I'm trying so hard to convince myself that's true?

A fat droplet of rain smacks my nose. It restarts my mind as another drops on Leon's forehead. The cool liquid is a relief to my warming skin, but as a swarm of them rains down on us I jump up, holding the small bag I also stole from Sofia over my head.

"Oh no, my hair," I say, glad to be able to focus on something other than the spiral of thoughts I'm drowning in. "It'll get curly." It took me two hours this morning to straighten. Then I stuffed it into a baseball cap before the aunts tried to force another deep-conditioning treatment on me.

Leon stands closer to me. "What's wrong with that?"

I ignore him, scanning for shelter, but there's nothing unless I jump into one of the shacks with an employee. As the rain picks up, the idea becomes more appealing.

Clearly not understanding the urgency, Leon just looks at me, so I grab his hand and yank him, running for the parking lot as the rain decides to continuously disrespect my effort by picking up.

When I spot his paint-chipped blue pickup truck, I let him go and rush toward it, pulling on the handle. "Unlock it," I yell as he *slowly* saunters over.

"What?" he says loudly.

"I said unlock it."

He moves toward me instead of the driver's side. "Sorry, the rain's so loud. Can't hear you." His voice lower now that he's near me and we can easily hear each other. It's not a freaking hurricane or anything.

I hurriedly pull out my hair clip from my bag, a large one shaped like an actual butterfly with a few tiny, colorful ones placed all around it. To prevent *all* of my hair from getting wet, I twist it and clip it in place.

"I said unlock—" When he grins like a cat that's just knocked over your favorite mug, I elbow him. "Are you messing with me? Why won't you open it? My hair—"

Leon pulls the clip from my scalp and his hands are in my waves—soon to be curls—and I forget the words I meant to finish with. He ties a strand along his finger, twisting it as his own hair flattens around his face. "Your hair is fine."

Every muscle in my body fights on whether it wants to soften or harden.

He seems so sincere, leaning down, close enough I can smell the banana he snacked on during the drive here mixed with the hot dog. I should have some kind of self-deprecating joke to share, something to ease the tension he built within seconds.

But words are hard.

I could wrap my arms around his neck and press my lips on his. A part of me wants to intuitively. Whenever Leon was this close, either he or I would pull each other in. But that was then, this is now.

He leans down, bending farther to clear any and all space between us. I know the whole point of this is because I want him to fall in love with me so I can break his heart like he did mine, become the perfect girlfriend for someone else. It's just . . . I couldn't have succeeded *this* fast.

Yet my hands move around him, my body falls into him. Maybe I'm underestimating myself. Who's to say I haven't charmed the hell out of him and he's already falling back into our own patterns?

Something shudders over his face, close to regret, before he jerks away from me, his body colliding with the car.

And the siren goes off.

We both jump and he scrambles for the keys in his pockets and presses the button several times before the alarm finally silences. At this point, the rain smacks the pavement hard enough we'll drown if we stay outside any longer.

I open the passenger door and hide inside. Because of the rain. Not because I'm scared of kissing Leon. That's ridiculous.

When he gets into the car, I make good on the promise I'm working on. Learning how to stop talking so much. And maybe Leon has the same promise to himself, because he doesn't say a single word the rest of the ride.

CHAPTER 14

HRBC Lesson #6: How to Be a Cool Girl™

Sofia: You're already a cool girl, but they won't know unless you learn how to brag about yourself. Tell them what you're good at. Tell them how fast you can complete a Rubik's Cube. Tell them how you can finish a puzzle of a thousand within an hour.

Titi Ivy: Being a cool girl is a state of mind. It's confidence. Stand straight, chin up.

Titi Ivy: When you get a compliment, accept it like you already know. (Mom: But do it politely.)

Despite the triple flip into a somersault my stomach performed during the silent ride back a few days ago to my house, the first thing I did when I got home was shower and then straighten my hair and brush my lips with my toothbrush though they didn't even touch Leon's.

These moments between us are getting muddled. I'm supposed to be hurting him. Not falling back under his spell.

Not this time.

When I got home last night and told Sofia all about me worrying I was losing some of my boot camp magic, she made me take a quiz she made on the dos and don'ts of being the perfect girlfriend. I failed. Twice. So, she organized emergency dates to get me back on the romance track, despite my protests and bribery of doing her chores for the week if she left me alone. I should have offered two weeks.

Sofia practically dragged me by the ear to the car where Titi Sandra was waiting to drive me to Willhill Mall. This place is large enough that even if any of my exes arrived early, they probably wouldn't be able to spot me from our different meetup spots.

The large warehouse is split into multiple levels, and when I finish smoothing down my straight hair, I move from the parking lot Titi Sandra dropped me off at into the first level—the food court. Though food court sounds more like a corner at a mall. This has full-blown restaurants spread throughout the open layout. Kind of like the casinos Titi Ivy would sneak me into so she could gamble when all the aunts told her to stop spending her money. She paid me in ice cream and french fries to say we went to "the park."

I put away my miniature Rubik's Cube in my cross-body bag and make my way through.

As I walk past the fancier restaurants, I rub the hairs standing at my arms. They must spend a fortune on electricity based on the air conditioner pumping through this place alone. If I had known it'd be this cold, I'd have worn something other than Sofia's pale blue romper and chanclas.

I make my way to Madeline's at the farthest side by the stained-glass waterfall, where my date, Jeremy, waits. As I pass it and notice the fish swirling within, I get a phantom taste of slime wetting my lips and shiver. I rush inside.

My eyes have to adjust to the change in lighting. It's not entirely black, but the only light comes from the wires of bluc and pink LED lights lining the walls and ceiling, gathering at the center of the room where it's thickest, like the veins of the root of a tree. Under that hangs a disco ball, and under *that* people clap for the girl standing on a stage the size of a bathtub whose performance I just missed.

It smells clean—but not. Like someone spilled rotten soup on the carpet and soaked it in Febreze before everyone walked in.

A curvy woman trades places with the girl and speaks into a mic. "Amazing job! Now, let's hear it for our next performers, Mimi and Alaa, singing a classic."

Oh God, I didn't realize this place had karaoke. Nerves snake up my spine when I spot Jeremy scribbling something down on a book by the host that stands beside it.

Then he sits down at a small table nearest the stage.

When I get to him, he smiles at me. His face is like a picture with an inverted filter, blue and purple and alien under these lights, making his normally red curls a pale color.

"Jeremy, how are you?" I sit down on the seat across him.

"Amelia, you look great," he greets me. "Surprised you didn't ask to meet somewhere else." He grabs his drink and gestures to the world around us. "Not really your scene, is it?" Well, he's *right*. I didn't know this was half-karaoke.

I mean, the most adventurous thing I ever did with Jeremy was join in on one of his pranks where he covered our principal's office with foil. I can still feel the Stare Titi Sandra burned into me when she got called into the office. "This is totally cool," I say as the mic does that horrendous blaring noise. "As long as you don't want me to do karaoke. Do you?"

He rolls his eyes. "Knew you wouldn't want to. What's the big deal? I picked this place 'cause I thought it'd be fun."

I don't know, I guess my idea of fun is different from his. Mainly because the thought of screeching into a microphone with so many people watching makes me want to vomit.

In an attempt to change the subject, I ask him, "Any good food here?"

He nods. "I ordered us some apps to pick on."

At the sound of a song starting, I turn away from him, my elbows resting on the table, and watch the two dark-haired girls start singing—one is good, the other horrible but cute, though the microphone's feedback and stuttering every other verse aren't really helping her.

Maybe if there weren't around twenty people in the tight space, my feet wouldn't itch with the need to run away. Well, I guess if there was less of a crowd, that'd be worse. Then there'd be nothing to watch other than whoever was on the stage.

Not that I'm going on the stage.

Jeremy laughs when the girl hits a particularly harsh note. I instantly feel bad for her. I don't have to look around to see other people are probably laughing at her too, especially because she keeps hitting the wrong key.

"You look different." He pulls my attention. "Nice hair." Somehow *nice hair* doesn't feel like a compliment anymore. Not since Leon said it was beautiful, even when it wasn't straight. Again, my brain decides to insert Leon in a situation that has nothing to do with him. I force a smile.

The waiter comes over and drops off a tray of fries, mozzarella sticks, tacos, and two waters. "Amelia?"

I look up, and it feels like my bones are trying to escape my flesh. I don't want to exist anymore. Not with *Arno* looking at me, at Jeremy, back at me.

"Arno, what are you doing here?" *Calm down, keep your voice normal.* "You have two jobs?"

He nods. "Yeah, saving up for college. Gotta work hard, you know?"

"Right."

"Right."

"Well," he starts, "I should get back to work."

When he walks off, I ask to be excused and follow him before he gets to the kitchen. "Hey," I point over to Jeremy. "That's not what it looks like."

"Huh?"

"I mean, I'm not on a date." When he only frowns, I go on. "Not that you would care either way. I know. I'm just making conversation." *Clarifying that I'm single so you don't forget about me. Trying not to drown myself in the nearest fountain.*

"Hey, no worries." He smiles. "It's good to know you're not on a date."

Oh my God.

Okay, good save. Next time I saw him at the Big E, I was planning on doing a few *cool-girl walk-bys* Sofia taught me.

"Basically, you purposely put yourself in their view," Sofia

said, stealing from Titi Ivy's style and wearing only a button-up cinched together by a thin gold chain. "But you pay them zero attention, like you don't even know they're there."

"I'm more of a visual learner," I said, snacking on a brownie from the platter of snacks Mom made us. "Can you give me an example?"

"It's all in the body," Sofia said, walking toward the kitchen. She placed a hand on her hip, then sauntered down the imaginary runway, her long legs swaying with her. "Shoulders back, chest out, chin always up."

After she did a little spin by me on the couch, I said, mouth full, "Sorry, one more time?" She rolled her eyes and strutted again. When she finished, I asked for another demonstration. I got away with it four more times before she grabbed a piece of a brownie and shoved it all over my mouth.

"Tighten up, Hernandez."

This almost tanked that, and any chance at a date with Arno.

"Well, I should get back to my not-date, then."

"Hey." He grabs my arm. "You know the grand opening is happening this week. My parents are letting me throw a party at our place the weekend after it opens. You're coming, right?"

"Is that an invitation?"

He gives me a funny look. "Yeah, I'm inviting you."

I nearly smack myself in the face. Of course it was an invitation. Some cool girl I am.

"That's awesome. I'd love to. Do you want me to bring anything?"

He tilts his head. "Like a gift?"

During Hernandez Romance Boot camp, Titi Sandra said, "I've heard food is the way into someone's heart."

"No, like food, you know?" I clarify. "A dish? I can get my aunts to help me. They can cook anything, really—" I pause to make sure I didn't slip into Spanish because he's so clearly not getting me, but he speaks.

"We're having it catered."

Right, not everyone has to spend hours before the sun is up cooking meals and keeping them in the oven until the evening for a party. "Well," I say, wishing we were closer to the window so I can fling my body out of it. "I'll just bring myself."

"Good, that's all I want." My stomach does a little dance at his words. "Anyway, you should try the steak tips," he goes on. "They're amazing. I ranked this number two on my Top Ten Restaurants in West Springfield. The only reason it lost is because of the ambiance. This place could really do with a facelift, right?"

"Top Ten Restaurants? Do you have a blog or something?"

He scratches the back of his head. "Yeah, Arno's Atmosphere. It started as a joke at the beginning of junior year. I had to take a journalism class and needed to build a site for a project, and I came up with ranking places. Not just diners, but activities, events, concerts, everything. I do news pieces on updates and renovations for upcoming venues. A lot. Anyway, suddenly, it wasn't only a project but fun. Now I'm majoring in journalism at Impact University this fall."

"Wow, that's amazing."

Someone else with a life plan, a future, and a passion. It's a reminder of how far behind I am to everyone else. It reminds me how bad I need this gap program, along with the terrifying possibility of me actually going. The thought of not being able to go makes my stomach feel like it's being flattened by one of the aunts' fondant rollers.

Will I really be okay off on my own?

I mean, the aunts have never strayed away from one another, and the Hernandez women before them hadn't either. If *they* have years of experience staying safe and together, who am I to break the cycle?

"Thanks. What about you? You just graduated. What are you going to study?"

Instead of focusing on me, I direct the focus back to him. "I'm sorry, it's just so cool. Do you have a newsletter or something?"

He beams. "Yeah, you should subscribe. I try to post stuff every two weeks, but sometimes it's once a month."

"I will," I say, a memory sparking to life. "You know, my junior year, I helped run my school's weekly magazine." Technically, it was Sofia's job, but she was so busy partying, and she knew I liked to write back to the people who submitted something in the advice section. I did it for her even though she was an entire year behind me. "We had this advice column I loved and sometimes I took one of the questions and made a whole essay about them, so it read like a blog. Is it something like that?"

He smiles at me sweetly enough that my neck warms. "That's cool. I think it's similar."

But I'm still a little nervous. I want to make the best impression, and Arno gets this spark of passion in his eyes each time I ask him about something he's interested in. It's nice to talk to someone who's thought it out, someone who's passionate about what they want do in their life. I feel inspired, like I immediately want to count my savings and figure out when I'm going to hit my goal for the gap-year deposit. But I can't do that now obviously because I'm still on a date.

Oh my God, my date!

"I should get back to my friend."

"See you around."

"Hope so," I say and turn around before I have to see his face after *that* embarrassing response.

When I return to the table, Jeremy asks, "Friend of yours?"

"Yeah, someone I work with."

"Cool," he says as I raise the water to my lips. "So, I was wondering, what made you text me anyway?"

I tilt the cup and the ice slides down so quick, it slaps my nose. The rest of the water, *all* of it, splashes over my face, drenches my top. I drop the cup down and hurriedly reach around for a napkin.

"Oh my God." I find one, try to blot it all, but there's no way this will dry with the air conditioner blasting. Jeremy holds his stomach in one of those laughs so hard it comes out silently. My body heats to an uncomfortable temperature. I don't have to scan the room to know all eyes are on me and my coated face and shirt.

Jeremy cracks up, his knee hits the table and nearly knocks the plates off.

"It's not funny!" I try to dry my face, but the napkin is soaked and rendered useless. I glance around, but the waitress isn't on the floor.

Each second, Jeremy's laugh gets louder, my throat burns hotter, and my fury boils over.

It takes everything, absolutely *everything* in me, not to bullet over to Jeremy, wrinkle the top of his shirt in my fist, and yank him up and crash my forehead against his.

"Is this why you agreed to hang out?" I say through my teeth. "To laugh at me?"

"Laugh at you?" He seems genuinely taken aback, and some of my anger settles into a simmer. "It's funny. You just spilled water. It's not the end of the world, Amelia."

"You don't find this to be embarrassing?"

He frowns, then leans in closer. "Come on, this is the furthest thing from embarrassing. Look around, nobody is watching you right now."

I look around, and, okay, he's *right*, but that doesn't mean they wouldn't be. And it's not like I can help the way my body's temperature decided to skyrocket despite the cold liquid gliding down my neck.

"That's just because they're too busy laughing at the girl on the stage."

"They're not laughing at her," he says seriously, like he can't believe he has to explain it to me. "They're laughing with her."

"How do you know?"

He offers me his napkin. "Look at her. *She's* laughing too."

That stole whatever remaining anger stirred in me and

shoves confusion in its place. She is laughing. In fact, she can barely get a full word out because her and her friend are laughing so hard, swaying together.

Honestly, they look like they're having a great time.

"Okay, maybe you're right," I admit. "I still like it safe down here."

"Safe is boring." He shifts in his seat. "Remember when we stole the school's mascot and had to run through the halls before the security guard caught us?"

"Yeah." I can still hear Mom's snapping at me to act like I was raised correctly. "I can't believe I did that."

"It was *fun*. Everyone was watching us run and cheering us on. Don't you remember? We couldn't stop laughing even when our parents got called." He leans over, grabs his cup of water, then proceeds to let it fall onto his face like I just did. But on *purpose*. "Who cares what people think?"

Okay, I'm officially softened like melted butter now. I'm also glancing around to see if anyone is watching the soaked pair sitting front row. Nobody is.

"Okay," I say. "I get it, seriously. I'm just not sure *how* you do this."

He rolls his eyes. "You've always taken yourself so seriously. You need to learn how to not care. Laugh things off."

Now, *that* makes me laugh. "Nobody has ever in my life described me as serious. Ever. It's like not my thing."

He looks at me with his eyebrows raised, like I'm missing the most obvious answer to a question he didn't ask. "See? Even now you're talking down about yourself."

"I'm not—" I pause. "You don't get it. I am joking, just about myself." I smile to really drive the point, but Jeremy throws me a look like he doesn't believe me.

"I don't get *you*," he shoots back. "The only jokes you make are about yourself, and they're not funny. It's not fun to listen to someone put themselves down all the time. You gotta learn how to laugh at yourself. Don't think of it as being at your expense, think of it as making yourself happy. How can you do that if you're worried about how other people look at you?"

The short month Jeremy and I dated, we didn't get deep into our childhoods, favorite things, topics that dove into why we are the way we are. It was a whirlwind of him pranking everyone around us, including me, and, okay, it was annoying, but his laugh was contagious. That's why I liked him. He made me laugh.

I never realized that I didn't try to do it too often for myself. "I guess I see what you mean. I never thought of it that way."

He gives me an encouraging smile. "It takes time to get to my comedic level, but you'll get there one day, I'm sure."

I mirror his smile. "Maybe I will."

Jeremy claps his hands together. "Anyway, give me a minute. I've got to go to the bathroom."

"Sure."

For something to do, I reach into the tote I brought filled with water and snacks for my shift and pull out the romance journal I've been using to jot down notes from my *lessons*.

I always carry a miniature Rubik's Cube, or a tiny sudoku notebook or word search in my purse. I like to have something to do, not just with my hands but with my mind. I hate the silence of it when it's not active. I always like to be trying to figure something out. And this book is actually helpful, plus Sofia added a bunch of funny doodles in it that Titi Sandra described as *inappropriate scrabble.*

When Jeremy returns, I put it beside me and blink when he grins. "Ready?"

Oh God. "For what?"

Mimi and Alaa are receiving their hefty applause and a woman joins them, taking the microphone as they exit. Then she introduces the next singer to the stage.

Freaking Jeremy.

"Hey, everyone," he says, and I wince. The girls didn't speak before *their* performance. "This is one of my favorite songs ever. Get your eardrums ready."

The music starts and I try to recognize the sound of snaps, or claps, or both. It's familiar, but I don't catch on until he sings the first line and the bass drops.

"Honey, honey, I can see the stars all the way from here."

Jeremy goes on, *incredibly* off-key, doing this two-step while singing into the mic, snapping his fingers in time with the beat.

Oh. My. God.

Jeremy is belting Beyoncé's "Love on Top."

To me.

He does this spin and snap, and the crowd goes wild. Some help by singing the background melody and the others clap along to the song and, oh—I guess I'm one of them. I can't help it. Jeremy is half laughing, half singing and wholly enjoying this, and my hands move on their own.

His shoulders are as nimble as his footwork as he gets to the chorus and starts pointing my way, veins popping out of his neck as he practically screams out the lyrics.

I've got to admit, it's my new favorite song. Jeremy's version of it, anyway.

He doesn't care what he sounds like. He only cares about doing whatever makes him happy. And right now, that's singing Beyoncé. And the people in the audience, they're having fun too. So am I.

Jeremy takes a dramatic bow, blowing kisses to his adoring fans as he runs toward me, his smile spread wide as the host asks if anyone else wants to go next.

"So," he sits back down, "what do you think? Did I *embarrass* myself up there?"

"No." I smile. "But I'm probably about to."

Then I rush onstage, grab the mic, and do the worst reggaeton performance the world has ever seen.

CHAPTER 15

Date Debrief #5

What Worked: Showed up early and ordered her favorite frappe to show her I remembered what she liked. (Sofia: Cute, people like when you remember the smaller details.)

What Didn't:

—Accidentally burning my mouth on my latte. (Sofia: What are you, a three-year-old learning to hold a cup for the first time?) (Titi Sandra: Don't be mean to your sister.) (Sofia: Pot, kettle.)

What Could've Gone Better: Not wearing a white shirt. Coffee stains. (Sofia: Isn't spilling coffee on yourself considered lucky?) (Titi Neva: That's a bird pooping on you.) (Sofia: That doesn't sound lucky.)

Total Rating: 4/10. The conversation was great up until I spewed coffee all over myself. She was really nice about it, but it was a little too embarrassing to not be awkward afterward. (Sofia: Maybe she found the awkwardness endearing.)

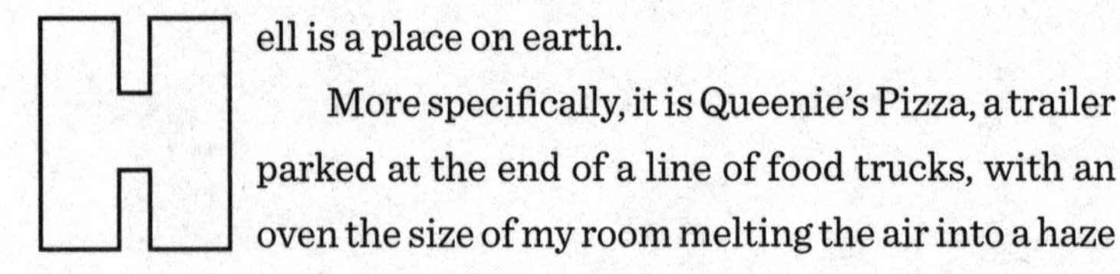

Hell is a place on earth.

More specifically, it is Queenie's Pizza, a trailer parked at the end of a line of food trucks, with an oven the size of my room melting the air into a haze burning my eyes as much as the pans burn my fingertips.

Seriously, if I wanted to run away and change my identity, it would be no problem. I'm pretty sure my fingertips are gone.

But it's the only thing I can do, get the ready-to-bake pizzas and put them in the oven. Every time I tried to stretch out the ingredients into a circle, the dough looked like Swiss cheese.

Knead the dough. Stretch the dough. Shrink the dough. Gently. No, not like that, softer.

There's still an hour left of my shift when Jorge offers me a slice of pizza, then gestures to the door. "All the kids ask for a break, but you kept working all day. Nice ethic. You can leave early. See you tomorrow."

"You're the best," I say, practically flinging myself out the truck. As soon as I walk out and feel real air, I wonder how the hell I didn't suffocate in that cage.

I check my phone and the last message is from my work crush, Arno.

This is an official invitation to my party 😉

7:15 pm

I bite down on my smile, then realize nobody is watching me, so I don't have to be chill-girl. I can just beam at the text and reply. I drop it into my tote bag and then frown. It's a little lighter than usual. I peek in it, move around the slice of pizza wrapped in foil, a half-empty water bottle, and my pen with a star at the top.

I wish I remembered where I dropped my Hernandez Romance Boot Camp journal after coming home last night. I couldn't find it this morning, and I could use a refresher.

There's a whole section inside about texting, and a legend of emojis and a rating on how flirty each is.

A wink. Not a smile, a single open eye. That's totally flirty, right?

I would text Sofia to confirm, but she's on some date, which means her phone is off, so I'm stuck under the evening sky on my own. Might as well take in the joy for my walk home.

I could call the aunts, but if—no, *when* the summer is up, I'll have to figure out things on my own. Making my way back home, that's going to be one of them. I should learn to read a map.

No, GPS is universal. I should remember to bring a portable charger.

Before I start my trek home, I walk down the line of food trucks trying to familiarize myself with the names of locations. I got lost twice trying to find my way from the arcade center, and the giant square blocked off into a maze by various shops setting up to sell whatever random product their company is forcing them to. I saw a booth selling hot tubs next to a tent selling slime. This place is as random as it gets.

Half the trucks are without lights. The only ones on are those with less help, like Queenie's Pizza, who don't have extra staff to work at the truck *and* at whatever restaurant they actually work at. Now that I'm out, my sense of smell returns, and I would kill for whatever they're frying up at Dowhop Donuts.

But my earnings are all going to the gap-year program, so I chew my slice of pizza as slowly as possible to really cherish it, though I never want to eat another slice for the rest of my life. At least I have pretty scenery for my dinner.

During the day, the Big E is a festival on steroids, but at night, under the endless string lights that hover above and wrap around every building, flash above every tent and ride, it's like a magical world.

Before I have to go home, I find a bench beside the lit-up teacup ride and allow myself a break. I'm sure my feet are a little sore from standing all day, but as I finish my pizza and sit down, my fingertips both sting and itch but every time I scratch them, the burning heats up, and it's an endless cycle of me clawing at myself.

As I'm fighting with my own body, I spot someone jogging ahead, looking around.

It's Leon.

I could let him go. I don't have anything planned for revenge today. I was just trying to get through keeping hydrated as fast as I sweat out all the water from my body. But Sofia says I should take every opportunity to make him fall for me. *Take initiative.*

"Hey," I shout after him as he peeks behind the corner of a truck, curiosity getting the better of me. "Leon!"

He turns to my voice, then jogs over. I stand as he gets to me. "Amelia, there you are."

"You were looking for me?"

"Yeah." He stretches his arms out. "I heard you were working at Queenie's and Jorge let you out early. I wanted to check on you."

Well, it doesn't take away me calling out to him. I stepped up. But I guess I can't complain if I already have him checking in on me.

It's a perfect spot to have him, in my hands. Especially since the last we saw each other, it felt like he was the one with a leg up. He's the one who pulled away from what I'm pretty sure would be a kiss. "Guess you'll have to find a way to make it up to me."

Back in familiar territory for him, for the Leon he is now, he smirks. "I can think of something."

"An air-conditioned room would be best at the moment."

"Jorge working you too hard?"

"No, actually, I think I'm in love with him." At Leon's wide eyes, I laugh. "Seriously, the thirty-year age difference means nothing to me. He's been the nicest person to me here."

Leon's frown deepens. "Have people been *not* nice to you?"

I blink, swallowing the lump in my throat. It's so easy to forget, to let myself be touched by his concern.

Before we dated, I had a pretty active summer working at Mari's summer camp. A lot of students worked there too, and I dated three of them. Something about a summer camp bubble makes emotions run high. I honestly fell for each one equally. Two of them dumped me, for each other, and one wanted to date me and everyone else with a pulse at the same time.

But when Leon first asked me out, someone started spreading rumors about how I was a serial dater. It was like the whisper game and eventually people started saying that I even tried to break up already-happy couples. People would mutter around me, move seats when I sat down.

When Leon caught me crying, sitting at the bleachers one lunch. He made it a point to correct everyone's perception of me. The next day, he had his dad order party pizzas and placed them next to me when everyone else was being served rubbery Salisbury steak. He shouted out I'd brought it for the class and everyone swarmed me with thanks, taking slices.

If he heard anyone talking about me, even utter my name, he'd walk right up to them and ask them to repeat what they said loudly and clearly. Turns out most people aren't as comfortable saying nasty things for other people to hear, and pretty soon people stopped talking about me, afraid Leon would appear from thin air and shame them.

We weren't officially together at that time. He just wanted people to be kind to me. Was upset when they weren't. His eyes right now hold that same determined and empathic heat they held the day he found me on the bleachers.

"Everyone is nice." My gaze lands on the sawdust clinging to his pale shirt. "Where'd you work today?" I thought his dad and the other employees only worked at the Big E during the day, and the work at the bakery is at a halt.

Without looking, he wipes the debris from his shoulder. "I picked up a shift here," he says, not mentioning where he was stationed. "Are you done for tonight?"

"Yeah, I was just on my way home."

"Cool. Sofia coming to get you?"

My phone vibrates. I pull it from my pocket. "Yup," I tell Leon before walking off.

As I near the exit, I feel the weight of someone's presence behind me. An extra shadow blocking the string lights lighting my path.

I turn, and Leon is a few steps behind me. Mainly because

he's so tall it's impossible for him to mask the sound of his footsteps. I frown as I face him. "Why are you following me?"

"When you lie, your right eye twitches, just a little," he says as my mouth drops open. "Sofia isn't coming to pick you up. So, you need a ride, Amelia?"

Where do I start? The fact that he knows when I'm lying by a twitch I can't even feel? The way he says my name with such *warmth* and familiarity and authority, like he's the only one who can call me by my name?

My mind is a mess, the organ behind my rib cage is wild, and it all makes me incapable of doing anything but stuttering a nonsensical answer.

As I struggle to steady myself, Leon says, "I'll drive you home."

I need water, lots of it. "You don't have to."

"I don't, but I want to."

He dumped you. You gave him every part of you, your body, your love, and he left you like it was easy. I repeat the chant in my head. Got to keep on track to complete Operation Break Leon's Heart. Not the most creative name, I'll admit, but direct.

Besides, if he's worried about me walking home alone, then he cares enough about my well-being. Another step closer to fulfilling my mission. If I keep up at this pace, I'll be breaking his heart in no time.

I link my arm around his. "Lead the way."

He leads me to what I recognize as his dad's truck. Whenever Leon's car gave him trouble, he'd always drive the house of a vehicle. He opens the passenger door and helps me up even though I'm tall enough to make it on my own.

When we get inside, he automatically turns off the music when he cracks the ignition on.

Why listen to the radio when I'd rather listen to you? That's what he'd always say when he drove me anywhere. I didn't need to think of something interesting, because he made me feel like everything I said *was* interesting.

I rub my eyes with the palms of my hands as he drives off. I'm doing way too much reminiscing. Maybe I should speed up this process, just dump him and get it over with. It'd be less messy for me. Less confusing.

Then I see an orange-and-red sign. "Hey, look!" I point toward it. "7-Eleven."

It takes him a moment to understand since it's been a while, but when he does his lips turn up. "No way, come on."

Instead of wallowing in the failed phone call, I'll take *this* as an opportunity. To remind Leon of the good times we had. Make him think we can have even more.

"Come on," I press as we near the parking lot. "Let's go in. Please?"

He glances over at me, his eyes hot. "Well, since you asked nicely." His voice is warm and smooth like a pot of honey as he turns into the parking lot.

I swallow, trying to ignore the way I can almost taste the sweetness of the words. "Yes way. You know the rules. Every time we see it."

"Those are dumb rules."

"You made them," I remind him as he finds a corner spot.

He hops out and opens my door before I can take off my seat belt.

"Don't be so boring," I say in a teasing tone as he grabs my arm to make sure I don't break an ankle hopping down.

Before I can respond, he pulls me toward the entrance easily, like we never stopped holding hands. Or maybe it feels as good as he remembers. Or maybe I'm projecting.

I greet the cashier before the cashier can welcome us and pull Leon toward the line of drinks. My stomach growls when my nose sniffs the corn dogs sitting beside the cashier in glass, but I won't even spend two dollars and twenty-five cents of the gap-year funds.

But you'll spend four bucks on a slushie with Leon.

Ignoring that ridiculous thought, I grab the largest cup available. As I do, Leon drops down a ten-dollar bill and starts at one end. My instinct is to open my mouth and tell him don't worry about it, but Leon grabs my arms and gently shifts my body toward the line of machines.

His hands are rough, almost like sandpaper, and yet it feels like the softest touch anyway.

There's extra effort in my first step, but they get easier once I make it to the stretch of slushies, beginning with the blue slush whirlpooling in the machine like a washer unit. I pour into the cup for a half second before moving down to the neighboring flavor, cherry, then orange, then blueberry. I keep going down the lines of juices and sodas. All different flavors mixing into the cup I hold like a championship trophy.

When I'm done, I nudge him with my elbow as he talks to the employee about whatever football game plays on the tiny TV by the counter. He says goodbye and keeps a hand at the small of my back, leading me out.

His hand feels like it's hot enough to leave a print of his palm there.

Under the LED lights, his smile brightens more than usual. He holds out the corn dog I eyed when we walked in. "Hungry?"

Suddenly, my stomach fills. There's so much movement, fluttering, flying happening in the pit of my stomach, it makes me a little dizzy.

I don't trust myself to speak, so I grab the corn dog and shove as much of it in my mouth as physically possible.

Mouth full, I shove the drink toward him. "You first."

"No way." He eyes the cup. "*You* made us stop here."

"You birthed this idea."

"I wasn't thinking."

Only he was, but not coherently. After one late night together, I was craving something to drink, but I couldn't choose what exactly I wanted. Part of me wanted Coke, the other juice, the other cream soda. We drove by a 7-Eleven, then Leon grabbed my hand and we ran in. He made me sample every drink possible and created the bomb Leon currently holds in his hand.

"All right, together, then. Hold this." He hands it to me, and I have no choice but to grab it before it falls. He shoves two straws in it, then holds it, nearing me as he does. "Ready?"

I nearly say no, out of spite, but . . .

I grab the straw and suck up the mixture as he does. I'm hit with an instant brain freeze, and rub my head with my hands as if that'll heat up the sting, but then I have to cover my mouth because I'm gagging.

There are no words to describe the taste of the gravylike

mixture. Sour but carbonated and sweet but spicy and, more than anything, *gross.*

Leon bends over laughing, shaking so much the drink spills along his hands and on the concrete below. Some of it splatters on his jeans, and I chuckle—I can't help it—as he fails to keep it together.

Before his jeans get drenched, I grab the drink to steady it but then the mixture spills on my hands. "Leon, pull it together," I say, but now I'm laughing harder and we throw our heads back.

"You're a mess," I say, getting away from him before I'm drenched.

He has enough sense to place the cup down. "Damn, I should get a napkin." He shakes the liquid off his hands.

I hold out my hand. "Yeah, for me too."

He grabs my hand, almost like it was a reflex as soon as he saw it held out. We both still, aside from his thumb slowly pressing its weight across my palm.

There's no brain freeze anymore. Everything in me sizzles then pools into a puddle.

Then he lets go. "Be right back." He heads inside the shop.

My hand remains up in the air as if Leon still holds it.

My heart thunders in my chest, and my throat dries enough I'd drink the bomb just to moisten the desert it's become. I have this plan to break Leon's heart, but I can't help but wonder who is really playing who here.

CHAPTER 16

Date Debrief #6
What Worked: Complimented his bike and proceeded to nod and act interested as he went on a ten-minute tangent on all the features. (Sofia: That's rough, buddy.)
What Didn't:
Knocking the bike over when I tried to get off it. (Sofia: I'm not entirely convinced there isn't something medically wrong with your balance.) (Mom: Should we take you to get checked for an inner ear problem?)
What Could've Gone Better: Note to self, I do not look good with helmet hair. (Sofia: Excuse me, you look good all the time.)
Total Rating: 5/10. The ride was fun and having to hold on to him while he rode was exhilarating, plus he swore the scratches on the side of his bike would come out with a bit of buffing, so I didn't hurt it that bad, right? (Sofia: Green flag, he wasn't mad at you for knocking the bike over, tbh.)

I love my little sister more than I love myself, but when she wakes me up before I'm ready, I have to tell the gods Titi Neva prays to I'm sorry because I honestly consider flinging her out the window like a rag doll. I'd never do it. But imagining it helps calm me down as I shove her off me.

My phone says it's *five* a.m. Usually, this time is nothing to me but only when I get, I don't know, more than a single hour of sleep. Nothing should be awake right now. Only demons. Mari is a demon.

I don't know what comes out of my mouth, just a string of vowels but I think there is a curse in there because Mari says, "Titi Ivy told me to wake you up. The aunts want you downstairs."

I wipe my eyes and the bliss that was my dream already fades from me. Then Mari's words hit me, swapping the bliss for fear and a numbing sensation in my stomach.

"Wait, the aunts? Why, is something wrong?" My brain automatically forms the worst situations I can think of and I nearly fall off the bed to lean over and make sure Sofia is safe and under me.

"I'm alive," Sofia says, her eyes half-open as she sits at the edge of her bed.

Okay, that's all my sisters accounted for—I already know Zoe is safe in Mom's arms—so what else would the aunts have us all up for?

Mari climbs down and skips away, leaving the door open so the music grows louder.

Like two zombies, Sofia and I groan and drag our feet out of our room, downstairs to the kitchen. For the first time in forever, the stainless steel table is without flour and pots and pans, and instead covered in plates of eggs, pancakes, fruits, and all breakfast pastries.

Not only that, but the stools that normally collect dust and spiderwebs in the garage now surround the long counter, each filled by the aunts and Mom holding a sleeping Zoe—God, I wish that was me—in her arms.

Sofia, a much stronger human than me, can already form a sentence. "What's going on?"

Titi Sandra at the opposite end of where Mom sits, says, "Breakfast."

"At five in the morning?" It sounds like Sofia has tears in her eyes. I'm about to join her.

"It's close to six," Mom says.

"When I was your age, I would still be up from the past night," Titi Ivy says.

"Time is a man-made construct none of us should follow too closely," Titi Neva says.

"This is hell," I whisper.

"No complaints," Titi Sandra says. "When you all have kids, you'll have to get up this early too. Get used to it." Her chin gestures to me. "This is how early you'll get up when you're working at the bakery."

"I don't *want* to get used to it."

Every single head turns toward me at the same time. I jerk back. I swear I meant to say it in my head. That's how tired I am. I'm risking the Stare. Too vulnerable to remember to be quiet and follow the Hernandez expectations.

"Try again?" Titi Sandra says harshly, but it's an offering. A chance to change what we all heard, to change what I wanted to say. A rare gift from Titi Sandra.

I take it. "I'll get up early." It feels like I'm betraying myself.

I don't want to get up early for myself or some imaginary child. I want to sleep in for hours, get up at night on days when I haven't done anything worth making me feel tired.

I want to bask in the lack of urgency. I want to live in the bliss of taking a break whenever I want.

But instead I shut my mouth and do what I'm told.

The free seats are all scattered, so I drop down next to Titi Neva, Sofia sits with Titi Sandra, and Mari by Mom. Even though parts of my body are still numb from sleep, my stomach immediately remembers how to work and turns with hunger when I get the first whiff of bacon.

"Is that apple-smoked?" I point at the pile of grease and love. When Mom nods, I start piling on my plate. Eggs, pancakes, French toast, hash browns—the works. I'm pretty much awake after my first forkful.

Sofia, who hasn't touched a dish, says, "Is there a reason for this?"

Titi Sandra answers, "Since when does family need a reason to sit and have a meal together? You spend too much time with your friends, you forget the meaning of family. It's all you'll ever have."

Titi Ivy adds, "We've all been so busy and our schedules haven't aligned. Sofia is always out, Mari has book club in the afternoon, Amelia has her work. We wanted to get together for a meal this week. Don't tell me you all are too cool for us now?"

"Not me!" Mari claps her hands together.

Titi Ivy mouths to her, *You're my favorite*, and she giggles.

Titi Sandra says, "Sofia, did you get the pictures I sent

you? The color scheme for the stationary set I found?"

"Yeah," Sofia takes a tiny bite of a pancake. "I already added it to my wish list."

One hand holding Zoe, Mom's other hand reaches out to my hair and twirls it around. "Nena, how many times you gonna straighten your hair? I already see some split ends. You have beautiful curls."

"I think you look pretty," Mari says.

I mouth to her, *You're my favorite*, and she beams, looking around as if she's wondering if she can get the whole table to call her that. I personally think the whole world should say it to her—the morning wake-up call already forgiven at the sight of that blinding smile.

Titi Neva sniffs my shoulder. "Mi amor, your aura is off."

I yank my hand-me-down pajamas to my nose, but it smells like the softener Mom always uses. "What? This is April Fresh scent."

"No, your aura. Something's off, you seem to be unbalanced, wavering, indecisive, shaky—"

"Nobody asked for a string of synonyms," Titi Ivy says with her mouth full.

"I know what I smell, what I feel." Titi Neva taps my shoulder. "You want to talk it out?"

"I want to finish breakfast."

Though now, and maybe it's because I'm already halfway done, my appetite fades. She could be guessing. Or maybe my eyes have been twitching and everyone along with Leon knows what it means, and nobody has pointed it out yet.

Sort of. I mean, I'm *not* indecisive, I know what I'm doing, and I know Leon deserves to hurt like I did. He absolutely does. He should get a taste of his own medicine and then I can move on, justice will be served, and curses will be broken. I know I have to separate myself from the Hernandez house. Not just for my future, but for myself, my emotions too. If I stay here, I'll resent them, I'll try not to but late at night I feel it stirring within me, preparing itself.

But I can't shake this unbearable feeling of guilt, like what I'm doing is wrong. I guess in a sense the act itself *is* since what Leon did to me was wrong. But I'm only doing it because he did it first. Two wrongs definitely make a right, and I'm going to prove it. Maybe just a little bit faster than I intended. That way I get what I want, Leon gets what he deserves, and I don't have to have an unbalanced, wavering, indecisive, shaky aura.

I drop my fork on my plate. "On that note, I'm going to shower and get ready."

"Don't you start at ten?" Sofia asks.

"Today is this huge meeting for all the staff at the Big E," I explain. "I have to get this week's schedule and staff shirts and do weird team bonding stuff with people I'm probably not even going to work with."

"Sounds gross, and I'm sleepy."

Titi Ivy gestures toward me. "I'll bring you, my firstborn."

"Thanks, Titi." I get up to leave.

Mom calls after me, "Wash your hair, deep condition." She doesn't look up from Zoe, scratching at her neck. A neck that should be covered since I'm pretty sure that top once was a turtleneck but now hangs loosely just under her collarbone.

She needs a deep condition. And some of that pink calming lotion Titi Neva uses on Mari's eczema. Mom doesn't flinch as Zoe digs her tiny nail into her already-red skin. I look around and everyone is either looking on their phone, at their food, or nails.

Anger fills me so quickly my vision blurs.

Instead, I walk over and place my hands on Zoe's body. "I think you need a break."

Mom blinks, then looks up at me with half-open eyes. "She's just fussy today. I was about to feed her."

Titi Sandra says, "Your mother is fine, go get ready. Being late is unacceptable."

So they can pay attention to me but not see Mom is morphing into a zombie.

My stomach churns. It's not like I've been checking in on Mom as much as I should have. One day she had bags under her eyes and today she has black holes holding them up. I somehow missed her not getting at least an ounce of sleep.

"I'll feed her." I grab Zoe, who starts to wail when I pull her away from Mom. "Why don't you take a nap? I have a half hour before I have to get ready."

"I'm okay."

"Come on, Mom." I roll my eyes, pretending there isn't a new ingredient of guilt swirling in the pot of the rest. This time, the realization that if I leave Mom, nobody will remember to give her a rest and she'll break. Wither like the way her skin cracks on the fingers that always hold up her daughter. "I miss my baby sister. It's selfish to keep her to yourself. Isn't that right, Zoe?"

At her name, my baby sister blinks, the surprise stealing her ability to cry. For now.

Mom looks at me, I can't tell if she's narrowing her eyes or if she's falling asleep on the spot. "Okay, but you wake me up in twenty minutes. That's it."

"Of course," I say, my gaze following her as she leaves to the back room.

When she goes, I glance at everyone. Not a single person offered to help Mom this morning, and I feel like trash because aside from today, I can't remember a recent time that *I* did.

Mom doesn't ask for help. We don't offer it. I wonder . . . I wonder if Mom somehow feels trapped the way I do. Not the same, not exactly, but in her anxiety. Stuck in this fear that if she's not taking care of Zoe, something bad will happen to her. The way I think if I stick around here, something bad will change inside me.

I bring Zoe to the couch and sit with her, rocking her until she quiets. "That's right, Beba, you're going to be a good girl now and for Mom *all* day today." Zoe blinks up at me, a smile playing on her tiny pink lips that somehow makes me feel like the sun is pouring over us even though the curtains are shut. "Isn't that right, pequeña? Isn't that right?" She giggles at my baby voice and I feel all right for the first time in a while.

Until Titi Sandra reminds me to get ready. Instead of finding Mom, I head up to my room and sit by Sofia. I pinch her awake and she jolts up, a curse she bites back when she sees a sleeping Zoe in my arms.

"You're on baby duty," I tell her instead of asking. Asking can get me a no, and I'm not giving her the option. "Mom needs a break, so you stay with her as long as she needs one. I mean it."

Sofia rubs crust out of her eyes. "Ugh, I hate it when you use your *older*-sister voice on me. Who do you think you are?"

The last time I used said voice on Sofia was when she thought it was a good idea to jump off the garage into a *kiddie* pool five years ago. "Just take Zoe."

"Fine." She takes our baby sister. "only because she's cute."

With that taken care of, I head to the bathroom. I go out of my way to wrap my hair, so the humidity of the shower doesn't allow a single curl to form and get ready as quickly as I can.

I take out my phone and text Leon to meet me sooner.

As I'm finishing getting ready, I grab Sofia's perfume on the bedside table and spray it all over myself.

"That's ten bucks worth of sprays," she mutters under the covers, Zoe lying on top of her.

"You'd make your own sister pay to wear your perfume?"

"I didn't choose you," she says. "Are you trying to entice Leon with your scent?"

"I'm using every possible method. I want to hurry up and dump him."

At that, she sits up. She doesn't *say* anything, but she unintentionally does the sister-telepathy thing. It's sloppy. I only pick up a bit. *What are you doing?* But it's accusatory.

I cross my hands against my chest. "What?"

"Nothing." She looks me up and down. "It's just, we know

he's attracted to you. He dated you. But you look supercute right now."

"What is that supposed to mean?"

"It means you look cute," she says, feigning offense. "Supercute. Date-worthy cute. Heartbreaker cute. I'm just checking in if it's because you want to be cute for Leon to dump him, or cute for Leon to like you."

I press my fingers into my temples. "Those both mean the same thing."

"No," she says dryly, "they don't."

My phone buzzes.

🏃🏃🏃🏃

Leon 6:10 am

Sofia whistles, and it's an extremely annoying melody. "What is with you?" I ask her.

"I'm not the one smiling at a text from her ex."

I bring my fingers to my lips, just to check. Maybe they were *slightly* raised. But that's because my plan is working.

"Has anyone ever said talking to you feels like chewing on broken glass?"

"Has anyone ever told you four out of five exes end up back together?"

My heart speeds an uncomfortable amount. "What?"

"I made that up, but your face said a whole lot just now."

"Eat dirt," I call as I leave the room.

Titi Ivy waits in the family car. I nearly have a heart attack as music bursts through the speakers when she starts the ignition. She's not exactly a speed demon, but she drives fast enough I consider practicing again so I can feel confident to drive myself places.

When we pull up, she drops me off at the designated entrance occupied by a few employees in a tent drinking coffee.

"Thanks, Titi," I grab the door handle.

"Hey," Titi Ivy says, "if you are any of the adjectives Neva described, you know you can talk to me, right?"

My pulse quickens, but I keep a smile on my face and eyes open. No twitching over here, thank you very much. "I'm good, Titi, swear it."

"But if you're not, I'm here. Siempre."

"Titi." My throat tightens. "I think you love me too much."

"That's impossible—"

"You love me too much, and I do nothing to deserve it," I tell her, and because it's a little heavy, I add, "I ate the chocolate bar you hid at the back of the fridge, not Sofia."

She pulls the car in park and I brace myself. "There's only one thing in this world that is entirely free, and that's love. And it's free because it's meant to be given easily. Free to give *and* receive." She says it with such clarity, such sureness, it only makes my throat constrict tighter. "So, my firstborn, take our love and don't worry about it." Then she smirks. "Seriously, you frown too much and you'll give yourself wrinkles. Value that pretty face while you have it."

The only thing I can think to say is "All right, love you."

She waves and pulls off, and I jiggle my hands and bounce on my feet, trying to shake off the heaviness of the conversation.

As I enter the open white gate, the guys greet me and I

wave, making my way through the festival in the town.

The sun hangs in the sky, but this place is pretty abandoned aside from some people in suits walking around with employees with staff shirts and doing more important things to keep this place together than me burning pizzas. But that's not my problem.

I walk through the animal section, and though it's kind of eerie walking past all the gated areas where animals will be, it's kind of nice. The animals don't belong here, and I know—since I asked the staff—a lot of them are considered "rescues," but now that they've been rescued, shouldn't they be set free?

I shake my head, clearing the thoughts that are unfortunately all above my nearly nonexistent pay grade.

When I finish making my way through the mini zoo area, I find a bench by an immobile ship that nearly flips you over when you ride. There are two guys manning it, pressing the buttons so the lights flash on, and a pirate theme song starts to play, then turning it off right after.

Very mature.

I pull out my phone and go into a deep dive of mindless scrolling, so deep I'm not sure how long it takes Leon to get to me, only that when he does I'm lying on the bench and his shadow startles me. I drop the phone right on my chin.

"Ouch, damn it." I sit up.

Leon coughs loudly as if that covers up his laugh and I automatically move my lips to tell him to shut up, but that isn't very chill-girl of me, so I press the skin under my eye as if it'll wipe away the pulsing beneath the skin.

When he finally settles down, he asks, "Are you okay?"

"Aside from my dignity, I'm fine."

He grabs my chin, his face closing in on mine. For a moment, I think he may kiss me. The shock of it has me dropping the phone again. When it falls, he lets me go and I rub my slick hands on my thighs.

It was nothing. All he did was touch my face but my feet feel like they're melting into a puddle. It feels so easy with Leon, which is why I need to come clean to him. Eventually.

"All right, then, let's start this over. Good morning, Amelia."

When he sits beside me, I spot a red heart with sunglasses on the side of his cheek that someone must have drawn on him.

I bring my finger to it, and it comes back to me stained with red.

Red paint.

It brings me back to our sophomore year, when Leon found out some annoying guy I rejected was pranking me every single week as some weird, loserlike payback. His name was Farris.

I was at my locker during class after forgetting to bring the right book. So, during a free period, I went to swap books in my locker. But when I opened it, red paint rained down. Some of it got me, but apparently Leon overheard Farris bragging to his friends before the bell rang and got to me right as I opened the locker. He wrapped me in his chest, taking most of the paint job.

Before I could fully process what was happening, Leon was off. I gathered my senses and caught up with him just as he found Farris, gathered his shirt in his hand, and reeled his fist back. Preventing that, I jumped in and dumped the remaining paint in the fallen bucket above the prankster's head.

Then someone shouted that the principal was coming. Before I realized it, Leon's hands were holding mine, and we ran till our chests hurt, huddling under a set of bleachers, laughing like we were escaped criminals.

It was one of the first times he made my heart flutter.

"I have to go," I say abruptly, standing and placing some much-needed distance between us. "I, um, forgot to water myself. My plants. My plant. Okay, bye."

Before he can call me out on my obvious lie, I run off. Literally run.

Because I was thinking about Leon, and only warmth bloomed in my chest. Fondness too. Not an ounce of anger or bitterness. I thought of him, sat with him, and felt comfort and safety and *love*.

I'm doing such a good job I'm fooling *myself*.

CHAPTER 17

HRBC Lesson #7: Don't Take Yourself Too Seriously
Sofia: If something wrong happens, it's okay, laugh it off! (This includes spilling something on yourself, stuttering, forgetting what you were about to say, dropping things.)
Sofia: If you go viral, just shrug it off. Embrace the follower count.

Trending again," Mari says beside me on Sofia's bed, watching the video of my zip-lining upside down like a dead body. "Are you famous, Amelia?"

"No." I snatch Sofia's phone from her hands. "Stop watching it. You're giving it more views."

Sofia takes her phone back. "I wish it was me. *I'd* be taking this as a marketing opportunity."

"And what exactly are you marketing?"

"My beautiful face and charming personality," she says, picking off the hair stuck on her lip gloss.

I rub the area where the harness dug into my thighs. "I don't understand, I thought that video finally died down."

"It's because some influencer stitched the video. Stirred it all up again."

"Dios mio."

Mari says automatically, like she was trained, "Don't say the Lord's name in vain."

"The Lord has more pressing issues than me, Mari," I say, desperate to get the attention off me while trying to maintain a cool-girl and good-humored response to it all.

Sofia just brought Mari back from gymnastics, so I ask her, "How was your morning of twirls and tumbles?"

"I can do a cartwheel now!"

"Can you teach me?" I ask.

"Sure," Mari hops off the bed—inches away from knocking her skull on the top bunk—then stands by the door. "Okay, watch this."

She takes a deep breath, then lunges forward. Her form starts off strong, but she loses balance, then tips over, slamming into the antique dresser, then the floor.

She raises a thumbs-up. "I'm okay."

"Hopefully the older you get, the more balance you find," Sofia tells Mari. "You get that problem from Amelia."

"She didn't get it from me," I say without thinking. "She's her own person. I'm my own person. We're all our own, separate, individual people."

Sofia snorts. "This family is the exact opposite of individual. We even share underwear."

"We shouldn't share underwear!" Both Mari and Sofia go wide-eyed at my sudden outburst. I'm not sure why my control seems too far for me to reach, but my nerves are on edge. Over the edge now. "Don't you think we should all just wear our own underwear? Don't you think it's weird that we don't have our *own* underwear? We can't even have that to ourselves."

Sofia holds out her hands like I'm a growling dog she's walking by on the street. "I mean, if it really bothers you, I won't wear yours."

"You say that, but you'll forget. Or you'll grab whichever pair you see first, even if it's mine. Because it's right there for you to grab. Because all of us are so on top of one another we can't differentiate whose is whose"

Sofia's brows furrow. "This feels very intense for a conversation about underwear—"

"It's not just about underwear."

"Then what is it?"

My saliva thickens and gets stuck at the center of my throat. I don't even know what I'm supposed to say. I don't want to share underwear or worry about it being used without me knowing. Just like I don't want to be stuck in this house forever.

But Sofia does. Everyone else does. This life is fun, endearing, even. She sees her future as *ours* in this house, bickering, working together, living together, breathing in every moment together.

And she's excited.

"I'm going to go for a walk."

"Amelia."

I'm already moving out the door. I slip on my sandals, then hurry down the path and onto the sidewalk, grateful for the cooling late-afternoon air.

With working, dating, and Mari forcing me to read every night, the caged in feeling my family unknowingly crowds me with hasn't felt as tight these days. But after that one conversation, it surrounds me, a vise around my bones.

I have the nagging urge to do a puzzle, but because I've been saving, I haven't bought a new one like I try to do every other week. Besides, since most of my nerves happen in this house, better to get out of it.

There's not a single person who will be happy with me when I go to the gap year program. At first, it was scary, imagining how isolating it would feel but still manageable. Now, though, it's starting to feel like they won't ever forgive me. They expect me to go to school for them, go to work for them, live in the same house for them, and Sofia, usually my number one ally in all things in life, wants to do the exact same.

Who does that leave me with when I wreck it all?

With so much I'm avoiding and my thoughts moving a mile a minute, I try to focus just on walking. Soon enough, it's practically crickets in my brain as I concentrate on one step at a time, putting a foot in front of the other. There's no destination in mind.

The longer I walk, the more I wish I wore sneakers and not the sandals sanding off the skin between my big toe and the others.

I walk so long, the sun starts to sink, but I keep moving. Then the streets start to seem familiar. When I turn the corner, I realize why.

A two-story house, painted a rich blue that matches the homeowner's eyes, stands on the plot of land before me. It's not the only thing standing on the evenly cut grass.

Leon and his dad are constructing some kind of giant

bench together, or tent, I can't tell with the mess of wood and cloth spread out before them. Leon frowns at a paper, and his dad has his arms crossed against his chest.

"We don't need instructions," his dad tells him. "It's my job. I can put together a swing chair."

"If that was true, we wouldn't have had to throw out the last one you messed up," Leon says very calmly, as if this is a common occurrence. "Don't worry, I won't tell the guys."

"Smart-ass," his dad mutters, half laughing. He stretches out, and as he does he spots me standing there at the top of their walkway like some kind of stalker. He blinks, recognizes me, then half smiles. "Amelia, what are you doing here?"

Leon's head whips up, and he flinches like he gave himself whiplash. "Amelia." He drops the papers and jogs over to me, telling his dad, "Build it however you want." When he reaches me, he asks, "Everything okay?"

"Yeah, um." How the hell did I end up here? Literally. "I was just passing by. I'll be on my way back now."

"You live half an hour away," Leon says, as his dad enters their house. "Where else were you planning to go?"

"A ditch," I smack my forehead. "Meant to say that in my head."

"Amelia." Concern etches into his face, weighs his words.

It's too much and just enough and all fake, so I shake my head. "See you around." Then I hurry as quickly as my awful chanclas will propel me forward.

Leon matches my step in an instant. "I can drive you home."

"I need the exercise."

"It's getting dark, and it's dangerous to walk by yourself. I'll go with you."

And what about the danger he poses to the incredibly confused organ pounding within my chest? I can't believe I walked here. I swear the thought didn't cross my mind, my subconscious just *hates* me. And the universe, which could have easily made it so Leon and his dad were inside so that he would have never spotted me and I could have made my way home *alone*, hates me even more.

"If you want."

"Of course I want to. More time with you is always better," he says. "But my car would be a lot more comfortable."

I speed up until I tire out and my gait slows and I suck in a breath as my sandals steal the last remaining flesh between my toes. I yank them off and grip them in my hand and walk on the uneven pavement, Leon behind me.

"Here." He blocks my path and holds his shoes out for me. "Use mine."

I blink. "What?"

"I know they're big, but it's better than being barefoot." When I look down at his feet, he adds, "I'm wearing socks, I'll be fine."

The same surprise that slapped me when I found myself on Leon's doorstep strikes again when tears spill down my cheeks as quickly as they formed. Leon's eyes widen as he jerks back, then looks around frantically, like the reason I'm upset can be found somewhere around him.

He fails to figure it out, then nudges me. "Put them on."

A laugh tears out of me, and the mix of crying and laughter has me choking. "I'm sorry," I say in between coughs. "I just had a weird day."

He moves to stand next to me and rubs circles on my back until I settle down. "Want to talk about it?"

Not *let's talk about it.* As if he knows a part of me doesn't want to. Then again, when I avoided it my brain malfunctioned, and I ended up walking straight to him, so maybe I need to get it out.

The sprinklers in front of the house we stop at go off and—oh my God, their sprinkler must be a freaking fire hydrant because it blasts us. We're both so shocked, we remain in place, getting soaked before Leon gains his senses and drags us away.

We take one look at each other, then burst into laughter.

"Sorry." I shake myself like a wet dog. "My bad luck is rubbing off on you. Better stay away."

"Not possible." He smiles, then kneels down and grips my ankle. I drop my hand on his shoulder before I lose balance. He lifts my foot, then puts it in his shoe, tying it tight, and does the same for the other.

How the hell does this feel so *intimate*?

I move first, because I'm losing feeling in my leg and Leon falls into step with me. As we turn the corner, on my street, I start to tell him what happened today—including the date but excluding the whole romance boot camp thing—mainly because it'll exhaust me to explain it right now. He laughs, until I tell him how I freaked out about underwear, and how overwhelming my aunts' expectations are feeling to me.

"I feel so horrible," I say, dragging my feet, but that's probably because Leon's shoes are like ankle weights. "They've done everything for me, but I'm mad at them. They want me to be like them and get upset when I can't. I don't know why they keep wanting things from me when they know I suck at *everything*."

"That's not true." He doesn't stop walking but grabs my hand as we cross the street. "You're good at *trying*. So many people give up as soon as they fail, but I've never met someone who is always picking themselves up. It's like you're immune to failure."

I never thought of it that way. It feels strange to even think like him. My brain doesn't work like that.

"Remember when you couldn't figure out how to parallel park so you stuck on water noodles to the ends of your family's car so you didn't leave any dents?"

I shake my head. "I didn't learn how to park."

"Yeah, but you kept trying and were pretty innovative."

"How do you even remember that?"

"I remember everything about you."

My heart feels trapped in an endless cycle of déjà vu, speeding up and warming like it used to preheartbreak whenever it nears Leon. It's too confused to realize it shouldn't behave the way it once did anymore.

I have to look at my feet, because suddenly my head feels too weighted to meet his gaze. "Well, no matter how much I try, I can't be like them."

"And you shouldn't have to be. They're all individuals as much as you are. And they love you. Maybe you should be honest with them and tell them how you feel."

"I'd rather lick rust."

He laughs softly. "I know it's scary. It's hard disappointing people you love. Feeling like they're upset with you and there is nothing you can do to change their mind." Now I meet his gaze.

"If I don't meet their expectations, they'll never be happy with me."

"I don't think that's fair to any of you."

His words are like a balm on my skin. Still, getting comfort from him, even if I want it, feels wrong. "Life isn't fair."

"Don't I know it."

We make it to my house, but I would have stopped at his words anyway. "Is everything okay?"

Something like hurt flashes on his face, but his smile is quick to mask it before I place why he would react that way. "Of course."

Maybe I never knew Leon the way I thought I did, and maybe all of this between us is fake. But it takes a liar to know one, and something has been off—or bugging Leon since he's been back.

"I think you're lying."

He smiles slightly. "I've always loved how honest you are."

I can't help but snort. "I think I've just outlined for you how not so honest I've been with my family."

"Being too scared to be truthful doesn't make you a liar."

I lean forward, trying to get a better look at every part of his face, checking for any movement or emotion that I may miss. "Is that what you are?" I ask him. "Scared?"

He shakes his head. "Not scared."

"Then what?"

He rubs his lips together, avoiding my gaze. I think he means to avoid my question too, with how long he's quiet.

Then he says, "Embarrassed."

I straighten. "Why would you be embarrassed?" There are so few times I've ever seen Leon be embarrassed, and when I think back on them, I'm not sure if he ever was. Nervous, maybe, when it came to admitting his feelings for me, when he was late to pick me up because practice ran late, when he first kissed me.

But embarrassed? Never.

He places his hands in his pockets and faces the ground. "You know, whenever you decide to tell your family how you feel, your dreams, no matter what, they're going to support you. Because they love you. No matter how scared you are of disappointing them, you have to know that's true. Right?"

I'm not sure where this is going, only that my heart speeds up rapidly. It feels like finally, finally, Leon is going to be honest with me—maybe not about our relationship, but about something as personal. My head knows I shouldn't brace myself with anticipation for it, but my heart has become this pendulum swinging back and forth between the need to care about Leon and the urge to crush the vital organ beating in his chest.

I only nod.

"Some families aren't like that—"

The front door screams as it's swung open. I jump away, but Leon and I are still so close, and Titi Ivy smiles knowingly as she leans on the doorway.

"Leon, it's good to see you. I didn't realize you and Amelia had plans."

"Neither did I," I mutter, once again meaning to keep it in my head. But we're together now, and it felt like Leon was ready to open up to me. Of course Titi Ivy intervened. This is the story of my life. No matter what I do, my family will be there, whether I want them to or not.

"Good to see you, Ms. Delgado." Leon, smiles as if he wasn't just too shy to meet my gaze moments ago, "You look as lovely as ever."

Titi Ivy fans herself dramatically—Leon laughs, and I want to die. Since the universe agrees my life is a joke, Titi Neva pops her head beside Titi Ivy.

"Leon, what a treat. I sensed a kind aura nearby."

"Ignore her," I tell him.

Titi Neva adds, "You two together are giving off such a warm glow. Let me get my crystals so I can soak this energy up." She hurries away.

Since he walked me all the way here, and for no other reason but that, I ask Leon, "Want to stay for dinner?"

Titi Ivy asks, "Want to stay forever?"

Leon chokes out a laugh, and I want to die: The Sequel.

"She stole that from a movie," I say frantically.

Leon smiles at me, then presses a kiss on my forehead. I gasp as he pulls away, as if kissing me is still natural to him. I swear if I didn't think the aunts would humiliate me further if I showed any signs of sickness, I would have fainted. "I need to get going. My dad and I are cooking ribs tonight."

Titi Ivy offers, “I can drive you.”

“No thanks.” Leon winks at me. “I need the exercise.”

“Wait,” I say as Leon starts to pull away. I kick off his shoes, then hand them over to him. “Thank you.”

“No worries,” he says, and puts them on before heading off.

Titi Ivy whistles as he does, as I stand there staring at his back trying to form any coherent thought. Leon turns, and even from the distance he’s at, I see his smile perfectly. He waves as he catches me staring, and I jolt straight, then fly up the steps.

“You look like you’re going to be sick—lovesick,” Titi Neva says.

“Horrible joke,” I gasp, slamming the door shut.

But I *am* sick. I have to be to be falling for the guy who broke my heart, while pretending I’m still in love with him in order to break his. The worst part of it all is that there’s no way I can end this well.

Not that I want it to. Leon deserves all the heartbreak . . . doesn’t he?

What have I gotten myself into?

CHAPTER 18

Date Debrief #7
What Worked: Standing behind him to show him how to swing the putter. (Sofia: Oh, classic move.)
What Didn't: Showing up fifteen minutes late because I couldn't find my favorite lip gloss. (Sofia: My bad, I lost it last week.)
What Could've Gone Better: Checking the traffic report at least an hour before I need to be somewhere. No one likes to stand around waiting for a date. (Sofia: At least you're self-aware.)
Total Rating: 6/10. Felt terrible about being late and I could tell he was a little upset about it at first, but I think I made up for it with my jokes and footing the tab for our cheeseburgers and cherry slushies. Plus, getting a hole in one in mini golf is always a great way to impress a date. (Titi Neva: Your confidence is growing!) (Titi Ivy: He should have paid, though. Men should foot the bill.) (Titi Neva: Don't be so stereotypical, Ivy.) (Titi Ivy: Surprised you know how to spell that, Neva.) (Sofia: How do you guys fight even on paper?)

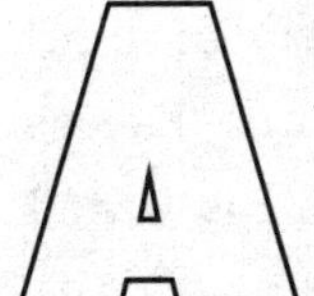

After tugging on the blue, oversize top covered with a pattern of pink and green confetti, I check myself out in the skinny, full-length mirror hanging on Sofia and my's bedroom door.

"You look like the seat of a Greyhound bus," she looks up from filing her nails.

"It isn't great, but it's not like I can tell them to change the uniform so my sister can design it."

"No, you totally should do that," she says, looking way better than me in a crochet top and jean miniskirt.

"I'll send an email." I tug the end of it and twist it into a knot. "Maybe I can make it a crop top."

She puts the nail file down. Uh-oh, full attention. "Why? You want to make sure you're cute for when your paths cross with *Leon*?" She sings his name.

I roll my eyes. The aunts just had to go and tell the rest of the house they found me outside with Leon. And I had to calm Mom down before she thought of an upcoming marriage proposal when they said we *kissed*. We didn't kiss. He kissed my forehead. Very different.

"Why'd you say his name like that?"

"Oh, sorry, did I offend you? Making fun of your boyfriend? Here I was thinking that you were only fake-dating him to get your revenge." At my groan, she adds, "Not that I'm blaming you. He sure is . . ." She wolf-whistles as an adjective.

"I'm going to say this once, and once only. Leon and I aren't together and never will be."

"Sure." Sofia gestures to me. "That's why you're trying to alter your outfit an hour before you have to go in for your shift."

I settle for tucking the shirt into my jean shorts. "Excuse me, I have a reputation to uphold as the hottest Big E staff member."

"That's because I don't work there."

"Thank God."

She gets up, and though her face fills with innocence, years of siblingship have taught me better. I dodge her right as she reaches for my hair, but she's so fast that she manages to snag the end of my shirt. Before it stretches, I bring my body closer to hers, which is a rookie mistake.

She digs her hands into my hair, ruining the perfectly lined parting that took five minutes to get right. Each time I flail and try to get away, she pulls it. I pinch her side, but she only pulls harder. In another life, we would have been great wrestlers.

Only when her hand covers my fresh mascara do I shout, "Okay, mercy. You're going to mess up my makeup."

"Ha, so you do care how you look."

I try to clear my voice so I don't sound so obvious. "Doesn't everyone?"

Her lips move, like she's chewing on the inside of her mouth. I don't like the way she looks at me, her eyes narrowing and all-knowing like she's got a hidden X-ray in her retina.

Just as I'm about to turn away, she speaks.

"I'm sorry," Sofia says, and when I see the look on her face I know she's more serious than what I expected. "I know who you are. I know how easily you fall in love. I should have talked you out of this whole revenge plot on your ex."

"I'm not falling for Leon." I feel my jaw tense and if Sofia notices it, I know she thinks it has everything to do with Leon and not at all because of what she just said.

Five thousand dollars.

That's how much I need, and then I'll have a year around people who know nothing about what I truly want, who don't know what to expect from me. I won't hear I need to do this, be more of that, and *You're not strong enough*.

"I didn't say you were." She gestures to me. "So that's your subconscious telling you what you already know."

"Shut up."

"Amelia." Her tone is so soft and cautious that I know I won't like what I hear.

I try to plug my ears but she gets up and pulls them out of my eardrums.

"It's enough now," she starts. "I mean, even if he isn't in *love* with you, someone willing to walk barefoot for half an hour, then walk another back home, for no other reason than to keep the other person safe? Well, he has to at least *like* like you."

"Okay, so the plan is working. Thanks for the update."

She grips my shoulders with her nails. "Dump him—sooner rather than later."

Already, doubt has lodged itself in between my rib cage. Enough to rattle the bones there, but not enough to deter me. I don't need Sofia to strengthen its resolve. "Why?"

"The longer this goes on, the more hurt he'll be."

I shove her hand off me. "That's the *point*."

She doesn't understand. Nobody would.

So what if I'm so good at pretending to like Leon back, it's muddling everything up for me. Like last night, when he kissed my forehead, I forgot everything I was doing—hell, I forgot my own name for a second. That's because I'm a gullible mess, and exactly why he deserves what he's got coming to him.

He's able to have me in the palm of my hands whenever he wants. Why can't I bite back?

"Consider it mission half-success. Do you really need to crush him?"

I shove my hands in my back pockets. "You're on his side all of a sudden?"

"Whoa, whoa." She puts up her hands. "I'm always Team Amelia. It's just . . ." She bites her bottom lip and I know where my hands go now. I poke her chest until she answers me.

"Well," she goes on, "you know, everyone makes mistakes. And honestly, he doesn't seem like such a bad guy—anymore, I mean. Do you know he shows up at the bakery almost every day to help? Even when his dad isn't there. Sometimes he brings the aunts flowers or smoothies from that place they always order from. He brings Mari ice cream cones—"

"So he's *buying* your trust."

"But *why* would he?" she says, and it simmers the blood boiling beneath my skin. "There's no benefit of doing that for us. It's not to impress you. In fact, he's almost always there when you're not around. What if he's changed? What if he's a good guy?"

"So what if he is? That doesn't change what he did to me. Why should I forgive him when he didn't even say sorry?" My voice cracks on the last word.

"Oh, Mels." Sofia reaches out to me, but I step away.

There's a light tap on the door. "Come in, Mari," I call, desperate to keep my hands steady, to kill every hint of guilt snaking its way through me.

So what? That's all I can think of. So what, so what, so what. It doesn't matter how much he impresses everyone else. He still hurt *me*. Aren't I allowed to be upset? Aren't I allowed some kind of justice? Karma?

Why am I supposed to feel guilty for hurting someone the way they did me?

Why the hell am I feeling guilty?

Because it is there, it's aways been there, that sprinkle of it. It's not easy to hurt someone, but what's the alternative? Being the only one in pain? Letting someone go without consequences?

Maybe it's immature, but that isn't *fair*.

Mari pops her head in, space buns with pink confetti dusting her part today, and holds out her newest fantasy middle grade book. "Can we read before you have to work?"

Mindless words, that's what I need. Better that than to think, than to reflect. Sofia doesn't know what she's talking about. If she was really Team Amelia, she'd just go with the plan.

"Can you read aloud while I touch up my hair?"

She zooms in, plopping next to Sofia and opens her hard cover. I grab the flat iron Perri is never getting back and check if it's hot.

"Ouch." I nearly drop it. Yeah, it's hot.

"Karma for damaging your hair." She straightens up, holds out a hand. "I see split ends in your future."

Mari giggles. "Is that supposed to be Titi Neva?"

"Don't tell."

Ignoring them, and Sofia's attempt to lighten the mood and

get in my good graces, I flatten the pieces that bumped up overnight.

Mari narrates in the background as I finish up my hair, then I lie down beside her for the rest of the time I have left before Sofia nudges me that it's time to go. As we get up, Mari says, "Can I ride too?"

"Of course," Sofia and I say at the same time.

A declaration I regret when we're in the car, halfway there, and Mari asks from the back seat, "Amelia, is it true you kissed Leon?"

I groan and Sofia laughs.

"No, we didn't. He kissed me." I shake my head. "Actually, he didn't *kiss* me, he pecked me. God, that sounds worse. He kissed my forehead. It was nothing. Felt like nothing."

"Very convincing." Sofia nods annoyingly.

"I like Leon," Mari goes on. "He is . . . very nice."

"A lot of people are nice." I open up the window, letting the warm air blast me in the face.

"Not like Leon."

"What are you his number one fan?" I frown. "I'm nice, you're nice, Sofia's nice. The guy who gave me an extra nugget at the drive-thru is nice. Who cares?"

Both my *little* sisters share a quick look in the rearview mirror, and I ignore them because I know what they don't. Leon isn't as nice as he seems. And I absolutely do not like Leon.

I can't.

We stop in traffic right before one of the entrances to the Big E.

Sofia scans the lot beside us. "Holy shi—crap,"

Behind the thin metal gates, the parking lot is already nearly full. The Big E has been open only an hour and it's already this busy. It helps that it's a perfect day, sunny but windy, good for walking around for long periods of time. Farther ahead—at least what I can see when I poke my head out—is the same.

"I'll get out here. Maybe you can make a U-turn before you get stuck."

Sofia throws up a peace sign as I open the passenger door.

"Tell Leon I said hi," Mari shouts.

"He's not working today."

"Oh." Sofia raises her brows. "You know his schedule."

My response is to slam the door and make my way past the gate, avoiding the cars circling the lot for an opening and finding my way to the south entrance, away from nosy know-it-all sisters.

A line wraps around the sidewalk toward the two tents flanked by security guards manning the walk-through metal detectors, and the employees at the end of tables, selling tickets or scanning the preprinted tickets on a register-shaped device.

One of the guards recognizes me and waves me through so I don't have to scan my ID that I *definitely* didn't forget at home.

I'm a little early, because I was hoping to "run into" Arno before I had to join Jorge in the hell-temperature trailer. I need some fresh crush energy to get my sisters' choice of conversation topic out of my head. Arno is stationed at the game section, which is the easiest of jobs since you just take the money and let the people play the games rigged for failure.

At first, I was annoyed I wasn't put in the games section, and when I found out I'd be feeding people from a food truck instead, I was preparing myself for hell, but honestly, I really like working with Jorge. He makes suffering through the heat worth it. Maybe. I'll see how hot it gets today.

There's nothing different now than there was yesterday at the Big E aside from the people, and yet it makes all the difference.

With the heavy crowd, the space between each tent and truck and store feels more cramped. And though I can still hear one of the several expensive speakers spread throughout the Big E playing songs from every genre of music, all the voices together make it impossible to hear the lyrics exactly.

Since I have to dodge elbows, and avoid large families that walk as fast as I do homework, it takes me double the time to make it to the gaming section, which means I can't stay for long if I want to make it to Jorge in time.

And I'm not going to be late for the single human who sees any potential in me being good at something.

Luckily Arno is close by, leaning on a pole holding up the unoccupied tent above the ring toss. As I get closer, his already scanning face catches me before I reach him. I wave and he looks around, then jogs over.

"Hey," he says. "You're not stationed here, are you?"

I shake my head. "I thought I'd come by and say hi, if that's all right."

"More than." He grabs my wrists, then pulls me in between two separate tents. We go even farther until we're almost behind them. He looks me up and down. It's a quick enough check out I'm sure it's not meant for me to notice, but I do anyway. "You look good today."

The hair and the extra layer of makeup might account for that, but I just wave a hand like I'm bashful or something. Titi Ivy said, during one of my many lessons, "If you're on a date with a man, they are easily intimidated. You have to start off shy, sweet." The uniform looks a lot better on him since it brings out his eyes. "Thank you."

"Are you still coming to my party?"

Since I have so few brain cells left, I say, "Definitely." Instead of a more casual, cool-girl response.

"Awesome, I'm glad. I think it's going to be my best one yet," he eyes me carefully.

"Okay, I'm excited to go."

This could be the start of something good. I can do it. I can be the perfect girlfriend. Arno will see that and officially ask me—again. This time I'll be ready for him. I have some more experience under my belt, taken way too many notes during boot camp. And with Leon falling for me, I'm confident I can do the same to Arno.

This party is going to be the start of a new Amelia. Curse broken and nearing a year abroad.

He pulls away. "I have to get back, but I'll text you?"

I rub my lips together and nod, watch as he jogs back into our makeshift alley to his station. That was good. Arno likes me enough to invite to his party, to compliment me and all that.

When I pass the array of shops before the area where Queenie's Pizza waits, someone calls my name. My heart stutters and I spin, nearly tumbling into Leon, who catches me.

"Leon, what are you doing here?" Good thing the crowd masks the weird pitch my voice squeals out.

"There was a ride that malfunctioned last night, Dad and some of the guys came early to fix it. I was just leaving."

"Oh," I say, and must sound relieved because he frowns. "I mean, oh no?"

He just laughs, and it's this softer, younger sound. A near giggle. It sounds so pretty, a flush of warmth runs through me at the noise. "Do you need anything? Did you bring lunch? Do you have a ride back?"

I frown at him. "Careful Leon, I might think you want to marry me or something."

"Careful, Amelia, I might just ask you."

Shut up, heart.

He's only joking. Bantering with me. We used to always joke around, flirt. We're already back to that.

Testing the waters, testing how far I've come, if I *really* have gotten Leon where I want him, I bat my eyelashes at him and ask softly, "Should we set a date?"

He jerks back, supernaturally still. Then his eyes grow hot as he watches me delicately, his gaze locked on me like he's waiting for me to say something more. Daring me to. When I don't, he reaches out to cup my face, then leaves his hand in the air like he doesn't know what he wants to do with it.

My entire body tenses, and I'm aware of each bead of sweat sliding down my neck, can almost *hear* the fluttering coming to life in the pit of my belly, can feel the vibration of my heart beating in my chest.

I shake it off, metaphorically of course, so Leon can't see the effect his hands have on me.

"Is that what you want?" he asks softly, gently, yet the words make the hairs on my arm stand.

Now I watch him. He's not at all turned off by the idea. At least, that's what it seems like to me. If anything, he sounds . . . hopeful. Which means everything I'm doing is working. If I can get my ex to fall for me, I absolutely should be able to get Arno—baggage-free—to fall for me.

A part of me is shocked, another part surprised, and the tiniest bit is scared. This is what I wanted and now that it's almost time for me to end it, I'm getting nervous. I'm not entirely sure *why*, but I recognize the dizzyingly flapping in my stomach.

It's flip-flopping Sofia sneaking into my brain, overriding my brain cells. I swear I'll shave her eyebrows once she's asleep.

Better to keep an air of mystery, give him a little, take some back. So I pat his cheek gently. "We can talk another time."

But as I go, he grabs my wrist and pulls between a shop selling crystal necklaces I've been eyeing for Titi Neva, and the other selling hand massagers I've been looking at to give Mom a break from holding Zoe. "Now is as good a time as any."

I look at my wrist, even though there's no watch there. "I need to go help Jorge."

"We're not done with this conversation."

"Well," I start, stealing the same smirk he's been so easily throwing my way, "we are for now."

He mirrors it, and then his chest presses against mine. He

pushes a stray hair away from my face, leaving his hands there. "For now," he echoes.

Something about the feeling of his thumb, lightly trailing my cheek, makes my insides warm and my knees threaten to buckle. Not the time, not the place, not the universe. I *just* had the upper hand, and now he's making me all weak in my bones. *Tighten up, Hernandez.*

"Good luck today," he sounds on the edge of a laugh.

"Bye," I say, and he starts to walk away then jerks back for some reason. I tilt my head when he stares at me like it's my fault, then follow his trail of vision and—oh, it is my fault. I'm still holding him. *Dios mio.* "Sorry."

"No—"

"No worries," I finish for him, and he chuckles. I hate that the sound feels like a gift.

This time I let him go and he walks away and I have to take a minute to compose myself. It wasn't even a kiss, just a touch of the forehead. It's only my nerves, I know what I have to do and that's making me freak out. That's all.

I blow out a heavy breath—a good thing too because it stops me from screaming when a shadow pours over me and someone grabs my shoulder. I whirl around, hands out in the fists Titi Sandra taught me in case a man ever cornered me, and drop them when I spot a vaguely familiar face.

"You scared whatever years I have left out of me."

"Sorry, I just wanted to talk." She smiles in a way that reminds me of Mari when she's going to ask for a trip to the library, or Sofia when she needs an alibi to sneak out. "We crossed paths for a bit when you took over working at Jorge's truck when my shift ended."

Now I fully recognize the big brown eyes and chopped brunette hair. "Hiba, right?"

"Right! Anyway, somehow I got roped into pig duty, and I'm *super* busy day of. But I'm on my third strike. If I call out again, I'm fired." She places her hands on my shoulders. "Jorge said you were asking around about more hours so, please, *please* do me a solid and take this for me."

"Pig duty?" I try to back away. "I'm not sure how equipped I am for that."

"It's double the standard pay."

That makes me pause. "You have my attention."

The whispers around the Big E is that closing at the pigpen is a nightmare. You have to round up all the pigs, mud and all, into their pen, clean up any messes, and try not to smell like literal crap by the time you're done.

"Please," she says again. "Everyone I already asked said no." She holds up two fingers. "Second, I heard you were going around trying all the jobs. So I figured you don't have too high of standards for this."

"Offensive," I say, and then take a breath. But true. And I'll take any extra cash to hit the five-thousand mark. If I can hit it sooner, even better. Less stress for the end of the summer deadline. If it's not too bad, maybe I can work there after my shifts with Jorge. It's not like people are lining up to do it anyway.

I mean, how bad can it be?

"Sure," I tell her. "I'll do it. Tell me the details."

CHAPTER 19

Date Debrief #7
What Worked: Buying him nachos after I beat him in the go-kart race as a consolation prize. (Sofia: Risky wounding his ego by winning, nice save with food.) (Titi Sandra: Food is the way to someone's heart.)
What Didn't:
Leaning in for a kiss too quickly and smacking our foreheads together. (Sofia: Ouch.)
What Could've Gone Better: Honestly? He laughed and still kissed me, so not much. Plus, I won the race, so it was a pretty big night for me.
Total Rating: 9/10. The nachos were amazing and he teased me about my competitive side in a way that seemed like he thought it was cute. Got asked on a second date as soon as it finished. (Mom: Wow, they grow up so fast.) (Sofia: You're a star, bb.) (Titi Ivy: Tough crowd. What's it take to get a 10/10?)

"You? Driving?" If Mom wasn't holding Zoe, I think she'd slap her knee. "Nena, we can't afford to fix another flat tire."

"I promise I'll be careful." I agreed to work at the pigpen tonight without checking if anyone was free to take me. Sofia is using the Honda, and the aunts have the van. Besides, it will be nice to get comfortable driving myself around. I can't be independent if I can't even drive a vehicle. "The SUV is automatic, so I'll be fine. I'll drive slow. I promise."

Zoe, the good little sister she is, starts to fuss and freak Mom out. "I have no problem dropping you off and picking you up."

"Mom," I whine. "You don't need to drive back and forth. I'm fully capable of driving myself." Right on cue, Zoe cries, and I tack on, "And you know, it safest for Zoe inside the house instead of the road."

Mom's eyes go wide, then narrow. "I see what you're doing, just so you know. But it's working so fine, pero, don't you go faster than the speed limit, but don't go too slow either. Stop at yellow lights, don't rush through them."

I'm already hurrying out the door for my late shift.

She yells out, "Remember, a red hexagon means stop."

Since when did my family become a bunch of comedians?

I grab the keys hanging by the front door, take a look in the circular mirror above it and confirm the concealer I padded on did its job. Looks good. Not trying too hard, just enough for boys who don't understand makeup to think it's natural, and glowy enough a girl is sure to stop and ask what foundation I'm using.

It's been a few months since I've driven—the last time I picked up a drunk Sofia from a party she wasn't supposed to go to—so it's not too jarring. Even though my heart is in my throat from the moment I start the engine, to the slow pace I keep—horns honking behind me before ultimately going around me—to the Big E.

Can't lie, it is pretty cool being able to park in the

employees-only lot. No fighting for a spot one foot closer to the entrance. Last night, Leon texted me that a bunch of staff were called in to break up not one but three fights when dozens of spaces were available. Nobody is more cutthroat for a parking spot than those people with the stick figure family stickers on the back of their SUVs.

But it'll be fine. Hiba swore everything isn't as bad as people make it seem.

I yank the SUV into park.

I do nothing but bake pizzas with Jorge all day. Thankfully he brought a loud, ancient looking timer that makes it impossible for me to mess up. For my break, I sit on the floor at the end of the trailer and pep-talk with myself about backing out of the heartbreak plan.

Each time Leon texts a picture of something he built with his dad, a 7-Eleven stop, a flower that managed to sprout in a garden of weeds, I think of Sofia's annoying, useless words.

They've dug into my brain, planted too many seeds of doubt. I have a whole garden of it.

Does Leon deserve to get his heart broken?

It's a question nagging at me as much as an aunt fusses about whose turn it is to do the dishes. Of *course* he does.

It's wild to believe I wasn't doing the right thing. I mean, when I really think about it, I can't think of how I'm supposed to move on without going through this. Maybe if he said sorry, acknowledged what happened, I can think of another option, but he hasn't. And I'm not a good enough person to forgive on my own.

Since I'm working later at the pigpen, I stay longer than I'm scheduled—partly because it's busy and I feel bad for Jorge.

When Jorge closes for good, I'm forced to leave the hell that became my sanctuary for the day. Since I stayed overtime, night has fallen when I get out. The few people remaining are either employees closing up shops, staff cleaning up, or guests being ushered toward the exits.

My phone buzzes and I check the new notification, a text from Leon.

Hey, want to grab some late-night ice cream?

I purposely ignore the unwelcome flutter of excitement after I see his name.

Sorry, on pig duty tonight, I reply, then I read through Hiba's text of directions for the shift, and the location to a staff trailer nearby the pen I can hang out in for a bit.

I spot it, recognizing the doodle of birds on the door Hiba said would be on it. When I go for the handle, some girl walks out. "Oh, you must be the one covering for Hiba today." She holds the door open. "I already did most of the cleaning. You just have to wait until the pigs are done eating in the showroom, they take forever, then move them to the pen."

Less work for me with still the same pay? Amazing.

"Thanks," I say as she hurries pass me.

"Oh yeah," she calls as she swings a satchel over her shoulder, "can you double-check the gate for the showroom? It's been giving me some trouble lately."

In answer, I salute her and let myself in the trailer to drop off my bag.

My phone rings so I turn on a lamp by a couch with a concerning amount of holes and plop down on it.

"Where are you?" Sofia says when I answer, her voice loud over a pounding reggaeton song.

"Canada."

"Amazing," she yells. "Can you teleport back to the house? The aunts have invited all the guys helping at the bakery for dinner. I think they're nearly done with the construction."

"Can't." I explain my night shift.

"Pigs? You're rounding up pigs? You don't even like to season the meat because you hate the texture on your hands."

"Good thing I'm not rubbing adobo on them."

There's a shuffle of movement, and the background noise becomes more of a chatter. Like Sofia moved to another room. "Hey, we're good, right?"

"No, I hate you, I wish we never met." I put my feet up and it feels like bliss after being on them all day.

"Good, so I'll say it again, since you're in such a good mood. Consider giving up the plan."

"Now I really hate you." I close my eyes and try to ignore every single thought of Leon.

It's the worst, because a few weeks ago if someone mentioned him, I'd pull up the lonely nights I spent eyeing the phone waiting for a call. I'd count all the money I spent on concealer to cover up the redness around my eyes. I'd remember the weight of my hand on my chest, pressing against it like it'll numb the aching throbbing beneath it.

But now my brain plays out the sweetest memories

between us. Like when he wrote our names in bubble letters on wood, then cut it up into tiny pieces in his own makeshift puzzle for me. Or the time I stayed home from school, and he snuck in the second story window of my house to bring me snacks and hot-hands to use as a heating pad for cramps. Or the time he let me practice painting nails on him, when I wanted to learn to do them on myself but didn't want to ruin my own.

I even see his smirk, smiling down at me after I fell in the hole when we met again for the first time this summer. And if I looked deep enough at the memory, I'd remember relief. From me, from seeing him in one piece. I'd see some of it in his eyes too.

Like we both shared the secret, *oh, there you are* feeling.

When I don't answer, Sofia says, "You're thinking about it, aren't you?" It's not an *I knew you would*. But a sound of relief. Like she was holding on to all this weight just *knowing* what I was up to.

Let's say I did give it up . . . Would I feel that same relief?

"He's at the house, isn't he?" I ask.

"He brought this fudgy layered hazelnut cake. It looks a mess. Like an erupted volcano, but it's—"

"My favorite," I finish for her.

"That's right," she says. "And unfortunately, *you're* my favorite, so hurry and get home."

I hang up and shut my eyes.

My insides feel like they're all scrambled up. When I first thought of getting revenge it felt right and just and it made it easier to be around Leon. And now there's this weight on my shoulders, but it's different. Like maybe Sofia is right.

Maybe it's not that Leon doesn't necessarily deserve to get away with what he did to me. Maybe he doesn't deserve forgiveness, but maybe it doesn't have to fall to me to care much whether or not he gets his karma.

That's a little easier to swallow than this newfound worry that if he found out what I've been planning all along he'd be mad at *me*. An actual joke. He wouldn't have any right to. And I shouldn't care if he was.

Ugh, my annoying sister and her annoying thoughts.

I press my eyelids tighter and pretend there is a puzzle in my mind. A sunset. No, reminds me of a time Leon and I laid on the beach until we nearly passed out from dehydration.

The water reminds me of Leon trying—and failing—to teach me how to swim. So can't think of an ocean.

A picture of the aunts only makes me think of how they'll feel when I leave them.

I go for a tree. A sakura one, with all the pale pinks transitioning into darker petals. I piece together the image one by one in my head. I make it a thousand-piece puzzle, to really empty out my brain.

When I finish, I start again with a different tree. It relaxes me enough that the tightness in my shoulders eases, and my breathing is longer and deeper.

My phone blares into my ears. I shoot up, the world spinning as I do.

I feel around for it, and my hand comes back with white

fuzz. I blink away my sleep, and the orange glow casts a light on the green plaid couch I'm lying on. I grab my phone just as the call ends.

It's past midnight. Twenty-four missed calls. Even more texts.

Whatever piece inside me in charge of tethering my heart snaps, and it drops.

I tumble off the couch and bullet out of the trailer.

I run, and not just because without the lights and people it's like walking through a haunted city and fear-induced sweat beads at the base of my neck.

When I get to the showroom, a tiny, covered tent where people can come and feed the pigs, I check the coast, and nobody is around. I push the curtain aside and walk in, my nose wrinkling at the stale smell of wet, yet unwashed, animal.

Relief pulls my beating heart back up where it belongs as I spot a pile of pigs sleeping on, the side of, and under a mound of hay.

I ease the gate open, but it creaks hauntingly anyway.

Some of the pigs stir awake, but I close it behind me and tiptoe my poor boots already mucked in dirt and what I hope is not crap. As they wake, some spot me and immediately get the zoomies.

Squeaking and oinking and rolling over.

My brain naturally begins to count them all, and my heart begins to shake again.

Hiba said there were seven in total. A lucky number. My brain immediately sees it and thinks: *BTS*.

But when I count, one is missing.

Just in case, I hurry closer. They spread apart and I move the hay, hoping to see the tiniest pig alive—Jimin—I've decided to name him, but there's only a sleeping pig too unimpressed with me to move. That's definitely Yoongi.

The creaking gate startles me.

I whirl and catch the literal tail end of a pig rushing out the gate. My feet propel me forward but the mud beneath is unsteady, and I nearly slam my body on the concrete but thank the gods, for the first time in my life my reflexes save me, and I throw my hands out to stop the full impact of the fall. Still, my palms sting with pain that shoots up my arms.

Before the largest pig gets too close to the gate, I gather my balance and push myself to a stand. Hurriedly—but carefully—I waddle out. I close the door, lock the gate and yank with all my strength to make sure no pig can ram it's way out.

Then I open the door, the bell above jingling as I do, and pop my head inside the darkness.

This can't be real life. I can't be missing two pigs in a giant carnival. I'll for sure be fired for this. I can kiss my gap year goodbye. What a night to remember.

Before I can move, a shadow scurries a few strides ahead of me.

"V?" I ask the shadows gently. I near a closed-up hot dog stand, dragging my feet, bracing myself to run at any moment.

Something heavy slams *right* behind me. I scream, spinning on my heel. A garbage can rolls by my feet.

A squeal screeches through the air—and I screech along

with it. Louder when a freaking *pig* dashes along my line of vision.

My hair whips behind me as I hurry after it.

Luckily, he reaches a dead end, a building connecting to another brick one. The pig has his nose poking around the ground, trying to smell a path he can follow toward food or something else that drives pigs to wander in the night.

I creep behind him.

Just before he senses me, I wrap my arms around him. He's a smaller one, but his whines are piercing to my eardrums. I pull the pig into my chest and when he flails, I relax my grip. When he realizes I'm not trying to choke him, he settles down.

Though small, V isn't exactly light, and my arms begin to ache. I don't want to drop him, so I waddle-run back to the showroom. "Let's bring you back to your brothers," I tell him.

Then I'll set off to find the seventh.

CHAPTER 20

HRBC Lesson #8: Always Ask about Books (Mari's Version)
Mari: You should ask them about their favorite book. That will say a lot about them. (Sofia: Surprisingly good advice from a child.)
Mari: Make them read you their favorite line.
Mari: If they don't like books, dump them. (Sofia: Nvm.)

After leaving V with his brothers, I'm alone as I drag my feet along the cement, whistling as I look for the last one. Whistling works, right? There are dog whistles. Naturally, there have to be pig whistles. I'm sure.

This time, I have a stick I found by some bushes in my grip like a sword, just in case there's someone in the shadows trying to get me so I can stab them in the eye with it. Maybe I should have kept V with me. Like an emotional-support pig.

There's been no trail of mud anywhere so far, at least not in the path of the flickering flashlight I found by the pig pen. No honking echoing between the booths of the game section. I need to get in the mind of a pig to find a pig.

What's a pig's brain like? My pig-brain can only think of two things. Mud and food. Trash food.

All right, time to make my way to one of the three food vendor sections. At least in the game section a lot of the booth's lights remain on—which is a lot for energy consumption, so sorry, climate change, but a benefit to pig-finding.

Still, the closer I get to the street lined with food trucks, the less light there is to help me peek around every corner, and the more sweat makes a puddle at the back of my neck. Ugh, I just know it's curling the baby hairs I took so long to flatten.

I make my way around a truck that during the day, sells fried cereal—seriously?—and near the back where the line of trash cans stand. My whistle cracks. I'm running out of breath and guts. How much longer can I wander in the dark without freaking out that someone is going to attack me?

There's no pig behind the round cans so I pull away. A clatter of metal steals my breath. I whirl, but there's nothing there. I whistle again and grab the handle of the lid, yanking it open before I wimp out.

God himself could hear my scream from heaven. Something small and furry spins at the bottom, then *jumps* up.

Arms wrap around my waist and yank my back as the little demon mouse scurries away. My scream breaks the sound barrier and my ear drums pop as I elbow the body and swing the flashlight at my attacker.

"Amelia—*ow*."

"Leon, Jesus Christ." I drop the flashlight and it flickers as it clatters. "Are you okay? I'm so sorry."

I had the strength of every aunt in that swing. I press my

hands on his shoulder where I slammed the light, rubbing it as if it'll ease the pain.

"I'm fine," he says through his teeth.

"Wait, what are you doing here?"

"Well," he says, still through his teeth but the hot look in his eyes makes me think it's not from the pain. "I'm definitely not here trespassing."

"I also am definitely not here trespassing." When his glare only heats, I add, "Fine, how did you know I was still here?"

"I wasn't sure. It's the last place you said you'd be. And your sister called me, said the same thing. But then you didn't get home or answer any of our calls. Even now, I just called again."

"I fell asleep." I try not to feel embarrassed. Feeling *more* embarrassed when I realize I'm still rubbing circles on his shoulder, I shove my hands behind my back as I step away. "Left my phone in the trailer."

He tilts his head to the side. "What are you still doing here?" Then his eyes widen. He gets a better look at me, the mud and dirt clinging to my skin. He crosses the space between us and grabs my wrist, pulling it up toward the moonlight. "What happened to you?"

The skin under his fingers is red and flamed. It's what caught most of my blow when I fell.

"Yeah, it's kind of a long story. You know the first part, but to fast-forward, I lost a pig, so now I'm searching for Jungkook to bring him back to his friends."

"Jungkook?"

"I thought he needed a name."

"Did you name the pigs after BTS members?"

Oh. He remembered. Usually, when I reference any of them, I'm met with blank stares. Even the aunts hear one of their names and say, "Oh, that band with the cool dances." But never bother to remember much about them.

But when I first fell for the band, deep-dove into every piece of media and interview about them, Leon sat with me and let me rant about every bit of lore I could find. I made him a PowerPoint of each member, facts about them, their achievements, their variety shows.

And he always watched with focused eyes, asked questions, let me play back my favorite moments. Always made me feel like anything I liked mattered to him because it mattered to me.

Two years later and he remembers one of their names.

"Anyway." I grab my flashlight, something solid fisting in the base of my throat. The most pressing issue is to find Jungkook. "How'd you find me in here?"

"What do you mean how did I find you? I followed your whistle. What are you even doing it for?"

"Pig whistle. I'm trying to attract him."

"Pig whistle is not a real thing."

"What are you, a pig scientist?"

"That's not a thing either."

"Oh my God, what are you even doing here?"

He gestures toward me, like I'm the answer. "To find you. I was worried. And Sofia said your location was still somewhere at the Big E."

I hate the flurry of movement it sends in my stomach. The butterflies he awakens whenever he unabashedly says something like that. It muddies everything. Makes my brain go fuzzy and my heart wish for more.

I tap my flashlight until it flickers back on. If only I was home. Home doing a puzzle right now, distracting my brain.

I turn and face him. "Want to help look for a pig?"

He opens his mouth, shuts it, then opens it again. "You know, that sentence should sound insane, but from you it's normal."

"Thank you?"

"Let me tell Sofia I found you," he says, typing on his phone. "All right, let's go look for Jungkook," he adds, like he's just accepted an offer to go for a casual walk around the block.

As we near the welcoming center, my ears perk. I grip Leon's arm. "Did you hear that?"

"Over your whistling? No."

"It's working," I pinch him lightly, then blow some more. "Jungkook? The boys miss you."

Leon follows me toward the cork board filled with advertisements, job postings, and brochures. "Won't walking scare it away?"

"Not an it."

"Fine, *Jungkook*."

"Well, you don't seem to be a fan of the whistling." I peek behind the tall wood. "Jungkook!"

Leon was right because at my squeal, Jungkook—double V's holdable size—dashes out, barreling toward me. Leon yanks me out of the way just as Jungkook smacks into the wall of one of the staff trailers. The sound echoes as Jungkook turns around and faces us, and for a pig, he has a real predator look in his eyes.

All of us freeze. Jungkook watches us carefully, like he might bolt any second.

"Are we seriously having a stare down with a pig?" Leon whispers beside me.

But my eyes are trained on Jungkook. Before I think it through—boy, do I rarely think things through—I open my mouth. "Oink, oink."

Jungkook's head tilts to the side.

Leon's face turns toward me as I let out another "Oink, oink."

"Amelia." He says my name like he's on the verge of a laugh. "No."

"Oink, oink." I slide closer to Jungkook, whose head tilts even farther as if to say, *You can speak my language?* I hope my next series of oinks translates to *You can understand me?*

Leon follows my lead, and I elbow him, but he says, "No way you can carry him back."

Point, so I keep speaking Jungkook's language as Leon and I creep closer and closer until Jungkook is just inches from his fingers.

"I can't believe this is working," Leon says as he wraps his arms around Jungkook, grunts, and lifts him into his arms.

My heart thunders when Leon keels over, as if he might drop Jungkook, but he rights himself up.

I hurry to match pace. "I can help."

"I got it." He's a little out of breath.

Just in case, I keep his fast pace with my arms at the ready. We get back to the pen quickly, and I blow out a breath of relief when I see I locked the gate and BTS eagerly awaiting the return of Jungkook without a chance to escape again.

For luck, I do a few more oinks as I speed ahead and open the gate, shooing the pigs back so Leon can easily drop Jungkook down. I hurry toward Leon.

"Come *on*." I grab him, pulling him out as V tries to run for freedom again. He sucks his teeth but lets me yank him out and shut the metal gate, then lock it. "Oh, thank God." I let out a heavy breath that turns into a laugh. "Wow, that worked. I'm actually a genius." I look at Leon, holding his lower back. "I'm amazing."

I am so used to letting other people handle serious situations. As soon as things get tough, my fingers tap on my screen, dialing up the aunts, Sofia. But I didn't even attempt to ask for any help. I had a problem, dove into fixing it—a little unconventionally—but still.

It's so strange. I've never felt this way before. Like, I'm capable. Smart. A problem-solver.

"You've always have been," he tells me, so warmly my body increases temperature.

Instead of acknowledging the heat flowing through my body, I grab his arm. "We should get out of here. I'm in desperate need of a shower." As I pull him, I catch him flinching in pain.

"Are you okay?" I place my hand on his lower back. "I

should have helped you. Jungkook was too heavy, wasn't he?"

"I'm fine," he says, but he doesn't shrug me off—or can't—as I bring my arm around him and help him move.

He doesn't push me away, so we keep moving, wrapped around each other. I step forward. We don't fill the silence, but it doesn't feel weird, only hearing our footsteps, our breathing. It reminds me how easy Leon always felt to me. How sometimes we talked until our throats were sore. And other times, we didn't say a word to each other, but being in the same room, feeling each other's presence, felt like comfort.

Funny how that feeling hasn't changed.

And I can admit, maybe Leon hasn't completely changed either. The good parts of him, at least. I mean, he just spent his entire night helping me gather a pig, hurt himself in the process, and hasn't complained once.

I blow out a breath of air.

The HRBC was all about me becoming the best girlfriend, building up qualities I already have. But there's one that was missing.

Being kind. I am kind. I am a good person. And a good person wouldn't intentionally hurt someone else, especially when they know how bad it feels.

But it also doesn't mean I'm not allowed to say my true feelings either.

Maybe knowing exactly how I felt, exactly all he did to me, could be a lesson for Leon. Now it's just me and him, walking together, the perfect chance to let him have it. To tell him how I feel. How he hurt me.

My balance shakes, and I stumble forward. Leon, already wrapped around me, manages to keep us both upright as I shut my eyes and wait for the hit of dizziness to pass.

Leon moves so he faces me. "What's wrong?" He presses the back of his hand on my forehead. "Did you forget to take your iron again?"

I did, but it's so incredibly annoying that not only is he pointing it out, he remembers how I forget all the time. I chew on my lip, my heart thumping harder than it did when we were running from the guard. I know I was seconds away from dumping him—wasn't I?

I'm not sure what I'm doing anymore. Not sure what I'm feeling anymore, either.

"Yeah." I give up on telling him the truth. "I forgot."

He's beside me again, this time linking his fingers through mine, leading the way. "Let's get you back home."

I don't say anything as he leads us out.

CHAPTER 21

HRBC Lesson #9: Learning When to Cut Things Off

Titi Sandra: Don't force yourself to do anything you don't want to.

Titi Neva: As soon as a date makes you feel uncomfortable, leave.

Sofia: If they try to make you feel bad, ~~ask them if their mother knows they failed at their job.~~ tell them your family of wrestlers is on the way and they better leave you alone.

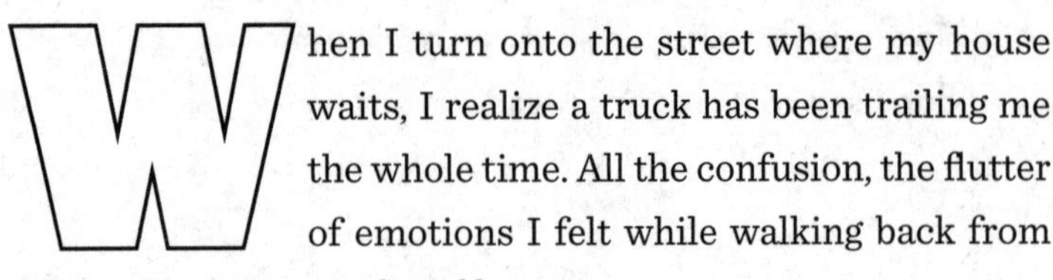

When I turn onto the street where my house waits, I realize a truck has been trailing me the whole time. All the confusion, the flutter of emotions I felt while walking back from Big E with Leon is replaced by anger.

The sudden switch of emotion is dizzying.

It's not fully directed at Leon, no. Some of it is at me. I'm mad at myself for feeling too many things, for being gullible. I'm confused too, and most of *that* emotion is because of Leon, because of this constant feeling of uneasiness and unwanted hope he evokes from me when he constantly teeters on friendship and romance after claiming he was only after the first.

Instead of pulling into my driveway I park the car on the side of the road. I almost forget to shut off the engine as I yank the door open and storm over to the pickup truck slowing right behind me.

I pull the drivers seat open before Leon can shift gears.

"What are you doing?" I ask him as he hurriedly pulls the truck into a complete stop before it runs my foot over.

Once he does, he hops out of the truck. "What are *you* doing?" he shoots back. "What if I ran you over?"

I shove my hands through my hair. It gets caught on a knot, which only pisses me off even more.

Of course I know what Leon was doing. I was a little woozy because of my lack of iron, and he followed me to make sure I got home safely. I know that part. It's more the why. There's always a bundle of whys in my brain when it comes to Leon. Whys I can't figure out so easily. Whys that keep me up at night.

I point a finger at him. "You want to be my friend, right? You think we're friends at this moment?"

He blinks. "Yes? I hope so?"

"And the caressing each other's faces, kisses on foreheads, midnight pig hunts? That's friendship?"

His jaw locks. "What are you getting at?"

"We're not friends. Or together." He jerks in surprise, and I add on, "Friends and partners don't keep secrets from each other. Like why you dumped me on my *birthday* with a single text, ghosted me for years. Why you're back, why you're *staying*. Why you take care of me, care about me, but still hurt me. You don't get the benefit of me when you've done nothing to deserve it."

He watches me for a moment, so carefully blank. I get it. I'm doing a complete 180 from joking and laughing while running around after a pig. But him helping me, being there, being so boyfriend material somehow snaps something in me. He's so good at being good, and I just can't understand why he *stopped*.

Leon settles on, "I'm not the only one with secrets, Amelia."

I blink. "What?"

"Things aren't the same between us," he says, and my stomach sinks. "You think I haven't noticed, but I have."

"No." I take a step back. "This isn't about me, it's about you. You're changing the subject. Deflecting." I tack on the word Titi Sandra uses during her calls with clients.

"It's late, I'm tired, let's talk about this another time. You should get home. Take your iron," the more gentle his words come, the more frustrated I am.

"No." My skin begins to warm all over. "By the way, I find it fundamentally unacceptable that you destroyed me, came back, and thought that I would just magically forgive you for everything without an explanation."

His body goes rigid. "I didn't think that, but you've been doing a good job acting like you have."

"Guess we're both good liars."

"Enough," he snaps, his voice clipped.

I flinch. He doesn't yell, but the harsh tone he uses feels almost like a blow. It's so final, so against continuing any conversation. Our communication was always open to extend as much as either of us needed. Even during fights, we'd always allow each other to say everything we needed so we didn't harbor any anger the next day or week or anytime after.

All this time I've been pretending so well that I forget that this thing between us is fake. But this is the reality, isn't it? Things are different, Leon is different, or I never really knew him at all. The shock of it silences me.

"Sometimes it's hard to talk. Can't you get that?" he asks. "It's not easy to turn on a switch and spill my life out for you."

"It used to be," I whisper.

He flinches like I shouted the words. "That was *two years ago.* Before I spent the past two miserable. Feeling like a failure. Desperate to come home. Too guilty to leave. Hating myself for wanting to. Being embarrassed that I had to."

"I don't understand—"

"Of *course* you don't, Amelia. You have a home filled with women who adore you, who think you rival the sun. And they're right about it, but that doesn't take away from the fact that you can't understand what it's like for a mother not to want you when you have four of them at your choosing whenever you want."

"What does that mean?" I ask, though I already know. It's just. Leon's right, I can't understand that at all. I don't have a father, but I've never had a father, never felt like I needed one. I've also never known what it's like to be . . . unwanted.

"It means that my mother regretted having me move in with her." He shakes his head. "No, not just that. She regrets ever having me in the first place."

"That can't be true."

His eyes dull. "It's not that I want to keep secrets from you. It's that I'm too embarrassed to try to get the words out. Going to Arizona was supposed to make me better. I was going to bond with my mom. Land a scholarship. Make my dad proud. I couldn't do any of those things. That's why I'm back."

"Leon." My voice cracks on his name. His words keep tumbling out like he doesn't know how to hold them anymore.

"But I'm better now, in a different way," he adds hastily, grabbing my hand in his, "I swear. I am going to take over my dad's business. I'm going to get a good degree. I'll remember to be kind. I'll be a good enough person to have a good future, and I'll be good to you, Amelia. I promise. I'm sure of myself now. I know who I am. I know what I can handle."

My throat dries, and my hand warms within his. I still have so many questions for him, and he's opening up to me now. But all I can focus on is the lingering pain from his words, how it hangs in the air, pressing on my shoulders. I want to ease it.

But I struggle to find the right words for someone who has no idea what Leon's gone through. Is going through.

"If your mother didn't make you feel loved, then I think that says more about her as a person than it does you." Even if I did bad things, I know my aunts would never make me feel unloved. I think there will always be a bunk bed waiting for me at home. It breaks my heart that Leon doesn't have that same kind of certainty. "I wish she didn't make you feel that way. I wish you had a better time with her."

He watches me quietly, his hand still covering mine.

"Me too," he says finally, his gaze darting up to the sky like he finds it hard to meet mine. "Sometimes I feel a little guilty, being so mad at her. I don't think she ever wanted to be a parent, and that's why she ended up divorcing my dad. She hated being stuck. Hated this town. And having me tied her down here longer than she ever wanted. But she still took me in, still tried."

She shouldn't have to try, but I'm not sure if that will make Leon feel better or worse.

"Was she mean to you?"

"No," he says, after a moment. "She was polite, always, but too polite. I was never comfortable because it was so obvious she wasn't. She treated me more like a stranger she let have a meal in her home. She never spoke to me more than a hello and goodbye. And if I asked her anything about her day, she'd say I wouldn't understand. That's on the few occasions I saw her. She was gone first thing in the morning most days, working as a dental assistant. And then came back to shower, left to be with her boyfriend. Some days she wouldn't even come home. Some days, I swear she forgot my name."

His gaze remains on the sky but goes a little glossy as he recalls the memories. "She didn't want to know anything about me. Didn't care to. I was just a reminder of the life she left behind—and an anchor away from the new life she built." Now he meets mine. "I would never want to trap you, Amelia."

That gives me pause. I'm not sure why he would think *I* would think that.

"What do you mean?"

He lets go of my hand and shoves his own through his hair. He shifts his body so I can't get a clear look on his face. But he's not fast enough that I don't catch the quick wide eyes of worry.

I'm not sure how to point it out, because I'm not sure what else to say.

We stand there, staring at each other, the space between us thick with unsaid words, unresolved emotions, and this agonizing urge to reach over and press my hand on his chest and feel his heart beating. In my brain, he left and lived this happy, adventurous life without me and it made hating him a little easier. To know he was in pain from the moment he landed in Arizona doesn't feel so good.

Finally, I settle on "I thought you didn't want to come back."

"I wanted to come back." He faces me again, steps toward me. "And I didn't. Coming back would mean that my mother truly, one-hundred-percent didn't want me, and that felt too hard. And then I injured myself after a rough tackle on the field." He rubs his arms absentmindedly. "I'm fine now, but the damage wasn't minor enough not to affect my throw. I'll never get it back full strength, so my dad sending me to get a scholarship failed, which was another thing I couldn't do. It was like wherever I was placed, I couldn't fit. I couldn't do what I needed."

My heart aches. I never had a dream, but Leon *did*, and it was taken from him when he hadn't even reached his prime. And he's here now, talking with me, working with his dad, living a new life that's so different from the one he planned for and is still able to smile. I'm not sure if I could do the same. "I'm sorry."

"Me too." He sighs. "But I also realized if I could get through that, I could get through anything. My mom was always working, and I started to at one of my uncles' chain auto shops out there. I spent most of my time on my own."

"Sounds lonely." Sure, I want to live away from my family, but I don't want to live absent of them. I want them within reach. It doesn't have to be physical, but knowing they're around and they love me somewhere.

"It was, but sometimes it was nice too. To focus on myself, think about what I want, what I want my life to look like."

Curiosity fills me. "What does it look like now? Your future."

His gaze travels me, from top to bottom, in a way that makes blood rush to my cheeks and ears. "I'm not going to be some big-shot football player. I don't want a flashy life. I want to be okay." He lets out a breath. "I want to have a steady career, never worry about money. I want to build a house on a lake. I realized a simple life will be a good one."

His gaze is warm where it lands on my face. "There were times I wish I never left."

So do I.

Those are words I've secretly wished to hear for so long but now that I have them, they don't hit me the way I fantasized they would.

Maybe because nerves and jealousy override my emotions. I'm still figuring out exactly what my future will look like, what I want. But Leon found his own way, without me. Though his plans don't seem bad at all. It's a future I wouldn't mind, possibly, but the time I spent without him, however painful, made me realize how much I still have to learn about myself. It made me really think about my own dreams or better, the lack of them.

It used to feel sad, not knowing what they were, but now all I am is determined to find and make them. Maybe they're with Leon. Maybe they aren't. But it's for me to figure out.

He goes on. "I know that I hurt you. I know that breaking up through text was the worst thing I could do. I was being a coward." He jams his hands in his pockets. "After I sent it, I had to turn off my phone to keep from calling you, from reaching out. I know you deserved better than that, but I let my embarrassment come between us. And when I saw you on your birthday so happy—"

"You saw me on my birthday?"

I remember, viscerally, the morning of my first birthday after Leon moved away. I was so angry because Leon didn't call me at midnight, or in the morning, or answer any of my not-so-subtle follow-up texts asking if he knew "what today was." My hand cramped up from holding the phone all day, waiting to feel a vibration in case I couldn't hear a ringtone.

And then, that night, while I danced in the café the aunts had rented out for me and my friends to party at, I got the text.

Amelia, you're the best person I know, but I think we need to end it here. The long-distance isn't going to work. I have to focus on football, on my mom, on my life here. And you have to focus on yours. Take care.

He stills, then lets out a deep sigh. "Yeah," he admits, "I did. I know we weren't texting as much. We were working on different time zones, different schedules. And honestly, the times we did talk, speaking to you felt good, but it also made me so homesick. And I couldn't tell you what was going on with me. I didn't want to be another person you had to take care of, when you're always doing that for your entire family. Always being there to help them, whenever they need you."

My head feels light enough I start to get dizzy. All I've wanted from Leon is answers and now that I'm getting them, they're nothing like what I concocted in my head.

Leon goes on, "But I put that all to the side. I wanted to surprise you for your birthday, and my mom bought me a late-night ticket back here. Then I saw the—" He shakes his head, seemingly changing what he was going to say. "I went to the party, saw you dancing with some guy. It wasn't jealousy, I swear. But I thought, *I'm holding her back. That's all I'll be doing, keeping you attached to me when you have a whole life here, filled with people who could actually be there for you.*"

He crosses every bit of space between us. "Amelia, I am sorry. I mean it."

I have the strangest sense of someone dropping weights on my chest. It's a similar sensation to what I feel when I look at the aunts now. Guilt. Different but familiar.

Each word is saturated in this slight desperation, like he needs me to forgive him.

And standing here, listening to him, feeling the weight of his gaze on me, I know he means it.

I should tell him. That the only reason I agreed to start hanging out with him was to hurt him.

I just freeze. I failed the ruse. I can't play the games anymore. Honestly, in hindsight, I'm starting to question if I was ever playing them at all.

"Amelia," he says gently, his hands cupping my face.

God, what is happening?

"Hey." He pulls me closer. "I'm really sorry."

"I believe you," I manage to get out, "and I think that I made a mistake thinking I could be around you and not fall for you. Again."

I'm supposed to be crushing him the way he did to me. How did we get here? Me confessing my feelings that should have never bloomed, hoping he feels the same. Or it's more like after they intially bloomed and he left, my feelings withered away, but never died. Now they've been watered again, revived into something stronger.

Everything is such a mess.

"You fell again." Leon's thumb trails my cheek, leaving a warmth in its wake so hot it almost burns. "I never got back up."

"Really?" I ask, my voice barely a whisper. Somehow I need his words to be true. When he nods, I add, "Prove it."

To do so, it's so gentle, barely a touch and everything in me softens—melts. My heart pounds, and he presses his lips on mine again, and again, feathery touches filled with such heat I wonder how it's possible for me to be warm without them, without him.

This is a complete disaster and there's no way for me to survive it.

He grips my face, tilting my head as he looks at me, eyes glimmering with heat and happiness, like peeking at a wrapped present, cutting thin lines on the gift wrap, peering into every angle trying to see what it could be.

He pulls back—a good thing, since I don't think I ever would have—and brings my hair behind my ear. "Let me follow you home, make sure you get there safe," he adds, like things are normal between us, like I still can't feel the pressure of his lips on mine, or see the redness of his freshly kissed, full lips.

Now, how am I supposed to admit to him what I did? What I've been doing?

Again, something between us shifted. I know now, we both feel the same, me unwillingly so. But how can I let this go any further without admitting what I've done? And is a sorry enough for me to move past all the hurt I have?

I'm not so sure.

"I'll get home safely. Speed limit, stops at red lights, watching out for deer. It'll be fine."

"Okay."

Leon grabs my arm and leads me to my car, like he doesn't want me to ask any further questions. "Believe me, Amelia."

But the farther I drive from him, the more it feels like I'm doing the opposite. I think about that fact the whole drive home.

It's a wonder I get back safely. I can't remember a single green light, a stop sign, anything other than the feel of Leon's lips on mine. The realization that I'm still so deeply invested in him, that two years wasn't enough for me to be over what we had.

It's way too late by the time I get home. My nerves bundle in my throat as I get out the SUV and go up the stairs. I don't bother being quiet because I know the aunts are waiting up for me. At least one of them.

But when I enter, the lights are off.

Wow. I can't remember a single time in my life where I've been out and someone hasn't waited up for me.

Holding my breath, forcing my eyes to clear of tears, I use my phone's light as a path to make it up the stairs. When I enter the room, Sofia is laying sideways, her tablet propped up and I hear the background noise of the latest anime she's been into.

She flicks her gaze up. "Covered for you. Tell me I'm the best, prettiest, kindest, most giving, amazing sister in the world."

I burst into tears.

She gets up so quick she's a blur, or maybe it's my vision hazy from crying. "What did he do?" she asks, her voice sweet and meaning every word. She holds my face in her hands. "I will rip out his spine and wear it around my neck."

Which makes me cry even more. Here she is ready to kill for me, and she doesn't know I want to leave her. That, along with the miserable realization: "I still love Leon," I confess to her.

"Oh, I know, Mels." She wraps me into her. "I know."

She brings me over to her bed, consoling me as she does. I can barely pay attention to her. I only focus on the warmth of her hands as she runs her fingers through my hair, singing along to the theme song coming from her tablet.

She doesn't ask me to explain anything, or ask details on what happened. Just lets me cry until my eyes swell enough I shut them. And then my thoughts get fuzzy, and sleep lulls me away.

When I wake, a line of light peaks out from the above bunk. I rub the gunk from my eyes. I'm not sure how long I was out for, but I prefer sleeping on my own bed. Mainly because of the bundle of fur pillows I like to pile under my back.

I get up and climb the ladder, pausing when I catch Sofia holding her phone flashlight above bundles of money, my gap-year brochure.

That clears some of the misery churning in the pit of my stomach.

"Sofia," I say, but my voice sounds distant even to me.

"When were you going to tell me you were planning on leaving?" She holds the Gap Year Program's brochure in her hands. "I came up here to get your pillows. Saw this hole in the frame." Panic claws its way up my spine.

"I—you looked through my things." I try to grasp on to anything else.

"You've been busy." She looks at me with this weird mix of disbelief and betrayal. "The wood on your headboard was poking out, I thought it was strange. Found it stranger when I found the money. It was less strange finding the brochure. More. I don't know. I can't think of the word yet."

"Sofia."

"*Traitorous* comes to mind."

"I was going to tell you about it." My feet go all staticlike, as if they're incapable of holding my weight. This is not how this was supposed to happen. This wasn't supposed to happen at all.

"*Selfish* is another." Sofia shrugs, like the words are no big deal, but her gaze burns on my skin. "So you were just going to disappear, leave the aunts with the bakery, leave Mom." She laughs, and the sound feels like sandpaper on my skin. "Wow, you made me watch Zoe as if we all needed to give Mom a break. I guess I'll have to do it more often since you're abandoning us."

"Sofia."

"You said you'd go to school, work at the bakery."

"I never said I *would*."

"You never said you wouldn't." She throws the brochure on the carpet. "I can feel myself getting ready to say things that'll really break us up, *sister*." The last word feels like an accusation. Or a curse.

"I don't want anything broken between us, Sofia." My eyes start to burn. "I haven't sent the payment yet."

"Yet." She tosses the word back at me. "So you are."

"Let me explain."

"Unless you're going to say this is all a joke and you're not planning on abandoning us, *me*, then it doesn't matter. So is it?"

Miserably, I shake my head.

She nods, like she expected it. "There are sheets on the couch. Good night."

"Please don't tell—"

"Get *out*."

Unable to find any fight in me to do otherwise, I move off the bunk and out the room. I hear the click of the lock we both know doesn't work and stand there in the dark, my chest tightening and tightening until I let out a ragged breath.

I really messed up. Only this time, I'm not sure if there's a way to fix any of it.

CHAPTER 22

HRBC Lesson #10: No Self-Deprecating
Titi Neva: You are your own harshest critic. Whatever mean thoughts you have about yourself, erase them from your mind, and don't you dare say them aloud.
Sofia: For every mean thing you think about yourself, you can't do anything else until you say two nice things about yourself instead.

The only good thing that happened to me last night is that I fell asleep. The only good thing that's probably going to happen to me is that my shift was early early enough that everyone was asleep, except for Titi Ivy in hair rollers and a face mask, who dropped me off.

Now I drag my feet under the unbearably hot sun to Jorge, my mood dragging along with it. That's how I know somehow, someway, while working in the hell-like heat, I've built a bond with Jorge. Otherwise, I'd have called out and found something else to do with my day, but seeing as nobody else ever volunteers to help him, I can't exactly abandon him even though I'm running off very little sleep, not enough breakfast, a traitorous heart, and guilt-swollen stomach. I'm trying too hard to focus on literally anything other than Leon, and what I'm going to do.

It's impossible for me to deny that I—at least some small part of me—developed feelings for Leon. Or maybe they were always there, dug six feet deep, and I've yanked them back up. Regardless, this whole break-Leon's-heart operation is leaving a foul taste in my mouth.

I can't work without messing up. I can't focus enough to do well in school—okay, maybe I don't try that much—but that's another character flaw. I'm cursed to die alone, and I can't even get payback on the guy who broke my heart then reappeared like nothing ever happened. I can't just be happy with the life given to me by a family who loves me.

Whenever the gods Titi Neva believes in put me together, they forgot to use glue.

When I join up with Jorge in the truck, he's stretching out a disc of dough.

"You look like sunshine."

I frown and pointedly ignore the greeting. I use my chin to gesture at the empty glass. Usually, Jorge has it filled with slices first thing. People apparently don't care if it's ten in the morning; pizza is an all-day thing. "Running behind?"

He blows out a breath as I wash my hands. "I have my kids over this week. Somehow I forgot that giving sugar to a set of eight-year-olds isn't the best bedtime routine."

It makes me smile, the love behind the exhaustion, the way his eyes glow in a way I've never seen them before. I move beside him and gather up a lump of dough and start slowly, to prevent rips or holes, stretching it out.

"My aunt used to crush up kids' melatonin in my apple juice when I was too hyper to go to sleep."

Jorge laughs so hard I *literally* hear bones crack as he throws his head back. This strange bundle of pride bursts in my chest. On dates, I purposely try to be funny. But here I am, miserable, and still manage to make Jorge laugh.

"Well." He rubs his lower back, moving away from me as I take over his disc while he remembers he's aging. "Maybe I'll have to do the same."

When I finish up this stretch of dough, I begin the process of putting it all together. My technique is a mix of Jorge's lessons, and the way the aunts line up and fluidly move their hands like they know what they're doing. There's no reggaeton blasting, so I start humming songs in my head, spreading the sauce, the toppings, and shoving them in the oven.

It's actually . . . nice. It's not exactly mindless work, but it's work that feels good for my mind. A break from overthinking while not overworking my next set of dough. I don't even burn myself when removing the finished pizzas.

A pattern develops in my head, my hands. Even the heat becomes second as I keep the process going, prep the pizza, bake the pizza, cut it up, refill the glass.

It's not rocket science, but it's something I started off bad at and now am pretty good at. It's nice. Each of my movements become a little more confident. It's cool to be good at something. I might be good at other things too, if I try.

I've sung two full-on concerts when Jorge drops his hand on my shoulder.

"All right, kid, time for a quick break."

I blink and drop the dough I was working. Jorge offers me a

bottle of water. I watch the way the condensation pours down its sides. Suddenly, I'm parched. I grab the cold liquid and down it in a few gulps.

"Honestly." Jorge pulls down the shutters so another customer can't walk up and order. "This has been one of the best days we've had so far."

Now that I'm no longer performing, I look over at Jorge. Unlike me, there is very little sweat clinging to his all-black outfit. Not even the usual powder dusting his clothes.

"How many slices did we sell?"

"Too many to count," he says, pressing buttons on the register. "If you ever need a full-time job when the summer's up, you've got a place at my restaurant."

Tears burn my eyes. I'm as shocked as Jorge, who steps back, looking around as if the cause of my sudden outburst is hidden among the ingredients. Poor guy did nothing to have to deal with me, but I'm a bit of a crybaby and haven't learned to stop myself from doing so once I feel the urge to.

"I'm sorry." I wipe my face roughly before the tears come. "It's just, I did a good job, didn't I?"

"An excellent job. So why do you look so sad?"

"Not sad." I shake my head. At least not working here. "Happy, actually. I was beginning to think I wasn't going to ever be good at, well, anything."

Whatever he sees on my face makes him sigh. He leans over the stove, reaching over to the shelf holding a giant tip bottle—filled to the brim. He grabs it and hands it over to me. "I've never managed to fill that thing up. Not even halfway."

I hold it, inspecting all the bills in there, surprised at how much we gathered. "Wow, someone left a ten-dollar bill!"

"Do you think they left that for the cranky old man with the messy hair?"

It makes me smile.

"No," I say and try to think about every smile that I matched and every smile that matched mine while I worked here. All the conversations I had were short in length but high in energy. "They liked me. Either they liked the way I complimented them or they laughed at one of my jokes or . . ." I place the jar on the counter and frame my face in my hands. "They thought I was cute."

"I'm sure they did."

He *knows* they did. Jorge believes in me. I have done good here. I know that.

Maybe I'd be good at more than this, if I didn't have people making me feel like I couldn't be great—including myself. Mainly myself. I'm my own enemy. There's no *reason* I should be surprised I'm good at service work, because I shouldn't have been so sure I'd be bad at it. I shouldn't think I'm going to fail at something before I try.

Who knew working in a boiling food truck would be so good for my confidence? "Hey, Jorge, you're not cranky, and your hair's got charisma. Character."

He crosses his arms against his chest, lets out a laugh that sounds aged with years of joy. "That kind of flattery filled up the tip jar." He pauses, takes a breath. "In the beginning, you struggled a bit, but I trust you. You know what you're doing.

And you charm people within a few seconds of meeting them. Your smile doesn't falter even if it's the hundredth customer of the day."

When I give him finger guns, he throws a nearby rag at me. "All right, get back to work."

By the time I'm done, the sun has fully fallen as I make my way out of the Big E. I haven't called anyone to pick me up. I'm willing to walk the length at night, if only to extend my time before I have to go home and face my family. Sofia hasn't answered any of my texts, and I've been ignoring the ones sent from Leon.

I can't believe what a mess I've made of things. And what the hell am I supposed to do about Leon? Everything is so muddled and messy and I feel like I've caught myself in the thickest web, impossible to get out of—at least not unscathed.

Someone grabs my arm. It's Arno. "Hey," he says. "Going to get ready for the party tonight?"

I'd completely forgotten about the party. Mainly because, somehow, I'd completely forgotten about *Arno*. I clear, or hope I do, my face of any confusion. "Oh, um."

He grins. "You forgot, didn't you?"

"No, of course not," I lie with a smile. "I just don't have a ride. I don't even have a ride home. I'm walking."

He frowns like walking anywhere is unheard of. "Ride with me. I was heading out anyway."

"You don't have to set up anything?" I ask. The aunts wake up at four in the morning for any event they host and spend *hours* preparing way too much food, arguing over decorations, and calling people to remind them being late will lead to their food being cold even though the aunts always warm up guests' plates.

"I told you it was being catered." He gives me a funny look. "There's no setup. We just show up."

"Right." I bounce on my feet. I don't want to go, not exactly in the party mood, but it sounds better than going home to face whatever is waiting for me. I gesture to my outfit, ripped shorts and the bus-seat shirt. "I'm not exactly dressed for a party, though."

"You'll match with, like, half the people there." He grabs my wrist. "You have to come."

Well, it's not like I have much else to do. "Okay, then."

I mean, how much worse can my day get, anyway?

CHAPTER 23

HRBC Lesson #11: Compatibility Test (Titi Neva's Version)
Titi Neva: Just ask them their sign and come to me. I'll tell you if you're compatible enough.
(Sofia: I'm sorry, I was running out of ideas, so I let her have this one.)

We pull up to the Victorian mansion and there are people throwing a football in front of the rosebushes circling the house, girls chatting on the steps to the front door, and someone on the second deck cheering to the people below, pouring a drink they all try to catch with their mouths.

"Uh, looks like the party started without you." Though it looks more like the party has been going on without him for a while.

He shrugs and gets out. I follow and he explains, loudly, to be heard over the music, "I let my friends come early. I didn't mean to be at the Big E so long."

The bass is so loud, the pebbles by my foot jump with the rhythm.

I make my way inside, and as I turn the knob, the door comes off its hinges. I grab it before it falls on the carpet, then hurry to push it back up.

As I walk through the hall, heads turn toward me—like a lot. No, like, all of them.

It keeps happening the more I move through the party—how many people does Arno *know*? I turn to ask him, but he's gone, lost in the crowd that *has* to be some kind of fire hazard. This place is huge and yet people are elbow to elbow. I scan the bodies, but Arno is gone, so I make my way to the open and airy kitchen filled with boxes of beer and pizza. A couple girls see me enter, nudge each other, then mumble as I debate about grabbing a slice.

Most of them are in a Big E uniform, so I'm not sure what exactly it is about me that's sticking out.

I text Arno to ask where he is. He replies he made a quick run to get some more food, even though whatever is in this room could feed the people at this party twice. So, for the wait, I grab a slice and start to chew.

More people pack themselves in, grabbing food and drinks and spilling liquids all over the white marble countertops. Some guy sees me finishing up my slice and pushes a beer in my hand. "No drinky, no entry."

I'm about to point out I've already entered, but I need to wash the pizza down, and I've drunk plenty of beers during our track parties, so I take it. I was too nervous to eat breakfast, so I grab another slice and another beer to down it, too.

Okay, I'm more nervous than I thought because somehow I end up with a third beer. Maybe it's because, aside from the guy talking to me about *World of Warcraft* as I eat the supply of food, I keep feeling like everyone is coming in and checking me out.

And not in a *you look hot* kind of way. But a pointy-finger, mumbling kind of way.

Maybe I'm hallucinating.

When the guy shifts from *World of Warcraft* to *Valorant,* I take my beer and elbow my way through the crowd of bodies way too sweaty for how much the air conditioner is blasting. I squirm through, breaking the crowd when I get to the living room, which is the size of my entire house.

I scan the crowd and spot Arno. He's hunched over, looking at something some girl is showing him on her phone.

It doesn't make me feel a pang of jealousy. It doesn't make me feel anything. Does that mean the crush is gone?

I thought the party would be better than being home, but now that I'm here, I realize I'd much rather be anywhere else. I wish I could rewind time to before Sofia became angry with me, so I could lie in bed as she explains the plot of the cursed sorcerers show she got me into last week.

I'll tell Arno I'm feeling sick, call Sofia, and go back home and drink water because as soon as I take a step, I think maybe I miscalculated how much pizza could soak up the beers I drank.

My phone vibrates in my hand, but more people turn my way and my neck gets unbearably hot. I need to hurry up and get this over with.

I approach them. When the blond girl spots me, she nudges Arno. He looks up and smiles, but it's not as nice as the ones he's given me before.

She glares at me, but I face Arno. "Can we talk?"

"Of course," he says. "Honestly, I need to thank you. I haven't had this many hits on my website in a while, and I'm getting so many followers. It's crazy."

I stare at him, trying to make sense of the words, and when I can't, I say, "I'm sorry, what?"

"Right." He shakes his head. "I never ran it by you. Listen, it's journalism. Any story is up for grabs. I hope you can understand, but this is my dream. Every story of mine brings me one step closer to it."

"What are you talking about?"

The girl, practically beaming, holds out her phone. It's Arno's page and a series of videos of him sitting down, holding a familiar book in his hands, the text *Hopeless Romantic Redates All Her Exes—My Craziest Date Ever: Part 1* written on top.

This can't be real life.

"I don't understand," I murmur.

Arno winces. "I know, the title is a little harsh, but it's clickbait, really. I *promise* it's not too bad. I tagged you too, so you'd get the clout with me. This is good for both of us, a chance to build our platforms early. Whatever you want to do, whenever you figure that out."

"I mean." The girl joins him, maybe his girlfriend, from the way they press into each other. "That's what I told him. Especially when he added in you were dating even *more* of your exes. What is this, like, your third time trending? The first two times it was for getting stuck on the adventure course, now this?"

Was this really happening? Was I going viral for my desperate attempt to be in a relationship? Were Arno and this random-ass girl standing here like it wasn't a big deal? Like it was a *favor*?

"How did you know?" I manage to get out. "About my exes, about the others."

Arno sighs. "That day I saw you on a date at my job, you left your journal there." The book that had the words *Hernandez Romance Boot Camp* written across it. Along with every lesson I took notes from . . . and every single ex of mine. Even the ones I didn't date. I wrote them all out, numbers included, to narrow down who I would reach out to." The room tilts. "It was easy to piece it together, especially after I reached out to some of the highlighted exes. I saw you around Leon a lot too. Honestly, I've never had so many views. This is sick. It's going to look so good when I finish building my portfolio."

"Why—why would you do that?"

He honest to God looks surprised. "Amelia, wait, you look upset."

"Is that a joke?" My voice cracks. "Why would you do this?"

His mouth opens, then shuts before he says, "I thought this was an experiment for you. I mean, when I'm researching, I gather the same kind of notes you did. You used other people for yours, and I used you for mine."

"That's not true." I want to make myself as small as possible so I can no longer feel everyone watching me. "I liked you. You didn't ask me."

"I didn't even think you thought of me as a person." His brow furrows. "I read it. It was like you thought of everyone as projects, not people."

"That's not true. I had fun with everyone, even if they were helping me try to become a better girlfriend, even if I used them for information. I didn't do it to hurt anyone. I definitely didn't use it to hurt you. I had this stupid little crush on you."

"Yeah, right," he says. "You're amazing, though. I couldn't handle dating so many people at once. I haven't finished going through the journal yet."

My stomach bottoms out. "Where is it?" I manage to get out. "Give it back."

"I will. Whenever I find it." He looks around the room. "Last time I saw, someone was reading it in the kitchen."

Panic drums through me so quick, it steals my breath away. It's enough to be a joke to thousands of strangers online, but to have to deal with it face-to-face? Isn't it plenty embarrassing for them to have seen all they have already? Do I have to let them know I'm so pathetic I redated my exes just to impress a guy who only wanted me for some views?

Not only that, but my journal. People are reading my personal thoughts written in pink glitter by a gel pen bought for my birthday. Some of the papers dotted with my tears, some from being sad I had to even go through this, and some from laughing so hard at the doodles Sofia left me throughout. People making fun of the lessons my family worked hard to prepare for me to try to just be . . . better. Something born by an abundance of love for me becoming a joke to people feels like lemon juice pooling behind my eyes.

"You're horrible." My throat grows heavy. My eyes start to burn.

"*I'm* horrible?" Arno repeats, pointing his finger toward

me. "You're the one hopping from person to person. Seriously, doesn't it get tiring? How do you manage it? Do you only stop at first base? Second—"

A hand drops on my shoulder, guiding me to the side. Their body's a blur as they storm past me. I only see his fist fly, landing right against Arno's jaw.

Luckily for Arno, the couch catches him as he falls over.

The crowd grows silent. Some asshole shuts the music down, and I know for sure all the eyes are on me—and now Leon, who turns away from a moaning Arno, is locked in on me. Whatever rage was in the punch he had fades when he looks at me. In its place is hurt and betrayal and nothing I have ever seen from him before. Not toward me.

"Leon."

A flash goes off. Then another, but instead of flickering, the light remains on. Right when I scan the crowd and spot the person recording me, Leon's body blocks my vision and the recorder's line of sight.

Don't cry, don't cry, don't let any of these people see you cry. I try to open my mouth to speak, but not only do words fail me, the moment my lips part I have to fight a sob.

Leon closes the distance between us. I brace myself for him, for whatever words he wants to unleash about betrayal and lying and cursing, anything to get all the anger he has to be feeling out. He has a right to. I know that, but my heart still feels the trample of his words before I hear them.

He grabs my wrist and then pulls me away. Everyone carves a path for him as he moves, dodging us as he rushes us out the door. The whole time he leads us down the sidewalk, I'm waiting for *him* to speak, trying to figure out how *I* can speak, but neither of us do.

When we reach his beat-up blue pickup truck, he opens the passenger door.

"Leon—"

He gently pushes me toward the seat, and shame from the party, from my actions, from my guilt, seals my lips. I hop in and he leans over, his arm pressing against me. Normally when he's this close, a tingle of awareness shoots up my spine, and warmth spreads throughout my body in tiny circles of heat. But his movement is quick as he grabs the seat belt and buckles me in.

Warmth gone before it could spread.

"Wait here." He shuts the door without giving me the chance to speak. If I could speak. If it didn't feel like a crab's pincers were slowly tightening around my throat.

My gaze trails after him as he strides back to the house, until he disappears within it. As soon as he's out of my line of vision, I press my hand on my chest, trying to massage the area, trying to loosen the tightness so it doesn't hurt to breathe.

I can't process what happened, not fully, not in detail.

It's like I was in that house for hours and at the same time, only in the blink of an eye. Walking in, talking to Arno, it's already blurring, but Leon's face when he saw me, the hurt etched into his brows, the smoothness in his cheek, where his dimple didn't dare to show—that image is crystal clear.

I hurt him. It's exactly what I wanted to do, but nothing,

nothing, feels good to me right now. He's so hurt and mad, but he's still willing to put me first, to make sure I'm safe. He pulled me away from any more potential humiliation when he could have joined in on it.

But of course he wouldn't want to. Of course he cares about me.

I can't believe I would think otherwise.

The driver's door swings open, and Leon climbs in. He doesn't look at me but gently places something on my lap. It's the Hernandez Romance Boot Camp journal.

Tears fill my eyes and I slap my hands over my face, muffling the sob that escapes right as the engine shudders on. I keep my face covered while I cry as Leon pulls off and turns on the radio—and the soft melody to one of my favorite songs, an artist I recommended to Leon years ago, begins. Like he was listening to it as he drove earlier today.

Even when the truck comes to a full stop, the music turned down, I stay with my hands covering my face.

I'm not sure how much time has passed like that, in tears, when I finally manage to pull them away. But when I do, Leon looks right at me, and the urge to cry all over again settles into me.

"I read it." There is no emotion in his voice, no emotion on his face. I'm shocked my chest has the ability to get any more knotted. "Maybe it was wrong, an invasion of privacy. But I read it, and I read what you wrote about me. About your plan. You just wanted to hurt me in the end."

"I do—I *did*." I shake my head, try to clear my thoughts but everything is all scrambled. "That was before. When you first came back, and I was so angry with you, with the idea of you being okay when I wasn't."

"Then why didn't you say that?" If he had any emotions coating his voice, or if it raised from the monotone level it was at right now, I might say he was snapping at me. I wish that he was. This quiet, steady anger feels scarier and final. Like it doesn't matter what I say next—he is already pulling away from me. Already folding me and my memory up like a shirt that no longer fits and he'll soon rid from his closet. "Instead of this grand plan of making me fall in love with you, just to dump me in the end. You didn't *have* to agree to be friends. Why say you changed your mind at all?"

Because I was angry. Because I made a mistake. Because I felt like you deserved it. Because it was better than to face the realization that after all that time my feelings never disappeared.

I open my mouth to speak, and then I replay his words. Get stuck on them.

Not "grand plan of *trying* to make me fall in love with you" but "making me fall in love with you." Present tense.

My heart beats wildly in my chest, a beat-up organ that doesn't know when to quit. Ever since our kiss, I've known Leon still has feelings for me, but I haven't known if they are as strong as *love*. Not again.

"Did you? Fall back in love with me?" I whisper.

Hurt crosses his face before he turns away, before I can really see every line of it. "I never stopped."

A sense of relief floods me, and a wave a happiness settles

over me, while a storm of guilt hurricanes inside me.

"Leon—"

"Please." He unlocks the doors. "Just leave." When I call his name again, he reaches over me, the heat of his body warming me for a single second as he opens the door. "Go."

His voice is so broken, my body moves automatically. It takes me three tries to unlock my seat belt before I stumble out of the truck. I head toward my front door, looking back several times as I do, but Leon doesn't look my way. Yet he doesn't leave either.

Only when I manage to unlock the front door, enter, and shut it behind me, do I hear him drive off.

And that last bit of kindness hurts too.

CHAPTER 24

HRBC Lesson #13: Honesty Is the Best Policy (Sometimes)
Mom: If something genuinely makes you uncomfortable, say so.
Titi Ivy: If a date asks you if you like their hair, outfit, et cetera, and you don't, it's okay to lie. Lying gets you far.

It's eleven at night and my family is up, waiting for me, waiting to tell me off for being the most ungrateful daughter on the planet. Maybe this is a good thing. I can get out all the bad things coming my way at once.

Bile climbs my throat. I breathe through my nose as I let myself in. A mixer is whirring, that's the first buzz I hear when I shut the front door. I follow it and find my entire family there.

Mom is on the end of the couch. Of course, Zoe is asleep in her arms. Sofia is beside her, her nails clicking on her phone, and Mari must be asleep in her room.

"Amelia Ivelisse Hernandez," Titi Sandra says from behind me, all hard-edged.

I swallow before I turn to face her. She's in line with her sisters, all making empanadas. Titi Neva stands at the center, creating the fillings in the mixer, separating them by flavor, slapping them on the dough. Titi Ivy is to the right of her, her black dress shirt barely covering her stomach as she crimps and puts together the crescent moons.

Titi Sandra is at the starting line, slamming dough onto the counter, beating it with the roller before smacking it in front of Titi Neva. None of them stop when I walk toward them, but they move harshly, slamming ingredients, whacking containers together, a way of speaking without speaking.

They're pissed.

They *know*.

Titi Ivy says, "Look at the clock, Amelia. Three hours late, no call, no text. You sent us straight to voicemail."

Titi Neva says, "You know better than that."

Titi Sandra says, "Don't stand there with that face. Get in line."

I'd assume they were all just stress-baking, but watching them add to the one of the five trays filled with food by the fridge, it's like they're preparing for something.

Instead of joining them, I take the opposite side of the counter in front of Titi Neva, who is the only one whose back isn't stiffly straight. Without looking at me, she pushes over a large bowl of strawberry filling and a pile of flattened dough.

I grab a spoon and fill one, half an inch so it doesn't spill out when fried. I learned how to eyeball measurements before I learned the full English language. There's not a single measuring cup in this house.

"My phone died." It's not fully a lie. It died on the way here. "I went over to a friend's. Well, I went over a coworker's house." Turns out, I don't have a single friend who went to that party.

Not Arno, nor the people who stared at me. And, worst of all, not Leon.

"You know our numbers by heart," Titi Ivy says, but at least there's no knifed edge to her words. "You should have asked to borrow someone's phone."

"You know better," Titi Neva adds, and like an echo, Titi Sandra whacks more dough on the counter so hard, it vibrates all on top of it.

I flinch. "I'm sorry."

I fill another empanada, bracing myself for them to demand my next apology. The bigger one. When it doesn't come, my nerves double. They're all probably so angry they can't even form the words yet. Or they know the longer the wait, the more I'll brace myself for it until it makes me sick.

It's not enough that I feel guilty already. They have to know that, they have to know *me*. Is this how it's going to be from now on? This cold, angry, air heavy with unsaid words and anxiety—the latter all my own.

Automatically, I fill another empanada. "What's all this for?" I ask nobody in particular, desperate to fill the weighted atmosphere.

"For the people helping with the bakery," Titi Sandra says, but what I hear in the clipped tone is *You know, the one you're not helping us with. Us, the people who gave you life, raised you, saved money to buy you a mini piano in middle school when you swore you wanted to be a composer and then you never touched the instrument again.*

My brain tells me to retreat. I can't handle this, not anytime, but especially not after tonight. I just need to sleep. I need a break. As if nothing is wrong, I ask, "How is that going, by the way? Any updates on when the bakery will be ready?"

"Not soon enough," she says just as casually.

Without thinking, I smash the spoon on the table. "I'm *sorry,* okay? I'm sorry I was late. I'm sorry I was planning to leave next year. I'm sorry I'm a mess."

All movement ceases.

Titi Neva is the first to speak. "What do you mean 'leaving next year'?"

My stomach free-falls. No, no. They are staring at me wrong, like they have no idea what I'm talking about. I turn, and Sofia looks at me with the widest eyes possible. We haven't spoken all day, but I read the *I didn't tell them* words in her gaze.

Oh God.

"Explain," Titi Sandra demands.

But my throat is in the process of tying itself into several Girl Scout knots. I reach for the spoon to fill another piece of dough, for something to do other than acknowledge all the eyes burning into my skin, melting into my flesh.

"Nothing to explain." Sofia speaks fast to cover up my silence. "Clearly she's out of it right now. I mean, look at her, she looks like she hasn't slept in weeks."

That pushes me right over the edge. I hurt Sofia so bad. Betrayal was clear in the glint of her eyes last night, in her words. I can't believe I thought she would tell on me.

How could I think that when she's never done so before? Every time I snuck in home after a date or tried to make my F's look like A's on my tests, or ate the leftovers in the fridge that didn't belong to me, she never said a word. When I dented the cars multiple times, she took half the blame. When I forgot to take the meat out of the freezer when the aunts asked, she said she put it back in. She's never given me a reason to think she'd betray me.

Even when she's mad, she is still willing to have my back.

I can't let the aunts think she is a liar like me. And I can't keep lying. I mean, seriously, it's played out now. I can't expect everyone to clean up after me, to cover for me when I screw up. If I want to be able to be on my own, I have to be able to stand on my own—even if it's scary.

"It's okay, mi amor." Mom looks at me with clear eyes, like she knows exactly what I'm about to say but isn't going to blame me for it. "Whatever it is, you can tell us."

It's her I look to when I speak. The warmth in her eyes, and the slight nod she gives me, has bravery wash over me.

I take a deep breath and speak. "For years now, I've been saving up money to leave. First, it was to move in with Leon after graduation. But when we broke up, I kept at it. I found a gap-year program that lets you travel outside the US instead of going straight to college, and I want to go. I got into the program, which starts in January, but I needed five thousand more dollars for the payment, which is why I started working at the Big E. The deadline is coming up at the end of the month."

I don't think it's ever been silent in this house before. Completely quiet so I can hear my heart drumming in my throat, the sound of a breeze reaching the windows, the buzz of the fridge.

It's eerie. This house has spent decades filled with life and in this moment, it mimics a graveyard.

I can barely look anyone in the eyes.

Titi Sandra wipes flour on her already-coated apron. "And cuando you were going to tell us?" When she weaves in and out of English, it's a telltale sign that her composure isn't as she usually controls it.

"Honestly, I don't know."

"Amelia," Titi Ivy says, "how could you have been planning this all this time and not tell us?"

Titi Neva holds a hand to the crystal around her neck. "I'm shocked."

Mom appears beside me, Zoe resting against her chest. "It's late. Why don't we finish up here and speak about this tomorrow?"

"We will discuss this now," the lawyer says, harsh enough I wince even though her words land toward Mom and not me.

"Look at her," Mom points her chin toward me. "Look at her, really. Her eyes, her shoulders, her *face*. She's not having a good night. Why make it worse?"

My heart rate speeds up enough that I couldn't count the pace if I tried. She's talking about right now, but her words help me realize something. That despite all the love and attention I receive from my family, I've never felt *seen* by them. I could never articulate it, because it sounds like it doesn't make any sense.

Even now, my brain is trying to tell me the thought is incoherent.

They speak to me every day, all the time. We spend hours together, cook together, eat together, sleep under the same roof. Titi Sandra knows I have to have something sweet after every single meal or I don't feel complete. Titi Neva knows I get instantly sick during rides on twisty roads and have a deeply weird fear of perfectly shaped holes. Titi Ivy was the first one to know I liked guys and girls. Sofia can tell how I'm feeling by watching my face for two seconds. Mari can pick a book from a shelf and predict how much I'll like it.

My family knows me so well and yet they don't. They don't see how lost I am, how lost I've *been*. I'm not sure they've tried to. It's like they're so used to this idea of me, of my future in the family, they don't realize I've never said I wanted what they did. They don't see that it doesn't fit.

They don't see *me*. At least, not completely.

I'm not invisible, and I think that makes it worse. That I'm visible to them, yet overlooked.

Titi Sandra doesn't acknowledge Mom at all. "You forget what family is, hija."

Daughter. The word is a punch in the gut.

Titi Neva comes over and places a hand on my shoulder. "Now, let's not go that far. So you take this trip for a few months, then come back?"

"It's a year," I manage to say.

"Oh." She lets me go. "I didn't read this in the cards."

"Neva, please," Titi Ivy snaps. "The cards don't speak."

"No, they don't," Titi Sandra agrees, "because if they did, they'd tell you, Amelia, that you're being foolish. First you think to leave your family to move in with some guy, then you think to leave on your own to a different country? Unacceptable."

"Leon isn't just *some* guy." But I feel as foolish as she accuses me of for defending him when they know it didn't work out. "He's incredibly kind, like I sometimes worry he forgets to eat because his brain is always filled with the urge to help anyone with in a ten-foot radius. You all have met him. You know that." As soon as the words are out, I realize I'm speaking about present and not past Leon. "And it's not for some guy. It's for me. The guy was just a plus. That's not the point. It was *my* decision. Me. Amelia. Stop trying to place the blame anywhere else but on *me*."

It's like she can't even realize I can be a fool all on my own. Like every single emotion and action I have is because of some outside influence and not my own. It's another way the aunts don't *see* me.

"It was back then when this seed was planted," Titi Sandra says. "He may have matured now, but then he was just another foolish kid with no idea how the real world works. He thought he could be some star football player and you'd follow after him? It's a good thing Connor shipped him off when he did."

Everything freezes. My heart, my body, time, sound. The only thing ping-ponging in my head are her words.

When there's a semblance of moisture in my throat, I manage to get out, "How do you know that?"

Her eyes grow wide then twitch like she's trying to get them normal again. "It doesn't matter."

Everything moves again, including my brain fighting to

piece together her words, what they mean. And I never told them about Leon, never mentioned his dream of being a star football player.

Titi Ivy grabs Titi Sandra's arm. "Adults talk," she says, a little too quick to be normal. "Connor has been working at the bakery all this time. We talk about our kids, always."

"Yeah," Titi Neva jumps in. "We know all about Leon."

I turn my attention to her. "If you did, then you'd have known we dated before I told you."

Guilt frames Titi Neva's heart-shaped face. She stutters, then steps behind Titi Ivy.

"Stop," Titi Sandra demands, shrugging off her sisters. "Since we're talking about keeping secrets, then we should lead by example. I take full responsibility for my actions." My heart plummets and swells all at once. "We knew Connor back in the day. We all went to high school together. He and Ivy had feelings for each other, fleeting. But they went away as soon as Kelsey, Connor's ex-wife, transferred to our school. He dropped Ivy like she was nothing, so when we found out you were dating his son, we didn't doubt the same would happen to you."

"What?" I try to meet Titi Ivy's gaze, but her own is on the floor. "I don't understand." I feel like I've been dropped into a show that's run three seasons and I'm watching the finale, trying to piece the plot together.

Titi Ivy, cheeks red, tells Titi Sandra, "That doesn't matter much to the story."

"Maybe," Titi Sandra goes on, "but it was how it started. And two years ago, when Connor came to this house for advice on how to raise his child when his wife left him, *we* were the ones there for him. He was lost as a single dad. Struggling to find enough work to pay the bills for him and his son. A son who was talking nonstop about moving in together with a girl straight out of high school he knew he wanted to be with forever." She holds me in place with her gaze. I never admitted we were dating to my family, but Leon was totally open with his father. "And when he asked for advice, we gave it to him: The boy needed his mother. Women are the pillar in any household."

My mouth hangs open and a dull, constant buzzing sound starts vibrating throughout my skull.

"This can't be true," I say, mostly to myself. For someone known to never shut up, I can't think of a single thing to say. I can barely think of how to feel, let alone any words for the aunts. For two years they kept this from me.

What the *hell*?

My palms begin to sweat. "So you're saying all this time you knew Leon and I dated?" So when they called me out about it before, it was about *me* keeping it from them. Not because they didn't know. "And *you* told Leon's dad to send him away?"

Titi Sandra says, in a quick, harsh tone, "We didn't tell him to. We advised him."

"Don't speak lawyer to me," I snap back.

She gives me the Stare, but for the first time, I don't feel my shoulders cowering. I don't feel any nerves in my stomach.

When I don't back down, Titi Sandra crosses her arms. "Sixteen years old is way too young to know what you want.

Connor agreed. His wife left because this town was too small for big dreams. He didn't want Leon to feel trapped and pigeonholed. To be stuck like his mother was. We both wanted the best for our kids. For your education, your future, your mental health. You were barely passing your classes. You wouldn't reach your full potential with a boy who had unattainable dreams. How could you take over the family business if you were following him around? A football player? I knew he wouldn't make it and see, he's come back and he's realized it too. He's going to follow after his father. Like you will us."

"Why?"

"Because it was what's best for you."

"Oh my God." I stand, rubbing—so hard the skin starts to burn—my temples. "All this time, I've been blaming Leon, throwing it in his face, trying to hurt him and *you* convinced his father to send him away."

Steam rises under my skin and tears well up. I can't even be embarrassed right now. I'm so mad, heartbroken, and confused.

All this time I spent angry at Leon, wondering what I did wrong, hating him—trying to anyway—for a separation that began with my own family? For the aunts to have snuck around and led me right on the path to the most miserable time of my life?

I rub my arms as I try to calm down, but I have all this anger inside me, growing and growing.

All I can think to say is, "You had *no* right. What else are you keeping from me?"

Nobody speaks, but Titi Neva looks to the floor so fast I know she's hiding something.

"What is it?" I demand. "Tell me everything now, or I won't forgive you."

"Amelia—" Titi Ivy begins, but I cut her off.

"Tell me."

"On your birthday two years ago, Leon came to the house," Titi Sandra says, lacking any emotion as if she's not telling me world-flipping information. It only enrages me more. "We told him he'd only hold you back. That you were already moving on, and he'd only take that from you."

"What?"

"I called his father," Titi Sandra says, "and we spoke to him about coming all the way down here when he should have been focusing on his training. Again, you wouldn't understand, but it's what was best."

Titi Neva grabs my hands. "Mi amor, do not forget we are cursed. All we want is to protect you."

Titi Sandra grabs my cheek. "That's right, my firstborn. Wouldn't it have hurt more when it ended between you if you tried to hold on? This way, with all of us beside you, you were safe, you could heal. We stick together so nobody has to hurt."

I shrug them off and gain the space I need to breathe. But it's not enough. It won't be, not if I stay in this house.

Titi Sandra speaks. "If we hadn't done that, if you never broke up, would you have gone with him? Moved away and left us?"

"I don't *know*." Now I'm the one snapping. It's overwhelming, feeling their gazes, the guilt, the nerves, the hurt. "God, I don't know anything, don't you get it? That's the whole problem. How am I supposed to know what I want when you guys don't give me a single second to think about anything other than what *you* want for me?"

Titi Ivy looks dumbstruck. "Haven't we always said we're here for you? To listen to you? Where did you get the idea that you couldn't come to us if you felt that way?"

I feel something in me crack. Not a single one, but a tiny one in the right place that creates a domino effect and it grows, breaking off in a dozen different branches until nothing holds all the emotions I've stored up and it doesn't flood, it hurricanes.

"When could I say I don't want the same thing you all did? That I don't want to stay in this house the rest of my life? That I don't *want* to work at the bakery? That I don't want anything while still not knowing exactly what it is when there's no room for anything that isn't for the family?"

My voice rises, and I cross my hands against my chest to keep them from shaking, but my whole body vibrates. "All you guys do is talk about me and my sisters taking over the family business. Having kids and raising them side by side like you all did. Adding another set of rooms for said kids when the bakery that I'm supposed to work at does well. Expanding and expanding for a growing family. Do you know I don't even *want* kids?"

"Amelia," Titi Ivy says, "where is all this coming from?"

"Everywhere." I feel like I'm running out of air. Or maybe I'm speaking too quick, breathing too little. "Tell me, please, *one* time you ever heard me say I wanted to work at the bakery,

take over the business, have kids, live here, stay here. If you can think of one, I promise to never complain again. I'll work at the bakery until my last day, I swear."

None of them speak because none of them *can.* All these years, even when I was a kid, all I've done is smile and nod and change the subject. It's true that no one in this family has bothered to see me, but have I been trying to be seen? I can't stop myself from communicating who I am now.

So I go on. "Why do you think I'm so obsessed with breaking the Hernandez curse? I don't want to live the same life as you all. I want to have a partner, I want to be out on my own, I want to explore. I may not know what I want to do, but I'll never figure that out here."

"That's enough," Titi Sandra snaps, but her voice cracks. Her eyes bore into mine. "You will not raise your voice in this house."

I open my mouth to do exactly that, feeling a scream bubbling out of me, but Mom blocks my view as she steps in my path. "No, you will not speak down to my daughter. *Listen* to what she is saying. Really listen. If you do, you'll realize this is not the first time you've ignored her."

Titi Sandra falters. "We have never ignored her. We've given her everything she could ever need."

"No," Mom says. "What she needs is to be seen as herself and not another member of the Hernandez family. There are eight people who live under this roof, but you, and all of us, seem to think of eight as one."

"We *are* a family," Titi Sandra says, but the bark is seeping from her bite, softening into something close to exhaustion.

"Made up of *different* people with *different* needs," Mom snaps, stealing the authority I'm so used to Titi Sandra speaking with. "The safety of this house stops being a gift when it's presented as the only option for our futures."

It makes me pause. Not just because of my sweet mother, standing up for me, standing up to the head of the house. *Our futures.* Like I'm not the only one being overlooked. Like Mom is standing up for herself too.

Mom goes on. "Being a family should be a gift, not an obligation. We fear the curse, so we keep one another close and don't think anything else is possible. Is our family cursed? Or are *we* doing the cursing?"

Titi Ivy walks between the sisters. "Now, let's calm down."

"No," Mom says. "Think about it, sleep on it, but you will not shut down Amelia when she's telling us how she feels. Or any of us."

My vision blurs. It's the first time I've ever seen Mom stand up to Titi Sandra, the first time I've seen anyone do so at all. Even with Zoe in her arms, she stands straight, chin up like she's daring her sister to disagree.

Nobody says a word for a few moments until Mom blows out a breath. "Good, that's enough excitement for today. Everyone, go to sleep." There's another breath of silence. *"Now."*

We all move.

I go the fastest, taking the stairs two by two, reaching the top of my bunk before Sofia shuts the door behind her. I want to close my eyes and pretend so much hasn't happened, but she flicks the light on and I don't hear the creak of her bed, which means she's standing there, staring at me.

I sit up, cross-legged, and meet her glare as she stands with her arms against her chest.

"You're a real dumbass for that. I might have been pissed last night, but I'd never sell you out. That's not what sisters do."

My stomach has fallen so far, I can no longer feel it. "I know. I'm sorry. For so much, but right now, for that the most."

"Yeah, well, I'm sorry too. Hearing them speak to you like that, knowing that's how *I* sounded is gross. You're not abandoning us. I know that."

"Thank you."

"Why didn't you tell me? Were you going to disappear and keep a hologram here in your place? Hope nobody noticed?"

"It's hard to explain."

"Try anyway."

I blow out a puff of air and stare up at the little popcorn flecks of paint on the ceiling. Sofia and I have always been each other's confidants. She's always been the easiest to talk to. Nothing was ever too embarrassing to tell or shameful to admit.

If anything, she should have been the first person I told when I got the idea.

"Disappointing the aunts doesn't feel great, but it's not exactly new." I try to put together the separate pieces of an answer into one. "I never got the grades they wanted, never could cook pernil to perfection, never do anything right the first, second, tenth try. I'm not *impressive*—"

"That's not true."

I hold up a hand. "Let me get this out. I don't mean it in a self-deprecating way." And as I say this, I realize it's the truth. Before, not being good at anything felt like a failure. Like I was just this walking mess of a disappointment, but now, it feels so small. So insignificant to what I care about.

"I think I'm not impressive because I've never *tried* to figure out what I could be, in everything. In sports I like. In hobbies. Even in food. I did track because the aunts said it'll build discipline into my schedule. I didn't bother taking any art classes because they told me it wouldn't matter in finishing off a business degree. I never tried to see if I liked to paint, or build furniture, or sing, or fish, because I was too busy trying to bake the best flan, or perfect the aunts' rice and beans recipe.

"So of course I'm not good at anything because I never really tried anything for a long time. But because I'm bad at the things the aunts expect me to be good at, they love me but they don't think I'm impressive." I look down from the ceiling to Sofia. My best friend. "But you've never made me feel that way. I tell you I'm unimpressive and you're so ready to disagree. I'm sad, and you explain to me the plot of some complicated show. I get dumped and you make a two-page bulleted list on why my ex is a loser."

"All your exes are losers," Sofia says stiffly, like she's trying to keep her voice leveled.

"I guess what I'm trying to say here is, I'm used to disappointing the aunts, but I'm not used to disappointing *you*. I never knew what it would look like and a part of me was scared of that and scared of placing you with the aunts."

"But you do place me with the aunts," she says quietly. "Because you thought I'd want to live our lives like the aunts too."

"Don't you?" I keep my voice soft. I don't want it to sound accusatory. Just like me, who never got a chance to find myself in this house of wonderful women, Sofia hasn't either.

"It's not like it sounds so horrible," she says, "but I guess I never asked if you wanted something different."

It sends a pang in my chest. "I never asked you, either. I'm your older sister."

She rolls her eyes, but she quickly wipes the space under them. "By one year."

"Seven in dog."

"Are you a dog now?"

"Woof, woof."

She laughs, and everything in me loosens, like every joint in me was overly tightened with screws and they all got released at once. If she's laughing, she's not too hurt, too mad. That, I can work with. Maybe I haven't broken things between my family and I completely. Not with my sister, at least.

"I think I understand and . . . I'm not mad if you go away for a year."

"You're a good sister, Sofia."

She holds a bit of heat in her gaze. "Yeah, well, don't think I'll forget this. You're taking my dish duty for a month."

"Deal."

"Okay, I'm just going to say it." She hurries up the bunk,

hops over, and sits cross-legged with me. "That was *fucked.* I can't believe Titi Sandra did that. And the aunts too. Maybe they didn't lead the charge, but they supported it. And they helped keep it a secret from you."

"Stop." I press my hand to my chest. There's only so much heartbreak I can take for tonight, and I can't think of the betrayal, of what it means for Leon and me. What it changes. I can't. "Not yet."

"I mean, I understand them a little," Sofia admits. "Whenever things don't work out for us in our individual lives, where do we end up for comfort?" She holds out her arms. "Here. Where we have one another. The aunts all do, and when they grow old and annoying, it was supposed to be me and you and Mari and Zoe."

I chew on my bottom lip. So, this is why Sofia was so hurt, so betrayed. I knew, of course I did, but I guess some part of me was hoping maybe deep down she was like me. She wanted to be on her own, explore, do all the things we planned, only alone.

"I don't think moving away or going off to travel puts a stop to that," I tell her. "It just makes the future different. I don't want to get *rid* of you all. I just want some distance to learn who *I* am. You think if you called me, even if I was across the world, and said you needed me, I wouldn't swim across the ocean to be with you?"

For the first time in my life, I see Sofia's eyes glisten with unshed tears. "I don't know. I'm not sure what's possible anymore."

"Exactly." I grab her hands. It's hard for me to ever feel

the older, protective-sister link between us, because Sofia has always been so much more put together than me, she always seemed strong and independent. I guess the aunts weren't the only ones who didn't see their sisters fully. "It means that *anything* is possible, Sofia. We can do literally whatever we want, be whoever we want. Isn't that beautiful? It'll make it so whenever we're together, we can be fully happy and fully ourselves."

She holds my gaze, or I think she does. My eyes burn with tears and it's hard to see her.

Finally, she says, "You did a real Disney *it's not my dream, Dad, it's* yours. You're a walking cliché."

"What does that make you, my hilarious, all-knowing sidekick?"

"Please," she scoffs, making her way toward her bed, "I'm a leading lady. Always."

"You are," I say, lying down. One day, I want to be one too.

As I stare up at the ceiling, I think of all the leading ladies I've seen, particularly the ones from all the rom-coms Sofia had me watch. Some were sarcastic, badass. Others were shy, soft-spoken. A few mysterious and sexy. But no matter who they were, what situation they were in, by the end of the movies, they *always* did the right thing. Even if it hurt.

I have no idea what the future holds, what I'll be doing in ten years' time, but I know one thing. I want to be a leading lady. And I'm not going to hold myself back because I'm scared of the unknown.

If I can stand up to my family, there's little else I can't do.

CHAPTER 25

HRBC Lesson #14: Don't Be Afraid to Initiate Things
Titi Sandra: Sometimes your date will be shy, and you've got enough Hernandez blood to suck it up and take initiative on conversation.
Sofia: If you think a date went well and aren't hearing back, why not follow up? Don't be embarrassed.

When I wake up, the silence that was so foreign to me last night strikes again. There's no reggaeton blasting, no pots and pans banging, no little sisters begging to read or aunts arguing over what flavors go with what. To a stranger, this noiseless Hernandez household at noon may seem typical. For me, it's as strange as waking up in a spaceship.

After rubbing the crust from my eyes, I go through the entire house and there's not a single family member here. Even Mom and Zoe. My nerves rumble, but I know they have to be gone because they wanted to. Which, them wanting to be completely away from me does hurt, but at least I know they haven't been kidnapped by aliens or something.

I do another sweep of the house to make sure nobody is hiding, then I head back up to my room and slump on the carpet.

Like a flash of lightning, relief and hurt jolts through me, and I pull my knees up and cry. I can't believe what the aunts did. I can't believe Leon didn't tell me. I'm a mess of joy and pain and my chest aches with the weight of it. And of course I've forgiven them, but now that they're not around and I'm not worried about hurting their feelings, I let the hurt sink its claws into my chest.

It wasn't fake. I hadn't made any of it up. Leon *did* love me. He always loved me.

All this hurt was misplaced. All this anger I've been storing up to use against him should have never existed.

No matter what happens, at least I have that. All this time, thinking someone I loved with everything I had gave me up like nothing ended up twisting something nasty inside me. This anger and insecurity and pain. Is it okay to finally let it all go?

How can I feel so good and so horrible all at once?

My phone rings. Only the aunts, Sofia, and Leon—though I don't expect, only hope for a call—can reach me. Other than that, my settings are on do not disturb. I don't need anyone calling or messaging me about Arno's videos. Or me stumbling upon it online. I deleted most my apps. I want to be off the grid for a while.

I haven't even told Sofia what happened. It's less about keeping a secret and more about keeping her from prison because she *will* fight Arno. She doesn't care about height or weight or muscles. She will make anything around her a weapon and try to kill him. I need my sister in my life, not in juvie. I just have to hope she doesn't see the videos before I can delete the app from her phone.

Speaking of my sister, I answer the phone. "Hey, Sofia."

"I tried to get you out of it," she says, annoyance saturating her voice. "But the aunts have to do some last-minute shopping for decor, and Titi Sandra wants you to come help clean before the grand opening next week."

I sigh. "Is she standing there, staring at you, making sure you get me to come?"

"You know, you're a much better psychic than Titi Neva."

"How many times can we clean that place? Doesn't she know *some* germs are good ones?"

"I think she thinks of them as tiny green blobs who have pitchforks and are anti–Marc Anthony stans." Her voice goes far away, then returns, and I'm guessing she's dealing with the Stare. "Anyway, I'll be here poisoning myself with Fabuloso."

"Has anyone said anything about me? About the program?"

"No, they're operating on a strict *if we don't talk about it, it didn't happen* method."

"Wonderful, be there soon."

"Try not to crash the SUV."

"Eat glass."

When I hang up, I head straight for the shower and get ready while trying to figure out what to do.

This whole pretending nothing happened goes strictly against how we were raised, and how we as a family have handled any sort of conflict. I think that means I broke them or broke something in their brains that they don't even know how to react.

It makes me nervous that it's permanent.

It also builds this new resolve within me. The aunts not

knowing what to do, how to fix something, that is a brand-new experience. Which means I've gone my whole eighteen years of living without disobeying, without speaking up for myself, without saying what I want.

It's about time that I did.

So much would be better if I learned that sooner. I wouldn't have fought with Sofia, I wouldn't have gone so long feeling lost. Maybe then, maybe things with Leon would have been different.

I certainly wouldn't have hurt him the way I have.

And maybe if I'd been more honest in the beginning, Titi Sandra wouldn't have done what she did.

With fewer nerves—though they're still there—I finish up and drive, without crashing into anything, to the bakery. The lot is less packed since most of the plaza is closed today, and there are only a few cars and a truck lined up.

I walk through the new, pale wooden and polished floors. The tarped walls and furniture a blur of blue as I head to the kitchen. Right before I make it there, Titi Sandra and Sofia exit. Sofia rushes toward me.

"TitiSandra'smakingmegowithhertogetsomeshelvingsheforgotLeonisinthereIwasjustabouttowarnyou." She says everything so fast in comes out in one long, nearly impossible-to-decipher word.

Titi Sandra just says, "You can clean the new stove," and doesn't look at me.

Off to a great start.

They walk off and I hurry to the back. If Leon is there I can talk to him and . . .

I don't know.

The aunts have been in the forefront of my mind, I haven't attempted to figure out what I'm supposed to say to him. I only have this pressing urge to talk to him, to be in the same room, to have him look at me and not be angry or hurt even though I still feel both those things.

When I enter, he and his dad are pushing a silver stove in between the fridge and counter. His dad stands up straight first, pressing his hand on the back of Leon's gray fitted shirt. "Don't bend too much. Use your knees."

"I got it, Dad," Leon answers.

They both turn and spot me at the same time. The way Leon's dad looks between us, it's obvious he knows something is going on, which makes me want to throw myself in the nearest trash, but I try to keep my chin up.

"Hi," I manage to get out.

Connor says, "Hello, Amelia." He looks toward Leon. "I'll go help Sandra with the shelving unit. It's too heavy for the girls on their own."

"Dad—" Leon calls out, but Connor scurries off, leaving the two of us here, alone.

Which is what I wanted but now I don't know what to do, or how words work, or how can I possibly think I can say sorry to Leon and have him forgive me.

I should at least *try*, but if I do and he doesn't, then it'll break my heart.

And I've had enough of that particular organ shattering and trying to piece itself back together again.

"I should start cleaning." I rush to the corner where the bulk supplies lean against the wall.

Gloves on, I dump cleaning solution on the nearest counter and start wiping it down like the harder I scrub, the more likely it is Leon, standing watching me, might start the conversation first.

Which is selfish and childish, but, man, I can't find any words that fit every emotion inside me.

He lets me finish several areas, and moves out of my way when I get to the newest stove and open it up to clean the inside. I feel his presence like a second heartbeat. Like for each breath I take, I feel his exhale on the back of my neck, his pulse at the base of my throat.

It's strange feeling so close and distant to someone all at once.

Then he laughs, and it's this dry sound without any happiness in it. I peek up at him, towering over me as I kneel across the oven.

"You're really not going to say a word to me?" he asks.

And I know I should. I should start a conversation. But my nerves are working overtime. Like they're riding a spinning teacup and the attendant won't turn off the ride.

I'm so nervous it's making me dizzy.

That, and all the cleaning solution marinating in the oven. I start dragging it from the base of the stove, to the inner corners with a rag that's seen better days.

"I said hi." Which is a ridiculous response. I don't know why it comes out. A lame attempt at lightening the mood.

One that, obviously, does not work.

"Figures." Leon laughs without humor.

Leon turns on his heel and starts to walk away.

"Wait," I say quickly, hopping up and slamming the oven shut. I press the self-cleaning button and hurry after him.

I catch him right after he exits, the door's hanging bells chiming as it shuts behind us.

"Hold on," I say as we both scan the lot. It looks like his dad already left to follow Titi Sandra and Sofia home to get the shelving unit.

He stills, but I can't figure out what to do. I pretended to forgive him, all to try to hurt him. Why would he believe anything I say now? And with how the aunts treated him behind my back, why would he bother to?

After all this, he probably thinks the whole family is rotten. That we're all a bunch of women who go around hurting people for fun.

Still, why didn't he tell me about being intercepted by the aunts on my birthday? All I can think of is that he didn't want to create a rift between my family and me, especially because he'd go back to his mom, and I'd only have them around. Or maybe, seeing how my family, my *mom* treats me compared to his mother was too hard for him to bare, and he didn't want to hurt the relationships we all have.

But doing that would mean he was the only one hurting.

I open my mouth to ask, but it feels like I don't have the right to any information from him. I thought hope was painful, but shame? Having shame is like trying to speak but you just chugged a mug of lava.

The words burn as they climb my throat, but they evaporate right as they reach my tongue.

We stand there, and it's like he's giving me an opportunity. *Say something. Before I go, anything.*

He gives me plenty of time to, standing in the warming sun, the windless day, as if even the weather wants my words to be heard perfectly clear as they reach him.

"I didn't move on" is the first thing I think to say. His brows raise slightly. "When you came to see me on my birthday, before we broke up. The aunts lied. I was just trying to have a good time, and I was so sad and mad because I hadn't heard from you."

Carefully, like he's not sure he should, he says, "So you know."

I nod. "I'm sorry, Leon." I try to swallow down the emotion rising in my throat. "They shouldn't have done that, got in your head. Even your dad's. They just came in between us, hurt you, so bad, and I never knew."

He doesn't say anything, just clears his face of any emotion, so I go on. "It must have been tough, having the aunts push you away while you were already struggling." As I speak, I start to think of how much hurt filled Leon for these two years—how much hurt probably still does. "Did you think they were right to send you away? Did you think it was best for the both of us?"

He turns away, but I catch the pain he's unable to hide from his face as he speaks. "It's not that they were right about us. I know we loved each other. I know we were young, but it was real." The use of past tense feels like someone with spiked shoes is walking across my chest. "But . . . we were living separate lives. And I don't know, back then, I thought maybe something was wrong with me. Your family didn't approve of me. My dad sent me thousands of miles away. My mom didn't want me. If everyone around me didn't see me as someone worth anything, I didn't want to be with you, when you're worth it all."

Both my hands grip one of his. "You've never been worthless."

He still doesn't look at me, but he doesn't move to let me go, either. "I know that now, anyway. But back then, I felt so lost, and I didn't really know how to fix whatever was wrong with me."

I squeeze his hand. "Did you know? That they spoke to your dad?"

"Only after your birthday."

"I'm sorry."

He swallows, and I watch his Adam's apple bobble. He's quiet for a moment, then he pulls his hand away. "I never blamed you. Not once. Not for any of that." Before any relief can flood me, he goes on, "But what about now? Are you even sorry?"

Right, because the aunts aren't the only thing I need to apologize for. And according to Leon, I didn't have to at all. But I can't think of how to bring up something that fills me with such shame.

They are just words, why are they so hard to think of? Or

it's more like there are too many words to say, and I can't piece together which ones will form the best explanation. A good enough reason to explain what I did, take responsibility, while also being enough to ask for forgiveness, while still feeling true to my *own* feelings.

I mean, I *am* sorry, but I was the only one in the dark here. Everyone got to know why Leon really left aside from me? Isn't it normal for me to have come to my own, worse conclusions? No matter how bad they warped my actions?

Or maybe I'm trying to make myself feel better. Ugh, I don't know. It's all so messy.

"I should finish cleaning before they get back," I say.

He turns away, doesn't say another word to me. I drag myself inside the bakery, hating how much of a coward I am. I mean, I was able to hold my own against my family, but owning up to my own mistakes seems like an even greater feat.

I suck in a deep breath to sigh, and my nostrils flare as I near the back toward the kitchen.

There is something off—enough that my nerves stab my insides. I bring my palm to my nose to see if they smell like a bad mix of cleaning supplies, but they reek of pure bleach. When I pull them away, I pick up on the strange, metal odor.

Like that time I forgot to check in on the pork chops in the oven and took a nap upstairs. I woke to Sofia screaming and gray smoke pooling from the living room.

Dread yanks my stomach down in one weighted pull.

Smoke slips from the cracks of the kitchen door, sneaking its way free, as I sprint toward the door. When my palm grips the doorknob, I yank it back with a scream. The heat jolts up my arm, and I can't close my hand in a fist as the shock wears off and the molten pain pulses. I grab the end of my shirt and use it to hurriedly turn the knob until I can kick the door open, a plume of smoke smacking into me as I do.

Fear freezes me in place.

Like thunderous clouds, smoke hovers above, clinging to the ceiling of the kitchen. It's both dead silent and deafeningly loud. Like a song with no instruments, only words but the words are this intense, hot, crackling.

I'm choking on it but throw my body forward.

Fire. Rising from the stove, licking the ceiling as its embers spark off and rain down around it. There's a bucket nearby, and my body moves automatically. I think, *Fire, liquid, put it out.*

But when I throw the contents of it, the fire hisses and pulses brighter—it was the cleaning solution I used earlier, not water. I choke on the embers, on the barrel of smoke that whips toward me.

"Amelia!" I hear Leon call out and my panic crescendos.

Now that he's here, now that he's in danger, everything hits me hard in one quick knife slathered with panic, slicing through my stomach.

His shirt is off, and he's slapping it at the fire. It's hard to think of anything but the shape of Leon.

My first instinct is to run and pull him from the flame becoming large enough to be his shadow, but he spots me before I move.

"GET OUT!"

With the fire clouding my senses more and more rapidly, all I can think is: *If I get out, then I won't be with you, and if I won't be with you, then you'll be in here, in danger, in the fire.* Just the thought makes my vision tilt.

My legs sway. I reach out, but there's nothing to steady myself. My knees buckle, and I fall forward.

Leon catches me before my head meets the ground. Titi Sandra's first, biggest purchase for the bakery. One that made her uncharacteristically squeal with delight. Why is it on fire? How is it burning? Electrical? All I did was clean it. I rubbed it down with my rag and then I—

I slammed it shut and stormed off. I put it on self-clean, or maybe turned it to bake. Either way, I left the rag inside.

"Hey!" Leon yanks me back as I reach for the handle. "What are you doing?" he screams at me.

It was me. I left the rag in there and now . . . Oh God. Now it's on fire.

"My fault," I choke out in tears while smoke invades my mouth, my nostrils, my throat. "My fault."

"You need to get out of here." He shoves me toward the door. Like he's going to stay and put out the fire and I'm supposed to leave part of my heart to burn with the flames.

Through tears and dizziness, I scan the room. The fire pulses and the extra light glimmers in the farthest corner of the kitchen. I make my way for it, but Leon grabs my waist.

He tightens his hold and I know in a second, he's going to drag me away since I won't listen to him. I point toward the corner before he does. "Fire extinguisher." He doesn't let me go to grab it but pulls me farther from the flames before releasing me and running for it.

Useless. I'm so useless standing here as Leon grabs it and rushes so fast toward the flames that, for a split second, it appears he'll be swallowed by them, but right before he is, the white plumes from the extinguisher spray out to battle the orange and red. He points it first at the source of the flame, shrinking it, but then there's a sharp *crack* and it lives again.

It's too hot. The sweat beading on my skin feels like it's bubbling. I have the urge to dig my nails into my flesh and rip it off.

Leon gets the flames to lessen. But the flames have burnt out the wall behind it and beside it. Where the electrical socket is.

I press my pulsating palm over my nose and lunge toward the side of the stove, narrowly avoiding touching the flames as they spread. My knees slam on the tiles with enough force my teeth smack together, and something in my mouth cracks.

"AMELIA!"

This close, my sweat simmers like oil on a hot pan. Too hot. The air isn't air. It's a curtain of water. Excruciating, scalding, lava water. I reach out, grab the charred plug, and yank it from the socket just as Leon grabs me and hauls me backward.

Leon drags me in one rough pull, then the extinguisher is back in his hands and he's battling the flames that I knew would grow once again. This time, when it shrinks, it keeps dwindling until it disappears entirely under the white mountain. Like he's unsure it won't burst again, Leon sprays the wall, the ceiling, the socket, repeatedly.

Now that it's gone, I can feel more than burning of my palm, but the rawness of my throat. Most of all, as I look at the scorched stove, melted countertops, and ruined walls, my chest feels like it's caving in.

I nearly burned down the bakery.

It's supposed to be a sob, but I choke out a series of coughs in time with Leon, who sounds worse than I do. Without any noise from the fire, each ragged cough he releases is loud enough it sends a pang in my chest. He lifts me up and pulls me away from the kitchen, outside where we can both breathe in less toxic air.

"Are you o—" He's cut off by a series of coughs. He needs water. And a doctor. Just to make sure he's all right.

Before I mindlessly go back inside in search of a bottle, someone screams my name. I turn just as Sofia tackles me. "Gracias a Dios," she breathes out. "We saw smoke. What happened?"

Titi Sandra appears, out of breath, her eyes wide and wild. I've never seen her like this, not even first thing in the morning. She's on the phone but hangs up when she reaches me, pulling Sofia off to grab my shoulders. "Are you okay?" She gives me a once-over.

I turn toward Leon, who's hunched over, catching his breath. My eyes burn. "He needs a doctor," my voice cracks. "He inhaled a lot of smoke. Because of me. I left the rag in the oven. I think I pressed bake or self-clean. I don't know. It's my fault. Can you get him to a doctor?"

"An ambulance is on the way," Titi Sandra's voice as calm

as if she was simply reminding me to clean up my room. "He'll be okay."

I duck under her grip and kneel before Leon. I grab his face with my hand that isn't screaming in pain, forcing him to look at me so I can check for any—I don't know. Something wrong. Something that the smoke did to him. His eyes are red, barely a hint of white surrounding the ocean and there's soot on his face, on my hands, in his hair. If there's something wrong with him, I'll *never* forgive myself.

"That was dangerous."

He clears his throat. "I couldn't let your family's bakery go up in flames."

"Better it than you." The guilt plummets from my chest to my stomach.

The aunts think of this bakery as another member of the family. Not only have I spent so much time fantasizing about a life without them, on my own, I just ruined their biggest dream of all. Maybe this is punishment. Maybe it's karma for thinking such useless things and it's the universe's way of making sure I don't change my fate, don't break the curse. Punishment for hurting Leon.

Still, I would rather have it burn to the ground than Leon get hurt.

"Hey," Leon says roughly, like he's battling with a cough. "You're okay."

"I'm sorry," I say to him, and look toward Titi who's facing the glass door like she's wavering on whether or not she can go in. "I'm sorry," I tell her, but she doesn't look at me.

Neither does Sofia, who fits her hand with Titi's.

They'll resent me for this. I don't know how long this will push back the opening, how much of an impact this will have. God, how much it will cost to fix it all. They poured so much money into this . . . do they have enough left? Even if they forgive me, this is too far. This isn't a mistake that a *sorry* can fix.

My fault.

Leon's hands grip the back of my head and he presses my face into his bare chest. His arms move around me, pulling me closer to him. I stiffen. I shouldn't be getting comforted. I put him in danger, God if I didn't go in and point out the extinguisher he probably would have stayed there and fought the fire with only his shirt. His body is slick with heat and sweat, and mine's pretty much the same.

But I can't help my arms tightening around him as I let the tears fall, hidden in his embrace. When our bodies shake, I'm not sure if it's from my crying or his coughing, but whenever I pull away to check, he squeezes his hold on me.

I can't believe that I *can* believe Leon would do this. I have no trouble understanding why he charged in, determined to save my family's bakery. That's the kind of guy he is. But after what happened at Arno's? After I hurt him? He should be nothing like the guy I fell in love with.

The problem is that I should be shocked, but I'm not—it's so Leon. And I can't believe I ever doubted his goodness.

The sound of sirens echo in the distance, but I remain intertwined with Leon. This way I can feel and hear his heartbeat, uneven, but still going. Nothing too crazy. I focus on it, until the sirens are directly behind us, and the doors begin to slam.

I yank myself free and dash toward the first uniformed man I see, gripping a duffel in his hands. "He inhaled way too much smoke." I point toward Leon. "You have to take care of him."

The young paramedic infuriatingly looks me up and down. "You'll need to be checked out as well."

"I'm *fine*," I grind out, waving a hand.

The paramedic reaches for it and flips it, so my palm faces up. He says something but his words turn mumbled when I finally get a look at my hand. There's no skin left. It's this runny mix of red and white.

"Oh." Bile rises up my throat. "Oh."

Everything fades out as I fall face-first into the paramedic.

CHAPTER 26

HRBC Lesson #15: Embrace Rejection

Mari: If a date doesn't go well, it's not the end of the world!

Sofia: Consider each failure a lesson, a learning experience. It's science. The more you test things out, the more likely your next experiment will succeed.

While most girls my age would fight with their family about being an adult, having freedom and extra responsibilities, today I'm glad to be considered a kid. Kids get to shake off problems and mistakes. That's what I've been doing since last night to this afternoon.

Sofia twirls my hair while I lay on her lap on the couch. Marisol's head rests on my leg as she reads another chapter in a high-pitched tone trying to muffle the aunts' voices in the kitchen. My hand doesn't hurt as much wrapped tightly in gauze, and with the ice pack currently on top of it. It doesn't feel great, but it's bearable. What isn't bearable is the guilt. I made the biggest mistake I could have possibly made, and what has my family done? Comforted me like I did nothing wrong. Even knowing I never wanted to be a part of the bakery's future, of *their* future.

But all I've been doing is pretending I hadn't almost burned my family's hopes and dreams because I was careless and wanted to make up with an ex-boyfriend, which I couldn't even manage to do.

As vigorously as I've been pretending not to listen, I haven't heard my aunts fiercely whispering about the costs, replacements, the bakery, equipment, potential loans. That, along with getting a flashback of Leon's face dangerously close to the flames, the sound of his coughs, and how the way then and now, it still makes my pulse beat to the speed of light.

I want to text him if he's okay. I know he is. Of course he is.

But he did inhale a lot of smoke. I should check in on him and make sure he's all right.

Yet there's this overwhelming urge to throw up whenever I find his contact name and I get the flashbacks of the night all over again. Worst of all, what if I call him and he's *not* okay?

In a burst of confidence, which I know I'll lose in thirty seconds, I hastily text Leon and ask for a phone call. That way I can hear his voice, know if he's truly okay. Then I toss my phone to the side and rub my quickening heartbeat.

When Titi Neva joins us with a solemn but not somber face—for Titi Neva, there *is* a difference—I know the time for fantasy is over.

As if sensing my unease, she presses a kiss on my forehead. "You've been up all night, mi amor, go get some sleep."

"What's the damage?" I sit up. "What's going on?"

Titi Ivy, still in her T-shirt dress from last night, waves at Titi Neva to follow her out the door. As she passes me, she says,

"Don't you worry, my firstborn. We'll take care of everything."

With Zoe in her arms, Mom joins us, Titi Sandra close behind.

I swallow, my throat tightening. My eyes land on the sleeping Zoe. She doesn't know how lucky she has it, napping in Mom's arms. Must be nice to be oblivious to the world of broken hearts and family debt.

"I'm sorry," I blurt out.

Mom sits beside me, pushing her shoulders against mine. "It was an accident. All that matters is you're okay."

My gaze lands on Titi Sandra. "Are we going into debt?"

"We? Hush, child." She looks me up and down as if I don't know what I'm talking about. Which, I guess I don't. I never have. "It's a simple matter of paying for repairs, new stoves."

Does she realize how her voice grows distant, just like her eyes do at that last word? Out of all the aunts, Titi Sandra is the one who loves to bake the most. The idea for the bakery came from her. The other aunts like to cook, talk to people, decorate pastries, but Titi, even after a shower and slicking her hair back with a pound of gel, always has a scent of flour clinging to her.

I remember the exact name of the model the stove was because it was one of the first times Titi Sandra's pitch skyrocketed from excitement. *Gas and electric. Efficient burners. Extra side dish warmers. Two hundred twenty volts. Porcelain cooktops.* She described it with a whimsical look in her eyes, the same as when Marisol talks about her books. Titi Sandra's never spoken that way about one of her cases.

And I destroyed that feeling for her in minutes.

"Okay, then, how much?"

For a moment, I think, *I'm working, and maybe it won't be so bad. Not enough to cut into my gap-year funds.* Then I throw the thought away. Yeah, I did make a mistake, but it's not enough that I need to sacrifice my own dreams to try to make up for it. I can pay it back, one day, but not at the expense of my future.

Titi Sandra gives me the Stare. The narrow, burning stare that will brand her wide eyes into your skin if you don't get away quick enough. "This is adult business. You're a child. In what world would a daughter be forced to spend thousands—"

"Thousands?"

"Enough," she snaps, and I flinch. "The only thing I need from you is to sleep and put some of my eye cream under those bags. You look as old as Ivy."

She stomps off and I try to let her words sink in, but thousands? The fact that she slipped up at all points to how this is affecting her. How *I've* affected her.

The guilt wells up within me, this time with the added worry of if Titi Sandra will ever forgive me. I can't blame her if she doesn't. Not unless I earn her forgiveness.

I turn to Mom. "What kind of thousands are we talking? A-couple-month's-rent thousands? Starting-up-a-new-business thousands?"

Sofia perks up from behind me, her green tea mask drying in spots around her face. "The-hot-tub-Amelia-and-I-have-been-begging-for thousands?"

Mom shakes her head. "Both of you, enough."

"I can donate my plasma," I say, and mean it.

"I can donate an organ on the black market," Sofia says, and I *hope* she doesn't mean it.

My mom flicks my forehead. "Nice try."

Everyone is acting pretty normal for having their dreams postponed.

Postponed, because I'll fix this somehow. Nobody has scolded me for my mistake or has looked at me like they wished Mom had never met the son of anarchy. I should be grateful. I *am* grateful.

But the back-to-normal personalities are giving me two things: whiplash. And this on-edge feeling like any moment someone might decide they hate me and will let me know.

A part of me would rather I get scolded already, so I won't be bracing for it. I can feel anxiety slithering under my skin, waiting to send panicked signals to all my extremities.

"Is nobody really going to act mad at me?" I ask anyone willing to do such a thing.

Mom is the one who answers. "*Mad* is for purposeful actions. Not for genuine mistakes. You being safe is all that matters to us."

I rub my temples rough enough to see stars. "Somehow that makes me feel worse."

Mom stands. "If you're not going to get some sleep, why don't you two get out of here? Find something to do. Get your mind off—"

"My horrendous night, the fire, my ex-boyfriend there to

witness it all, the family curse." My voice rises way too high for anyone to believe I'm feeling okay.

"All right." Sofia yanks my hair back, also done with me spiraling, "It's all going to be okay."

I turn to her. "Can you take me to Leon's house?"

"Of course."

We head out, and Sofia opens the door for me. Even waits for me to get in, buckles me in, then shuts it. Like I'm fragile.

The drive is silent, and Sofia's hand is linked in mine the whole time. When we reach Leon's house, his dad sits outside, having a cigarette.

"Dad smokes sometimes," Leon told me once when we were dating. "He tries to hide it, and even told me only idiots smoke. But he does it when he's stressed. And I pretend not to know so he doesn't feel guilty."

We arrive at Leon's house, where I see Connor smoking outside. When I don't move, Sofia gives my hand a squeeze. "Go on."

"Can you come with me?"

"Why?" she asks gently. "You know how to stand on your own."

It sounds like such a lie. But I get up when Connor stands, hurriedly putting out the cigarette under his boot. I stop just before the front step he stands on.

"I'm sorry," I tell him. "I'm the reason he got hurt."

He looks at me for a moment, and I brace myself for a scolding, for him to tell me to stay away from his son and his house. But his hand is gentle when it reaches the top of my head. "You're a kid. You're allowed to make mistakes." He points a thumb behind him. "Leon is fine. He's been up all night, so he just fell asleep. That's all that matters."

The softer his voice is, the more my bottom lip trembles. Waiting for a blow and being met with kindness instead feels undeserving.

"If I'm quiet, may I see him?"

He taps my head twice. "Course you can, kiddo." He moves out of my path, tells me the direction of his room like I haven't been hundreds of times.

But when I enter the hallway lined with photo frames and sculptures his dad makes in his free time, it feels like hundreds of years. Unlike my house, it smells like hard work here. Like sawdust and musk and freshly sanded wooden panels.

I pause at a frame just before Leon's green bedroom door. It's golden, and a tiny heart sits at the top of it. Leon passes this every day to enter his room.

A photo of him and me, our arms fighting with each other to be the one to hug the other more, my homecoming dress caught in a slight breeze, and his too-big-for-him-at-the-time tux unbuttoned.

We spent that night eating snacks and dancing in circles, even when I was embarrassed to get the steps wrong, and kissed in the rain when we were supposed to be home.

He had to have remembered the night every time he glanced over at this picture. Every time he needed to go into his room. And he never took it down.

My feet feel like bricks as I let myself in.

Leon sleeps on his side, facing me. His dark comforter covering most of his face, and his hair teasing his forehead with the tiny fan on his bedside blowing at him. He can never sleep without the noise.

I tiptoe over, pulling his bottom drawer open. There, like he never moved it even once, is the tiny cactus-shaped humidifier I got him when I worried his fan obsession would give him a sore throat, along with all the essential oils and bottles of water.

Swallowing the lump in my throat, I pour a mixture together in the device and switch the fan for it.

As softly as I can, I sit on the edge of the bed. In this position, he's curved in a way that makes it feel as if he made room for me. Here, I can pretend like it's just us two, with no baggage or pain between us.

And it brings me back to the love I had for him before and makes me realize that I have so much more of it now.

I peel back the covers, giving his nose more room to breathe. My thumb brushes across his forehead, pushes his hair from his face. It makes room for the smallest scar to reveal itself at the side of his head.

A memory he formed without me, but one I want to hear about. I want to hear about every single thing I missed. I want him to trust me enough to confide in me. I want to press my lips on his skin.

I want him to love me too.

"I'm glad you're okay," I whisper. "I'm mad at you for not leaving me to deal with it myself. I know I should be grateful. I *am* grateful. But I've never been more scared in my entire life."

Here, in this tiny room, with nobody to hear me, it seems safe enough to say words that feel scrambled in my head. Here, it doesn't matter if they don't make sense. It's not embarrassing to get them out.

"I love you. I know we're young, but we were young when my aunt sent you away, and she thought the distance would make that disappear. And two years went by, and it's as present as ever. So just because we're young, doesn't make it any less true, right?"

I watch his brows press together and pause. I don't want to speak loud enough to wake him, but I want to reach his heart here, even if he doesn't know it.

"I wish you never left. I wish I wasn't a coward. I wish you told me about my aunt. I wish I told my aunts off. I wish I never started a fire."

He makes some sleep-induced groan as he shifts his position. His knees pull up, and it brings me closer to his face. His hand snakes around my wrist so that I nearly fall on top of him. Instead, I close my eyes, trying to not put too much weight on him.

Like we're normal. Like everything is okay.

And he is fine, and I am fine, and nobody is hurt. That *is* all that matters. And so is doing the right thing, even when I'm scared too.

So I untangle myself from him and walk back to Sofia and ask her to take me home. To do the right thing.

CHAPTER 27

HRBC Lesson #16: How to Be Yourself in the Best Way
Sofia: At the end of the day, you can only be you. If you feel like you're working too hard on being impressive, instead of being impressively you, then take a step back. Eat some French fries. Chill out. You're lovable the way you are.

Night begins to fall by the time we get home. Everyone is showering, cleaning, hushing Mari and Zoe into sleep. So I get unready from the day too. Sofia doesn't ask what happened, just tells me about another anime she's watching and I lay on the top of my bunk, counting the pieces of popcorn on the ceiling until Sofia begins to snore.

I can hear the distant movement of metal against metal. Of course it's Titi Sandra. She's stressed, and she *always* stress cooks in the middle of the night.

For hours I've been thinking about how to make things right with my family, even Titi Sandra, who doesn't realize how much losing Leon hurt me. But I also am waiting for my own apology too. I'm owed one.

When two parties need to make up for different reasons, who goes first?

With a sigh, I gather what I need and tiptoe out the room,

which is ridiculous since Sofia can sleep through a fire alarm. Just like she sleeps through my loud curse when my toe knocks into the side of a stair.

Limping, I make my way down toward the kitchen's light.

Titi Sandra is alone, continuing the empanada production line. Gently, from her phone resting somewhere among the mess on the counter, Beethoven's *Moonlight Sonata* is playing. When she spots me enter, we hold each of our gazes.

"If you have something to say, say it."

I don't flinch. "I'll pay you back. One day. When I'm back from my gap year."

Her mouth moves, like she's chewing on the inside of her cheek. And then, shockingly, Titi Sandra looks away first. "We don't need your money."

"You do," I remind her, "or money in general. Why does it matter if it's mine?"

Tired and all, my heart rate rockets. Despite the sudden confidence I have, it's a foreign feeling speaking this way to Titi. Even despite that, I feel sure and confident in myself.

I used to be so caught up in trying to rush through everything, to fix all my "problems" to fix me, but I don't think I was broken enough to need that. I wanted to break this women-made curse I let hang over me, blamed it for my own bad luck. But I know now that it's okay to slow down, to not put so much pressure on myself, on my life. To do whatever I want, even if my family doesn't understand.

Things may not have worked out the way I thought they would, but that's okay. It's probably going to keep happening to me, and I'll keep taking missteps, and I'll keep thinking I'm on the right path and maybe have to hop on another one but that doesn't seem too scary anymore.

At least, no matter what, I know that I'm in charge of my life, and I can always pick myself back up. And when it's hard, I *can* have the freedom to deal with it on my own—or reach out to my family.

It's all my choice.

Titi Sandra watches me, no heat in her gaze, no tension in her shoulders. I feel her looking at me, *really* looking at me, before she says, quietly, "The adults are supposed to take care of children, not take their money. We have insurance. And you don't need to give any more money 'out of principle.'"

"If adults take care of children, they should let them make their own decisions," I counter. "Whether it be paying money for things they broke. Or going away for a gap year."

Titi Sandra sighs. "Do I have to hear about this program again?"

"You don't have to, but it will be nice to get used to it since I'm going." Titi Sandra shakes her head and opens her mouth to disagree, but I go on. "I'm my own person, and it's time I start acting like it. It's time you started treating me like it too."

She sighs, drilling circles into her temples as she leans back against the kitchen sink. Titi still hasn't even taken off her pant suit, her heels. It must be exhausting having to always keep it together.

I go on, because the more I talk, the more weightless I feel. "I'm going to do the program. I'm okay with the unknown. I'm not scared."

Titi Sandra closes her eyes and I can't tell if she's processing the words or shutting me out. "I suppose you want an apology for sending Leon away."

"I don't suppose. I know I deserve one," I say, "for that, and for hiding it from me all this time. You helped send Leon away, regardless of why you *thought* it was best for us. And when he came for my birthday, you sent him away again. He deserves one too." *I know because I'm still working on my own.*

"I am not sorry, though, not completely. You both were sixteen-year-old, unfocused, children. As an adult, it's my job to take care of you, to do what's best for you even if you don't see it." When I open my mouth to interrupt, she goes on. "And I have already apologized to Leon."

I blink. "What?"

Her lips pull into a small smile. "When he came back this summer, he confronted me about what we did. He said he understood why we did it, but he was and still is, a good person, and we made him feel like he wasn't. Then he told us he wouldn't tell you the truth, because he'd never want to put a rift in our relationship, but said *we* should tell you—if we ever had the confidence." She lets out a light laugh. "After that, I found myself warming up to him. He managed to stand up to me, demand an apology, offered to keep our relationship with you untainted, and called me a coward all in one breath."

I rub my face. It's like every new thing I learn Leon had to go through behind my back, everything he did, makes me fall for him more. And all I've done is wreck our relationship, and all he's done is secretly take care of it, of me.

"You've only apologized once in your life, haven't you?"

Her smile widens. "Maybe." She goes back to the station, starts filling dough like she needs something to do as she talks. "I'll tell you a secret, one I'll never admit to ever again." My curiosity peaks, I lean over. "I'm the oldest of the aunts."

I forget to be mad and my eyes widen. "No way."

She chuckles. "Erase that from your memory now." She folds the dough in a crescent moon. "Our mother passed away when the girls were teenagers. Neva was thirteen, and I had just hit twenty. It left us all messy, unsure. Her biggest fear was us growing apart without her, and I thought it was my responsibility as the eldest to make sure that never happened. To take care of everyone, make the decisions, go to law school, get the highest-paying job I could—all so we could stick together and my sisters wouldn't have to worry about anything. I never wanted to be a lawyer."

My eyes widen. "No way. I thought you came out the womb saying *objection.*"

"That's not how a divorce lawyer works." She shakes her head. "And it's true. Before we lost our mom, she always picked me first to knead the dough. Or season the meat. Or flour the cutting boards. It was our bonding time." Her eyes go a little glossy. "Our mother worked two full-time jobs to take care of us, so we only saw her before dawn and after dusk. Cooking became a form of love to me. Taking some of the burdens of my mother, feeding my sisters, figuring out everyone's taste and watching them smile when I made their favorite. I may have trouble saying 'I love you' to family, but it has always been easier for me to feed them, and to me, that means the same thing."

"So you wanted to be a baker." It dawns on me, watching as she makes two empanadas without messing up, barely looking down at what her hands are doing. Since its conception, the bakery had always seemed like a group effort. Everyone cooked and baked well. Everyone liked to do it. Why not start a business?

But of course, the dream had to have been formed by someone *first*.

"Yes." Her eyes glazing over. "It may seem like I only care about the business side of things, but it's because I'm good at it. If I could roll up my sleeves and spend my days cooking, I would."

When I think back on it, Titi Sandra has always been the most attentive to the smallest of details. Managing the budgets on ingredients, not wanting to spend too much money, but willing to shell out more for quality ingredients. Spending weeks hiring and firing different designers until someone's vision aligned perfectly with hers. Every detail needed her approval, the tile in the bathroom, the entry doorknob, the tablecloths, and vitrine shape to hold the pastries.

I thought I was the only one who wasn't seen completely, but I realize that we're all guilty of it in some way.

"Why didn't you just become a baker?"

"It was too much of a risk, and there were too many people in this house." She gestures toward me. "And babies on the way."

"I'm baby."

She smiles at that. "Our first one. All this time, because I was the oldest, I thought it was my responsibility to be in charge, to head the house, and I expected the same of you. I'm sorry. For that, and for not telling you the truth. I should have."

Something in me eases, deflates. I think it's most of my anger. There's still some swirling within me, but not enough to stop me from circling the counter and wrapping my arms around Titi Sandra.

"I'm still mad at you," I tell her stiff body, "but I forgive you. Only if you forgive me for not telling the truth either. And only if you promise not to do anything like that again."

She raises a brow. "I can't promise not to look out for you."

I narrow my eyes at her. "Look out for me sure, as long as it doesn't sabotage my happiness. Or hurt people around me. Or require two-year-long secrets."

She looks at me like she's trying to hunt through every piece of my brain and keeps finding new corners within she's never discovered before. Then she relaxes into the hug. "Deal."

The sharp clapping of applause startles Titi Sandra and I out of our hug. Sofia pops her head in, smiling widely and the aunts follow in behind. Sofia wraps her arms around Titi Sandra and I, squeezing tightly. "See? Look at us, one big happy family. Knew it would happen."

I try and fail to wiggle out of her grip. "You guys are freaks. Were you really just listening in the hall?"

"Maybe you two were speaking too loudly," she says as Titi Neva and Ivy pull me in a hug.

"We're sorry," they say in unison.

Titi Ivy says, "We only want what's best for you."

Titi Neva says, "Even if what's best isn't here with us."

It's a little embarrassing, how quick the tears fill my eyes. I manage to clear them enough I spot Mom standing by the doorway, smiling at me knowingly. I think that's her look, I can't tell because I'm just shocked that Zoe isn't in her arms.

Titi Ivy lets me go and pinches Titi Sandra's cheek. "Our eldest learned how to stand her ground. The insurance money went through. We haven't throttled one another throughout all of this. Aren't we the loveliest family?"

"Sure," Titi Sandra answers, shifting which foot she leans on, uncomfortable with the sudden audience.

And in this moment I realize that family isn't obligation but a borrowed gift between us. We can seek it out for comfort when we want it, we can prioritize whoever needs it the most, we can leave it alone, but it never fades. It may feel like it wavers, but the foundation is always steady.

Forgiveness is always available, but only when asked for.

Relief pulls the weight off of my shoulders, and I let the aunts smother me in hugs and compliments until they tire out.

"All right," Mom says, at the end of a sigh. "Let's all love one another tomorrow. It's time for bed."

Mom presses a kiss on my forehead as I pass her. "I'm proud of you, hija."

"I'm proud of you too," I tell her, walking past her confusion. Proud of her standing up to Titi, standing up for me, for loving the mess I am.

When I get to my room, Sofia follows close behind. "Wow, I can't believe that just happened. I've never witnessed Titi

Sandra apologize about anything. Ever. You really are a curse breaker. Miracle worker. Built different."

I manage a small smile. "I'm still in disbelief too."

Sofia frowns, analyzing my face. "You look like someone ran over your BTS figurine. What's wrong?"

I nearly say nothing, already having an excuse climb my throat, but she has perfected Titi Sandra's stare and I'm all out of guts. So I tell her how I can't bring myself to face Leon, how I'm terrified he'll never forgive me.

"I've always thought you had only one brain cell, but now I think you don't even have the one," Sofia says.

I sigh. "Come on, I already feel bad enough."

She shakes her head. "That's not what I mean. You have something real with Leon. It's messy and delicate, but it's real. Don't screw it up."

My jaw drops. "Don't screw it up? Have you not listened to anything I've said? It's already ruined."

"The same way you made a mistake and fixed it with the aunts is the same thing you have to do with Leon. You messed up. So what? Join the rest of the world. If you're not going to try to say sorry, then you don't have a right to be sad about it."

She's right. I haven't thought about finding a way to tell Leon I'm sorry, truly sorry, and explain myself. I just thought, it's so ruined there's nothing that I can do about it, but I guess, even if there isn't, I still have to try.

"That's some strong tough love, you've been hanging out with Titi Sandra too much."

"I'm practicing my lawyer voice."

"I love you." My chest tightens. "You're a perfect sister, and I don't tell you enough. You are the bravest, smartest, funniest, prettiest girl I know."

She looks at me, her cheeks turning pink. "That is the most cliché thing you have ever said, I'm so embarrassed for you."

"I hate you."

"I hate you more."

It's a gift that when I climb my way into my bunk, my exhausted body falls asleep almost as soon as I lay my head to my pillow.

CHAPTER 28

HRBC Lesson #17: Love Yourself (Sofia's Version)

Listen, I don't believe in the whole *you can't love someone before you love yourself*. Sometimes the people around us can see us for how amazing we are, even when we can't. You are the girl who forces herself to read books for kids half her age to make her sister happy. A girl who loves so much she braces through humiliating viral moments and still leaves the house. A girl who remembers to take her baby sister from her mom when she hasn't showered. A girl who is freakishly observant and knows when someone needs comfort. Also sometimes funny. A girl who loves so deeply because her heart is never ending.

Love yourself because you are beloved.

I wake to Mari sitting on my stomach. "Titi Ivy said your days of being sleeping beauty are over."

I shove her off me and try to pull the covers above my head. "Tell her restart the movie."

But she climbs back on and sits back on my stomach. "Nope. Titi Ivy read with me yesterday."

"Oh, and now you're her little minion." I sit up, shoving her again. "Remember who taught you what a library card was before your loyalties change so easily."

She giggles and runs off.

"Little brat," I groan, and force myself up before someone else in this house, someone heavier, decides to dive onto my stomach. I adjust my sweatpants back to the middle, since sleep sent them to the side, and slide on one slipper of mine and one of Sofia's when I can't find the other in the pair.

I half sleepwalk downstairs, where the aunts are bickering and *The Nanny*, Mom's favorite show, plays on the living room TV.

"Amelia," Titi Ivy shouts when she spots me walking over the carpet. "You're the final vote. Lottery ticket or scratch."

Titi Sandra makes coffee behind them, and I'm tempted to finally try some. "Who wants which?"

"I'm feeling lotto," Titi Ivy says. "I had a dream. I know the numbers. Lots of fours."

I look toward Titi Neva, who shakes her head. "Your aura is pale this morning, untrustworthy. The energy today is vibrant, energized. Let's do the golden scratch tickets. Seven of them exactly. My crystals hum when I think of that number."

"I vote Titi Neva's choice," I mumble, finding a place on the couch beside Mom.

Titi Neva and Ivy head off to the bodega to buy tickets, and it takes me the entire theme song before I look over at Mom and realize my little sister isn't on her chest.

"Where is Zoe?"

Mom tenses, and she starts picking at her nails. "With a babysitter," she says, and I would have expected an entire crowd to start a mob dance to the tune of Beethoven's *Moonlight Sonata* before I thought those words would come from

Mom's mouth. "Titi Ivy's friend runs a day care. I'm . . . going to start bringing Zoe there once a week."

Now, *that* makes my eyes fill with tears. "I'm so proud of you."

She shakes her head, pressing a kiss on my cheek. "That's my line."

"Amelia, come help prep," Titi Sandra calls me over. "You think because you're going away for a year you can skip on cooking duty for the rest of the summer?"

She says it casually, like she's scolding me . . . but it's an acknowledgment that I'm leaving. An acceptance that I want to go.

My smile fills my face.

"Yes, ma'am." I join her, grabbing an apron.

Sofa leaves with Mari to the library, and Mom falls asleep on the couch. Titi Sandra and I work together, humming along to the classical music lightly playing from her phone.

It's a smooth operation, and when it's not, when I inevitably spill something or drop a plate or put too much adobo on the beef, Titi Sandra sighs and says, "The graceful cooking gene really skipped you."

But it's nice to know she realizes how different I am from her, even if it's in just a small way of being a failure in the kitchen.

I'm sweating by the time she gets a phone call. She takes it in the corner while I try to cut up chicken breast thin enough for empanadas without adding to the tiny scars already denting the skin on my fingers where I've cut myself throughout my life.

"Right, of course," Titi Sandra says. "No need to bring it over, I'll come pick it up in a few days. How heavy? Ah, I see. Then I'll have the girls help me, no need for you boys to come over." I stand up a little straighter. "Oh, oh, is that right? Well. Yes, if that's what he thinks is best. Do you need anything? Okay, thanks, Connor. Goodbye."

When she sees me staring at her, she says, "Another skill you failed to master: subtlety."

"It's not one I care to learn."

Her smirk vanishes as fast as it appears. "Connor was going to drop off one of the new stoves I ordered. Wanted to do it while he still has his staff on the clock since Leon's going away."

The knife I'm holding stills midair. "What is that supposed to mean?"

"Connor said Leon's leaving."

"He's *leaving*? Where?" *What?*

"I didn't ask too many details. He said he wants to take a year off." Am I making up the guilt at the end of her words, the aftertaste of it? "Connor's brother's got his own shop down south in Florida. Leon wants to see if he feels at home there."

It feels like hands are kneading my stomach like its dough. I'm a part of the reason Leon didn't feel welcome here, in the place he was born. That feels so heavy, I'm not sure how I'm supposed to come back from it. Me, along with my aunts? It's a wonder Leon even spoke to *me* at *all*.

Everything is happening so fast. Fully realizing my feelings, fully messing things up, and now Leon leaving before I can even attempt to explain myself. I need some time. I need to speak to him. Catch him. If I want to.

Your choice. It's time I start making them.

"When is he leaving?" I ask.

"I assume he'll be dropped off soon—"

I barely let her finish before I spin on my heel. I hurry toward the door, then run back to the kitchen. "Titi," I say, but she's already holding her keys up to me.

"Remember, red means stop."

"Bye."

Getting in the SUV, driving off, it's all a blur. It only comes into focus when I turn the corner on to Leon's street. I speed up toward his house.

I don't remember if I put the vehicle in park before I'm out, pounding on the door. Connor answers, his eyes wide. "Amelia, what—"

"Where's Leon?"

His eyes fill with understanding. "You missed him." Cement churns in my stomach. "The train leaves in an hour. I just dropped him off at the station."

I barely catch the end of his sentence before I'm back to driving, speeding, praying not to be pulled over. It's like the universe is testing my resolve, my determination. I catch every red light, get stuck behind every slow car, yield to every pedestrian.

Do you really want to catch him? Or are you going to get scared again?

It's like each stop is an opportunity to turn around, go back home. But screw that. Screw being scared. I keep going, keep moving. I park in the first open space I find at the end of the station in case it's all filled.

I realize I'm a walking—well, running—cliché right now. Trying to catch the person they care about before they travel thousands of miles away. But I will happily be a cliché if that means I get my happy ending.

Maybe I hated it to begin with, but thank God the aunts made me do track. I *fly* through the lot, weaving through cars honking at me as I sprint toward the automatic doors.

I move so quick, I ram into them before they open fully.

The force of it knocks me back, and my teeth rattle. One of my slippers flies off behind me.

I rub the side of my face that got the brunt of the blow, but I pick myself up anyway. I'm slower, but just barely, with a bit of a limp, being shoeless, and my bones still rattling under my skin.

Elbows and bodies press into me as I get into the thick of the station.

It's rush hour, and everyone is leaving or entering or lost and trying to find which gate signs to follow or sitting on a bench inconveniently placed under the high-ceilinged, fully glass building.

Florida, where is Florida?

There, a sign that reads train 612 is heading to Miami. I rush over to the lines making their way, and when I reach the turnstile, it locks up. I push it again, but it doesn't move.

Someone in a uniform snaps at me, "You need to scan your ticket."

I look over beside me and catch a man holding his barcode

on a black circle. It lights up green, then his turnstile allows him through. I move my gaze back over to the older woman. Around her sixties, I'm guessing.

I rack my brain and run through the list of older celebrities the aunts are into and settle on "Oh my God," I shout, pointing behind her, "is that *Denzel Washington*?" I swear this woman almost falls flat on her face as she whirls.

I grip the edges of the turnstile and hop over it. Of course, I am no longer on the track team and my balance is not up to par. My legs get tangled up behind me and my knee slams on to the silver marbled floors.

Pain rattles up my leg. My teeth grind together, and the pain is so strong and quick, nausea climbs my throat. But I swallow it down and limp-run my way forward.

The train has already pulled up, the doors open. Several workers stand by each opening, a device in their hand that pours a red light over each passenger's tickets stub. If Leon is already on the train, I'll have to bulldoze my way through the workers, and I will, but I'll end up on the train equivalent of a no-fly list. No-ride list?

My heart pounds as I call out Leon's name, working my way down the platform. Some people jump as I go, my voice startling them. Separate from the station, there are fewer people here, less chatter.

Just my annoying voice filling the air, desperately shouting for the person I love to answer me.

Hope dwindles in my chest as I make it toward the end of the platform. I haven't seen him yet, and he hasn't heard me yet.

Unless he has.

And he hopped on the train faster, to get away from me. I can't blame him. If that's the case, then he has every right to do that.

Just like I have the right to keep moving forward.

At the very end of the platform, I see him. In jeans and a loose-fitting sweater, his backpack in one hand, the other extending the ticket out.

"Leon!"

He jerks back. He looks to his left, then his right, where I'm doing my waddle-run. My heartbeat skyrockets. Right as the employee brings the red light over the ticket, I reach them.

And snatch the paper from them both.

"Amelia?" Shock coats his voice.

"Excuse me?" The woman holds out her hand impatiently.

My brain tries hard to keep up with the rest of me, but it's too slow to use critical thinking skills. All it can compute is ticket equals Leon on train. We don't want that.

So I shove the ticket in my mouth.

They both stare at me. My brain starts to catch up to logic. My tongue tries not to convulse at the taste of fingers and ink and paper.

"Ma'am," the employee says, but that's all she says.

And, like, valid.

Leon grabs my arm, pulling me toward the edge of the platform, away from the employee holding a hand to her chest as the next passenger holds out their ticket impatiently.

Like after a child puts a crayon in their mouth, Leon holds out his palm expectantly.

"No," I say, my voice half a cough as the taste makes me gag. "If I give you this, you'll go on the train."

"That's kind of the point of the ticket," he says slowly, "but right now I'm concerned with you choking on it."

I chew on it, enough that I'm sure the barcode would be ruined, then I let it fall from my mouth to his hand. He doesn't even seem grossed out. He just looks at the wet and invalid ticket, then sighs.

"Really? What are you doing?" He looks me up and down and I realize that I'm one slipper down, in pajamas, hair matted, and wearing a shirt four times my size. But I can handle the embarrassment that comes with it. It feels so small compared to how I feel about him.

"Trying to fix things."

He looks down at the ticket. "It's ruined," he says, "I guess I'll download the app."

"No, I mean *this*." I gesture between us, trying to catch my breath, hoping he doesn't download the app, because a phone will be a lot harder to chew on than a piece of paper. "I'm trying to fix *this*."

He frowns at the movement. "There's no need."

I can *feel* every pore in my skin growing hot.

It's hard to look at him for too long, so my gaze travels down to his feet, but that feels inauthentic, so I force myself to meet his stare.

"You're leaving. Again." Okay, horrible start, seeing as last time my own aunts sent him away. "I mean, were you going to go without saying goodbye?" Another bad start. Why am I accusing him? I should have rehearsed this on the car ride over.

"Would it have even mattered?" he asks quietly and my heart sinks.

"Of course it would have."

"Doesn't seem like it." He looks at the street while he speaks. "Not that I care. I'm used to it. My mom didn't want me, so I went away. Your aunts didn't think I was good enough, so I went away. You don't want me either. Who cares if I go on a trip without saying goodbye?"

"*Me,*" I say without thinking. "I care about you. I've always cared about you."

He steps back. "I'm fine. Besides, I'm only—"

"I'm sorry," I say, a little desperate at the lack of emotion, the lack of . . . well, anything in his face. "I realize now, though, even though everything happened like it did, if I still believed it to be true, I did the wrong thing. I should have never tried to hurt you. You never deserved it. No matter how mad I was, trying to hurt you wasn't the way to go. I know I'm better than that."

When he doesn't say anything, I go on. "I hope you know that you being back, it all was the same for me. I fell hard again, or maybe I never stopped falling and I knew I had to tell you the truth, but I was scared."

I grab one of his hands in both of mine. His hand in my palm, my soft fingers in his hardworking ones. Rough and cracked and covered in splinters from helping his father, helping my family, helping me.

"I'm sorry, Leon. For everything."

Strange how those words were what I wanted to say all along, yet they were the hardest to force out. Now that I've said them, I feel as if I can say them a hundred more times if that's what it would take.

He looks at me, heat in his gaze, and a little hope too. That breaks my heart, that he thought I didn't care, wouldn't care, at all. "It's okay."

"I'm *so* sorry," I continue, will continue for as long as it takes for Leon to believe me. "I know that's probably not enough but I am. I know everything that happened with my aunts now, I do, and I've had this anger toward you for so long and it grew into this nasty thing. I thought the only way I could get rid of it is if I made you feel the same. I mean, you ran toward a *fire* for me. And I have been so horrible to you."

"Amelia," he says again. "I said it's okay."

But I shake my head. "Doesn't feel like it. Not yet."

He grips the bottom of my chin so I can face him. Hope dangerously flutters in my chest, that, and so much love I have no idea where to put, so I drop my hands into fists at my sides.

"I'm sorry too." He gently runs his thumb across my jaw. "I know I should have told you the truth, especially after I saw how much it hurt you, me leaving, but I know how much your family means to you, how scared you were about how they'd react when you told them you wanted to go off on your own. I didn't want to mess that up. Especially after . . ." His voice cracks and he clears his throat. "My mom regretted having me move in with her. She probably regrets having me in the first place. You have four versions of a mother, and they all love you so much. I'd never want to ruin that."

It must be exhausting caring so much about other people. I can't believe he'd keep the secret, allow me to hate him, so I wouldn't fight with my family about it. He's way too good for me, but that's not an excuse. I need to step up and be someone he deserves too.

He's so hurt by his mother, and I wish I could soothe that pain. I'll never be able to understand what that feels like, but I know I want to make it better, even in the slightest. "I don't think your mother regrets having you, Leon." I place a hand on his cheek. "Maybe there is love in giving up what you can't properly cherish."

His breath hitches. He lowers himself so our faces are nearly touching. "I can cherish you."

Now my breath snags. It feels too good to be true. A part of me worries he may harbor some resentment toward me, but I think of how quick the aunts and I made up. I don't think forgiveness is completely letting go of the hurt. Forgiveness is accepting someone's apology and working toward healing together. I'm willing to do that. It seems like Leon is too.

"When you first got here," I say, "I didn't see it, that you cared about me."

"I know." His thumb runs across my cheek. "I guess I thought, at first, if I didn't ask for your forgiveness, you couldn't deny it. As long as I could annoy you enough to stay around you, it wouldn't be as bad as you not forgiving me for leaving.

I thought if I pushed too hard, I'd push you away. Lose you for good." He blinks. "Do you, though, forgive me?"

"Of course," I breathe out.

Leon was there before all that, before things got messy and I lost myself. And he loved me. I realize now that I am worthy of love as I am. From others if they want to, but more importantly, for myself.

Leon was just quicker to pick up on it.

"It was always going to be you, wasn't it?" I ask him, and he cocks his head to the side. I shake my head. "No, it wasn't, but it can be." If I want it to be. My choice, who I love and who loves me. "I love you, Leon."

He sucks in a breath, holds my gaze. Wordlessly, I see his inner thoughts, see him trying to find the truth in my face, in my words. I let him too, because I mean it. I always have.

"Can I say something?" he asks suddenly. When I nod, he goes on. "You have never looked more beautiful to me than you do right now."

A little embarrassment floods through me. "I know, I look ridiculous."

He grabs my arms. "No, I'm not joking. I mean it. You're beautiful. You're honest. And you're brave." He comes closer. "And really weird for eating half of my ticket."

My left ear heats up. "You're the worst," I tell him.

"I love you," he tells me.

"Oh, thank God," I say, "because it'd be so awkward if I was the only one."

He laughs, then grabs the back of my head and presses his

lips on mine. This time he is not soft and testing. His mouth is desperate as his hands tangle in my hair and his tongue marks every part of my mouth as his.

"Wait, wait, wait." I pull away with tremendous effort. "Before this goes literally any further, I need to tell you I'm leaving in a few months."

He frowns so quickly, I almost laugh. "You wanted to stop me from leaving to tell me *you* were?"

"I'm going away for a gap year. My choice. I want to figure out who I am, what I want to do, be. If you want, you can come. There is still time to apply. You were going away for a year too. Come with me, but only if you do it for you."

He tilts my chin up, his eyes hot on mine. Confusion flashes in his face, then he tilts his head. "And if I said no?"

I don't hesitate. "Then I'll miss you while I'm away."

He smiles widely, knowingly, and proud too. "Good. Now, can I ask something?"

"Sure."

"I loved this huge, dramatic confession you've injured yourself to make because you thought I was leaving, but why do you think I'm going away for a year? I wasn't going to leave permanently. I just wanted some space. I thought it would be good. And my uncle has been asking me to visit him forever. But I wasn't ghosting. Not again. I was only going to be gone a week."

My brain glitches and I look him up and down, my gaze snagging on his stuffed backpack. Right, that definitely isn't going to last more than a week. But that's what my aunt said. "Well." My cheeks heat as I try to figure out what's going on.

"Titi Sandra said so. She was on the phone with your dad, then told me you were going away for a year. Today."

He chews on his lip, like he's fighting a smile. "So before, she lied to you and sent me away, and now she lied to you again to send you *to* me."

I rub a hand over my face. "Amazing," I let out a breath. "She sent me here in a panic. I could have come less urgently, maybe avoided the bruises forming on my body." The train rumbles the floor, speeding away. "And now you missed your train to see your uncle."

Maybe Titi Sandra and I have a lot more in common than I thought. Good intentions—messy executions.

"I'll take the next one." Leon reaches for me. "You should come with me."

He snakes one hand around my waist, bringing me closer, but it is not close enough, as his lips find mine like that's their entire purpose in life, just to meet with my own. Breathing? Don't need to do that. No, I only need Leon's mouth on mine, fingers knotting my curls, heartbeat to heartbeat. I only need this to survive.

If there was ever a Hernandez curse—it was never a match for me.

EPILOGUE

It's hard to breathe with the entire weight of Leon on my back.

Literally, he's lying completely on me, crushing my body as he tries to get in the frame of my FaceTime call with the aunts. The bed creaks below seeing as it's meant to hold one body. But this is our third hotel since we've been traveling on the gap-year program together and we're used to sharing twin beds at this point. The twin beds just aren't used to us.

He snatches the phone right before I drop it on the carpet. "Wait, where's Mari?" he asks, and Titi Ivy pans the phone to Mari sitting on the floor against the new, fluffy couch. She peeks up from the pages and smiles. "Mari, how is it?"

"I love it," she tells Leon, who has made it his mission to get her to read every Percy Jackson book. "I can't believe the sequel is better than the first."

"Wait till you get to the fourth book."

Titi Neva steals the phone, and her face fills the screen. "Mi amors. My dreams told me to look out for you both today. Stay inside, order in."

"Oh my *God*," I hear Titi Ivy say in the background. "She was right *one* time about some scratch tickets and she's been telling everyone about her dreams every night since."

"*One* time was all it took to win us double the money to

replace the stoves and repair the smoke damage *and* get you a new nose?" Titi Neva says sweetly to Titi Ivy out of the frame. "Are you sure you want to speak to me that way?"

"Of course not," Titi Ivy replies just as cavity-sweet.

"Anyway," Titi Neva says, concern creasing her brows. "Did you guys spread the crystals I sent you? You know they need to be recharged during the day. Too much travel without cleansing is bad luck."

Leon presses a kiss to the side of my head. "No bad luck with this one."

There's a sound of someone dramatically vomiting. The screen pans again, and Sofia is sitting by a new round table made of marble, but that's not what catches my attention. It's the girl I've never seen before, sitting across from her, frowning at Sofia, who does.

"Sofia," I call out, "did you get the night-light I sent? Are you still having trouble sleeping in the dark by yourself?"

"Bite me," she shouts to the screen, then turns to the pretty-girl brunette grinning like she's going to use this information against Sofia. "She's joking. She's lying," Sofia tells her.

"Doesn't sound like it."

When Titi Ivy is back in control of the screen and her perfectly made-up face fills it, I ask her, "Where are Mom and Titi Sandra?"

"Your mother is still at the bakery because she refuses to close on time in case someone wants to purchase an empanada after five." She rolls her eyes. "Hardworking woman, that one."

"She sure is." I grin.

"As for Sandra, who knows? She hasn't come home for three days since staying over Jorge's house. Too good for us now." In in the distance, Zoe starts crying. Titi Ivy jumps up. "Oh, I'm on Zoe duty today. Okay, you two lovebirds, stay safe. Love you!"

A chorus of *love you*s all join in before the screen goes black.

When it does, Leon angles himself so I can move (and breathe properly) again. But when I make it onto my back, he positions himself on top of me once more, straddling me, the scent of our shared lavender shower gel circling us.

"I *also* love you," he tells me, the end of his gold locket—a picture of us hiding within it—falling over my neck.

"They were saying it to you too, you know," I say, my breath becoming erratic even without his full weight on me.

He presses a kiss on the side of my neck. "It's not a competition." He presses another just under my chin as I lose the ability to breathe, to think. "But I love you the most."

"Yeah, right," I say hoarsely.

He brings his lips to my ear. "Should I prove it?" he whispers.

I can do nothing but nod.

And he does.

ACKNOWLEDGMENTS

First and foremost, thanks go to the brightest star of my galaxy: Emily Anne. My rock, Miss Approachable herself, Emily Erin Forney. Emily Anne the Third. Emily Furney. Bee to my boo. Daisy to my strawberry. "Eight" Shorty. Can I call you Shorty? My person. The occasional Schmidt to my Nick Miller. The occasional Nick Miller to my Schmidt. Unfortunate platonic soulmate. There's no greater person on earth to me than you.

To my editor, Dainese, I'm so grateful to you. For, of course, loving *BAG* and acquiring it (shout-out to you), but also for the thoughtful and fun perspective you brought with every round of edits. Thank you to everyone on the Simon team who has done anything for me. Thank you Justin Chanda, Krista Vossen, Hilary Zarycky, Morgan York, Amaris Mang, Chrissy Noh, Lisa Moraleda, and Alex Kelleher-Nagorski (I love seeing your name in my inbox).

To my sister, Jay: You have been with me longer than anyone. Thank you for giving me the gift of being an aunt, which has been the greatest joy of my life. I can't believe I never get sick of you, that I can sit with you and do nothing or go insane playing a *Super Mario* game (that I always win). DJ, you're the best brother-in-law I could ask for. Thank you for always making me feel like family and, most importantly, taking my side when I bully my sister. Joe Joe, you're the coolest kid I know. You're confident and outgoing. You're everything I wish I could be.

Ethan, you were the first one I held, and I love it when you randomly hug me. You're so helpful, thoughtful, and sweet, and you remind me to be kind by just being you. Ella, looking at you is like looking in a mirror from when I was a kid, only you shine brighter than I ever could. Mason Jar, you're so loving and so clever. I seriously think you're the smartest human on the planet. Please get rich and take care of me so I don't have to work anymore.

To my brother, thank you for always checking up on me, offering me lunch when I'm at work, and caring about me. Papi, thank you for the books that birthed my love for reading and led me to my writing, which brought me here. I remember every time you took me to the bookstore; they're my favorite memories. Mami, I love your random doorbell rings with a shopping bag full of food in one hand because you worried I hadn't eaten. You're the hottest mom on the block.

To Diana, my friend, ARMY (soon to be Carat?): first thing's first—without you, I wouldn't have fallen in love with BTS, and for that alone, I owe you my kidney. Truly, both you and they have brought such joy to my life. Thank you for being one of my biggest supporters. You mean so much to me. You truly give and give, and I hope to do the same for you, but I fear I can never repay all you've done for me.

To Michelle: forever the light of my life. I think we ALL know I can't smile as wide as I can with you, from being a box on the screen, to karaoke bars, to being called ugly in Philly (me), to a house in Charleston, sitting and watching *Bloodhounds*, streaming *Zelda* for an audience of one (you). You are a light not just to me, but to everyone. You radiate so much "joy, love, friendship."

Thank you to my online friends who became IRL friends (I can't name you all, but I love you all). Thank you Anthony Nerada, Shreya, Gabriel, Amanda, and more. Em and Darci, thank you for all your support, love, and the fun we've had these past years. Jeremy, for all the game nights (and buying *BAG* every time I posted?). Thank you to my agent siblings for your support!

To Kay: I cannot believe that, at one point, you were a stranger, and now we're such enemies. I'm sorry that you felt the need to lie and say the seagull pooped on me when it did on you. Thank you for being you, and the frequent "Spell-check this for me?" and the much-needed vents. I'm so happy we're friends, despite my constant inability to emote about it properly. You're a star. You're so Middle Coast.

Thank you to my friends for being around to distract me from writer's block: Aylin, Mimi, Chris. Cheska, my partner in crime and chaos, being with you always leaves me feeling healed. To Hiba, for telling absolutely everyone about your "author friend." Thank you to all my friends at Harper for cheering me on; it really warms my heart. Sari, thanks for being my manager and mentioning my book every opportunity you saw fit, lol.

To Ellie: You've always felt like a big sister to me, and I thank you for always supporting my writing. I hold you in my heart so dearly. Hannah Cookie and Andy! I can't believe you're parents now—read the baby my book!

It would be impossible to name all my friends, coworkers, acquaintances, and the people who have made me feel good enough to be a human. (Seriously, I have a page limit; this was originally thirteen pages long.) If you have ever made me laugh, asked me how I was doing, or uplifted me, even just once, not even about writing, just because: thank you. The only thing I hope to have done in my life is to have made someone laugh, to have made them happy, even once. Each time it was done to me, I carried it with me forever.

To the readers: I love you. I'm not popular or anything, so you picking up this book and taking a chance on me means more than I can type out.

To BTS and SVT and every *Run BTS* and *Going Seventeen* episode that got me through editing this book: I love you.

And to myself for sticking it out through all the rejections: I really am that girl.